THE AMULET OF CANANEA

Song of Carmelita

Raymond F. Cavanagh

Raymond F. Cavanagh

This book is dedicated to my wife Dianne who has always supported my dreams.

The Amulet of Cananea
Song of Carmelita

© 2014, Raymond F. Cavanagh

Table of Contents

Table of Contents
Prologue
   The Priest & the Amulet
     1756
Part I
Chapter One
   Manuel Díaz Carreras
Chapter Two
   Opportunity
Chapter Three
   Edelmida Ríos Castillo
Chapter Four
   La Fiesta en la Casa
Chapter Five
   Declan Cassidy/
   Thom MacMurrough
Chapter Six
   Investors
   William Cornell Greene
Chapter Seven
   Manuel & Edelmida
Chapter Eight
   The Enemy Within
Chapter Nine
   Turning Point

Chapter Ten
  Retribution
Chapter Eleven
  Te Quiero
Chapter Twelve
  Revenge
Part II
Chapter Thirteen
  Cananea in Conflict
Chapter Fourteen
  El Paso
Chapter Fifteen
  Rail Wars
Chapter Sixteen
  Revolution in the Air
Chapter Seventeen
  Carmelita María Ríos Carreras
Chapter Eighteen
  Blood and Water
Chapter Nineteen
  Truth or Consequences
Chapter Twenty
  Discovery
Chapter Twenty-One
  Strike
Chapter Twenty-Two
  Confrontation
Chapter Twenty-Three
  Loyalty

Chapter Twenty-Four
    Justice
Chapter Twenty-Five
    Farewell
Chapter Twenty-Six
    Freedom
        1911
Chapter Twenty-Seven
    Resolve
Epilogue
    Tucson
        Acknowledgements
        Author's Note
        About the Author

Prologue

The Priest & the Amulet

1756

Padre Javier Pachero, S.J. clutched the golden Cross of Cortés to his breast as he journeyed on his secret mission through the harsh and barren land in Sonora, New Spain. The cool desert dust caked the exposed parts of his feet that his woven leather sandals didn't protect, as his long brown woolen robe scraped along the ground and kept him warm in the morning air. He knew though that soon enough the sun would rise up to bake the land, and the robe would steam him slowly until he could no longer bear the heat and would have to return to camp.

Padre Pachero was leading a group of volunteers who had journeyed with him from Spain to spread the word of God to the natives of this new land. His journey had taken him and his flock over miles of thorn scrub, and into the chaparral surrounding the valley on his approach into an area known to contain a small and sparsely populated village containing a collection of native wikiups. They knew nothing of the secret he had come to unearth.

As he continued on his journey, the April morning sky showed no signs of trouble and the sun burned bright with a yellow and orange corona as it rose over the hills of Sonora.

He squinted into the hot sun at the mountains looming in the near distance, and climbed on the back of his horse, a patterned Spanish Jennet that he rode with a hand-tooled, soft leather vaquero saddle. The horse and saddle were gifts from his parishioners in his native Spain for the journey to the New World, and seemed acutely out of place in this savage and barren land.

The priest was a ruggedly handsome man, with shoulder length brown hair, clear brown eyes, and a trim, but long, mustache which altogether gave him the appearance of being taller than his five foot eight inch height.

He had an innocent air about him and made good counsel to his flock, who warmed to his easy-going demeanor. His gentle personality made people feel comfortable talking to him, and encouraged them to discuss their most personal thoughts, fears, and sins. Encouraged by the teachings of his Jesuit faith, he had an insatiable appetite for learning and was a voracious reader, always looking to learn about new places, which is part of what had led to his assignment in New Spain.

As they reached the foothills of the Cananea mountain range, Padre Pachero motioned to the volunteers from his parish to move ahead.

"Please continue on, and I'll catch up later," he called out to his congregation. "If I don't catch up with you at mid-day, or if you see any signs of a village along the way, send someone back to remind me to move on. I believe we still have many miles to cover, but I can't be completely sure. I have a special request from the Bishop that I must attend to."

His followers readily accepted his explanation, as the Padre was noted for his absent-mindedness and often seemed to disappear for periods of time on one mission or another.

The priest had come to the area known as *Pimería Alta* to extend the work of Padre Eusebio Kino, who had brought Christianity to the native people of the land. Kino had travelled extensively throughout the region, converting virtually all of the tribes who lived in the area by the time of his death.

Kino was one of Padre Pachero's heroes, along with his own recently departed father. Kino had founded and built twenty-four missions in his sixty-six years, a remarkable feat by any standards.

Padre Pachero worked his own miracles and had established a strong bond between the indigenous people of the region and the religious institution he symbolized.

The Jesuits' charter on this day was to extend east and into regions which had not been well established yet, to further spread the word, continue to develop and reinforce the disparate tribes as disciples of God.

The Padre had come into possession of the Cross of Cortés, a gift from his uncle who was one of a long line of explorers in the Pachero family. The cross had been handed down to the first born male of each generation of his family, since the days when Cortés conquered the Aztecs over 200 years before. His uncle and father would regale him with wild and mysterious stories of the cross and those it touched, embellished through years of retelling. Since his uncle had no children of his own, he gave the cross to his brother to give to his son, the only remaining boy in the Pachero family. The artifact had a long and storied history, and would come to spark a chain of events in the new land that none could have anticipated.

The precious item he held was a 24-carat, three quarter inch thick, solid gold cross, encrusted with a ruby at each of the points where Jesus' hands and feet had been nailed during His crucifixion. It measured twelve inches tall and eight inches across and the gold itself was filigreed and shaped in an ornate style, with softened, rounded corners at the end points in the form of a clover representing the Catholic Trinity of the Father, Son, and Holy Spirit.

The cross had always been viewed as a good luck piece, and his father had given it to him to keep God watching over him during his journeys, to keep him safe from harm, and to always remind him of Christ's sacrifice. Just after he gave his son the cross, he died suddenly of complications from pneumonia.

The priests' family had explored this region for decades, and Javier had direct lineage to the Pachero who had gone to the new world with *Hernán Cortés* when he explored the Baja Peninsula and first set foot in New Spain.

Legend had it that Onorio Pachero, Javier's ancient ancestor, came back from that trip with the cross in his possession. He had been given the cross by Cortés himself as a reward for his efforts in conquering the Aztec nation. Onorio claimed that he had interceded when an attacking native had swung a makeshift sword with a jagged edge at Cortés head and Onorio dove at the attackers' legs and sent him flying, disrupting the arc and thus saving Cortés' life. The conquistador was so grateful he gave the precious artifact to Pachero expressing his eternal gratitude.

Onorio's neighbors in Spain had been led to believe that Cortés had captured the cross from a warring native tribe that had worked the mines that were plentiful in the region and held vast riches of gold and silver. In reality Cortés had brought the cross with him from Spain. It was a gift from a benefactor who helped to fund exploration of the area and had been commissioned just for this trip as a good luck charm. Time would tell if it brought good luck or bad.

Padre Pachero was one of a contingent of missionaries and their congregations, who had arrived the year before, in the summer of 1755.

They struck land after a long journey that began at the Port of Cádiz in Andalusia, an autonomous community of the kingdom of Spain, circling around Cape Horn at the tip of South America, and up to the Baja peninsula in *Norteamérica*.

The journey had been slow and arduous, and many of the passengers and most of the animals they brought with them fell victim to illness from a variety of diseases and had died, some quite tragically, during the journey which had taken 12 months to complete. The ship carried 8 missionary priests, and each of them were to take their disciples and migrate out in a pre-designated direction, after spending a few weeks in the port city of La Paz to rest and recuperate, renew their supplies, and acclimate to the new area. Although the golden cross had been handed down from generation to generation as a good luck piece or amulet, just as many of its owners had fallen victim to misfortune as had benefited from it, and yet the belief persisted that the cross was a blessing.

Padre Pachero's mission to continue to spread Christianity to the natives in New Spain, which was fast becoming a burgeoning Mecca of expansion created by the promise of wealth from the untapped resources of the land and its people, was challenging at best. For centuries, word had spread throughout Europe of the vast reserves of gold, silver, and precious stones in this part of the world and had inspired most of the recent spate of explorers from Spain, Italy, and Portugal, all driven with the same desire to find and return with the lost treasures of Portugal, and the Seven Cities of Gold.

The myth of the Seven Cities came to light after seven Catholic bishops, led by the archbishop of Porto in Portugal, fled the continent in massive fleets of ships carrying colonists and supplies, and most importantly, the gold and silver religious treasures from their churches. They left to seek asylum from a marauding band of Moors, a nomadic band of the Muslim faith who had invaded their continent and pillaged their lands.

They sought new lands and the chance to spread the word of Christianity wherever the winds of chance took them.

The desire to protect their faith, and their gold and bejeweled religious artifacts, dictated the strategy that took each of them each in a different direction around the globe, many to areas not previously explored.

It was said that when the Bishops reached their respective landfalls, they burned their ships to avoid discovery. For centuries, the ensuing drive to find the lost gold forced subsequent explorations of the lands farther and farther west and south, which spawned a competitive and aggressive push expanding the New World.

As the legend grew, and returning conquistadores extolled the riches of the lands they claimed the bishops founded, stories began to unfold confirming sightings, and the stories of these cities and their incredible wealth increased and proliferated. The whereabouts of the cities was never documented, but it was assured that they were located to the west in the New World and thus inspired a plethora of explorations funded by wealthy leaders, royalty, and private businesses.

Javier, for his part, had long heard the stories of the Cities of Gold, and had been chartered by the Bishop to examine all possibilities of the existence of gold and silver mines while in the region, and to keep this part of his mission confidential between them. The Bishop was not interested in publicly turning the core responsibility of sending dozens of missionaries into hostile native lands to spread the Word of God into a side journey to look for mythical treasure.

Javier waited until the rest of his party was out of sight, climbed down off his steed, and walked slowly over the area surrounding the foothills, searching for the location that would match the description of the place his uncle had described to him.

As Padre Pachero continued his trek, he moved in the direction of an area he had identified on his crude, hand drawn map, as one that housed precious metal mines. His thoughts centered on the various natives he had met since coming to the region. Most of the tribes were somewhat sedentary and were not aware of other tribes or lands outside of their purview.

His was a personal mission today, not sanctioned, or even known about, by the contingent with whom he traveled, or the bishop who approved his trip. Padre Pachero was looking to find the source of the gold he believed was used to make the amulet his ancestor had brought back with him from his conquest of the Aztecs with Cortés in 1521. He believed in his heart that this item had helped him to survive and was a source of good luck to him and everyone who had ever possessed it.

To the people in Javier's hometown, it also served as further proof of the existence of the Cities of Gold, and his ancestor Onorio, for his part, did nothing to quell the speculation. In fact, his reputation as an explorer had only been enhanced by his story, and his ability to attract his own funding for further exploration was ensured by the evidence of riches found.

So went the wheel of life; artifacts uncovered in New Spain that were originally brought from the homeland, but once identified and returned, reinforced the notion that there were untold riches to be found in the new territory.

Padre Pachero had marked an area in Sonora at the foothills of the Cananea Mountains, and set out to find a mine filled with silver and gold, which it was said, the ancients had found just prior to their return.

Javier had been making trips out into the hills of Sonora for months, and came to befriend many of the native tribes of the region. While the common belief back in Spain was that all of the tribes were wild pagans with a ferocious desire to kill those of other cultures, most of the native tribes were peaceful, and, in the majority of cases, weren't even aware of the existence of one another. One exception to this was the Apache tribe, a nomadic and warring nation that traveled throughout the region and would engage in battle with anyone, native or otherwise and often stole horses and food from the more pacifistic tribes.

Padre Pachero had been gone with his parishioners for over three weeks and found himself in a land that had little detail on any of his maps and appeared not to have been explored much by previous expeditions. He couldn't know for sure, but he felt he was close to the area as described by his uncle, which was characterized as a place with a flat peaked mountain and was one of the highest mountains in the area.

Javier had been sent to New Spain, because as a child he was often sickly, suffering from difficulty breathing, a condition that might have been asthma, but was never diagnosed as such. This difficulty kept him indoors much of the time and led him to spend his childhood learning about art and music, and reading about new and exotic places. In spite of his physical challenges, Javier never gave up his dream of following in his family's footsteps and traveling to far off lands. The Pachero family had always been deeply religious, but Javier was the first of his clan ever to enter the priesthood.

The search for gold in the New World, and the desire of the European countries to explore, conquer, and broaden their empires, offered great opportunity for a man of Javier's background. His ability as a priest, and his family background of explorers made him an ideal candidate to go to New Spain to increase the number of Missions and use the opportunity to continue the search for the Lost Cities.

Although Javier possessed superior intelligence, his mind was often lost in thought and he was not always as aware of practical requirements as he should be, and now found himself poorly outfitted for the terrain of Sonora. The landscape here was very different from his home, which was located in the Basque region near the coast of Spain. Pachero had come to this particular area, in part, due to the desert conditions in Pimería Alta, which his doctors had thought could be beneficial in helping with his respiratory ailments. He convinced his bishop to approve the trip, which he did with the caveat that Javier take on his special and confidential request.

Under normal circumstances, his health issues may have prevented him from the journey, but it proved to be a very positive experience, and since his arrival nearly a year before, his breathing had improved considerably and he was able to get

11

out and explore the region on his own with little discomfort.

The environment was different and fascinating to him here, with an incredible array of plants and animals like he had never seen before, such as the huge saguaro cactus – some as high as 18 feet tall, which stood like sentries guarding a treasure. And that they were, if you were to believe the *corridos* and legends that the natives sung, which glorified the rumored stories of treasure throughout the hills.

While settlers from many European countries began to arrive in the New World, the vast majority were content to dwell at land's first sighting, settling on the shorelines while battling the elements and hostile native tribes.

The Spanish missionaries, however, continued on further and further into remote regions throughout the south and west, where the land was challenging and ever changing. The unrelenting terrain, aggressive wildlife, hostile native tribes, and abrupt shifts in weather afforded them a slim chance of survival and many had died from one or more of these threats. The land was littered with evidence that few had survived.

The Sonora region was both beautiful and challenging, and throughout the millennia the flora and fauna evolved as beautiful, but tough, with many only surviving through sheer will. The land was defined by predatory creatures; scorpions, snakes, roadrunners, buzzards, arachnids – all evolved with the single intent to survive. It was kill or be killed, and if you weren't bigger and stronger, than you had to be faster or more poisonous. Some had the ability to blend in with the environment and escape other natural enemies with chameleon-like traits, but most had to fight to survive which made them all formidable opponents.

As evolution in the environment dictated, both hunter and hunted honed the unique traits that helped them survive the years, and the land was ruled by the law of survival-of-the-fittest, in nature's cruel version of the children's game of rock, paper, scissors. This was a finely tuned contest of superior athletes played out on a field with no boundaries, and the end game was survival.

The area in which he now found himself was destitute, with nothing more than cactus, tumbleweed, and all manner of God's creatures that had survived centuries in this harsh and hot climate by killing and eating anything it could. He moved cautiously towards that mountain peak and came upon a number of smaller hills, one of which held an opening to a shallow mine. As he approached what appeared to be the crude entrance with caution, not knowing what surprises might be lurking inside, he bent to pick up a fallen timber, which was apparently designed to shore up the roof of the mine that had fallen directly across the opening and hindered his path. He bent down and reached his left arm far under the heavy timber log

13

to leverage it up so he could get a grasp on it with his right hand. As he did this he felt a sting, like a needle-prick on the soft, fleshy inside part of his arm near his left elbow. His first thought was that it was a nail that had been sticking out of the underside of the piece of wood, but as he turned it over, he saw a small, brown scorpion scurry away. Javier was familiar with scorpions; as a child he had been bitten by the Mediterranean scorpion, which was the most common in Spain. It had caused him pain and took a few days for the itching of the sting to go away, but a doctor had promptly treated him and he had recovered with no long-lasting effects.

This scorpion, however, was the bark scorpion, a species that is venomous and indigenous to the Sonora desert. It is very small, this one being only two inches long, and it has a tendency to live on wood and under rocks. Scorpions are nocturnal animals and rarely active during daylight, and, unfortunately for Padre Pachero, he must have awakened this one from its rest with nasty results.

Not knowing how lethal the sting might be, he decided to take caution and fashioned a crude tourniquet, using the rope that served as a belt for his heavy brown robe, and tied it just below the muscle in his arm, slit a cut near the sting with his knife, and attempted to suck out the poison. Walking back towards his horse he staggered and collapsed, most likely from the effects of anaphylactic shock, which may have been introduced into his system by the venom of the sting, triggering the reaction by releasing massive amounts of histamine into his blood. His breathing became difficult, and the mid-morning sun, which was just beginning to bake the area with the dry, arid effects of the desert, made breathing difficult even under normal conditions. He was still alert and knew something had to be done quickly, but he was incapacitated, isolated, and he was well aware that the effects of the shock could be fatal if not treated promptly.

As the priest lay there contemplating his fate, renewing his vows, and reviewing his legacy, a native woman in a long, flowing, multi-colored serape-type covering approached him on a horse. The priest was certain this was an apparition, for the woman was alone in this desolate area and he thought he was witnessing a hallucination. As the priest took in this specter, he thought to himself that it is a very dangerous and unwise thing to do, a woman traveling alone in this part of the world. As evidence of his concern he had only to recognize the situation in which he now found himself.

As Padre Pachero's vision began to fade, he was aware that the woman had taken his head in her hands and poured a little bit of cool, clean tasting water into his parched mouth, perhaps the sweetest tasting liquid in his memory. But before he could say a word or ask a question, he succumbed to the heat and shock and passed out.

15

Chevor (an ancient tribal name which translates to Willow) was a member of the O'Odham tribe, an agrarian tribe which had arisen from the Hohokam culture, Hohokam meaning "People of the Desert." The O'Odham tribe was composed of the Tohono O'Odham (Papago) or desert people, and the Akimel O'Odham (Pima) or river people. These were a peaceful people whose culture revolved around the Santa Cruz and San Pedro rivers in an area of Sonora that was destined to become critical in Mexico's drive for independence. They were all descendants of the Sobaipuri, the first native tribe to meet the Spanish explorers when they arrived in this land.

The Papago were friendly to the 'whites' and were willingly converted to Christianity, a faith they embraced and maintained. The name the explorers gave them, Papago, refers to their agrarian diet and translates loosely to "bean eater" a derogatory term used by the Spanish who conquered the land and enslaved its people. The Sonora region offers a vast cornucopia of climate, vegetation, and terrain that encourages both wildlife and plant life as food sources for the native populations, and the Papago or Tohono O'Odham took full advantage of the fruits of the land.

As Chevor tended to Padre Pachero, she noticed the puncture wound and the crudely made tourniquet on his arm. She wondered why he apparently had such a strong reaction to what appeared to be a bite or sting. As she was contemplating what she should do, she noticed a small, brown scorpion scurrying through the dust, and surmised this was the source of the sting. She herself had seen many scorpion bites and knew that it was extremely rare for them to be fatal, but the reaction that Padre Pachero was exhibiting was something she had never seen before.

In her memory she recalled a time when an elder of the tribe was stung by a brown scorpion, went into shock and died. But it was thought that this occurred because the elder was frail, and that it was a rare exception. Generally, the scorpion bite was simply very uncomfortable and caused a rash. It was rarely deadly.

However, Chevor was concerned. This young man seemed to be of good health and yet, apparently he passed out from the effects of the sting. His breathing was shallow and his skin cold and clammy to the touch. Although Padre Pachero was not the first European to ever come in contact with a member of the tribe, he was the first they had seen in a generation. Chevor herself had never seen a person who looked like this before. His clothing was heavy and odd, made of a fabric unlike any she knew, and his complexion a much lighter tone than those of her tribe. This man's face was narrow and lean and he had a strange growth of dark hair over his upper lip. This was very different from the men in her tribe who had smooth skin and broad, open faces.

Chevor poured more cool water from her calfskin canteen onto the priest's forehead and lips. She removed the rope tourniquet, extended the small slice in his skin where the scorpion had stung, and gently tried to suck out any of the remaining poison that may still have been in proximity to the wound. She cut a branch off a nearby creosote bush, which grew abundantly in the region, and used the sap to disinfect the wound. She then took a length of cloth from her blouse and tied it around his arm above the muscle and tightened it by twisting it with the stick.

She somehow needed to get this stranger back to the medicine man in her village. She took the piece of wood which the priest was lifting when he was stung, located another one similar to it lying nearby, and with the priest's rope belt she quickly fashioned a lattice for support and placed her horse blanket on top of the makeshift stretcher. She tethered this to the stranger's horse using the leather reins. Even though the provisional gurney would need to be dragged along the ground, she would get him back to the village fairly quickly. The encampment was less than a half-mile away over the ridgeline and timing seemed to be critical.

As Chevor worked, she was thinking furiously of an excuse for how she came upon this stranger. She had gone out toward the mines to meet with Ban, her secret lover. Although the tribe was not monogamous, they frowned on close relations between a man and a woman until the man had his

18

first kill of the hunt. Ban was still untested and would not be allowed to join the hunt until his sixteenth birthday, which was in a few weeks. He was expected to do well, as he was strong and athletic, like his namesake the Coyote, but until he had his first kill, the liaison between Chevor and Ban must remain clandestine.

When Chevor got back to the village, there was considerable commotion surrounding her arrival with this strange man, the likes of which they had never seen before. She quickly explained that she had been out to the mines exercising her horse when she can upon him in this condition. She had seen the rope tourniquet on his arm, and the mark of the sting, and assumed from the mark that he had been bitten by a scorpion. The medicine man was summoned and identified that a scorpion had indeed stung the young man, who seemed to be in shock.

He had the stranger brought to his tent, where he fixed an herbal paste, and applied it to the wound. He then mixed a potion that he split into two separate portions. One portion he placed on the open fire and waved the steam towards his unconscious patient. The other he placed in a container with a rough-hewn cone top made of parchment. He had one of the tribesmen hold the stranger's head up while he poured some of the cooled liquid into his mouth.

The priest sputtered and coughed. His eyes flew wide open and he sat upright quickly. He was momentarily confused and disoriented, but then he remembered where he was and felt the itch of the scorpion's sting. He looked around to see himself surrounded by the strange faces of the Papago. They had broad, open faces, some with markings, and some had piercing in their noses and ears. He had met other natives in his six months in Sonora, but none of this tribe.

What Padre Pachero could not know was that this tribe had worked the mines for decades, but only as a source for tools to use in their gardens.

The tribes had no use for traditional currency and while the metals from the mines were valuable to them for their tools, it was also community property and not something to be bartered. Since mining was not a priority for them, they were only scratching the surface of the potential that the mines could deliver. By the time Padre Pachero arrived, the mines had been dormant for some time. The native tribes had essentially carved out crawl space to get to the raw material which they could melt down and fashion for tools, but stopped exploring as it became too dangerous to crawl into the confined spaces where other creatures made the their home.

The medicine man pointed to the swelling on the priests' arm, then to the cup and his mouth, indicating he should drink the rest of the liquid. It was bitter and difficult to swallow, but he somehow managed. The priest then laid back down to rest. His breathing was still labored and difficult, but he seemed to be improving.

As he gently laid back down on the makeshift gurney, he looked up and saw Chevor standing there. He smiled, nodded, and mouthed the word "*Gracias.*" She didn't understand the word, but she knew his meaning. Although it appeared to the tribe that he was quickly improving, he knew in his heart that he was suffering internally and could not survive. With great difficulty, he motioned for his saddlebags. He had a great deal of trouble communicating in his current condition, but Chevor finally came to understand and went to retrieve the bags and handed them to him.

He reached into one of the bags and pulled out the beautiful, hand hammered gold cross that was bequeathed to him by his ancestor, Onorio on the advent of his journey from Spain. It was inscribed in Spanish, "*Vaya con Dios*"- "Go with God." He believed that this Amulet was the reason he successfully made the journey, helped him through rough seas and long stretches of loneliness, and helped him find this mine, the place he thought to be the source of the gold used to make the cross and inspire decades of exploration. It was a source of comfort to him on his land journeys over the desert areas where there was little food and no water. It never occurred to him that its possession could have anything to do with this latest predicament which had befallen him.

But Javier knew he had reached his final resting place and that his legacy would be secure in finding the source of the Amulet and one of the sources of gold and silver that his countrymen had been searching for since the days of Cortés.

He had to get word back to the others in his party so the word could be spread back to his native Spain. It would cause tremendous excitement and give Spain its rightful place as having re-discovered at least one of the long-lost cities.

He was desperate to find a way to communicate this back to his disciples at camp. He cursed himself silently for taking on this mission alone and not bringing others in the event he encountered hostile tribes or environmental issues such as he now faced. It never dawned on him as he lay dying that the Amulet could also be a source of bad luck in his demise.

As he handed the Amulet to Chevor, he wondered to himself "where did Cortés obtain this cross?" Certainly Javier believed the gold came from this lost mine, but who had the means to fashion such a beautiful piece of gold and jewels? Where was the City he had heard so much about where artisans of this caliber could be found?

These natives only had primitive methods and would never be able to make such a fine item. As his vision began to fade, his belief that this area could be the source of precious metals was not in question, but who could have made it and where certainly was. Was this truly a relic of Cibola, the city that Cabeza de Vaca came looking for and proof that the Seven Cities of Gold, did, indeed exist?

As Padre Pachero thought about his ancestor and the stories he told, he reflected on the fact that, as a Priest, he represented the end of the line for the Pachero family. He felt at peace with himself, however, and knew in his heart that he would not survive this last adventure. As he recounted his sins and asked God for forgiveness, he knew what he must do.

He motioned for something to write with, and the natives brought him a piece of tree bark and a feather quill with a small container made of hollowed out wood and applied with some sort of lacquer that held an ink manufactured from plant dye. He hastily scribbled a note in Spanish which read "Fatal scorpion bite. Cross is gift. Build the church. Cross on altar. God bless all."

He handed the note and the cross to Chevor, telling her it had brought him luck and fortune and he knew it would do the same for her. He tried explaining to her and the others surrounding him, as frantically as he could with hand gestures and spoken words the natives could not possibly understand, that this place was the source of the gold and silver, but he knew it could not be the place where such finery was made. He tried, and failed, to communicate this before his body finally gave out on him. He looked up at Chevor and with one final gasp of breath whispered *"Adios"* and passed away peacefully. The effects of the anaphylactic shock were too much for his drained body and he welcomed his reunion with the Lord almighty. Chevor didn't understand a word that he said, but she knew his meaning.

The following day, a small group of Padre Pachero's disciples, in search of the missing priest, came upon the native tent sites and were shown the priests body. They read the note, thanked the tribe and put him on his horse to take him away for a proper burial, noting the location of the site so they could return later to preach the word and build his church. As they were about to depart, they noticed the cross hanging outside the largest of the tents' and assumed this was where the chief lived.

They had not yet learned the language of the Papago, and, as had Padre Pachero just hours before, the tribe tried to communicate through hand signals indicating this was a gift from the priest. They feared that this new group would try and confiscate the gift of the cross.

None of the priests' followers had ever seen anything as ornate and beautiful as this in the new world, and its existence was a secret which Padre Pachero had held dear to his heart. They vowed to honor his dying wish and build the church and hoped the natives would be willing to use the Amulet as the cross to be housed at the apex of the altar.

The natives did not understand, and although they were a peaceful people, they were protective of this item, which now belonged to them and was offered as a token of thanks, so the thought of returning it was not acceptable.

They did allow the flock to examine the cross and hold it to see its weight, which enabled them to assess the value of the object. It was immediately apparent to them that this was one the relics of the Lost Cities and that they must be in the vicinity, which they would report back to their parish as soon as they returned to Hermosillo, their headquarters in this new country.

They left the tribal colony with a promise to return and bring the word of God, and with the use of the cross, believed they had communicated that message to the tribe effectively.

Chevor watched closely as they rode off to the southwest and thought to herself "These strange new people will not take my gift. The one with hair on his face meant this for my people and we will protect it with our lives." Then she turned and entered the chief's tent and sat with him and the medicine man in silence to honor the memory of their departed friend.

The missions of Padre Kino in the western part of Sonora, which he spent a lifetime constructing, were used to help educate new tribes and convert them to the Catholic religion. The beauty and splendor of some of the missions were erected with such magnificence that the natives could not help but be impressed, and it did seem that a greater being had a hand in this work. The Pima tribe, who were closely related to the Papago, were disciples of Padre Kino, and instrumental in helping to convert Chevor and her branch of the Papago tribe to the new religion.

The year after Padre Pachero died, the tribe was recruited by Padre Alonso Espinoza, who would become the pastor of the congregation, to help construct a small, flat roofed adobe church to serve the needs of the community and hold religious services. It was a poorly constructed building, as the priest was not an architect and did not employ the help of building experts, but it served the needs of the people and helped to spread the word of God.

Not only were Chevor and her people willing to help in the construction of the church, they did, indeed, use the Amulet as the cross at the pinnacle of the roof above the altar as a tribute to Padre Pachero and his memory. Still, the question about the Amulet remained – was it a talisman of luck or a harbinger of evil?

Part I

Cananea, Mexico

1889

Chapter One

Manuel Díaz Carreras

A sudden, harsh, clanging noise jolted Manuel awake just as the first rays of sunlight streamed through his window. Explosions were common in the copper mines in Cananea, Mexico, and also the most feared of all the dangerous things that occurred on a daily basis. As he ran towards the explosion, he wondered how many of his friends were trapped down there this time and who might they be.

Manuel had been awakened not by the sound of the explosion, but by the clanging of the iron triangle as it bleated out its alarm. He dressed quickly in a white collarless cotton shirt which had yellowed with age, twill work pants, and heavy, reinforced-toe boots. He rushed down towards the mine to see if he could help with the rescue efforts that he knew must already be under way.

As he approached the site, Manuel saw the last remnants of smoke emanating from the mouth of the excavation. It was now eight a.m., and operations had been working at full capacity so the potential for disaster was great as the mines would have been full of workers. Fortunately, it was still cool enough, and early enough, that the new day brought verve and vigor to the rescue effort.

As Manuel hurried down the path from the company barracks, he was struck by the noise, dust, and confusion that always occurred after an "incident." The peel of multiple alarm bells indicated the severity of this collapse. In this case, bells were ringing at each of the barracks, as well as the mess tent, outbuildings, and at the tunnels themselves. Although mining collapses were a common occurrence, pandemonium was rampant. People were rushing towards the mouth of the newest vein of the mine, and there was smoke and dust everywhere. Supervisors were screaming out orders and creating more confusion than they resolved, and the whole area was marked by a general feeling of disaster and despair.

Manuel ran towards the scene of devastation, just as he saw his fellow worker, Pedro, emerge through the smoke. "Pedro, what's your assessment? How many down?" he called out.

"It's never good, Manuel. The first day shift was fully staffed. But the collapse is at the deepest section of the mine. Only the men working in that section should be affected. We are waiting for a count now. But it's never good," he repeated, "you know that." Manuel looked at his close friend and nodded his agreement silently.

Pedro and Manuel were both strong workers, and many of the other miners looked to them as leaders in the camps. They talked briefly about the approach they should take to organize the

29

teams, and together they corralled a few of the strongest workers and began the process of coordinating the rescue effort. Manuel and Pedro split the team into two lines; one line to dig, and one to remove the earth. It was a team effort and once the line began the process they fell into a kind of rhythm that took on a life of its own.

The men tore into the task, removing rocks and debris at a furious rate, and literally clawing at the earth to get to their *compadres*. The primitive tools of ax and shovel made the rescue effort a near impossible task, but the determination of the men afforded them superhuman strength, and they continued unabated through the day. Realistically they all knew that a rescue had to occur within hours of the collapse to have any hope of uncovering anyone alive, but there was no way of knowing the extent of the cave-in or whether there were any air pockets in the mine to allow for the workers to breathe.

Regardless, the natural gases in the mine along with the darkness and fear combined to create an environment of death, with no light, no sound, and little hope of rescue. The trapped miners could do little more than wait.

For ten hours the laborers worked the mine, shoveling out dirt, and moving the earth to a series of mounds, which would later be sifted for any vestige of precious metal. The work was tedious, and much tougher on the backs and shoulders of the teams than the work they did day in and day out.

Tension crackled in the air, and the rescuers all hoped that, if they ever found themselves trapped, the rescue teams would work just as hard and as tirelessly as they did now. Shifts were crudely devised as workers tired from swinging the axes and moving the earth.

At the tenth hour, with nerves frayed, backs breaking with the effort, and hope beginning to wane, the miners heard a cry from within the cave.

Someone was alive, and calling out for help. This re-energized the troops and a flurry of movement drove the effort to break through to their trapped colleagues.

Manuel and Pedro led the team of sweat stained, dirty, and tired miners, and with one final swing of the ax, a wall of copper colored earth collapsed and a tiny hole formed, showing a pocket of space with the miners within. Workers on both sides of the wall frantically scraped away the dirt, and one by one, seven of the miners crawled through and were dragged to the mouth of the cave to safety.

Two of the miners had been killed when the roof first collapsed, but these seven had been able to run back towards the mouth of the mine, and were trapped in a three-foot space between two bracings.

As the injured miners were reunited with their families and loved ones, the work of burying the dead and moving on with the daily mining effort settled into an all too familiar and difficult routine.

31

Manuel, Pedro and the team of rescuers went to the mess tent for food and tequila, as early as it was, and commenced to discuss the ongoing challenge of conditions in the mines.

"Something has to be done about this" one of the rescuers griped loudly, "this is the third collapse this month. Next time, we may not be so lucky. We risk our lives to save the lives of others, but that is not the answer. The mines in *Norteamérica* are using advanced machinery to dig the mines. They use premium tools to keep the workers safe. Miners there are paid better wages. The owners know that it is the workers who are most important to continue to bring out the precious metal, but they treat us as cattle."

"If things are so great up north, why don't you go there?" one of the other rescuers shouted. "You can put up with the cold, rain, and snow. I'll stay here where the weather is warm and the senoritas, warmer." The crowd laughed and raised their glasses in salute, but underneath the camaraderie many of the workers harbored the same thought.

The potential for revolution was in the air and a groundswell of sentiment was growing for the workers to take matters into their own hands.

Manuel had only recently begun working at the mine, but as he sat listening to his fellow workers, he reflected on its long and troubled history. The Cobre Grande mine had previously been owned by General Ignacio Pesqueira. His

32

widow had recently sold the property to a prospector named William Cornell Greene of the United States for development.

Pesqueira was a former Governor of the State of Sonora, Mexico, and a military hero who helped defeat the French and drive them out of Mexico after the Franco-Mexico War, also known as the Maximilian Affair.

He had tired of both military and political life and retired to the sleepy community of Arizpe, a small village a few miles south of Cananea. Pesqueira had fought the Apaches for years while trying to settle the area. He happened upon the mines which the Jesuits had abandoned decades before and turned it into a money making hobby.

He mined minerals on a small scale, employing the help of local native tribes, but never recognized their full potential. Mining in the State of Sonora had been active since the days of the Aztecs and although the area was remote, ongoing operations at a number of mines kept the population employed.

The Europeans quickly tired of the mines in Sonora, primarily because the French and Spanish who had developed the area had only been looking for gold and silver - metals that were sparse in these particular mines. Copper, which could be mined in Cananea and elsewhere in the region, had been considered a nuisance due to the large amount of ore that had to be handled in order to yield a relatively small amount of the metal.

It had also historically brought a much lower price than gold or silver. But with the advent of electricity and expansion of the railroads, it was coming into great demand, and smart entrepreneurs like Greene saw this and capitalized on the opportunity.

The mines were one of the few places to find employment in Cananea, outside of the service businesses, such as the cantinas and hotels, which had long been established. These were usually owned, worked, and managed by families who had inhabited the area for generations.

Life in Mexico under *Presidente* Porfirio Díaz had changed the face of Mexico dramatically during his rule. Prior to his Presidency, named the *Porfiriato*, the country was rampant with bandits and crime was commonplace. Díaz vowed to bring peace and prosperity to Mexico, and at this he was successful, although at a very steep price to the people.

There was essentially no middle class, and the lower class families constituted the working poor, so opportunities such as working the mines in Cananea attracted people from all across the region, both in Mexico and the United States.

Education was considered the privilege of the rich, and Díaz had hoped to effect a change for the peons, but this never proved to be a successful endeavor during his tenure.

William C. Greene was not the only one lucky enough to take advantage of the Díaz regime and its aggressive policies designed to bring new capital to the country. There were a multitude of foreign investors coming into Mexico helping to generate money and jobs. Unfortunately, most of the money went back out of the country, and the jobs that were created were primarily menial or dangerous.

However, the politics of the situation worked for both Díaz and the investors, as Díaz effectively eliminated the threat of the *banditos* who had previously roamed the countryside, aided by the help of the *Rurales,* who instilled fear of reprisal. Businesses thrived as they reaped the benefits of tax incentives and waived compliancy requirements, and no longer had to worry about the safety of their goods being hijacked.

It was exactly this juxtaposition of events that would ultimately lead to the peons' revolt against the Díaz regime, and create the environment that would lead to the Mexican Revolution and drive for equality.

Manuel was lucky. His family was well established, and due to his family's connections, his first position was working directly in the mines, where the pay and prestige was higher than in some of the more menial jobs. He was a mestizo, part Spanish blood and part Indian, although physically he took all of the features of his Spanish father, He was of average height with raven black hair and dark brown eyes that seemed to smile even when he was angry.

His father had come to New Spain on a land grant, and built a comfortable business selling grain in northern Mexico and Arizona, but he, like all in the area, were impacted by events at the mining operations.

There were not many workers who had completed their Catholic elementary education as Manuel did. Most had to work as soon as they were of age, contributing money to their families for food and clothing.

The miners worked hand to mouth, and as the town grew, competition for jobs soared, pay remained low, and goods and services became comparatively more expensive to the average worker. The miners constituted the working poor, the proletariat, and the undercurrents of revolt against the politics in Mexico City had been brewing for years. For decades the ability to work the land had been taken from them, as the Presidency of Porfirio Díaz encouraged foreign investment to the benefit of the rich, but the detriment of the poor.

The number of deaths in the mines was unconscionably high, and many young men had to take their fathers' places as head of the family. In this catholic, conservative, family oriented country, there were no other options.

Besides the obvious health and safety concerns, one of the problems facing the mine's owners was the challenge to deliver the amount of product that was ordered in a timely fashion. Even if the mines could produce at the level required, there was an enormous challenge facing them in distribution. The delivery system was severely overtaxed between the poorly constructed roads and the lack of adequate trains in the region. Due to these challenges, the mines were worked hard, and the men to the point of exhaustion, thereby exacerbating the potential for danger.

The copper mines in Cananea had eleven separate tunnels from which the miners were to extract as much ore as possible in a day, and they were selling all of the ore it could process, so each delay cost the company money, and pushed back fulfillment.

Manuel was a personable young man; well-liked by his co-workers and managers alike for his affability and dedication. He liked to work, but even more, he liked the money, so he took additional hours or filled in for workers unfortunate enough to take ill or become injured. He knew how dangerous his occupation was, but vowed that he would one day make it out of the mines and open a dry goods store of his own.

Manuel was sturdily built, with strong arms and hands from swinging a pick ax to dig for the precious metals that had been culled from the unforgiving earth for decades.

Cananea was a melting pot and microcosm of the entire country. There were laborers from Ireland, the United States, China, Japan and elsewhere. The majority of the workers were natives and although the system had layers of classes, it really all boiled down to a caste system split between the rich developers and the poor laborers. While the classes in Mexico were battling amongst themselves, the country at large was also still struggling with their recent independence from Spain. This area of the country had been settled by diverse native tribes for centuries, and when the Europeans came, the natives suffered under Spanish and French rule, and had ongoing battles over U.S. expansion.

The earliest Spanish explorers, who eventually conquered and wiped out the entire Aztec nation, mixed with native Indian tribes and the homogenization of a new nation evolved, although they struggled for centuries to gain independence and a common voice.

For the Carreras family, the mines were the center of their lives, providing money for their necessities and adequate schools for them to send their children.

Manuel's thoughts drifted back to his father, a strict disciplinarian who had worked hard his entire life, only to be killed in the aftermath of one of the mining collapses, when he had been called to help in a rescue effort.

As Manuel sat with the others drinking tequila, he was lost in thought about his father who had died there only 12 years earlier. Living in a mining town, Manuel had lost many friends and relatives over the years. He would try, but could never get over the heart wrenching experiences, or forget each and every one of the episodes which he lived over and over again in his mind. He never got used to the pain and suffering it caused, although it became a normal part of his daily existence.

Manuel and his father had been very close, more like older and younger brothers than parent and child. His memories of his father were one of a strong, proud man who did little for himself, and always gave to his family. Manuel was an only child, and his father gave him all he could and more. He was afforded as much love and opportunity as it was possible for a man in his fathers' position to offer.

The Carreras' were a close, tight knit family who embraced the Christian principles and family values that the Jesuits had instilled in all the natives throughout the region. When Christianity had arrived in Sonora decades ago, the Jesuits brought with them the core Christian principles of family, faith, and forgiveness.

The Carreras family, along with many in the community, followed these principles without question. After Manuel was born, however, things changed radically, shaking their belief. His parents were told there would be no more children. Manuel's mother, Rosita, was a small woman of great humor and passion who was not afraid to speak her mind. She had vestiges of Aztec blood and was proud of her heritage.

She had experienced a very difficult labor and medical facilities at the time were virtually non-existent. There were only native medicine men that treated all ailments using natural remedies that were close at hand. Their most difficult tasks were stitching wounds and setting broken bones. There were no experts to help with difficult pregnancies and births. Manuel's mother was sturdily built, but small in stature. Her birth canal was severely constricted, and she experienced a very difficult birth that kept her in hard labor for 17 hours before delivery.

His delivery had to be assisted with a tool that substituted as crude forceps, and Manuel was extremely lucky that he suffered no permanent physical damage. However, during the delivery his mother's organs were torn, and she learned that she would never be able to conceive again.

While this was devastating to his parents, it ultimately proved something of a blessing for Manuel, who, as an only child, was given all the love and attention his parents could offer. However, they were quite poor, even by the standards of their time and place, and Manuel had to start working the mines as soon as he was physically able.

The copper content when Manuel started working the mines was still fairly high, as much as thirty percent, meaning one ton of ore would contain six hundred pounds of copper. Over the years, as the mines were continually worked, extraction of the materials required an effort to drive deeper into the earth. The ore content declined as a volume of the overall materials, making it difficult to get the amount of copper required, and with increasing demand, that meant hiring more workers and drilling additional mines.

In the short days of winter, the shift started before sun up and ended after sundown, but to the miners this hardly mattered. The mines were pitch dark and without the artificial light that the candle lanterns shed, they wouldn't be able to work at all. Manuel was surprised they didn't task the workers 24 hours a day in different shifts, but supposed it was because management didn't want to work those grueling hours. The potential for rescue would also be nonexistent, causing a situation in which the workers would revolt.

Work conditions in the mines were harsh with temperatures so hot that the workers routinely took off their clothes and worked in their tee shirts and shorts.

Conditions in the smelters were even more intense, and many times a day a miner, or smelter, was taken from the workplace and brought to the infirmary suffering from heat exhaustion, dehydration or worse. The physical work was grueling, and the tools that the workers used to cut into the hard clay soil could weigh up to six pounds, and swinging this weight all day long was equivalent to lifting hundreds of pounds each and every day they mined. The work was backbreaking and breaks were few.

Water was plentiful in the mines, however, since it was used for damping down the dust and mixing with the raw material for excavation. But it was not drinkable, and after ten hours in blistering heat, with little potable water, no bathroom, and no fresh air, the environment took its toll on many who worked there. The task was impossible for those who suffered from a fear of enclosed spaces.

The tasks were rotated to keep away boredom. One day swinging the ax, one day hauling out the residue, one day sifting for metal and one day weighing and packaging, then starting all over again. Each week was different from the one before allowing for the illusion of combating boredom. The mines operated six days a week, which was one of the primary grievances of the workers. The only real family time or time for leisure activities was Sunday.

Manuel's reverie in thinking about his family was broken as Pedro called for attention and stood to declare an impromptu eulogy. "A toast to our dead brothers, who died because the rich owners of the mines do not care enough for our safety," Pedro declared.

"The time has come for us to stand up for ourselves and demand better working conditions. This has gone on for too long. The wealthy owners live in their fancy mansions and we work and slave and can just barely put food on our tables."

This was a common cry of late. The workers were being stirred by anti-government sentiments. The lack of benefits, poor medical attention, and serious ailments from working the mines, too many hours and not enough pay were all complaints that were being heard more and more frequently.

Pedro had a particular reason to be bitter, besides the death he had witnessed this day. His brother had recently died of the miners' disease silicosis, a condition that affected a large percentage of the workers and was a chief cause of death for those who were not killed in the accidents that seemed to occur on a weekly basis.

It was a hideous disease, caused by silica dust, the most common mineral element on earth. As the earth is mined, silica is kicked up, and workers are exposed to its effects with disastrous results. Even very small amounts of silica can lead to the disease, which occurs when the silica embeds itself into the lungs. Once ingested, the body cannot expunge the element with natural processes such as coughing, or sneezing. The effects can accumulate for years before the disease is detected, and then it is too late for its effect to be reversed. The lungs form fibers around the silica, and lead to monstrous fibrous tumors that can cause chronic pulmonary obstruction and eventually, death.

As vocal as he had become, Pedro was not the only one to complain. Lately many workers were taking up the cry of revolution. The world at large was changing, with people around the world fighting for their rights, and the freedom to choose their destiny, and the argument raged that Mexico should be no exception.

Tonight, they were all physically exhausted, and the outpourings of grief turned to thoughts of their fallen brothers, and the care their families would need in this time of sadness.

As Pedro continued his soliloquy, others took up the cry, "*Viva Magon*," referring to the anarchist Ricardo Flores Magon, who, along with his brother, Enrique, incited Mexican workers throughout the south and west from their headquarters in St. Louis. Flores Magon was an important figure in voicing the concerns of the workers.

His newspaper, *Regeneración*, served as a platform for anarchistic practices, and was a bible to those who opposed the *Díaz* government and the caste system that developed out of its policies.

In Cananea, there were approximately 5300 workers of Mexican and native decent, and 2200 American workers. The inequity in pay and benefits was taking its toll and skirmishes occurred on a daily basis throughout the town. Men who were coworkers in the mines fought with each other for no other reason than the color of their skin, which was the badge of prejudice.

As the night wore on and the tequila continued to flow, the workers all took up the cry and became ever more belligerent in their drunken ravings. There were three in particular that seemed to be leading the cheers, Juan José Ríos, Manuel M. Diéguez, and Esteban Baca Calderón. These were all Magonistas, as the followers of the Magon brothers were called, and spent their days stirring up the workers with talk of revolution and anarchy. They all favored the rise of the Mexican worker to join the fight and overcome the long and iron-fisted reign of Porfirio Díaz.

Manuel, who was well respected by his peers and noted for keeping a cool head in times of conflict, cried out "*Compadres*, it is true we need to stand up to the wealthy landowners and politicians, and fight for our rights and our freedom. But for now, let us bow our heads and pray for the memories of our lost *hermanos,* who died in the mines while trying to provide for their families in the only way they knew how. Bow your heads in silence and pray." And this they did.

Chapter Two

Opportunity

The night passed by uneventfully, and the next day Manuel was called into the mining manager's office. The management at *Cobre Libre* had recently brought in a new overseer, Thomas MacMurrough, a ruddy-faced Irishman who was recruited because of his work with indigenous personnel on the Southern Pacific railroad.

As Manuel stepped into MacMurrough's office, Thom called out "*Buenos Días*, Manuel" in his broken and brogue-accented Spanish. "I understand the miners had a bit of the devil's brew last night, and started up talking in revolutionary tones again. This is something I can relate to."

"*Sí, Señor* Thom, yesterday was a very difficult day for us all and the men were blowing off steam. I'm sure we will all be back to business today." Manuel replied.

"Well, Manuel, you seem to be a voice of reason to these men. It is important that they understand their roles here and do their work without complaint. Please make sure your friend Pedro, in particular, understands this."

The mines owner, "Colonel" Greene, as he came to be known, knew he would eventually need to build a railroad to transport and distribute his

46

copper effectively, and a man with MacMurrough's skills would be necessary.

All of the other managers at the mines were Americans, but not necessarily because Greene did not trust his Mexican workers; it was more a question of the experience required to run mining operations. Colonel Greene had been prospecting and working mines in the Sonora region on both sides of the border for years, and made many friends along the way. He had learned to speak Spanish almost as well as a native, and married a woman of Spanish blood. He was a *compadre* to the miners, and this background would serve him well as owner of the mines, just as his education while growing up in New York would in the boardrooms of his various businesses in the future.

Greene had been condemned as a fool by his peers on Wall Street, who insisted there were no new mines, or any mines of value that were not already claimed, and in a sense they were right. But Greene found that although silver and gold in the Sonora mines had petered out, there was plenty of copper to be had. He was able to shrewdly acquire large holdings in the commodity relatively inexpensively.

Greene found that other companies simply did not offer Mexican workers the opportunity to show their capabilities for management. And most of the Americans who came to work the mines throughout the region had a prejudice that was prevalent in the south against anyone with dark colored skin.

As an Irishman, Thom was the first non-American to join in the exclusive club of influencers and leaders at the mining operation. He was prone to drink, was diminutive in stature, and had a freckled face that was long and lean, with a front tooth chipped halfway, and a shock of orange hair that seemed to stand straight out from his head.

He had the Irish gift of gab, and regaled all he came in contact with of stories of the "Auld sod" and his ancestry. Many of these stories stretched credibility, but he was so glib of tongue, that it was difficult not to at least be entertained by his stories, even if you didn't always believe all that he said.

He claimed to be a direct descendent of Dermot MacMurrough, King of Leinster in twelfth century Ireland, a King whose melodramatic story appealed to Thom.

He loved the passion of the story of the King and spent parts of his life emulating the drama of the story, which he would tell to all who would listen and pretend they were not bored.

When he first landed in Boston, after coming over from Ireland under suspicious circumstances, he would often recount his fabricated story in exchange for a free pint in the pub or a snootful of whiskey, and he would recount the history as if it were really his own.

"Sure it is, I am a descendent of the great Dermot MacMurrough, King of Leinster, who ascended to the throne at the tender age of sixteen, when his older brother, who would have been King, died unexpectedly. No one knows if his death was of natural causes, but let's just say you can draw your own conclusions. The MacMurrough blood has always run hot and we look out for ourselves. At any rate, his sovereignty was vociferously protested by the High King of Ireland, Turlough O'Connor, an evil man who was jealous of me ancestor and sent a rogue named Tiernan O'Rourke, chieftain in a neighboring county, to dispatch with Dermot."

"MacMurrough!" cried out the saloon keeper, "Are you going to tell that tired old story again? No one believes your story and if you were truly related to a King, what would you be doing telling lies for free beer?"

"Aw, keep yer trap shut, O'Shaunessey. Can't you see I have a couple of fine, upstanding Gaelic brothers here who know the truth when they hear it? We all know your mother was a Brit."

O'Shaunessey couldn't argue the point, but he hated to see his clientele taken for booze, but then again, the Irish were always a generous lot and if the story made them happy, so be it.

MacMurrough continued "O'Rourke proceeded to ravage the countryside and me ancestor's land in Leinster, plundering villages and violating one of the three sacred laws of Ireland, Daire's Law, which forbade the killing of cattle during battle. That horrid act, which would deprive the people of a critical food source and their livelihood, was a crime above all else. This transgression infuriated young Dermot, and led to a longstanding feud between the two. While O'Rourke was away on a pilgrimage, me heroic ancestor, Dermot, took captive O'Connor's wife, Devorgilla, a calculating and conniving creature if ever there was one.

Many had voiced suspicions that Devorgilla had actually orchestrated the abduction to get away from O'Rouke, and that Dermot was merely a pawn in the game. Nevertheless O'Rourke retaliated, and forced Dermot to escape to England, where he enlisted the help of Henry II.

Henry sent the Earl of Pembroke, known as Strongbow, to help reclaim the title that was rightfully his.

Yes, I am a direct descendant of this great and powerful King, and although our family's claim has been denied unfairly, I deserve all the respect of royalty. A toast to Ireland, land of the people, who continue to fight oppression to this day."

Thom was quite delusional about this so called history, but the lie came easily to him, and he was an accomplished liar. He had heard the story in the pubs back home before his sudden departure for the U.S.

When he came to America, he embraced it as his own and used the story to deflect any doubt about his adopted name. Thom came to sincerely believe the story, and was very proud of this ancestry, although it had nothing to do with his own family's saga. Still, he reveled in the fact that people believed he came from a long line of pugnacious and fiercely independent fighting Irish.

Thom had been born Declan Cassidy, and had grown up in Castlebar, County Mayo, Ireland. In his teen years, he joined up with a "band of brothers" who fought colonial rule in Ireland, which led to the real reason he came to America to help build railroads. A warrant had been issued for his arrest after a terrifying incident, forcing the young man to expatriate.

Declan finished high school at 17 in 1881, and could not find a job for which he considered himself suitable. He was a smart lad and did well in school, although precocious and headstrong, with a very sharp mind and excellent recall of events. Cassidy was always much smaller and thinner than his mates. He learned to compete using his intelligence and his gift of gab, both of which were plentiful. If he could not succeed using these god given talents, then he was not above using trickery and any weapon he could get his hands on to win his way.

He became acutely aware of landowners' rights through the stories of his parents survival during the Great Hunger, also known as the Irish Potato famine in the mid 1840's. That dark period in Irish history made many Irish farmers destitute. They generally did not own the land they tilled, but rather leased it, and when the crops became tainted, they could not pay the landlords or feed their families and were forced to emigrate.

Declan's parents each came from one of the few families who had not evacuated during this disastrous period.

It was as he was looking for work that he fell in with a group that called themselves the Green Brigade. This was a radical group, loyal to the Irish Republican Party, which was newly formed, and promoted a platform of self-rule and independence from Great Britain. They had developed a reputation as a secret fraternal organization, whose charter was to provoke armed revolt against the British state in Ireland.

Declan and his cousin, Sean Flaherty, had been accused of the murder of a British policeman. It seems that they had spent the evening at the Lamb and Lion Pub, plotting a way to break into the British Armory at St. James Gate to avail themselves of weapons that had been stockpiled by the British to be used in the event of insurrection. Violent revolt was an increasing probability ever since the British response to the famine, or non-response as the Brigade contested.

The ensuing destitution resulted in scores of Irish dying or emigrating, if possible, causing the population of the country to fall to only three million people, a third of its' pre-famine existence.

The Green Brigade was a ragtag band of crazed brothers who were a well-kept secret of the revolution. They operated with a total absence of fear of reprisal, and would do whatever they could to incite the British.

After several pints, Declan and Sean left the pub to scout the armory for a scheduled break-in the following night. The plan called for Cassidy to distract the night guard by creating a diversion, while Sean would slip behind and render the guard unconscious. When they arrived at the armory for their test run, they attracted unwanted attention, the stout doing its' work, and requiring relief. Sean stumbled while relieving himself, drawing a guard to see what the commotion was about. Just as the guard turned the corner to confront them, Declan seized a rock the size of a large grapefruit, snuck up behind him, and cracked him hard in the skull. The guard crumpled like a dropped sack of potatoes.

"Jaysus – what did you do that for?" Sean asked incredulously.

Declan dropped the rock and looked up with a smirk on his face "I didn't want him to be able to recognize us tomorrow night when we come back."

"Well, you gave him a good crack – I doubt he'll be here tomorrow night with the pain he'll have."

They ran back to the pub to establish their alibi, and stayed until closing. No one would have noticed the brief period of time they were gone.

Later that night, at a nearby hospital, the guard died from his injuries without regaining consciousness. The incident drew screaming headlines condemning the ongoing violence and the leaders of the Green Brigade were incensed, since the mission would now have to be postponed for several weeks.

Declan and Sean went on the run and were taken off any future missions. The Brigade, however, stuck with their bothers, and arranged for passage on a freighter to Boston where they split up, each with new identities; Declan as Thomas MacMurrough and Sean as Robert Keane. Declan, now known simply as Thom, headed out West to put the past behind him, and work the railroads, which were expanding across and throughout the United States.

He eventually found himself in El Paso, which was a hub for all railroads heading west. The city boasted seven different rail lines converging in the center of town, making it a nerve center for the railroads, and a place that was always hiring new workers.

Thom proved himself to be a hard worker, and was promoted to a supervisors' position in a short time. He managed other workers well, and he was tireless, although he had a reputation as a hothead, and there was a rumor, correct of course, that he had once killed a man.

His reputation was legendary and he needled his workers cruelly.

"Li, pick up that spike maul now and drive more of those rail spikes." "Dumb shite coolie" MacMurrough muttered to himself.

"MacMurrough, lay off Li. He's one of the best we have on the rails. Look after the lazy ones" one of the other supervisors shouted.

"These heathens need to be driven. Yes, he's the best, that's why I drive him harder. I have a job here and that's to lay track. The best ones need to make up for the lazy ones, which is mostly all of them. I'll say one thing for them, the coolies make up for the other riff raff. Ever since the dumb arses up in Congress in Washington passed that stupid law, laying track has become more and more difficult. I drive Li to increase output to set the bar for the other shitheads. You'd be wise to do the same."

The supervisor that was sparring with MacMurrough just shook his head and moved away.

The workers who helped to build the railroads came from a wide variety of countries, but had been mostly Chinese, until the Chinese Exclusion Act was passed seven years before in 1882, virtually stopping the rate of immigration from that country. New workers were being imported every day from all over the world; Japan, Mexico and Africa, among others, due to the railroads rapid expansion.

Thom had shown a flair for getting the maximum amount of effort out of his workers and eventually left El Paso for a better position at the mining company in Cananea. He was attracted to Mexico because the pay went a lot farther, and he could stay in one place and be virtually certain no one from the "auld sod" would ever find him in the godforsaken place. Plus, he loved the warmth of the people, particularly the *Señoritas* who flocked to the mines to make money off the wealthy American businessmen and workers.

A whole new subculture evolved out of the mining community in Cananea. The economy was geared to servicing the workers and their families. As a mining town, there were cantinas, bordellos, and places to gamble to let off the tension created by the difficult and dirty work at the mines.

Now Thom was in Cananea and took no time in forcing his will on his workers. He looked at Manuel and awaited the reply to his directive to keep Pedro in check.

"I will, *Señor* Thom. Is that why you called me here"?

"No, Manuel, I have a more important item to discuss with you. As you know, now that Colonel Greene owns the mines we are most concerned with improving results. Copper is at a premium these days with the expansion of the railroads and the telephone in the U.S. You seem to have a steadying influence on the men, and lately, this talk of revolution is a distraction. I need the men focused on the task at hand, which is mining copper. You have shown yourself to be a leader and I have spoken to Colonel Greene about the possibility of promoting you to a position of supervisor in the mines. We can use a person like you to manage the mining operations and keep the workers focused and in check."

Thom was being disingenuous with Manuel, who was flattered by his smooth words and complementary assessment. Up to this point in time, operations management at the mines had not only decided that only Americans were to be supervisors, but had recently decreed that each supervisor would select his own workers, thus virtually ensuring that Americans would be selected first.

To many of Colonel Greene's investors and advisors, this seemed to be a terrible mistake for several reasons, but the primary one was, of course, money. The use of Mexican labor was one of the advantages the Cananea Consolidated Copper Mines had over similar mines in Arizona, Michigan, Utah and elsewhere across the U.S. The cost of labor in Mexico was much cheaper and gave them a strong competitive advantage. They also reasoned that the Mexicans were already on the cusp of a class revolution, and any movement of favoritism for American labor could only exacerbate the situation. The Flores Magon brothers were rallying citizens all throughout the country with the views they published in *Regeneración,* which was resonating with the proletariat.

Greene was not directly involved in day to day operations at the mine, leaving that to his trusted cadre of managers who he had brought in for the task. These operational leaders had been doing the company a disservice by taking any little bits of power the Mexican workers had away from them, thus helping to set the stage for a revolt. So, the concept of promoting Manuel was one of a conciliatory nature, and designed to help stem worker discontent. It had the added benefit of lowering overall costs as the prevailing theory was that Mexican managers would pick Mexican workers who were paid less than their American counterparts.

"Well, *Señor* Thom, this is a very great honor, but one that carries great responsibility. Mining operations is responsible for the safety of the worker, and the safe operation of the mines. Will I be able to do what is necessary to ensure the workers safety?"

"A very good question," said Thom, adroitly sidestepping a direct response. "Of course, Manuel, you know that no Mexican national has ever been put in this position of responsibility before. It is important to the owner of the mines, and the shareholders, to show the workers the potential for growth, and to put an end to all this talk of revolution. I have been assured that you will be able to make appropriate changes, within reason, and based on cost justification. I, myself, will help you position these suggestions with the owners."

"And, *Señor* Thom, with this new responsibility, will I receive an increase in pay?" Manuel held his breath. He expected Thom to tongue lash him for his audaciousness.

Thom looked at Manuel hard and breathed deeply in and out through his nose.

He smiled and said, "Of course, Manuel. I have been authorized to offer you a 10% increase in pay, and you will have the option to move into the managers' barracks with the other mining supervisors."

Manuel knew this was a pittance of what the other managers made. The Mexican workers made only three pesos a day, compared to five dollars for the American workers, and regardless of the fact that the cry of 'five pesos for eight hours of work' was still more than a decade away, the unrest among the native miners was apparent, and increasing day by day.

Even with a ten percent increase, Manuel still made much less than four pesos a day, even as a supervisor. However, it was more than any other native worker, and he would be the first Mexican with a title.

The additional advantage of moving into the managers barracks was a surprising and tremendous concession. "If a revolution were to happen," he reasoned to himself, "wouldn't it be better to be on the management side of things?"

"*Señor* Thom, I will do the best job I can as mining operations manager. I accept your offer. "

They shook hands and Thom said, "I will announce your promotion next month after *Presidente* Díaz's visit. I'm sure the *Presidente* will be pleased that we are promoting a Mexican to a position of importance."

Manuel left with mixed emotions. On the one hand, he was being given a tremendous opportunity. The mines were the largest in all of Mexico, and one of the largest companies in the country overall. On the other hand, the talk of revolution was real and presented a concern to him. *Presidente* Díaz had been in office for over a decade, and his politics were increasingly being questioned by the people. The world at large was going through tremendous change and Mexico was in constant turmoil. He wanted change for his country, and it seemed the chasm between rich and poor was growing larger. The country needed to spread the wealth and he was hoping that his promotion would be viewed as a movement in that direction. But he knew that Pedro's anger of the night before, and that of the workers in general, was minor compared to what he heard was happening elsewhere in the country.

He had an ominous feeling that he just couldn't shake.

Chapter Three

Edelmida Ríos Castillo

"Child, please kneel properly when you say the rosary. Back straight, head bowed, eyes closed," said the nun to Edelmida. Sister María Ignatius was not nearly as strict as some of the nuns at the convent. The order of the Sisters of Saint Joseph was noted for their disciplinary ways, and it was said that while the Jesuit priests brought Christianity to the Sonora region, it was the nuns who enforced it.

Edelmida was just sixteen years old, but had been alone her entire life, leaving her with a fiercely independent streak. Her father had worked at the Cobre Grande mine in Cananea and had been killed during a mine collapse, just weeks before her birth. During a rescue effort, a timber he was leveraging to bolster an opening in the mine close to the entombed workers, snapped, and a large splinter from the creosote soaked log, the size of an arm, pierced his upper torso severing an artery. He bled out quickly and died almost instantaneously, causing untold grief for Edelmidas' mother, and resulting in a premature birth. As baby Edelmida was exiting the birth canal, her mother ruptured her uterus and died shortly after due to internal bleeding, leaving the infant with two lost parents at the time of her birth.

Edelmida was immediately placed with the nuns at the convent, and from that point on the nuns cared for her and raised her as though she were one of their own.

The convent was well financed by the mining company for just this purpose, helping families of the mining catastrophes that happened on a regular basis.

It was a mutually beneficial relationship. The mines appeared as a caring, benevolent company, and the Sisters were doing God's work and reinforcing and expanding the Christian parish.

It had always been the rule that when a child turned 17, she would return to the mining company and be given a job. This was not indentured servitude. If you choose to leave the job and go elsewhere, you were welcome to do so. The convent had to make room for others and, at 17, it was expected you were an adult who had been brought up in a good Christian environment and were considered capable and self-sufficient.

Edelmida was being prepared now to go back to the mining company. She was a precocious girl, but she had shown a knack for cooking, and proved to be an excellent chef. She excelled at dishes of the local cuisine, *empanadas*, *chile verde*, and roasted quail particularly, but also with foods from other lands that she had only read about;

France, Italy and Spain. This would make her an outstanding addition to the cooking staff at the home of the owner of the mines, Colonel Greene, and particularly for his American managers, and even for the resident Irishman, a supervisor named Thom MacMurrough.

Edelmida finished her prayers and went to the kitchen to start preparing for the midday meal, humming to herself as she prepped. Edelmida had a modest voice, but she loved music, and would sing, or hum, all through the day, earning her the nickname, "The Sparrow."

She was a very pretty girl, receiving the best features of her Indian blood with high cheekbones and coal black hair, and her Spanish heritage which gave her height making her one of the tallest girls in her circle of friends. Her height also imbued in her a sense of humor, which was necessary when you stood taller than most of the boys.

As she was chopping peppers to be used as a salsa side dish, the knife suddenly twisted, slipping and slicing a piece of skin off the knuckle of the middle finger on her left hand, which began to bleed profusely. She quickly wrapped her hand tightly with a piece of cloth and applied a hastily concocted paste of cayenne pepper and water to cover the wound and mask the color of the blood. Cayenne had long been used for treating a variety of ailments, and was known to stem bleeding quickly. The color also made it easy to hide the wound. If

63

the nuns ever noticed Edelmida with a cut, she could lose her place in the pecking order in the kitchen. Too often a person was replaced by a subordinate for less important reasons than a cut hand.

Lunch was the most important meal of the day. The nuns would tend to the school after morning prayers and at one o'clock take a meal followed by a siesta. At three o'clock, they would have activities followed by evening mass. Then the children would do homework while the nuns tended to their personal business. A light meal would follow, and then free time until bedtime at eight thirty. The cycle would start again at six a.m. the following morning.

The convent was not very big. There were 5 nuns and, at any given time, between twelve and fifteen girls staying at the orphanage. Still, as a percentage of the population of the town of Cananea, this was a tremendously large number of children without parents, and it pointed up the dangerous nature of the work.

Edelmida would be moving to the owners' kitchen in two weeks' time, and because of this, she decided to spend that time concentrating on cooking non-native dishes. The range of culinary ideas which came from Europe through the Jesuits, was new and exciting. She felt that her people relied too much on hot spices and she was interested in working with subtle flavors of the herbs and spices that were being imported more frequently with each passing day.

Of course, Edelmida was hampered by the lack of availability of choice meats, fresh vegetables, and, particularly, fish. The nuns did have funds from the mining company for the school, but this was used mostly for clothing and books. There was money for basic cooking, but not much more. Edelmida had to be very creative to find ways to prepare the meals in different fashions and tastes, and relied heavily on local spices.

She knew that things would be different when she got to the Casa Greene, and had heard they had a huge, modern kitchen, with two fireplaces and a stove for cooking indoors. These were kept stoked with wood, creating a very hot flame which she would need for some of the new cooking methods she had read about. The Casa had the luxury of bringing fresh vegetables and meats from the port and storing them in a cabinet that stayed cool and kept items fresh longer. Sometimes, she heard, they even had fish, which was brought in from the Sea of Cortez. Edelmida had never had fish for cooking before, and couldn't wait to try it.

Tonight's dinner would be more common, and consisted of chicken cooked with tomatoes and onions, maize polenta with honey, and greens from a small and sparsely populated garden she kept behind the convent.

Edelmida's garden was fenced with wooden stakes and gauze cloth to keep out the critters, and more gauze cloth over the top to keep out the hot sun. She watered constantly, but felt it was more like a vegetable tent than a garden.

Water was scarce in the Sonora desert in spite of several rivers that ran through the region. These were little more than streams and the water it provided had to be shared and used sparingly. The area is fed water by the San Pedro River whose headwaters begin in the Sierra Madres, and is most unusual as the water flows from Mexico in the south up to Tucson in the north.

The nuns had their own well, however, which helped husband the precious resource. The Papago were known to be excellent farmers, and the existence of the well enabled them to keep their gardens full of fresh vegetables and herbs throughout the year. The high desert challenges of farming in the area caused the tribe to be somewhat nomadic, sowing the seeds of their crop deep in the earth prior to the rainy season, and once the rains came the flash floods would force them to move to higher ground. After the rainy season passed, their crops would flourish and be harvested and dried, prior to the onset of summer heat whose high temperatures could cause the crops to die.

Edelmida made her way to the kitchen and heard her friend, Anna, who was doing prep work for the meal, speaking to one of the nuns about the unrest at the mines. "I heard there was more trouble today at the mines, Sister. That new gringo manager they hired, the one with the hair like fire, was screaming at some of the men as they slaved in the heat at the belly of the mine. He says all Mexicans are lazy and good for nothing and that's the reason all the managers at the mines are gringos."

"Well, What about Manuel Carreras? Didn't they just say they were going to name him manager and move him into the manager's barracks?" The nun replied.

"That's true, and Manuel's a good worker and well respected, but many say that it is a ploy to calm the workers down – to make it look like there is hope for advancement. Most of the men barely make enough money to feed their families while the owners live in huge homes with servants, and have gold, jewels, and artwork that could feed a family for years. I agree with Pedro, the workers need to look out for themselves and the wealth of this country needs to be shared."

Edelmida burst through the door and tried to change the mood. "Yes, and they have fish," Edelmida exclaimed as she entered the kitchen. Anna and the nun laughed out loud.

"Edelmida, you do have your priorities," said the nun.

"Yes, and my priority now is not to think about the troubles at the mines. In two weeks I will go there and feed them with such delicious meals that they will realize that our people are good and talented and they will give us all higher pay."

"You do dream, girl," said Anna. "Let's get cooking and make today's meal."

Chapter Four

La Fiesta en la Casa

Edelmida began work at the Big House, Casa Greene, on a bright warm Monday morning in April, 1889, just two weeks after her 17th birthday. As she climbed the hill and passed the newly planted trees, she marveled at the recently completed structure. The Greene home was perched on a hill overlooking the town and was isolated by a wide expanse of land that was barren up to the property line, where scrub brush and Chihuahua pine trees had been strategically planted so anyone walking by would have a difficult time seeing into the windows of the home, giving it an appearance of privacy, in what was, in reality, a very public setting.

Her heart was beating rapidly, not from the climb up the gently graded slope, but from the excitement she felt as she approached the building in anticipation of what she knew would be a wondrous experience and the most exciting thing that had ever happened to her yet in her short life. Her name was a bit unusual, being a derivative of the more common Edelmira, which translates to "princess," which is exactly what she felt like at this moment.

The town of Cananea in the late 1800's offered little in the way of comfort and elegance with the sole exception of Casa Greene, the home of Colonel William Cornell Greene.

Having been raised by the nuns at the orphanage, Edelmida had only been exposed to the bare basics in her living quarters and rarely to other amenities in her lifetime, and she was raised not to expect any more than what she already had. In fact, she was taught that greed, as one of the seven deadly sins, specifically reinforced the requirement for a sparse existence, lest she be doomed to eternal damnation. Up until this moment, she had been satisfied with her lot in life and what she had, although she often wondered what it would be like to have more. She was taught not to give in to worldly desires, but often bristled at what she considered to be the antiquated ways of the nuns, and harbored dreams of a better life no matter what they taught her. Her upbringing, and the fear instilled in her against the commitment of sin, had her repressing her urges, but now, seeing this bounty before her, she wondered why she could not also have such finery. As she wandered through the deserted kitchen and into the pantry, she thought to herself, "Colonel Greene cannot be a devil; he has all this beauty surrounding him. Why is it that the nuns insist on teaching us that we cannot also have wonderful things and still maintain a Christian life? I wonder if their vows of poverty and celibacy have embittered them and made them jealous of others who have so much more."

Colonel Greene had spared no expense on his domain. The floors were Italian marble, the foyer composed of marble, granite, and mahogany. The wall coverings were flocked velvet wallpaper, and the hardware was 14 karat gold plate. The kitchen was quite large and very well appointed, and to Edelmida this was nirvana. She had never seen anything like it, with rows of cast iron pots and pans, knives of every size and type, cabinets full of accoutrements, and a pantry that one could walk into, stocked with almost any type of herb, spice, or dried goods one could imagine. Since Colonel Greene entertained so often, the kitchen was designed to accommodate food preparation for a large number. Parties were held often and he frequently had investors come to Casa Greene for tours of the mines and visits to discuss financing.

There were four separate work areas for preparing the food: three large sinks made of porcelain-coated cast iron, three stoves, and two ovens, both heated with wood. The hearth was large enough to stand in with a huge cast iron pot balanced in a hanger mounted on the back wall, which could be swung in an arc from one side of the hearth to the other for adding new logs to the fire. It also had a fine mesh grate built on legs stretching waist high to allow cooking of meats and tortillas.

There were pots and pans hanging from hooks above the stoves and cutlery, gleaming and polished, on rows of wooden pegs. Many of the items in the kitchen Edelmida had never seen before; colanders, tools for shaving cheeses, pastry tools. Different sized and shaped spatulas, whisks, and measuring cups. The array of equipment was staggering and she couldn't wait to get started.

Suddenly, a harsh tone interrupted her thoughts. "Edelmida! What are you doing here?" It was Luisina, the head chef that Colonel Greene had brought in from Spain to oversee all kitchen activities, and who was Edelmida's boss. Luisina was known as a taskmaster and handled many of the most important kitchen duties herself. She sourced all the food, maintained her own garden of spices and herbs, and insisted on only the freshest ingredients, shaping her menu around the items that were the best on any given day.

Although Cananea was in a remote location, the town had grown dramatically over the past several years and there were now nearly over 1000 people employed at the mines. The trains brought fish, produce, and other foods from the United States, and imports from overseas.

Luisina had a scowl on her face as she said, "Girl, you are not allowed in the main kitchen until I tell you. All help is to meet in the pantry, each morning, one hour after sunrise. There I will assign tasks for the days meals, and schedules for the week. You will be able to learn everything about preparing meals, but you will start, like all the others, with the most basic tasks. I will be watching you closely. Those with talent will be able to do some cooking and enjoy the more creative aspects of the culinary arts. Those who are less talented will continue to work the prep and cleanup areas."

Colonel Greene had brought Luisina to Cananea from Spain by way of New York, and it was said she had studied in Paris, although no one could verify if that were true. While Edelmida never imagined traveling so far from home, she had heard many stories of these places, and imagined it must be very exciting to be a part of something so big and vibrant. However, her dreams were much more humble, and all she really longed for was a home of her own, and a family to care for someday. Edelmida was a homebody, a person who loved to cook and clean and stick to a specific routine, although now that she had been exposed to the kitchen of Colonel Greene, she wanted to be able to afford the best that she could, and vowed to work hard to make her dream a reality.

"*Sí*, Luisina, I apologize – I just wanted to see the place I heard so much about for so long."

Luisina was not moved. Her experiences in New York and Barcelona had toughened her, and made her a demanding and stern taskmaster. She was brought to Cananea, primarily because of her culinary skills, but also due to her language skills and strict demeanor in the kitchen. Colonel Greene had always believed that the best chefs were stern taskmasters. The language spoken in Cananea was primarily English, but there were still vestiges of the native Papago tongue, and a large majority of Spanish, imparting upon the town a patois that was somewhat unique in the region. Luisinas experiences in the various cities where she worked had taught her many dialects giving her the ability to adapt quickly to variations on a tongue.

Luisina brought Edelmida to the pantry where she was introduced to the other women who would be her co-workers. Each had a specific task and the kitchen was as well run as a military operation. Edelmida was immediately assigned to prepping the vegetables for the evening meal, which made some of the girls jealous, since it was considered to be the last step before the chance to cook. She would chop onions and potatoes and place them in a bowl of water until they were ready to be cooked, and prepare other vegetables, depending on the season. She diced tomatoes and peppers for salsa, and chopped cilantro, and was amazed at the bounty and of all the different types of vegetables at her disposal. As she chopped, she puzzled why her hand had not healed more quickly. The wound she had suffered in the kitchen at the orphanage was certainly caused by the dull knives they had, so different from what she was using now, but the wound persisted, and did not heal as quickly as she would have expected. "No matter," she thought to herself, "I doubt that will happen again –

this cutlery is incredibly sharp, and will certainly not slip in my hand." She took out her large jug of sweet tea, which she always carried with her, a brew she made every day at home and set out in the sun to steep. She added a good amount of sugar, which she seemed to crave lately, and went back to her task.

While at the orphanage, she had learned how to slice, dice, and chop in various styles, but the techniques were crude and rudimentary and she knew from watching the others that she still had much to learn. Fortunately for her, the volume of effort with the nuns was not much different than that required at the Casa, except where there would be a big event, as the Colonel often hosted large parties of visitors and investors.

She was shown a book of recipes and was truly amazed at the variety of ways food could be prepared when you had the right equipment.

As she and her colleagues worked in the kitchen, they talked about the newest buzz, which had come over the town like none before, when word got out that *Presidente* Porfirio Díaz was coming to Cananea at the request of Colonel Greene. Díaz had recently been awarded the Legion of Honor from France, which he proudly displayed on the uniform that he wore on a daily basis. The dictator was well decorated and proud of his military background. As one of the heroes of the Battle of Puebla, he always attended events in full military uniform, including his precious white gloves, so the affair at Casa Greene would be decidedly formal.

The economic policies of the *Porfiriato* had been both a blessing and a curse to the citizens of Díaz' Mexico. During his reign, lands were taken from the indigenous population and *Haciendas* were created, consolidating wealth for the few and further exacerbating the caste system which proliferated throughout the land. The *hacienda* system was not new to *Porfirian* Mexico; Cortés was awarded huge tracts of land by the Spanish Crown, including the practice of *encomienda*, a system of forced labor whereby the *Hacendado or patron* (owner of the *hacienda*), used the native tribes for the manual labor, and were instructed to convert them to Christianity. The common belief of the Crown was that the natives were incompetent savages and had to be converted and taught the skills necessary to make the land productive.

This leftover concept from the past was employed by Díaz, enforced by his military using strong-arm tactics, and produced great economic wealth for the few, while keeping the majority at low income levels, and largely ignorant and uneducated.

Colonel Greene was one of a number of outsiders who took full advantage of the economic realities of *Porfirian* Mexico. Greene was a pragmatist who worked hard for what he had, but also knew how to leverage whatever advantages were laid at his feet.

The *Porfiriato* encouraged economic expansion and use of the labor pool to build the transportation system necessary to bring Mexico to modern prominence as a world power. It almost worked. Mexico vastly improved its rail system, and was noted as a major producer of precious metals and markedly increased exports during his reign. But Díaz had failed to understand the overall power of the people, which eventually became his downfall.

Meanwhile, Colonel Greene was playing by the rules. In fact, he did pay better than most employers in Mexico and was a good friend to the people of Cananea, but as his enterprise grew, it became more and more important to align himself with the rich and powerful politicians of Mexico City. He was already making a name for himself on Wall Street, but his operations were located in Mexico, so currying favor with the leaders and top businessmen of the day was important for his success, as well as his safety. A decision was made that the time was right to invite *Presidente* Díaz to Cananea to view the operations and see how well the people were being treated.

This led to a lunch conversation between Díaz and his top advisors, or *cientificos*, a group who adhered to the idea of *Positivism* as originally advanced by the French philosopher, Comte. This

77

philosophy embraced the concept of advancing the fortunes of Mexico under the *Porfiriato*, through logical assimilation of social mores and economic expansion. The self-important *científicos* loved to quote from Comte, believing it lent them a sophisticated air and gave them a more worldly status then they actually enjoyed.

The date was set, and the meeting was a good strategic move for both Greene and *Presidente* Díaz; Greene to improve his visibility and set up expectations for future development and expansion, and Díaz, because the groundswell of unrest among the peasants and peons was stronger in the north, further away from the center of power in Mexico City.

As the day approached when *El Presidente* was set to arrive, the kitchen was buzzing with anticipation. The event would be short-lived, only two hours of cocktails and appetizers, but the Colonel had asked Luisina to fix the best foods she could find using fresh, local ingredients. Pickled quail eggs, bean salad, empanadas, and guacamole, accompanied by the finest *añejo* tequilas.

The event was expected to be very well attended, and included many investors from New York, as well as the most influential and wealthy of those from Sonora State. The evening of the event, word came down that Díaz would only make a very brief appearance, as he had to leave for a meeting in El Paso/Juarez to discuss expansion of the Mexican rail system into the United States.

The affair went off magnificently. The food and drink were superb, and the atmosphere festive, with strolling bands playing well-known tunes that extolled the virtues of Mexico and its' leaders. All of the men were turned out in their finest suits, with starched, high collars, cufflinks trimmed in gold, and cravats held in place by tie pins of rare stones. The women dressed in long, flowing gowns of crinoline and lace that hissed along the floor as they walked, with narrow waistbands and exuberant bosoms, enhanced by the latest in fashion, the S bend corset. Their hats were large and flowery with bands of satin, and plumes of brightly colored feathers, and they carried parasols, ostensibly to keep the sun out of their eyes during the day, but which became a fashion accessory in the evening. Several of the women dressed in more traditional Spanish garb, with flouncy dresses of multi-layered fringe, adorned by ribbons and topped by mantillas on their head.

Colonel Greene formally greeted *Presidente* Díaz as he exited the new, sleek black carriage that the Colonel had sent for him and had ordered especially for the event. *Presidente* Díaz was nearly as imposing a figure as Colonel Greene, with a mane of silver hair and an opulent moustache that curled at the corners, although his expression was always stern, and it did nothing to add an air of humor.

They ascended the stairway together and upon their entry at the head steps leading down into the ballroom, Greene introduced *el Presidente* in a loud and booming voice to the entire ensemble. *El Presidente* passed through the room, greeting those he knew, and being introduced to those he did not, and was gracious and enigmatic to all he met, although still somewhat aloof and reserved. After the initial enthusiasm of the entrance of Díaz, Colonel Greene invited him, and his Secretary of Finance, José Yves Limantour, to meet with him and his senior management team in the parlor to enjoy cigars and fine cognac, while the fiesta kicked into a higher gear as the liquor flowed and the band swung into music designed to encourage people to dance.

"*El Presidente*, I welcome you to our humble town and hope you were able to view a bit of the mining operations on your way to see us." Greene had sent the new carriage to greet the *Presidente*, with instructions to take him on a route to give him maximum exposure to the surroundings and, particularly, the mines.

"*Sí*, Colonel Greene, very impressive. I noticed several of your workers along the road calling out to me. They seemed to be angry and had signs demanding higher wages, but, in fact, that is why we came to see you. *Señor* Limantour?" In fact, wages were of primary concern, but just as disconcerting to many of the workers, and the reason the turnout for protest was so high, a politically dangerous thing to do, was because Díaz had announced that he would outlaw the bullfights in the coming year.

"Colonel, as you know, Mexico has long been behind the times and considered a second class country, particularly in comparison to our neighbor in the north. *Presidente Díaz* and his cabinet have worked tirelessly to bring the country into its' rightful place in the world as an economic power with vast natural resources. The economy has improved greatly, the exchange rate against the U.S. Dollar has grown, and exports have increased dramatically. However, none of this comes without a price. We are well aware of the concerns of the workers for higher wages. They see how the country has done, and expect, rightly so, to share in that wealth. However, the ability to share in this wealth takes time. If we were to increase the pay of all the hourly wage earners throughout the country, our economy would collapse. However, expanding expenses would reduce profitability, and the building of roads and rail service, which is badly needed to compete on the world stage, would come to a halt. We are aware that you came up through the ranks as a mine worker, and empathize with the plight of the wage earner, but we implore you to maintain the status quo and keep wages low, until this country is on its feet for certain. This is the main purpose of our visit, as the Cananea mines are not only the largest mining operations in the country, but proximity to the United States puts a magnifying glass on operations and sends a signal to the rest of our country and to the world at large."

Colonel Greene looked at the two men, and then at his staff. He was stunned. It was inconceivable to him that the *Presidente* of the country would want to talk to him about this. He knew that there was increasing tension and unrest, but it must be even worse in Mexico City than what he had witnessed to date in Cananea. Of course, Colonel Greene spent quite a bit of time in New York lately, much more so than Mexico, so, he thought, perhaps he was somewhat blind as to the extent of the issue and its impact.

"*Señor* Limantour, we here at the Cananea mines empathize with your situation. Certainly, we are hearing more often and vociferously from the wage earners to increase their wages and bring parity to the Mexicans. They are asking for other rights as well; shorter hours and more Mexican supervisors and managers. I want to help you and maintain order throughout Mexico, so here is what I can offer. I will talk to my staff and we will hold wages as you recommend. However, we will try to offer other concessions which will be local in nature, such as supervisory positions, to help appease some of their demands and keep the peace, and we will support *Presidente Díaz's* efforts through a contribution to his ongoing campaign. Fair enough?"

"*Sí*, Colonel Greene. Concessions of a local nature are your concern. We appreciate your support. Now, I believe we must leave for El Paso, can you call up your fine coach for us, *por favor*?"

"Of course, *Señor*. But before you go, I do have a question for you. You mention that you are heading to El Paso to discuss a rail line between Mexico and the United States. I assume there will be a bid placed for a company to build this line on both sides of the border, correct?"

"That is accurate, Colonel Greene," Limantour replied as he squinted his eyes in understanding."

"Well, *Señor*, as you know, moving the matte from Cananea to other markets is critically important to us, and we have worked to build our own transportation. I believe that the copper company would be an ideal candidate to build the Mexican side of the line, and my senior management team is composed of all Americans, which will make negotiation and cooperation with the U.S. authorities quite easy and amenable. Would you please consider us as a viable contractor for this project?"

Colonel Green offered his most ingratiating smile as he looked from *Señor* Limantour to *Presidente* Díaz and back again. A knowing look came upon *el Presidente*s face as he realized the *quid pro quo* that Greene was extending. He stood up and extended his hand, "Of course, Colonel

Greene. We would be happy to mention you as a premier corporation with the ability to compete in the bid process. I assume I can count on you to honor your commitment to contain wages and contribute to our campaign?"

"Of course, your Excellency – and may I say it has been a pleasure meeting with you and helping your cause."

Presidente Díaz, Limantour, and his staff then took a hasty retreat out the back door of the study to the Colonels' waiting carriage. "A wise man." Díaz commented as he looked back, smiled, and waved goodbye.

Edelmida was very happy with her new life and could not imagine anything more wonderful than the work she was doing in the kitchen at the mines.

One bright summer afternoon, as Edelmida headed back to work at the pantry after siesta, she was stopped along the way by one of Colonel Greene's managers. She recognized him by his shock of red hair and had recognized him from some of the dinners that she had served when Colonel Greene invited his management team to the Casa, which he did with frequency.

"*Señorita*, you are new here at mines are you not?"

Edelmida noticed he had a peculiar accent and a rough manner about him. It was unusual for a manager at the mines to address one of the workers, especially one of Spanish heritage. Virtually all of the management team were American or white European, and most thought the native workers beneath them.

"*Sí*, I just started here a few weeks ago *Señor,*" Edelmida replied.

"Well, me girl, you are a welcome addition and I hope to see more of you soon. Perhaps we can stop for a cool drink one day after work, eh?" he said as he leered at her.

"Perhaps, *Señor*," she replied, wondering what he meant by that, for it was unheard of for one of the managers to socialize with a native kitchen worker, and the feeling he gave was distinctly not pleasant. As she walked away from him, he stood watching her from behind and could feel himself stiffen with excitement. Edelmida thought that a cool drink would be a good idea, for it seemed to be unusually warm and she was always thirsty lately.

She could feel his eyes on her and when she turned around, he quickly turned on his heel and walked away as if he had not been watching her, but she had caught him and it made her extremely uncomfortable. The nuns had warned her to beware of the workers at the mines, but she didn't realize that applied to the managers as well. She walked on with a strange feeling of foreboding and hoped to avoid this strange little man at all costs.

<u>Chapter Five</u>

Declan Cassidy/

Thom MacMurrough

Thom MacMurrough had a secret. It was not the murder in Dublin, his obvious love of the drink, or his new name. He loved young women. No, not really love and not really young women, he lusted after adolescent girls.

Growing up in a Catholic country, as Ireland was, it was difficult to find someone willing to give up her virginity prior to marriage. The priests had ruined it for him – "weren't relations between a young man and a woman natural?" he thought to himself. Declan lost his virginity at fifteen years old, quite young for men in Ireland, and he always remembered it fondly.

The girl was from the neighborhood where he grew up and always seemed to be a tease, at least from young Declan's perspective. She was also fifteen and they attended school together. Anne Marie was her name and she had curly brown hair worn just to her shoulders, with light brown freckles and the liveliest blue eyes he had ever seen. Her breasts were small and just budding and when she saw Declan, she seemed to throw her shoulders back so they would jut out, teasing him.

Often, after school, they would play with their other neighborhood friends until evening. After dark, the teasing would start. It was innocent enough at first. Declan would tease her and begin to tickle her and they would roll around on the ground wrestling. He would feel her breasts and she would act like she didn't like it, but could never seem to struggle away, and Declan believed this was intentional. One time, during their tussle, he kissed her and she had kissed him back. Declan could not get her out of his mind. One warm summer night he arranged to meet her behind the stable at the church. For her part, Anne Marie really liked Declan and was excited at the prospect of being alone with him for a time. They could kiss and be close and maybe, someday, she thought, they could even be married. Her cousin had married right when they finished school at 17, and they seemed happy enough.

"Over here, Anne Marie," Declan called out. He had been waiting for her for nearly an hour. He brought with him a flask of whiskey to keep them warm and break the ice.

"Declan, you startled me. I'm never out at night by myself and I was starting to worry you wouldn't be here. I wish we could have met closer to home. My parents will be worried if I'm gone too long. I told them I was going to the church school because I forgot one of my books for homework. It's very dark out tonight, and I don't like walking all this way by myself. Maybe this was a bad idea."

Lord, she does prattle on, thought Declan. "Anne Marie, my dear, I am so happy you came. "Would you like a nip to keep you warm?"

"Oh, no Declan. My lips have never touched drink and I doubt they ever will. It's the devil's brew, it is."

"That makes more for me," Declan replied as he took a large swig from the flask. "Come, give us a kiss," he said as he came close to her, put his hands on the back of her head and pulled her close to his body, kissing her hard and pushing his tongue into her mouth.

"Declan, stop, you're being too rough," Anne Marie cried.

"Oh, Anne Marie me love. You told me you didn't have much time, and isn't this what we're here for?"

"Well, Declan, I do like you and want to be close, and maybe a kiss is all right, but I don't like it when you're rough."

"All right then, Anne Marie. I'll be good." Declan said as he took another large gulp of whiskey. He stroked her hair and told her how pretty she looked. Anne Marie was a tease, but underneath her bravado, she was a good Catholic girl with strong morals and a sense of propriety. As they sat and chatted, Declan continued to pull on his flask and became increasingly inebriated. He began to kiss her lightly, then reached down to touch her breast.

"Declan, stop, you promised to be good."

"I am good Anne Marie; let me show you how good." Declan rubbed his groin against her leg and pushed her down to the ground. He started to feel her all over and pushed his tongue into her mouth repeatedly in little darting motions. Anne Marie cried out for him to stop, but Declan was in his own world and only one thing would release him from the way he felt. He wanted her and he would have her.

"Declan, stop. I have to get home. Me Da will come looking for me."

Declan, in his excited and drunken state, took this as a sign to move more quickly. He put his hand up Anne Marie's skirt and ripped off her underpants. He pulled down his own pants and moved between Anne Marie's legs, pushing hard. The more she screamed and resisted, the more excited he became. He thrust and gained entry as Anne Marie sobbed and begged him to stop. As she kicked and screamed, trying to turn on her side so he could not penetrate, he held her hands down and pushed harder and harder, and tearing her apart with his thrusts.

She begged him to stop and he said to her, "This will go much easier if you just relax and enjoy it. You agreed to meet me here and you know as well as I do that this is what we both want, so just have a good time. This will be the best you will ever have."

She didn't take his advice and continued to struggle in vain, crying and sobbing, and praying that he would either stop or be finished, but he seemed to go on and on and on.

When he was done, he got up and took the last drop from the flask, "Anne Marie, me girl, you are a blessing. Me first love, and I will always remember you."

Anne Marie, sobbing and bleeding from below, sat up and with venom in her voice cursed Declan Cassidy, his mother, his father, and all his past and future generations. Then she ran home to hide, and vowed she would never be with a man again.

Since that time, Declan Cassidy would only be truly satisfied when he was with a woman who had never been penetrated. He didn't limit himself to virgins, because, of course, as he got older it became more and more difficult to meet and attract young, virginal lovers. Over time, Declan stopped worrying about the pretense of love, or whatever the girl imagined the relationship to be, and all he really cared about was finding a girl whose virginity was intact. His intent was to be the first to engage in sex with the girl, whether she wanted to or not. His desires carried him to dark and uncharted waters, and he found himself moving from place to place as he found, and raped, young, nubile, and guileless young girls.

Declan didn't think of this as a sickness or, indeed, anything out of the ordinary. He believed that a man and a woman were put on earth to procreate, and he never thought of himself as getting any older. He always remembered Anne Marie, and each time he had sex with a woman, he re-lived that first experience.

Of course, he knew that society did not approve of his behavior, but he blamed the priests for that, along with virtually everything else in the world. If only he knew the pain and suffering he would endure because of his perverted behavior, he would have thought twice before continuing his extended crusade.

Chapter Six

Investors

William Cornell Greene

The first Friday in May, 1889 dawned sunny and bright with the kind of hope and expectation that builds rejuvenated spirits. Spring in Cananea was typically rainy and cool, so the welcoming sunshine and warmth gave rise to a general feeling of happiness and contentment. Edelmida was settling into her routine at Casa Greene, enjoying her work and socializing with the crew in the kitchen. Some of the crew she recognized from the orphanage, but many were older and, although she did not know them, the friendly environment in the kitchen at the Casa sparkled with camaraderie and everyone got along quite well.

Colonel Greene had only just recently purchased the mines and business was booming, enabling him to build his beautiful home on a hill overlooking the grounds of Cananea. He regularly invited investors to the mines encouraging them to invest more money since he continually required new capital for expansion. The Four C's (Cananea Consolidated Copper Company) as it was commonly referred to, was now a publicly traded company with shares exchanged "on the curb" near the New York Stock Exchange. Colonel Greene proved to be one of the most successful and most prolific of the curbstone brokers.

A popular book about the wild and hectic times of the traders had just been published two years before. Written by William Worthington Fowler in 1887, "Inside Life in Wall Street or How Great Fortunes are Won and Lost," described the scene in the following manner "On a busy day, they are all eyes and ears, scud and scamper, their fingers quivering like aspen leaves, their mouths pouring out a stream of bids and offers disencumbered of all the spare syllables, while they telegraph signals with the ten digits, and with nods and winks." Thus it was, that Colonel Greene, with all the verve of a gambler, raised the capital he needed to build and expand the mines.

William Cornell Greene was born in Duck Creek, Wisconsin, but moved to Chappaqua, New York, when he was very young and was raised there by middle class parents. He was a precocious young man, and his yearning to move west and seek out his fortune caused him to roam away from New York in his late teens. He spent time in a number of cities moving steadily west, then south, in his search for fortune. He was known as Bill Greene, a sometime cowboy, avid hunter, gambler, and lover of women.

Greene continued his hunt for elusive riches for years, well into his twenties and early thirties, moving again and again until he eventually found himself south of the border in Sonora, Mexico. There he met up with a good friend from New York, and found work mining for gold, silver, and, sometimes, copper. He eventually made enough money of his own to purchase his first copper mine, although many thought him crazy and said that the mines were spent and the minerals had all petered out. Greene took a gamble, and because he had mined these hills surrounding the area for years, he believed they still had plenty left to offer. He worked the mines hard, extracting ore from veins that had not yet been tapped, reinvesting the money, and finding new veins in nearby mountains.

Greene was in the right place at the right time when he took over ownership of the mines late in 1889. The need for copper was at an all-time high due to the rapid explosion of goods driven by the industrial revolution and the immigration of people from other lands resulting in a dramatic increase in the use of electricity. Railroads were being built to move people and goods across the U.S., and all metals were in great demand, particularly the utilitarian copper, because of its tremendous properties as a conductor of electricity at a reasonable cost.

Greene's challenge was getting the copper from the mines in the rural countryside of Sonora to the markets in the United States. The roads were very poor and there were enormous challenges moving the raw materials across the streams and rivers, which swelled when the rainy season came. The Sonora region is typically very dry and hot, but when the rains visit the area, flood plains become impassable.

As a supplier, Colonel Greene had to find a way to make his goods available at any time of year in any weather conditions. His connections in New York enabled him to go back often to line up additional investment and float new shares of stock. These cash infusions enabled him to build the framework necessary not only to move the copper from the mines, but also to build new and more efficient smelters, develop other mines in the region, and build housing and food sources for the workers. He issued new shares often, and also consolidated operations of different mines allowing him to issue shares in the new company to help fund his transportation needs and build railroads.

The colonel was a very persuasive man. His gambling endeared him with the cigar smoking high rollers of the day and he often joined the likes of Rockefeller and J.P. Morgan at the Algonquin Club and other high-end venues in Manhattan which enabled him to raise capital to fund his expansion efforts. The Cananea mines continued to grow and thrive under Greene's leadership and he spent many years of his life living at the Waldorf in New York with his wife and family, traveling back and forth to the mines in Cananea. In time, Greene's son would be the first baby ever born at the exclusive hotel.

Raymond F. Cavanagh

Bill Greene became Colonel Greene when he first applied for a permit in Sonora to purchase the mines. The Mexican clerk had inadvertently misspelled his name on the form, transposing it to William *Colonel* (not Cornell) Greene. Greene loved the idea of being called Colonel and stuck with the name, which he was known by for the rest of his life. He never served in any branch of service, but earned his stripes by the sweat of his brow, and spent years working in the southwest, herding cattle, working the mines, and pursuing his lifelong passion for gambling. Gambling became a way of life for William Cornell Greene, not just the gamble he took in buying and growing the mines, but in everything he touched.

He was a shrewd and very smart businessman, although he did have a penchant for overextending his enterprises. Whenever he needed more money to fund one of his new ventures, which were innumerable, he would again go back to New York and float more stock to pay for the expansion, creating a need to generate ever greater revenues and profits to stave off investors. This inversed pyramid of money would lead to serious problems with his enterprises and his ultimate downfall. Greene was anything but frugal, and he was known to have lavish parties for his investors, both in New York, and at the mines in Cananea, and to his friends he could not be more generous. He shared his wealth willingly and often gave presents spontaneously to friends, allies, and business associates worth thousands of dollars. He loved horses and had dozens on his ranch, which he raced at Saratoga, and horses were one of the gifts he bestowed as a token of friendship and loyalty.

Colonel Greene experienced a life altering loss life during the time he was living in Tombstone, Arizona, and many believe it shaped his future, and drove him to achieve his successes to try and fill a void he could never really fill. Greene had come to Tombstone as a young man just twenty-nine years old in 1880, when it was still an uncivilized and untamed frontier town of 2,000 people, mostly prospectors looking to capitalize on Ed Schieffelin's silver mine discovery three years before Greene's arrival. Whatever semblance of law and order that existed in the town was provided at the time by the Citizens Safety Committee, a vigilante group who often took matters into their own hands and set the tone for the reputation Tombstone would eventually acquire.

Schieffelin himself, the founder of Tombstone, was an unusual man whose history was not unlike that of Colonel Greene's. They both had a hunch about their mines and fought to win the rights to prospect their finds, and both eventually became millionaires. Schieffelin was born in Pennsylvania, but his family moved to the southwest when he was still very young. For the first 30 years of his life he led a quiet existence, but then, suddenly, decided to strike out for California to try his hand at prospecting for gold. Along the way, he spent some time in the army camp at Fort Huachuca, where he became an Indian scout, which afforded him the time to prospect the land on the lookout for his "big strike" and the mother lode. The area surrounding the Fort was Apache territory, whose resistance to white settlers was led by Geronimo after the death of Cochise, and represented a serious threat to anyone, but particularly those who traveled alone.

Schieffelin would take his life into his hands prospecting the area and entering into areas that no white man had ever been before. He would come back from his scouting missions with stones embedded with minerals, which the soldiers believed to be fool's gold. They would ride him mercilessly, telling him "the only stone you'll find out there is your tombstone," and thus the town was named.

Tragedy struck several years after Greene arrived in Tombstone. There, he met and married his first wife, Ella Roberts Moson, the sister of his business partner at the time, Ed Roberts and divorcee of William Montgomery Moson of California. Ella was a convent-educated woman with fine tastes and not accustomed to the rough life that Tombstone represented. She and Colonel Greene fell in love and they spent the next several years living a quiet existence on his farm on the San Pedro River, where he cultivated crops that flourished due to the water source the San Pedro provided. He would bring his crops to the Copper Queen store in Bisbee, Arizona territory, where he and the owner, a friendly Irishman named, W.H. Brophy, became lifelong friends. He would also sell hay on contract to Fort Huachuca, which was located just twenty-five miles from his homestead. Water rights became critically important to him, as it was to everyone in this arid section of the country, and he was always concerned that someone would attempt to divert the river and reduce his flow. It was a common practice in the lawless west, and Greene recognized the value of his land on the San Pedro, and protected his water source aggressively, many times landing him in court over these rights.

Ella had two children from a previous marriage, and the Colonel raised them as if they were his own. Life was good for many years for Colonel Greene, although he still, occasionally, would go to Tombstone to gamble, but for a lawless town like Tombstone, his was a sedentary existence.

He and Ella also had two children of their own; Ella, who was born in 1887 and Eva who came three years later. He loved his little girls and was a loving and giving father, and the family of six lived a quiet life for many years.

While living outside Tombstone, Greene developed a long running feud with a rapscallion named Jim Burnett, a self-proclaimed sheriff who practiced vigilante justice in Charleston, a small settlement just south and downstream of Colonel Greene's farm on the San Pedro. Burnett was an ornery type who dispensed justice indiscriminately from the business end of a shotgun, which he always carried with him draped over his arm, threateningly. He used his power to build his holdings in cattle, and routinely fined Mexican workers who had no way of paying the fines, so he would put them to work performing "community service" on his land. Burnett had threatened Greene on many occasions, but the Colonel was not known to back down from anyone, and the two had altercations time and again.

Greene, however, was generally content to live his sedate life on the San Pedro cultivating crops, raising his family, and paying close attention to his water rights. He built a dam on his property to enable him to better cultivate the land and ensure the abundance and quality of his crops. Still, Greene was always searching for ways to generate more income, and he regularly combed the Sonora desert in search of gold and silver mines.

The delineation of the border between Arizona and Mexico was spotty at best, and people came and went without any regard for geography or politics. Burnett was not well liked anywhere in the territory, and he had used up whatever goodwill he had with the townspeople, when he leased some of his land to six Chinese farmers who developed a co-op farm and priced their goods aggressively, thereby diverting business away from other farmers, including Colonel Greene.

This expansion of land usage increased his need for water, and Burnett authorized the Chinese farmers to build a new dam on his property. Some say Burnett encouraged the workers to find a way to improve the flow of water, and one night the dam on Colonel Greene's property was inexplicably blown up and water rushed downstream, flooding the banks on Greene's farm, and cascading down to Burnett's properties.

Ella and Eva Greene, now ten and seven, regularly went to play in a shallow pool of water on the banks of the river near their home, and the following day, along with a friend, Katie Corcoran, received permission to go to the wading pool. At the time Colonel Greene was off in New York on business, to talk to potential investors in another attempt to line up funding for his excursions into Mexico in his quest for gold and silver mines.

The children went off happily looking to have fun in the sun and spend the day cooling in the flowing waters of the shallow pool. Eva jumped in first, and as soon as she did, quickly sank as water flowed over her head enveloping her. She bobbed to the surface, sputtering and choking out water, and she shouted out to the others "Go back! Go back!" but it was too late, and their friend Katie had already jumped in. None of them could swim, and the sudden depth and flow of water was too much for the two of them. The younger Eva ran back to the ranch house for help, but when they came back to the water hole, it was too late. Ella and Katie had been overcome by the water in their lungs, and both had died.

Colonel Greene returned to Tombstone as quickly as possible when he was notified of the death of his beloved daughter and her friend. He was despondent and overcome with grief, and as the reality of what happened sunk in, his grief turned to anger, and his blood boiled with a burning desire to seek revenge. He intuitively knew that Burnett was behind the explosion that had ruined the dam and flooded the water hole, causing the drowning of his child and her good friend. He posted a one thousand dollar reward for information leading to any proof of who was behind the explosion of the dam. Whether through an informant, or his own investigation, Greene was certain the culprit was Burnett.

Several days after posting the reward, Colonel Greene was in Tombstone on ranch business, where Burnett also was on this day. Whether this was serendipity or calculated is not known, but the Colonel went to John Montgomery's livery stable and corral, also known as the O.K. Corral, and asked Montgomery to take care of his team. He also handed over his pistol, which was always a prudent thing to do while in Tombstone, and went off to town to conduct his business. When Greene went back to Montgomery's sometime later, unbeknownst to him, Burnett was seated inside the office. John and the Colonel chatted for some time – Montgomery trying to keep the two apart - and it's unclear if either one knew at this time that the other was in town. Burnett eventually left the office and went out the side door which was on an alleyway leading to the corral. After he exited, he sat down in a rocking chair on the raised wooden sidewalk, and began to chat with a few of the local hands. Montgomery went into the office to get the Colonel's pistol to give back to him, saw that Burnett had left, and breathed a sigh of relief with the realization that he had avoided a confrontation. He handed the Colonel his pistol, and Greene said goodbye and left. With gun in hand, Colonel Greene, came around the building heading for the corral, and froze as he stared at Burnett seated there talking to the hands as casual as could be.

Greene confronted Burnett and accused him of blowing up the dam and killing his daughter, which Burnett vehemently denied. The two exchanged words and, as Burnett put his hands on the chair to rise up to confront Greene, the Colonel raised his pistol and shot him dead with one shot. "'Vengeance is mine, I will repay' saith the Lord" he intoned.

Colonel Greene was acquitted of murder, based primarily on the strength of witnesses who stated that Burnett appeared to be rising to reach for his gun. The Colonel would never be the same after the drowning, and he was only driven harder to ensure his business success, life-long drive toward wealth, and the safety and security of his family. A short time after the incident, he and his family moved out of Tombstone and permanently settled in Mexico where they built their home in Cananea.

Edelmida did not know any of this, of course. To her, Colonel Greene was the chief benefactor of all the wonder that the mines in Cananea had to offer. People here had good jobs at fair wages, and although there was an undercurrent of unrest from the miners due to unfair pay practices between the native workers and the Americans, she was happy, indeed, and loved both her job and her life at this point in time.

"Edelmida," said Luisina, "I need to go to the market to pick up some fresh peppers and fruit for the luncheon that Colonel Greene is hosting today for investors. I will be back in just a few minutes."

Once she was gone and out of sight, heading the few hundred yards down the road to the local market, Edelmida wandered out of the kitchen to marvel at the expanse of the dining room, the fine artwork on its' walls, and the beautiful table settings that Colonel Greene had imported from New York.

Edelmida wondered what it must be like to live in such a manner and be able to afford such luxury and finery. She vowed that she would work hard and save her money to build a nice home for a family she hoped to have someday, as she settled into her routine at Casa Greene. She was wise enough to realize she would not be able to afford such a lifestyle, but would create an environment for her children so they could grow up to believe and achieve things far beyond her reach. A life here at the Casa would expose them to fine living; artwork, music, fine wine and foods, elegant table manners and an upbringing that would not be available to the average person in Cananea. "Yes," thought Edelmida, "my children will know what it is to live a cool, quiet life with plenty of good food and money to spare. I will do all in my power to ensure they are well cared for and raise them to believe that they can become whatever they wish. Someday, maybe not in my lifetime, but someday, we will be equal to the Americans and also have fine things and live in a better world." Edelmida was happy with her thoughts and truly believed that the world would change soon and things would be different, but she had no idea how right she was and how soon this would occur.

As she thought about all this, she marveled at the beautiful pictures on the walls of the dining room. "Colonel Greene must have spent a fortune on some of these pieces," she thought to herself.

Edelmida went back to the kitchen and continued her prep for the evening meal, moving between the kitchen and the dining room to set the table and set out the appropriate serving pieces. She carried with her a flask of warm, sugared tea, for she seemed to crave the sweet fluid and needed to quench her perennial thirst, which she thought must be due to all the work she had to do each day. Edelmida primarily did the kitchen prep work for the meals, but she was a very attractive girl and her movements in and out of the main dining area often drew stares from visiting investors. It was apparent to her boss, Luisina, that this was to the Colonel's advantage and so she decided to give Edelmida more flexibility in her movements through the dining area than most of the kitchen help.

Now that Luisina was off to the local market to source fresh vegetables and herbs for the meal, Edelmida decided to branch out a bit and explore the drawing room, which housed many of the fine artwork that Colonel Greene had accumulated during his many travels to New York and elsewhere.

She had heard a rumor of one spectacular painting of a young woman from Spain for which Colonel Greene had reportedly paid a very great sum of money, and Edelmida would sorely love to see such a painting, which she could only imagine must be painted in gold, or encrusted with jewels.

As she made her way gingerly to the drawing room, she slowly opened the door and peeked around the corner. She saw no one there and heard not a sound throughout the Casa, and so she stepped inside the room to take a closer look at the paintings adorning the walls. She was surprised to see there were only two large paintings, one on

106

each end of the drawing room to the left and right as you entered, and two small ones, one above and slightly right of the other on the middle wall straight ahead. She could not tell which one it was that cost so much money, for they all looked similar to her. Pictures of people in various poses, one, a woman and a small child flying a kite, and the other, a woman in a Spanish outfit complete with mantilla sitting in a similar drawing room to the one in which she found herself now.

As she turned to leave, on the wall behind her as she entered, where the main leather sitting chair faced, there was a magnificent gold cross that sparkled and was encrusted with jewels, looking more spectacular than had been described to her by the other workers.

It clearly was the most expensive object at Casa Greene and without a doubt worth millions of pesos. Edelmida could only imagine that it must be an heirloom for it looked very old and yet it sparkled as if made only yesterday. She had only seen such objects in the cathedral where the nuns took her and the other girls to the *Mission San Xavier del Bac* in Tucson, back when it was common to cross the border in either direction.

As she examined the cross in awe, she was startled to hear someone opening the door behind her and suddenly say in a deep, booming voice that resonated throughout the room, *"Buenos Dias, Señorita. Por favor*, be sure to dust these paintings very carefully, they are worth a handsome amount of money, and pay particular care of that cross, it is an heirloom with a long and storied past."

"Colonel Greene," exclaimed Edelmida as she jumped backwards. Edelmida immediately recognized him. Colonel Greene was a man of great stature, six feet tall, with wavy auburn hair and an opulent moustache. "I am so sorry – I was just admiring the beauty of the Casa and was struck by the magnificence of this cross. It is the most beautiful thing I have ever seen, even more beautiful than the crosses I have seen at the *Mission San Xavier del Bac*." She had blurted this last statement out in her native tongue, which was a blend of Spanish and Papago. Colonel Greene smiled crookedly as he replied in Spanish, "Really? That's very interesting, child. I have not noticed you before, are you new to the Casa?" he asked.

"Yes, Colonel," she replied, switching back to English. "My name is Edelmida and this is my first week here. I come from the orphanage and will be working in the kitchen and serving meals. No one was here and I thought it would be all right to admire some of the works of art you have. They are beautiful indeed" Edelmida replied.

"Edelmida!" shouted Luisina, who had just come back inside from her errands, "you are not allowed to wander out of the kitchen without permission, and you are certainly not allowed to wander into other rooms at the Casa not associated with your duties."

"It's all right, Luisina," Colonel Greene replied with a smirk. He liked the spunk this new girl had shown in exploring, and it reminded him of himself when he was young and impetuous. "My new friend here was just admiring my golden cross. Please leave us to chat awhile, and I will make sure she gets back to her duties very soon." Luisina left the room hesitantly, thinking to herself that she would need to keep an eye on this new worker.

"You have a fine eye Edelmida, this cross has been handed down for generations by the natives in the Sonora region, and is believed to be proof that the cities of Cibola and Quivira, as well as the other Cities of Gold, really do exist. Its very presence is part of the reason the Missionaries continued to explore and settle the land centuries ago." "It is said that this cross has great powers and it was once owned by Hernán Cortés, the first person from Europe to visit our enchanted land centuries ago. It is very, very old, and quite valuable."

"How did you come upon such a treasure, Colonel Greene? Did you find it while prospecting the hills of Sonora for gold and silver?" Edelmida asked, for it was legendary how Colonel Greene had come upon the mines in Cananea and built his empire.

"Ah, that's a very interesting story, Edelmida. You see, when I first came to Cananea from New York years ago, I was convinced that the region was still ripe with the potential for gold and silver. Of course, I don't often admit this, but I really wasn't looking for copper, and at first I wasn't sure these mines were worth pursuing. Still, copper was a valuable metal and with expansion of the railroads I knew demand would increase, and if I could find a way to get it transported efficiently, it could be lucrative. For centuries, this area has been rumored to house one of the Seven Cities, and it is well known in certain circles that the Jesuits had been mining the area for decades. Of course, it was against their religion to own the mines and make a profit from its riches, and so they mostly worked them for the items they could fashion for the Mass. It has been well documented that one of the ways that Christianity was spread throughout the native lands was due to the extensive use of gold and silver to dazzle and enchant the people. The religion itself prides itself on simple living and Spartan existence, but the use of brilliant items to enhance the beauty of the Mass has long been an inducement to the poor and destitute, offering them hope that they too may someday have such riches. If only Jesus, who was himself a poor and simple carpenter, knew how the religion was spread, I'm sure he would offer a strong opinion on their methods. Of course, the missionaries had to keep the mines a secret from their superiors back in Spain, or they would have had to rid themselves of the mines, or send any money gained back to their church. It is rumored that some of the priests had mercenary tendencies and took some of the precious metals for themselves and became rich, but for the most part, the money was used to build new and beautiful missions which today are prevalent throughout the entire region, all the way out to the Pacific Ocean."

"But secrets always seem to have a way of leaking out, and while I was working on Wall Street in New York – have you heard of this place?" Colonel Greene asked.

Edelmida, with her eyes open wide and her mouth slightly open with the wonder of what she was hearing, shook her head yes. The nuns were very strong on teaching history and geography in hopes that some of their students would, one day, break the chain of events and move on to bigger and better things, traveling the globe and becoming not only worldly, but a model for others to follow.

"Good," Colonel Greene responded, "it is a wonderful place, and the liveliest place in the world – a place where you can do anything and become whatever you choose. At any rate, while I was on Wall Street, I would go to church at St. Peter's Cathedral, the oldest church in the State of New York, where there is a painting by the famous Mexican artist Jose Vallejo called *The Crucifixtion*, which hangs above the main altar there and was offered as a gift by the Archbishop of Mexico City in 1789. I became very good friends with a priest there, Father Julio Esperanza. We would have many discussions about religion and history, and, of course, being in the financial center of the world, our discussions would center around the effects of the search for wealth on both history and religion."

"Padre Esperanza had many, many stories of his relatives in Spain who came to the New World a century ago in search of gold and the cities of Cibola and Quivera. He told me of the mines that the Jesuit brethren had worked for decades until they were all called back to Spain, and told to leave the area where they had constructed their missions and were spreading the word of God. All this occurred back in the 1760's, well over one hundred years before I started my two-year excursion throughout the Sonora region in search of a productive mine."

"It was a very difficult and challenging time for me to be looking for precious minerals. All of the people I knew in New York thought I was crazy, and maybe I was. They were convinced I was on a wild goose chase looking for wealth in the mountains." Greene explained to Edelmida.

"'All of the mines have been found' ," they told me. " 'You are loco to be spending all your time, energy, and money looking for the elusive pot of gold at the end of the rainbow.' "

"In truth, Edelmida, I did not believe in the Cities of Gold, although Padre Esperanza was a great story teller and made the tales seem real. The folks I knew in New York weren't too far wrong. Most of the mines in the region *had* been found, but many were not being mined to their true potential and several had been abandoned after the Jesuits left the area."

"Finally, after years of scouring the desert and living off the land, with its beautiful, but harsh and arid terrain and proliferation of poisonous and dangerous animals, human and otherwise, I came upon the mines here in Cananea. They had once been owned by General Pesqueira, the former Governor of Sonora. He is the one responsible for naming the mountain peak "La Elenita" after his bride. The General believed the mines to be tapped out, but he was a politician, and a warrior, and knew nothing of modern mining techniques or of how to get the funds necessary to invest in continuation of the mining process. After he died, I approached his widow and convinced her to sell the mines to me for a nominal fee, which she was willing to do because she wanted to honor her husband's legacy and felt she could accomplish that by allowing the sites to be reopened. I went back to New York to line up funding for expansion. It was still a difficult battle, investors wanted gold and silver, not copper – but the U.S. was growing and expanding rapidly into the western territories and electricity was a critical factor in this growth. Copper became more valuable due to its excellent properties for conducting electricity at a much cheaper cost than other metals. Plus, the railroads were expanding, which not only drove up the demand for copper, but also made it easier to bring it to the lucrative

113

markets up north. So, I guess I was in the right place at the right time, and capitalized on my new found fortune."

Edelmida was astonished that Colonel Greene was telling her all this. He seemed to be almost talking to himself and obviously relished telling his story to anyone who was interested. He was certainly a gregarious and expansive man. "But, I am digressing," Colonel Greene continued, "so how did I come into possession of this beautiful cross? Well, as Padre Esperanza told me his stories, he recounted a tale of a relative on his mother's side who spent some time with Cortés on his famous excursions throughout the Southwest in his own search for the Cities of Gold. As I'm sure the nuns must have taught you, the reason the conquistadors came to this area was specifically to find the elusive cities. Cortés, as perhaps the most infamous of them all, was not a nice man, and he pillaged each tribe and area he came to trying to locate the gold. Cortés had been convinced that the local tribes were hiding the existence of the cities from him and he did all he could to extract from them the location of the precious areas. He truly believed that these cities existed and that he would not only be wealthy when he located him, but also the most famous explorer in history, since so many before him had tried and failed to do that very same thing." Greene continued.

"According to Padre Esperanza, Cortés conquered a tribal encampment somewhere in

Sonora, not too far from Cananea, and took a wealth of gold and silver items, including this cross. He would often bestow one of the captured trinkets from his plundering on one of his key people in battle as a reward for bravery, and it turns out that Padre Esperanza's ancestor had struck down a native who was just about to swing a makeshift sword at Cortés. The cross was given to the ancestor on his mothers' side, Onorio Pachero, to be passed down to the eldest son of the family as an heirloom and reminder of the bravery exhibited while at the side of Cortés. It had always been considered an Amulet, a good luck charm, although it seems both good and bad luck have followed it wherever it went. From here the story gets interesting. You see, the last person in the Pachero family to own the Amulet was Padre Javier Pachero, who died suddenly and tragically while spreading the word of God to the pagan Indians who inhabited these lands centuries ago. Padre Pachero gave the Amulet to the natives to be placed at the apex above the altar of a church to be built. The church *was* built, but was not properly constructed, and within fifty years it needed to be completely redone. During that time, King Carlos III of Spain recalled all of the Jesuits from the region, and opened the way for the Franciscans to come to continue the work of conversion of the pagans. A Franciscan priest named Padre Juan Bautista Velderrain, rebuilt the church with a loan from a local Sonoran rancher, employing a large workforce of Papago to help him and the architect he hired. However, there were not enough funds to fully complete the structure, so he spoke to the Archdiocese who agreed to broker the cross to a Catholic benefactor to generate the additional funds to complete the building. This unnamed Samaritan then donated the cross to his local church - St. Peter's in New York City where my good friend, Padre Esperanza, is pastor."

Edelmida was mesmerized. To her small and contained world, this story was the most exotic she had ever heard, and the fact that it was real made it all the more incredible. However, she had to ask "Colonel Greene, this is a fascinating story. So, did Padre Esperanza offer it to you since he is a priest and will have no children?" Edelmida asked innocently.

Colonel Greene smiled and said "No, Edelmida, nothing as magnanimous as that, the cross didn't belong to Padre Esperanza, but to the church. However, Padre Esperanza truly believed, with all his heart, that the Cities of Gold existed, and that he would be sent to the region one day to build a monastery and spend his time looking for the elusive lost cities, but he could not know when, or even if, this would ever happen. So, I proposed a deal to my good friend and confidant. He would allow me to use the cross as collateral for a short term loan to fund my trip to Sonora to search for the lost mines. If I was successful in finding a mine

116

that would produce precious metals, I would pay back the loan, purchase the cross at a premium as a benefactor of the Church and the Diocese, and offer both the Church and Padre Esperanza fair compensation so he could fund his trip to Sonora to look for the lost cities himself. If I failed, I would have to go back to New York and my job as a stockbroker, pay off the loan, and the cross would remain at St. Peter's with Padre Esperanza. He was willing take a gamble on me and convinced the Bishop that the risk was minimal, and he approved the transaction. Well, here we are, and there is the cross, so I guess you know how this all turned out. I have named the cross *The Amulet of Cananea*, because it has brought me such tremendous good luck" Colonel Greene concluded.

"Why, *Señor* Greene, that is a wonderful story."

"Do you know what is most remarkable, Edelmida? The foundations of the church built from the proceeds of the Amulet, which was sold to the benefactor in New York, became one of the most beautiful Missions in the land. It is called the White Dove of the Desert. Do you know what I am referring to?" he asked her.

Edelmida's face brightened and she felt as if she had been called on to answer a difficult question by the nuns in a history class. "Oh, yes, Colonel. It is the Mission I told you we visited with the nuns, *San Xavier del Bac* in Tucson. What a wonderful

117

coincidence! Thank you for telling me all this. You are indeed a smart and lucky man and I thank you for coming here and building this beautiful place and allowing me to cook for you and the staff. I will do my very best to make sure you always have fresh and delicious meals. What is your favorite dish Colonel?" Edelmida inquired.

"Thank you for your kind comments, *Señorita*, but I truly believe it was the passion of the cross that helped me find the mines. They say it is a lucky amulet and I believe that to be true. As to my favorite food? Well, as I mentioned, I am from New York, where you can get any kind of food imaginable, and you know that Luisina is from Spain and has worked and studied in Paris and New York, so she can make anything, and make it wonderfully. But I am a miner first and foremost and have spent many years now in Sonora working the mines, ranching, and traveling this great land, so my tastes still run to the local foods, rich with spices and fresh from the land. I would have to say my favorite dish is *Pozole Rojo con frijoles*. I have not yet asked Luisina to make this - I believe she may think it does not challenge her culinary skills enough, but perhaps one day I will. It was nice meeting you, Edelmida, and I look forward to seeing you again soon."

Colonel Greene then walked out of the drawing room leaving Edelmida speechless and in awe of the man and the Amulet. She thought to herself "He is a very lucky man indeed. It seems this cross must be a truly blessed item."

Edelmida returned to the kitchen and her duties. Fortunately, Luisina was not there, so she avoided her wrath for the time being.

Edelmida didn't realize she learned things about Colonel Greene that very few people knew. The risks he took and the story of how the mines evolved to what they had become were fascinating. She felt that some of the stories she heard about Colonel Greene could not be true. He seemed to be a hardworking and decent man, obviously religious and personable, even to his servants. The complaints she heard from some of the men had to be wrong. They always complained of unfair wages and put the blame squarely on Colonel Greene. She would learn more about their complaints and see if she could help Colonel Greene stem the issues he was facing from the workers.

Edelmida would never know the complete story of Colonel Greene. He was one of the richest men in America during the height of his success and owned several mining companies throughout Sonora, particularly in Cananea.

His holdings, however, were much more extensive than that. He had built an empire around the mines which included a lumber company to process the wood needed to extend and enforce the mines; railroads, to bring the finished goods to market; ranches, which supplied horses necessary for the workers to travel the mines, bring goods to and from town and just general transportation; and a farm to produce fresh fruits, vegetables, and chickens for eggs and food, and cattle for meat.

Colonel Greene started with the mines in Cananea and, as a former prospector and horse rancher, earned the respect and admiration, not only of his workers, but also of the press, investors, and dignitaries throughout Mexico and the United States. He was clearly a "cowboy" in the sense of the word that he enjoyed the country and riding, and he associated himself closely with his workers. He was also very adept, and, frankly, lucky in his financial dealings on Wall Street and in the boardrooms of the investment community.

Still, all of this good will and hard work could not prevent him from his involvement in the center of an event which sparked the Mexican revolution.

Chapter Seven

Manuel & Edelmida

One bright and hot spring day, as Edelmida made her way to the pantry, humming one of her favorite *corridos* of the day, a ditty that had a happy tune but dark and disturbing lyrics about revolution and death, she noticed a smiling face approaching her and whistling a tune to himself as he headed towards the main mine at the camp. As he approached, she noticed that the tune he was whistling was the same one she was softly humming to herself. She met his eyes and he smiled and nodded hello.

He stopped and said "Buenos Dias, *Señorita*, it's a lovely day today, no?"

"*Sí, Señor*, quite beautiful" Edelmida replied.

"Are you new here?" Manuel asked her politely. "I have not seen you before and surely I would remember you."

Edelmida blushed and lowered her head so he couldn't see. "*Sí*, I only started here a few weeks ago. I work in the kitchen at Casa Greene."

"Well, you must be very special; Colonel Greene only has the best of everything, so you must be a wonderful cook."

As they chatted and became acquainted with one another, the path became busy with other workers hustling to their jobs at the mines or one of the other businesses that had sprung up in Cananea, driven by the growth of the community. Manuel was smitten and fell into her eyes, and in a rare and exuberantly spontaneous moment, Manuel boldly asked Edelmida if she would like to join him at the company dance on Saturday night. She looked askance at him, for this was a very unusual request since they had only just met, yet Edelmida saw something in Manuel's demeanor and she had an instant liking and trust for this plain looking, yet somehow attractive man.

The Saturday night social was a well-attended affair where nearly all the workers from the various mining operations went to dance, drink, and blow off a little steam after the long and dangerous work week. The social often got quite raucous, as the men far outnumbered the women in Cananea, and arguments ensued as the men postured for the ladies. It was out of character, but wise, for Manuel to ask Edelmida before someone else did. In Cananea, it was not unusual for the first person to ask you to a dance to eventually become your spouse.

Edelmida replied "But I don't even know your name."

"My name is Manual Díaz Carreras" he said as he bowed deeply at the waist. "And you are?"

With a giggle she responded "Edelmida Ríos Castillo – and what do you do here in Cananea, Manuel Díaz Carreras?"

"I work in the mines, the Cobre Grande. I have been there since before Colonel Greene owned it, as a watchman, since it was not being worked, but now that he has purchased it, I am digging out the ore. It is a lot of work and we work long hours, but I am happy that the mines are active again and the town is growing. Many of the men are unhappy, though, because we make much less money than the Americans, but I am happy to have a good job and I think Colonel Greene is a great man. So, now you know a little about me, and I would like to learn about you, but I have to get to my job. So, will you tell me more when I take you to the dance Saturday?" He grinned.

"You are not bashful, *Señor*. Let me think about it, and I will see you here tomorrow morning and give you my answer." He said goodbye and continued on his way humming that same tune.

When she got to the pantry, she asked one of the other girls, Juanita, about Manuel, and explained what had happened.

"*Sí*, I know him Edelmida. He is a fine man, but he mostly keeps to himself. I'm surprised he was so forward with you. He must be in love" Juanita said with a smile.

123

"Well, perhaps. During all those years at the orphanage I only met a few boys from the town, and the nuns did not encourage us speaking with them. I felt a little uncomfortable and didn't really know what to say" Edelmida replied. She was only seventeen, after all, and, although she had the demeanor and poise of a much older woman, inside she was emotionally still a child. Her sequester at the hands of the nuns after all those years gave her pause when it came to speaking with men her age. She felt very comfortable speaking with elders, because she had been trained in the art of conversation, but something about the emotions she felt when talking to Manuel left her tongue tied and embarrassed. In spite of all this, she could not wait to go to the dance with Manuel on Saturday night.

All week long, the other girls in the kitchen teased Edelmida good naturedly. Of course, they were all jealous, and even though some of them had their own dates and suitors, it was the newness of the budding romance that caused their jealousy. There is nothing like newfound love, or at least the idea of newfound love, to make even the most hardened person yearn for that feeling.

All the women who worked serving the mines in various capacities were looking forward to the end of the work week and the dance. These were always well attended, and virtually everyone attended for the food, music, and dancing.

The past few months, though, tensions had grown thick and almost palpable throughout Sonora state, as talk of revolution, change in the political landscape, and the rift between the Mexican workers and their American counterparts became wider and wider.

The men did not dance much, but mostly drank their stress away and would occasionally become too aggressive with the women who attended, or with one another. The ratio of men to women was nearly fifteen to one, and Colonel Greene had to employ an army of enforcers to ensure that peace was kept in the town. This was part of the reason that the brothel was not only tolerated, but encouraged. Fights would often break out at the dance as men vied for the attention of even the most homely looking women.

The miners in particular were a rough breed, and they were primarily Mexicans, although a few were native Indians who had moved to Cananea to work at the mines, which were paying fairly well compared to other work that was available anywhere else in the country. It was becoming increasingly difficult to continue to work side by side with the Americans, who were paid nearly three times as much for the same work, and it drove a wedge between the races, creating an atmosphere of fear and distrust. Interestingly enough, Colonel Greene was well respected by all sides, and although pay was unequal, his mines had brought money, jobs, and purpose to those in Cananea and the entire Sonora region. Colonel Greene was looked at as something of a hero in this regard, although he had a vast and diverse background and the many stories that were told about him were quite incredible.

The mines employed hundreds of workers overall, but even so, they all got to know each other well over time, and new workers were hired every day and came from all over the region to work at El Cobre as the primary copper mine was known.

The Spanish conquistadors who had arrived in search of gold brought settlers from other countries in Europe as well. When the Jesuits arrived in the 1700's to spread Christianity, they created the first common bond between the disparate tribes who lived in the region, and while many resisted this new religion, over time it was embraced and proliferated, as Spanish settlers and natives began to marry and breed, and Spanish was adopted as the common language.

For centuries the native tribes had co-existed peacefully, although they were generally unaware of one another. Their numbers were small and they were geographically separated, but when the Spanish brought their horses to America, it dramatically increased travel and exploration added to the melting pot effect.

The lack of travel prior to the Spanish intercession helps explain why the country had so many different tribes, with none dominating the landscape. This clearly made it easier for Europeans to conquer the lands and impose their will on the people.

The day started out hot and sunny, very different from the recent slew of rains that had blanketed the region. Rains were important to Sonora and the natives counted on this weather to feed the crops and fill the rivers with water, which was such a rare commodity during most of the year. The Papago would move away from the riverbanks during the spring season and return when the rains subsided to cultivate the land and store as much of the water as they could for the coming dry season.

Edelmida was just beginning to settle into her routine in the kitchen at Casa Greene. She enjoyed her work and the crew she worked with, and in spite of the trepidation she felt when she first started, realized that this was where she belonged, doing the thing she loved best and contributing to an important cause, the cause of helping grow the economy of the region through the work at the mines. Many of her co-workers were women she recognized from the orphanage who had left in previous years.

There was a great sense of camaraderie in the kitchen at the Casa, because most of the workers had come from the orphanage and it was akin to a feeling people have when running into old friends at a class reunion, a mixture of fond remembrances and ennui. There were the usual school stories which everyone shared and remembered

127

affectionately, in spite of the fact that at the time a particular incident might have been an embarrassment, but there were also cases of running into someone who had been more an enemy than a friend, which sometimes led to experiencing both ends of the emotional spectrum. At Casa Greene, old grudges would dissipate in lieu of new relationships and everyone had a very specific role, and were very good at what they did. There were few petty jealousies as a smooth kitchen required everyone to do their particular job and work to get along. Luisina would not tolerate anyone who caused problems, for there were always new graduates who wanted nothing more than to work in the kitchen at Casa Greene.

Edelmida, like many of her classmates was the center of one such prank at the end of her junior year at the school that the nuns ran near the Casa.

As classes came to the end of a school year, the graduating class, who would soon be released to the world to find work and make a life on her own, would play pranks on each other, and, sometimes, if they could get away with it, on the nuns themselves.

The Sisters, of course, found no humor in this whatsoever and would take great pains to keep a watchful eye on the graduating class and keep each other informed of any mysterious behavior or apparent collusion.

Edelmida reflected on this with a smile on her face as she worked her way down the path from her apartment to Casa Greene to begin work in the kitchen.

When she got to the pantry, Edelmida asked one of the other girls if she knew anything about Manuel Carreras. She was surprised at what she heard.

Chapter Eight

The Enemy Within

Colonel Greene's right hand man at the mines was Albert Bacon Fall. Just as everyone called Will Greene the Colonel, Albert Fall was known simply as A.B. A lawyer by trade, he was born in Kentucky, and worked various jobs during his youth, including time in a cotton mill, which led to a life long battle with various respiratory issues.

A.B. made a decision early in his life to move out west, as so many had before him. Some went for the prospect of money and many to escape the cold, with the hope that the dry climates of the southwest would improve their health. A.B. Fall was no exception. He hoped that the dry air of the southwest would ease the difficulty he had breathing in the moist and cold air of the east, and moved to the Sonora region of Mexico with hopes to improve his life and health while in his early twenties. Thus began his love affair with Mexico. He traveled throughout the country and became fluent in Spanish, just as his friend and colleague Colonel Greene had done. He also began acquiring mining properties, and found the Mexican people to be warm and friendly. Like the Colonel, he befriended all that he encountered and had good relations with workers in the mines as well as connections throughout the political spectrum, including a friendship with Mexican *Presidente* Porfirio Díaz.

He would later move to New Mexico where he set up permanent residence and would become a United States Senator. From there, he would become Secretary of the Interior under President Harding, where he met his downfall as the architect of the Teapot Dome scandal. Fall was a smart man, a shrewd businessman, and a person who was loyal to his friends.

Surprisingly enough, Fall met Colonel Greene during a trip to New York, not in the mines of Sonora, where they were both working on trying to line up financing for their business ventures. Like Greene, Fall had spent time as a prospector in Mexico while he was finding his way in the business world. There were many similarities between the two men, moving from the east, traveling throughout the southwest in search of their fortune, working as a laborer on the mines they encountered and eventually owned, and working themselves up to positions of prominence and wealth in the burgeoning southwest. They shared a love for Mexico and its people, spoke Spanish fluently, and expanded their interests from mining into other, equally lucrative businesses.

While in New York, they met and discussed mining rights that Fall had purchased from a grubstake miner named Sam Dedrick in the Sierra

Madres. During the course of discussion, the Colonel's relationship with Fall strengthened, and in just a few days Greene had retained Fall as his personal lawyer. Fall would later say that being in the Colonel's sphere of influence was like being caught up in a hurricane. The Colonel was known for making snap judgments and working out the details later. A.B., as the Colonel's lawyer, was often the one who had to straighten out the finances and details of decisions the Colonel made. Years later, this "shoot from the hip" approach would prove to contribute to the Colonel's downfall.

Fall spent many years at the mines with Colonel Greene and was one of his most trusted lieutenants. He was adamantly opposed to the hiring of Thom MacMurrough because he felt it would drive a further rift between the management staff at the mines and the Mexican workers. MacMurrough's reputation had preceded him, and his handling of immigrant workers during his time at the transcontinental railroad was part of the reason he came highly recommended, although he was known to be heavy-handed.

Since Mexico had gained its independence from Spain in 1821 after decades of struggles, and during the next 71 years, leading up to this date in 1892, the constant struggle was between the working class, and the rich and powerful. Fall was certain that bringing on MacMurrough to manage the indigent workers was certain to further drive a wedge between them and management.

At the mines, this was exacerbated because the American workers made so much more than the indigenous workers, whether Mexican, Spanish, or Indian, and had created an environment of mistrust and contention, bordering on revolution.

There were still the remnants of influence from the Spanish rule, and constant threats from the United States to overtake sections of the country. The indigenous Indian population had never been cohesive, as each tribe had developed independently and exhibited no commonality of purpose. However, the arrival of domesticated horses from Spain in the 1600's did much to help consolidate the country, but Mexico was so sprawling, and the means of communication so primitive, that it took centuries before the land came together with any type of common bond. It seemed this land was only united in its common purpose to defend itself against intruders and attempts to govern itself without the distractions of graft and corruption.

The Mexican workers were not only paid a pittance compared to what their American counterparts were paid, but they were segregated into their own barracks and had a separate restaurant, bar, and other services, and were restricted from any of the establishments the American workers frequented.

Colonel Greene had recently brought on Thom MacMurrough, just after his acquisition of the Cobre Grande, and A.B. had a strong dislike for him, but didn't have the option to fire him, since he was the Colonel's hire.

The best he could do was to try and convince Colonel Greene that he was a bad apple that could only lead to trouble. To that end, Fall had his good friend and Colonel Greene's chief of security, Francisco de Torres, look into MacMurrough and his background.

Francisco was recruited by Fall after he left the *Rurales* where he served under Emilio Kosterlitzky, the Mexican Cossack of Sonora. Torres was a giant of a man, both physically and in his demeanor. He stood well over six feet tall, had a long drooping moustache, and one piercing brown eye, the other perpetually covered by an eye patch that he had earned during his stint in the *Rurales*. Torres was never seen to crack even a hint of a smile, and his gruff exterior hid a softness for women which he had developed after the murder of his sister, María, by the Apaches.

He had come to know A.B. when there was a skirmish in the Sierra Madres, which Fall was prospecting at the time, and a dispute developed over water rights. Torres was recommended to A.B. as a person who could persuade people to do his bidding, and Francisco helped Fall resolve his differences. They became well acquainted, and whenever A.B. needed a strong arm, he turned to Torres. Francisco turned this need for security into a company, and sold his services to anyone who had the funds. When A.B. was brought to Cananea, it was obvious to him that the Colonel needed a strong hand to help control the workers and he enlisted Francisco as the one to keep things on an even keel.

Francisco spent several weeks digging and tracing backwards from MacMurrough's arrival at the mines, looking for something to bring to A.B. as evidence of MacMurrough's ineptitude or unworthiness. But the trail went cold and ended in New York. Francisco assumed that he may have come from Ireland through Ellis Island, although, in truth, Cassidy took the name MacMurrough after he made his way down from Boston when he landed illegally. He had guessed, rightly so it turns out, that no one would question the lack of documentation, given the confused state that always seemed to occur when immigrants landed.

Torres and his men assumed that MacMurrough suffered the same fate as many who had come to America's shores during the periods on intense immigration, and that his name was transposed, or changed entirely, for no apparent reason upon entry. This assumption brought their investigation to a dead end, and they could find nothing of his history prior to his arrival in America after his apparent emigration.

There had been some reports of drunkenness, which were dismissed as an Irish trait and nothing more, and some of his escapades with women, but none of them resulting in arrest or incarceration, so Francisco could do nothing but wait until MacMurrough made a mistake again, and he didn't have to wait very long.

To say the mines were a tough place to work was a vast understatement. The hours were long, the pay short, and the work dirty and dangerous. So when the workers wanted to unwind, they would head into Ronquillo, a small shanty town on the outskirts of Cananea, which became the ghetto for the indigenous workers, where there was a choice between the cantina and the bordello to help the men relax at the end of a long day's work. Despite the fact that the mines were first worked by the Jesuits, there was no mission that had been built in Cananea, but only a small church and school, although these were also expanding rapidly as the town grew.

Right after his shift ended, Thom MacMurrough made his way down to the cantina in Cananea proper. Here, where the non-native workers congregated, he played a few hands of poker and drank some fine tequila, which had just been brought in barrels from Jalisco. This was sipping tequila. *José Cuervo Añejo*, which meant it had been rested in new French oak for one to three years.

Tequila had become very popular over the past 30 years in Mexico, and packaging created by the Cuervo company, which distributed the liquid in handy, round shaped five-liter bottles wrapped in agave fiber called *damajuanas*, helped the drink become pervasive throughout the region. These containers evolved, and at the turn of the century there were smaller flask-type bottles called *pachoncitas* that could easily fit into the back pockets of the workers' baggy pants, which had become so popular.

This was not the cheap mescal which also came from the agave plant and contained a worm in the liquid. This was really nothing more than a marketing ploy to attract macho consumers, who would show their prowess of chewing the larvae of the maguey worm, known as the *gusano rojo* for its red color, to prove their masculinity. This fine tequila was a distillation of the Blue Agave plant, which was deemed to be the best of the agave, for manufacturing the fiery liquid. Don Cenobio owned several distilleries at the time and is widely credited with defining tequila as being best made from the blue agave plant (also known as maguey) and was a major promoter of tequila. The newly independent country of Mexico was searching for its identity and there was encouragement from the government and all its people to promote and benefit from such homemade products. The Mexicans were tired of sending their money to Spain and France for exported goods and were eager to share in the wealth and generate new Mexican brands for export. They had learned from the wine industry to focus on quality and *terroir*, and, thus, Tequila, a small town located in the State of Jalisco, became the only place that true tequila could be made, just as only true champagne came from the Champagne region in France. The advent of bottles, and the

137

coming of the railroads to Sonora, was a major boon to helping export this fine liquor to the United States and beyond.

As Thom sipped his Tequila, he thought about Manuel and Edelmida. "Manuel has good taste in women," Thom thought to himself, "maybe a little old for me, but I bet she's a virgin." The more he thought about it, the more aroused he became, and after several more shots decided it was time to head down the street to the bordello.

Madame Conchita had been running her establishment for several years, and had been in Cananea since well before Colonel Greene bought the mine. The former owner of the mines, Colonel Pesquiera, was one of her best customers, so she never had to fear the authorities. In fact, Colonel Greene's Chief of Security, Francisco de Torres, always kept an eye out for trouble at the house, as he was doing this night when MacMurrough arrived. Madame Conchita did have a powerful fear of Thom MacMurrough. He was a cold hearted and mean son of a bitch, and every time he showed up at the house it was the same thing. He was always drunk and inevitably wanted the youngest girl. In fact, he complained time and again that not only were the girls not young enough, but there were no virgins among them. "No virgins?! In a bordello?! Stop the presses!" Conchita thought to herself.

Thom came in this night, but he was not drunk, although it was obvious he had been drinking. "Madame Conchita, me lovely girl," he said loudly in that strange mix of Spanish and English with his Irish brogue. "Have you found me a lovely young virgin girl?" he asked.

"*Señor* Thom," Conchita replied, "it so happens that there is one girl who has just joined our fine establishment and she has never worked in a house like this before. I don't know if she is a virgin, but she is quite young, only 16, and I think you will be very pleased with her."

Cananea at the time was a rapidly expanding area, and people from all walks of life were flocking to the region to provide goods and services to the workers of the mines. A mining town was a wonderful place for people willing to do what it takes to separate the miners from their hard earned pay, and there was little to do in Cananea and little time to do it, and, of course, a man had needs and certainly there were not many women in Cananea. Those that were there already were either nuns, wives, daughters, or prostitutes.

While Conchita went to get her new employee, Thom could not stop thinking about the girl that he saw Manuel speaking to that day. He began to swell thinking of her new, pink womanhood and how he could pluck that fine flower.

Sonora saw a strange mix of races, with people of native Indian, French, and Spanish extraction coupled with an increasing number of American fathers, who bred a new mixed race of beautiful mulatto women. Tall, with coffee-colored skin, sometimes with light colored eyes and sometimes with dark, smoldering eyes that reflected the fire within, high cheekbones from the native races, coupled with the features of European and American blood, all created an exciting mix of beauty and allure.

Edelmida was an example of this homogenization of disparate cultures. Tall, with the high cheekbones of her native heritage, and straight, raven black hair down just below her shoulders, she had a regal air about her and walked with her head held high and her shoulders back in an almost military-like fashion. Her eyes were a soft, light brown with tiny flecks of gold, and she had a full mouth with a slight overbite and a hint of a smile on her face at all times. She was not classically beautiful, and a wide nose, somewhat crooked, only enhanced her looks and made her oddly more attractive. Thom believed that since she had just recently come to the Casa Greene from the orphanage, that she must surely still be a virgin. The nuns were a doting bunch and watched their wards very closely.

"Yes," thought Thom as he waited, "I will keep an eye on this new girl."

"*Señor* Thom," Conchita said, interrupting his thoughts and his increasingly throbbing manhood, "here is Suato." Conchita stepped aside to reveal a young looking native girl with long dark hair, a flat nose, midnight dark eyes, and a smile that revealed white, but crooked teeth. She was not completely unattractive, but after Thom's fantasies of Edelmida, she was bordering on unacceptable. "And, yes, *Señor* Thom, she told me she is a virgin," Conchita continued.

Thom thought to himself that an ugly virgin was better than no woman at all, and took Suato by the hand and introduced her to a world she could not have envisioned, and certainly didn't deserve. He was more aggressive than usual, and although the girl professed to have never worked a house before, and claimed to be a virgin, she knew things she could not have possibly known if that were true. He allowed her the conceit anyway, however, and fantasized that she was a virgin after all, but in his heart it was not the same.

As Thom stumbled back to the barracks hours later, sated for now, his thoughts kept turning back to Edelmida. "Tomorrow I will speak with Manuel," he thought to himself "and see what I can find out about this lovely new girl Edelmida." Meanwhile, Francisco de Torres, who had seen MacMurrough arrive at Conchita's, made a note of his activity. He felt there was something sinister about MacMurrough, although he could not put his finger on what exactly it was, but the cold trail he left made Francisco more than a little suspicious.

While Thom was in town tending to his own selfish needs, Manuel, Pedro, and others were gathered at the *bodega* talking about conditions at

141

the mines. Their dissatisfaction was driven in large part by pay discrepancies, but also by the segregation throughout the community. The native workers had segregated barracks, restaurants, bars and other areas, including the bathrooms and kitchen.

The mood in Mexico, in general, was dramatically changing and becoming more militant. Porfirio Díaz, who had been ruling the country for over 30 years, had created an environment that encouraged capital investment from the United States and elsewhere, but created a caste system throughout the country. The Four C's was a microclimate of this environment, and the workers seemed to be moving past rhetoric and striking a more radical pose. The discussion at the *bodega* this evening was about the need to strike and ask for higher wages and better working conditions, a complaint that seemed to occur more and more every day.

The following day, Manuel ran into his boss in town while running errands. "Manuel, I know you have been talking to that new girl who works in Casa Greene's kitchen – what's her name?" Thom asked, as though they were two *compadres* discussing Saturday's bullfight.

"Her name is Edelmida, *Señor* Thom. She is a lovely young lady, beautiful, and the nuns raised her right. She is a wonderful girl and I have asked her to the dance on Saturday night," Manuel replied.

Saturday night was for drinking, dancing, and romancing, but many of the men went in for other entertainment. The bars were full and there were many places to go for a card game or a cockfight. The company did not condone this behavior, but there was nothing that could be done to stop it, money changed hands at the speed of light, and unfortunately the roosters would fight to the death for the benefit of a selfish and sadistic few.

The fights had been banned early in his tenure by *Presidente* Porfirio, along with bullfighting, but were reinstated because it had been such an important part of the culture in Sonora and all of Mexico.

Thom decided that sometime before the Saturday night dance, he would approach Edelmida to see if he could interest her in a tryst. She was young, although not nearly as young as he would like, but he was fairly certain she was a virgin. All of the girls who came from the nunnery were virgins.

That evening, Thursday, he went out of his way to find Edelmida at the end of the workday. Many people were traveling the road back from the mines at the end of the shift, past the Casa to the barracks, as the miners and service workers made their way to their homes. He waited near Casa Greene, for he suspected that Edelmida was not meeting Manuel by chance, and was, instead, lazily meandering about the area in hopes of meeting up with him.

Sure enough, about ten minutes after the shift whistle blew, Edelmida exited the side door of Casa Greene and wandered towards the road. Thom came around the corner, as if in a hurry, and bumped into her, startling her and knocking her to the ground, falling nearly on top of her. As he helped her to her feet, he said "Oh, *Señorita*, I am so sorry. I didn't see you. I was on my way to inform Colonel Greene of a terrible incident at the mines with one of the workers. Are you all right?" Thom asked.

"*Sí*, - I am really more surprised than hurt. Please - you have serious business – don't let me hold you up," she replied.

"No, I insist on buying you a cup of coffee or a glass of tequila to make up for my mistake. Please, come with me to the cantina. Surely, you are interested in what happened at the mines today?" Thom teased.

Edelmida was hesitant. She did not know this man, although they had met briefly, but he was obviously a man of some importance if he was going to confer with Colonel Greene, and she did not want to insult him.

"Please, lass. You will be safe with me." Thom said, interrupting her thoughts. "Colonel Greene brought me here to the mines to help him manage operations and I am responsible for all the workers here. Besides, I shouldn't really bother the

144

Colonel with a little thing like a knifing at the mine, after all, that's what he hired me for." Thom was being cagey and knew he would hook Edelmida with this lie.

"I'm sorry, I just started working here a few weeks ago and I was always taught by the nuns to be cautious with people I don't know, especially men. Forgive me for my lack of manners, Mr. MacMurrough," Edelmida replied innocently. Thom laughed softly and offered her his most sincere smile "Not at all, not at all, my dear. Look, I insist, let me buy you a drink and I will tell you what happened to the worker Manuel Carreras today during the incident.

"Manuel!" Edelmida cried, fearing the worst.

"Do you know Manuel Carreras, my dear?" Thom responded. "You have been here such a short time – but – never mind that, I'll give you all the details over a glass of tequila."

Edelmida walked with Thom, chatting and asking questions. From behind a flowering coyote willow bush, one of many beautiful plants that thrive in the high desert of Sonora, Francisco de Torres had observed the entire exchange. "I have heard of no one being stabbed at the mine today" he thought to himself. "I had better keep a close eye on this one. Colonel Greene is quite fond of Edelmida," he thought as he followed them towards the cantina in town.

145

As Thom walked with Edelmida, he thought she was, indeed, a beautiful girl, but like all women, in Thom's mind, she talked too much. She kept asking him about Manuel and the stabbing, and while his ruse had worked in getting her alone, her incessant questions were driving him loco.

"Edelmida, my dear, we need to stop by my room so I can get my keys as I have to go back to see Colonel Greene later. It is only a short detour off our route and I will tell you on the way what happened today at the mine," Thom said.

"Oh, *Señor, por favor*, tell me now" Edelmida pleaded.

Meanwhile, Francisco was attempting to follow them, but the road to the cantina had only sparse vegetation, most of it low to the ground, and it did not offer enough cover for him to go unobserved. By this time most of the workers had already arrived at their destinations and there were almost no others on the road, so he had little hope of remaining hidden.

He had to put some distance between himself and Thom. MacMurrough was well aware that Francisco wanted to get rid of him, and the two had become mortal enemies with no pretense of friendship. Since Francisco knew they were going to the cantina, he decided to take a different route, figuring to be there before they arrived, thus avoiding any suspicion of his interest in the two of them.

As Francisco headed off towards the cantina, Thom steered Edelmida towards his room and began to expand on his bed of lies using all the charm he could muster.

The managers at the Four C's enjoyed comfortable living quarters and, although the building looked like a typical barracks from the outside, the inside was actually subdivided into individual living units. Each unit had its own front door, and offered a back door which opened into a common area, that was used for meetings and some socializing. The units themselves consisted of a small living area with a comfortable chair, standing lamp and table; a bedroom with a single bed, nightstand, and small, roughhewn wood bureau; and a bathroom in the back with a small shower stall, toilet, and sink. The backdoor of the unit was off the bathroom and the whole living area was arranged in train-like fashion, one room linked to the other, linearly.

"You see Edelmida, Colonel Greene brought me here to help manage the native workers because many of them act like animals and don't appreciate the opportunity they have here. They are generally not trustworthy and will do what they need to, to get money. It can be almost like a prison sometimes, with fights over the littlest things and occasionally stabbings, mostly over women, since there are so few here at the mines. How well do you know Manuel? Did he tell you I promoted him to team leader?" Thom asked, confusing Edelmida between his obvious discriminatory attitude and his self-satisfaction for promoting one of the "animals." Of course, Thom did nothing without motive, and he was trying to confuse Edelmida and distract her from his ultimate intent.

"No, *Señor*, I only met Manuel a few days ago. He seems to be such a nice man and he asked me to the dance on Saturday night." She replied.

"Well, Edelmida, be wary of these workers. Their whole life is the mines and the only women they know are the ones in the *taquerías*, bars, and bordellos – very rough and world wise women who know how to please a man," Thom explained. "Please come in, I'll be just a minute."

Edelmida was very leery of entering Thom's room; she was always taught this was not lady-like unless a couple was married, as it would forever soil her reputation. The nuns contended that men often bragged about their conquests and would name the women they were with, even though the truth was quite often exaggerated, or, perhaps, not a truth at all.

"*Gracias, Señor* Thom, but I will wait here for you – I need to get back to Casa Greene before dark to prep for dinner, or Luisina, the head chef, will be very upset with me," she replied.

"Don't worry about Luisina me dear, I know her very well and will explain your tardiness to her. We are very good friends and I'm sure she'll understand your concern about Manuel and what happened at the *taquería* today," Thom protested.

"The *taquería*?" Edelmida exclaimed, "I thought you said the stabbing was at the mines?"

Suddenly, Thom grabbed Edelmida by the wrist and swung her into the room slamming the door closed with his boot. He grabbed Edelmida by the hair and pulled her toward the bed.

"Stop" she cried out "You're hurting me! What are you doing?"

With that, Thom smashed Edelmida in the mouth with his open hand drawing blood and chipping a bottom tooth with a ring he wore on the pinky of his left hand.

"Shut up" he screamed at her. His eyes were stretched wide from the adrenaline that coursed through his body. He smiled wickedly and began to breathe heavily thorough his mouth. He licked the blood off her lip as he forced her down on the bed and began to fondle her roughly.

Edelmida screamed and kicked trying to escape his grip, but he hit her again, harder this time, and said "Not another sound out of you me dear. I have been waiting for a virgin since I came to this god-forsaken place and I will have you. Be still and enjoy a real man for you will never be with anyone like me again. Your first time will be your best. Now shut up and do what I say," Thom screamed. Thom moved his hand down to the scabbard on his right leg and unsheathed an eight inch long Bowie knife and held it up to her cheek. "One more word and you'll feel the pain of my friend here" he spoke menacingly.

Edelmida realized that she had been tricked and there was no stabbing, and she would be a marked and shunned woman who would forever have to live with her shame. She closed her eyes and said a silent prayer for this to be over quickly and succumbed to the brutal attack from Thom MacMurrough. Try as she might to squirm and squeeze her legs together, the wiry and rough MacMurrough was too strong for her. He forced his way onto her and with repeated thrusts forced his way into her and pounded into her like one of the drivers in the mines, pushing, pushing, relentlessly and hurting her beyond what she had ever imagined. Edelmida clenched her teeth and did all she could to prevent the penetration, but to no avail. She cried and screamed and prayed for this to be over quickly, so she could go to church and beg for forgiveness. She prayed all the while asking God in his infinite wisdom to grant her the strength to avenge this horror one day.

When Thom was stated, and finally rolled off Edelmida in what seemed to her to be an eternity, although it was only a few minutes, he said to her "You have just been deflowered by the Cur of Killeen. There will never be another time like this in your entire life, and I promise you I will never go near you again. But I also promise you, Edelmida, if you ever breathe a word of this to anyone, ever – I will kill your precious Manuel and next time the story of the knifing will be real. Go away now and say nothing, and tonight, after the dinner party, come back here and wash the blood off the bedding so on one knows what you did, and your sinful secret will be safe with me. I will be at the bar until midnight. When I return I expect everything to be in order. Don't make me embarrass you."

He slammed the door as he left to go to town, and once he was gone, Edelmida arranged her dress as best she could and ran out of the room, crying and praying at the same time, determined to find a way to pay back Thom MacMurrough for the evil he did to her.

All this time, Francisco was waiting in the cantina wondering what had happened to Thom and Edelmida and where they could possibly be. They surely should have arrived by now, unless something happened to delay them. He decided that if he were to retrace his steps, he may run into them or at least see if something happened to waylay them. It was a fairly busy night in town, Thursday being the unofficial start to the weekend, and when he left the cantina there were people everywhere, coming and going on seemingly important missions. Impromptu card games, drinking, loud arguments, and fights were common on the streets and a party-like atmosphere prevailed.

As Francisco rounded the corner at the end of the street where the cantina was located, he saw an image that appeared to be Edelmida running away from the barracks, clearly upset and looking frightfully disheveled. He ran towards her and called out her name, but she only became more animated and tried to run faster. Thom was nowhere in sight.

The next morning dawned bright and warm and Edelmida took extra time getting ready since she had not slept a wink all night. She had spent the night instead going through a whole range of emotions, many of which she had never felt before. After soaking for hours in the tub, scrubbing herself until her skin was raw, she cried and cursed God and man for what happened to her that fateful night. Her hopes and dreams were all but dashed because of what MacMurrough had done and she cursed her own naiveté and stupidity for trusting him. Her anger and shame gave way to a brutal hatred of *El Diablo* MacMurrough, as she thought of him, and in the early dawn after she had steeled herself to what was now her past, she called up all her inner strength and vowed to see MacMurrough paid back in kind for the sins he inflicted upon her.

As Edelmida lay awake, she prayed 20 decades of the rosary, corresponding to the 20 mysteries, although it seemed to her that there were no Joyful, Glorious, or Luminous mysteries, but for her only Sorrowful ones, and she drew on her faith to help her deal with the incredible physical, emotional, and psychological pain of her rape.

She reflected on Jesus Christ and the suffering He endured for her and committed to give up her emotional scars for those less fortunate than herself.

"Lord, my God, please allow my pain and suffering at the hands of the devil incarnate to be offered up so that others may not suffer as I have. I will regain my strength and resolve to fight evil throughout my life and offer my pain for others. God in heaven, you sacrificed for me and I will dedicate my life to eliminating evil in the world. Thank you for giving me the strength and helping me to deliver the word of God," Edelmida intoned to herself. "An eye for an eye," she continued "and may God have mercy on my soul."

And with that Edelmida got out of a bed that saw no sleep that night, a new and determined woman, and began to plan her retribution on the evils of man.

As Edelmida walked to the kitchen that morning, she was struck by how clear everything appeared to her. The sun was bright and warm and the sky had light, wispy clouds that moved rapidly across the sky. The birds seemed to almost flock, and sang and tweeted as though they were a choir of instruments, each playing a different song, but somehow all in the same key. The cactus was flowering and along the path everyone seemed cheery and bright. Like the first day of spring after a long, cold, wet winter, when the world smelled warm like fresh baked bread and all the cares and worries of the world are left behind as the shedding of a winter coat.

As she rounded the corner to Casa Greene, Francisco de Torres approached her. "Buenos Dias, *Señorita*," he greeted her. Edelmida immediately tensed up and was tempted to scream and run back to the Casa, frightened by this apparition of a man with a patch over one eye and a cold dark look over his virile moustache. But there were so many people around and the morning so bright, that she simply remained frozen on the spot, her soft brown eyes held open wide in anticipation.

"Allow me to introduce myself," he continued. "I am Francisco de Torres and I am chief of security here at the mines. I report directly to Mr. A.B. Fall who, as you probably know, is Colonel Greene's lawyer and partner."

Edelmida just stood there staring, not taking a breath, not even thinking of, or registering, what he was saying. She just stood and stared, a stone-like statue.

"Are you alright, *Señorita*?" He asked.

Edelmida came out of her trance and responded, "Yes, I'm sorry. What can I do for you?" she responded.

"*Señor*ita, last night I observed you speaking with Thom MacMurrough, and I couldn't help….."

At the sound of his name, Edelmida began shaking and could not control herself as tears flowed from her eyes and her whole body convulsed as if she were beads of water on a hot iron skillet.

Francisco put his hand on her shoulder and tried to calm her, but it only seemed to makes things worse and she turned with eyes burning into him and screamed at him "Don't you ever, ever touch me. I am a pure and chaste girl and no man has the right to touch me!"

He stepped away from her and asked her gently, "Are you ill, *Señorita*? Can I get you some water? Can I fetch you a doctor?" Francisco did not know Edelmida except by reputation. Her nickname, "Princess," from which her common name derived, seemed so apt for her and she was highly regarded by everyone she met. This seemed so out of character for what he knew of her that Francisco could not understand it. He waited as Edelmida held up her hand, which had a bead of rosaries intertwined in the folds of her fingers, and it seemed as if she were praying as she began to compose herself.

"No, *Señor*, I'll be all right. I have a touch of something, but I'll be fine." As she straightened up, took a deep breath, and wiped away the tears, she continued, "You had a question for me?"

Francisco was confused. She had gone off so quickly and without warning and just as quickly seemed to brush whatever it was aside and compose herself and act as if it never happened. He had no choice but to continue. "*Sí, Señorita*, I hope I'm not upsetting you, and please let me know if this is not a good time to talk. I am so sorry for touching you, I was only trying to comfort you."

"No, no, it's fine, really. Please tell me what you want," Edelmida responded quickly.

"As I was saying," Francisco continued, "I observed you speaking with the foreman last night and, as you know, fraternization between management and employees is strictly forbidden. Mr. Fall is very firm about that and I wanted to make sure you were aware of it. What was it he was discussing with you, if I may ask?"

Edelmida hesitated. This was a chance to talk to a high ranking official of the company and tell him of the sin that occurred the previous night. The fact that it was a violation of company policy for managers to fraternize with the workers meant that *El Diablo*, as Edelmida now only thought of him, might be punished for his crime, but *El Diablo*/MacMurrough had also come to her with a very credible story and professed to have Colonel Greene's ear. Who was she to trust? Making up her mind, she replied, "He asked me if it would be all right to have the fish prepared Vera Cruz style on Friday night, as it is his favorite recipe, and I told him I would be happy to suggest this to Luisina, but I was sure she would honor the request," she responded coolly. With that, Edelmida excused herself and marched off towards the kitchen with a smirk on her face.

Francisco knew immediately that she was lying, but for what purpose, he could not fathom. He had followed them long enough to know there was much more to it than that, but he sensed Edelmida's tension and felt that this was not the time to press. He would continue to follow MacMurrough and keep an eye on Edelmida. He knew, instinctively, that MacMurrough was a bad seed and would slip up soon enough. He also could feel the hate and distrust in Edelmida who he knew was a chaste and honest girl who would eventually do the right thing.

As Edelmida hurried toward Casa Greene and the sanctity of her kitchen, he called out to her "*Gracias, Señorita*, I will look forward to that myself."

He couldn't see the determined look on Edelmida's face or the smile that slowly appeared as she began to formulate her plan to take down *El Diablo*.

<u>Chapter Nine</u>

Turning Point

Friday was pay day at the mines and also the day when the workers let off steam from the long week and the pressures of the job. It was no surprise that Saturday saw more accidents, by far, than any other day of the week. Fatalities and injury were always highest due to the fact that after the paychecks were cut and the men paid, they flooded the town, taking advantage of the bars, bordellos, and various gambling pursuits like betting on the cockfights or playing poker and other card games. They drank too much, too fast, and were inebriated before the sun went down. Too often, one of the men would stay up all night, drinking, gambling, and whoring only to go to his shift immediately after this night of drunkenness and debauchery. The native miners always seemed to have the highest injury rate on Saturday, although there were no statistics kept to back up the claim. It was long believed that the natives could not hold their alcohol as well as the Americans or Europeans, although they would try to keep up, and that led to the disasters they faced on a weekly basis when returning to the grueling rigors that mining copper in Cananea represented.

The weekly dance, which was organized by the management team at the Four C's, and scheduled every Saturday night, was designed to keep the men focused until the work week was done and then allow them to enjoy their hard earned pay and do whatever they liked at that time, instead of starting the party on Friday. But since their paychecks came on Friday, that became the unofficial start to the weekend, and the beginning of the hard drinking times that were common with the miners.

It had been discussed many times that the payout should be changed and pay day moved to Saturday, so they would not have the money to drink on Friday night and might help limit the liabilities they suffered. However, paying the workers after work on Saturday would give the families no time to shop for their weekly groceries. In the staunch Catholic environment that was Cananea, nothing happened on Sunday except Church services, and on Monday everyone had to be back at work, so there would be no time to get the errands done that each household needed to accomplish. It was a belief held by management that the men should be smart enough, or at least patient enough, to handle themselves and wait until after the full week was done before carrying on as they sometimes did. The dance had evolved as a place where one could meet the type of woman to marry and settle down, and not designed to be a rowdy and hectic party, so the men had to blow off steam sometime and Friday night was it.

The caste system that existed at the mines also came into play. Almost all of the office workers and managers were American and many were family men who had wives and children at home and didn't live in the shacks and hovels that was the native miners' habitat. For the Americans, Friday night was a family time when the children would be done school for the week and most of the women, if they worked at all, were also free to enjoy a night together. These men were the operational decision makers at Cananea and they needed to have their pay to enable them to have a family night or just to prepare for the food shopping the following day. It was too important to keep these workers happy, as their skill sets could not be found locally and the native miners were generally considered dispensable.

Every day at Cananea, new, strong young men showed up from the villages surrounding the mining community from hundreds of miles away, just to try and win a job with steady pay and the advantages that living and working in Cananea afforded them. These men came from villages that made their own clothes, grew and raised their own food and meat, and did not have any real social opportunity. Cananea may have had workers who were unhappy, but there were many, many men who envied them their positions.

Working at the four C's, the camaraderie among the men was strong and the pecking order established quickly. The macho environment was a

160

place where a man was constantly challenged by his peers. Fights broke out routinely for no apparent reason, and if a person wanted to be accepted, there were certain initiation rites that had to be observed and passed.

The debate over pay day continued on an ongoing basis, and in the meantime, the family men went home to enjoy the beginning of a nice family weekend; the rest of the workers continued to drink too much on Friday night; the injuries and deaths continued to climb to new heights each Saturday; and new workers would come in from the surrounding villages. The cycle of life in Cananea.

Payday would have been a tension filled event in any case. While most of the managers at the mines were American, certainly all of the money handlers were. The miners would line up to receive their pay, and after any money which had been advanced for scrip was deducted for use at the company store, they would come away with their marginal income.

There was something much more insidious at hand in the pay structure at the mines. The Americanos would brag about how much they made, and, at the pay station windows, the money was counted out loud and so everyone knew what they received as a weekly wage. It became obvious why the bourgeoisie gringos were able to board a stage to the Arizona border a few times a year, while the native peons could barely keep

161

themselves and their families in good clothing and properly fed.

Manuel and Pedro were lined up at the pay station at 3:00 on Friday. Their shift had just ended and they were eager to get their pay so they could take it into town to the *taquería* for a cold beer and some food. The line was long and the day very hot, approaching one hundred and two degrees with a direct, unblinking sun beating down on them. The light colored clothing they wore and the *sombrero* was little relief from the oppressive heat. The roads were all hard crusted dirt, tamped down by the horses and carts that passed by day after day, and from the feet of the workers on their way to from the mines each day. When the rains came each spring, the road became a muddy mess, but today, it was dusty and flecks of dirt flew up all around them making it tougher to breathe.

They covered their mouths with their bandanas, but this was little help and didn't shield their eyes, so tempers were short and the miners on edge. An adolescent in tattered white pants that hung to his knees with a dirty and torn short sleeved shirt, that was once white but hadn't seen that shade in months if not years, stood by the side of the pathway at a makeshift stand made up of a plank of discarded wood set atop two different sized bricks giving the stand a decided tilt, as he hawked lukewarm sugar water with thin slices of browned lemon floating on the top for color and a hint of flavor. The concoction wasn't cold, but it was wet and sweet and made the wait a bit more acceptable. He always did a very good business and it was said that his outfit was more like a uniform to elicit sympathy than a representation of his station. The cost of this weak brew was obscene, but the men gladly paid it when the weather was this hot and oppressive.

Of course, all the proceeds from the salesmen's efforts went to his father, who had worked in the mines until he experienced a near fatal accident that left him with a debilitating injury to his right side, affecting his arm and upper body so he could no longer work. He had been working in the mines when one of the timbers holding up the ongoing expansion, splintered and came down on him, jamming the wood splinters into his neck and nearly severing his carotid artery. It had taken him months of recuperation, but years later he still had pieces of wood that would surface near the scars from time to time and his right side never fully recovered. He had taken to drink and become something of the "town drunk" in a burgeoning village, soon to be city, of town drunks.

This had been a particularly long week for the men at the mines. There was no break from the heat and the sun was high in the sky baking the earth and the exposed parts of their bodies. In the mines, the workers often stripped down to their skivvies to work, which helped keep them cool, but made them prone to injury with so much of their

163

bodies exposed to the elements. But here in the line, they all bundled up in the loosest fitting clothing that covered their entire bodies and their heads to keep sunstroke from affecting them. The clothes helped to keep out the dry dust which was stirred up by the movement of people and horses going to and from the mines, causing added respiratory problems for those that did not keep their noses and mouths covered.

After a long, strenuous week of swinging a pick and with temperatures cooking them from the outside in, tempers were short and the air fairly crackled with tension. The sun was so strong that they had to squint to the point where they eyes almost closed and a headache would start to form in the middle of the brow where the eyes pushed together.

Pedro, who was shorter and heavier than Manuel, began to breathe hard in short bursts and seemed to be laboring just standing in line.

"Manuel" he gasped out, "Look at the gringos taking their pay. They are falling over themselves and taking the pesos and counting it in our faces, dropping bills as if it meant nothing to them. They make three times the money we make, their hours are shorter, and the path to their pay station is lined with wooden planks to keep the dust away from them, while we smother here in the dirt. The Flores Magon brothers are right – we have to do something. I hear that some of the men are organizing a strike to demand higher wages and better working conditions. There is a meeting tonight at 7:00 at the Cantina and I will be there, do you want to come along?" he asked Manuel.

Manuel was torn. On the one hand he knew Pedro and the others were right; conditions at the mines were deplorable, but there were very few jobs that paid as well as this one, and those that did were still reliant on the mines for their work, serving the needs of the miners, their families and the owners. The lumberyards, ranches, and construction jobs were no better, and some were worse than the mines. Besides, Manuel had been offered the first management position for a native worker and he couldn't very well afford to be seen consorting with his disgruntled employees.

Things had seemed to be going well for Manuel just now; the promise of a promotion and more money, meeting Edelmida, his little Sparrow, thinking seriously about a real relationship for the first time in his life, and even the mines seemed busier and more productive than ever before. In fact, the mines *were* busier. Colonel Greene was a genius at lining up investors and getting more money to expand the mines. This was a time to capitalize, with growth and expansion in the U.S. and Mexico, and the railroads being built to connect everyone, everywhere.

"No, Pedro. *Gracias*, but tomorrow night is the dance and I will be meeting Edelmida. I'm sure you'll all have a great time without me, drinking all the tequila you can, to keep it from being exported to the United States, gambling your money away, and bitching about the conditions at the mines and your lot in life. I'll save my energy for tomorrow night when the girls will all look pretty, dressed in their finest outfits and I'll enjoy the music, dancing, food, and good times instead of spending the time complaining again about something you can do nothing about," Manuel replied.

"Suit yourself, Manuel, but know this, times are getting tougher and we can't take much more of this abuse. All over the world, people are rising up against oppressive conditions and governments that don't care about the people, and they are winning these struggles. Tempers are short and the Flores Magon brothers are building a strong following, inciting change, and forcing the government to pay attention to our needs. There is talk of revolution and soon we will see a change even here at the mines. Mark my words, things are changing, there is even talk of a strike if our demands aren't met soon," Pedro vented.

"Well, I hope not," Manuel said angrily, "I think sometimes we don't realize what we have, always wanting more and thinking only of ourselves. Before Colonel Greene came to the mines and built what we have today, conditions here in Sonora were much, much worse and we only had those things we could make or grow ourselves. We need to be grateful for what we've got."

And with that Manuel picked up his meager earnings and headed off to the *taquería* for a light meal and then off to an early bed, for he wanted the night to go by quickly, waiting in anticipation for the next day when he would see Edelmida again.

Manuel was right, the mines were very productive and bringing in more money than ever before, and because of this, the town was growing, buildings were going up at an enormously fast rate, the railroads were being built out and bringing more people and goods to the town, conditions were ever improving and, economically, Cananea was one of the best places in the region, probably in all of Mexico at this time. Of course, this led to greater diversity, and as the population exploded, differing factions with different viewpoints created confusion and unrest. Because there was more money, in all factions, it became easier to prey on the greed of all the citizens and encourage them to demand more.

Casa Greene itself became a symbol of this wealth and Colonel Greene, being the larger than life and the personification of excess, always lived large, importing items from all over the globe to show his investors who would visit often at his request, just how well things were going. These visitors, mostly from New York, but also other parts of the world, would arrive bearing gifts and dressed in the latest fashions from Paris and New York, thus fostering an impression on the locals that more and more wealth was being created while they

Raymond F. Cavanagh

continued to see the same wages and conditions with little improvement for them and their families.

The reality was very different; Colonel Greene did spend lots of money and put on great airs, and there were stories of his hunting trips out west and hobnobbing with Presidents and entertainers in New York. It was said he was a good friend of Jenny Lind, The Songbird, and had dinners with Rockefeller and J.P. Morgan. All of this was true, and it fed the belief that the rich got richer and the poor helped them get there. The perfect conditions, since time immemorial, to foment unrest and talk of revolution.

But Colonel Greene was seriously overextended, and during his frequent trips to New York, he was floating additional stock and setting up ancillary companies who fed off each other, providing goods and services to one another and creating the illusion that each of them were doing well, although cash was a constant struggle. His companies included the Four C's, Cananea Gold and Silver mining, the Sonora Lumber Company, railroads, ranches, and other businesses; all generating money, but more of a house of cards than truly profitable ventures.

It was true that Greene was friendly with Morgan and Rockefeller and that he corresponded with Teddy Roosevelt, both of them hunters who loved the outdoors, and Colonel Greene was oblivious to the issues surrounding him, leaving the details to others, such as A.B. Fall. It was his way to

168

borrow, build, and leverage, creating the illusion of wealth and borrowing more for yet another venture. He was taunting fate, and the conditions at the mines were only one of his many concerns. His was a life of constant movement, building, borrowing, traveling, eating, day after day after day. He told his management team what he needed, and trusted they would get it done for him, regardless of cost, in money or otherwise. A trust that would one day be violated, and eventually lead to disaster.

The next day, Saturday, dawned hot and bright, another typical summer day in Cananea. Manuel woke early, showered in cold water, and went out to the cantina to brace himself for the day with an early bowl of menudo, a spicy, smoky breakfast stew made of tripe, hominy, and chilies, which was standard breakfast fare before a long day at the mines. It was also known to be notoriously good for hangovers. The meal was a favorite of Manuel's as his mother made it as a special treat for him as a boy, but he couldn't stand the smell of the tripe cooking before the hominy and chilies were added. The dish was said to originate during the civil wars when the people on the Sonora ranches would kill the cattle, dry the meat for jerky for the soldiers to ship off to battle, and use the remaining cuts for themselves. Many of the world's most fragrant and flavorful dishes have been created out of less desirable cuts of meat tenderized and enhanced with spices, and such was the case with this regional masterpiece.

After finishing his meal, he walked back towards his barracks, glancing around, not expecting to see anyone but the nuns and a few people coming off the night shift. Security worked around the clock throughout Cananea to make sure no one entered the mines in off hours and to keep the offices secure, so he was surprised as he rounded the corner near his barracks and came upon a crowd gathered outside the cantina. As he approached, he heard someone speaking in Spanish to the crowd in a loud voice "last night was the last straw, we have to band together to fight this injustice. I say we strike today and show them how serious we are."

"What happened?" Manuel asked of a security guard he knew who had worked the night shift.

"Last night there was a meeting of some of the workers who are unhappy and demanding better pay and working conditions," he replied. "As usual, there was lots of tequila flowing and a couple of the men got loud and rowdy and started to talk about revolution. They wanted to make an example of one of the managers at the mine and went to Madame Conchita's to confront whoever they found there."

The one constant about Madame Conchita's was that it was too expensive for even the highest paid native miner to afford. Under the rule of

Porfirio Díaz, although the overall economic conditions were good in Mexico in general, the developing crevice between the rich and poor was growing increasingly uneasy. The people who worked the land were quite upset because the laws had been changed, and in order for them to continue working the land, they had to acquire leases and these were difficult to arrange and also expensive. In addition to the fact that the native miners made substantially less than the American workers, the natives were paid in silver pesos and the American in gold dollars. The exchange rate, which was never favorable to the peso, was at a historic low, creating an even wider disparity between the compensation of the Americans and other workers at the mines.

So, Conchita's, a high end whorehouse, was exclusively populated by Americans, either the managers at the mines or the businessmen who came from New York to invest.

"Unfortunately, they picked the wrong man - *Señor* MacMurrough. There was a scuffle and Luis Hernandez pulled a knife on him and lunged out in an attempt to stab him. MacMurrough defended himself in a way I have never seen before. He grabbed Luis by his wrist and twisted until the knife came free. MacMurrough had the wildest look in his eyes that I have ever seen. A crooked grin crossed his lips and he pulled them back over his teeth in a cruel smile. He looked positively crazed, and he tossed the knife from hand to hand and began to circle Luis. One of the others jumped towards him and tried to put a stop to it, but MacMurrough slashed his arm and he ran away screaming and bleeding into the night. Luis thought he would have a chance to take the knife back at that point and lunged towards him in an attempt to do what MacMurrough had already done to him, but MacMurrough turned back at just that moment and plunged the knife deep into his stomach. Luis looked up with an expression of astonishment on his face and began to sink to the ground. MacMurrough, instead of removing the knife, twisted it viciously, pulled it out quickly and drove it in once again, deeper, and closer to the heart. He again twisted the knife with a vicious thrust so devastating, that Luis almost flipped over during the struggle. There was no saving him and we all knew at that point that he was dead. Everyone knew this MacMurrough was a tough hombre, but last night he became the most feared man in all of Cananea," the guard finished, breathlessly.

"What happened to MacMurrough, did anyone call *la policía*?" Manuel asked.

"Not right away," the guard responded, "most of the men scattered as soon as MacMurrough pulled the knife out of Luis' chest. There were plenty of witnesses that swear that it happened just as I told you, but none that will go on record and none who wanted to hang around and be questioned by *la policía* and risk becoming the next victim of *Señor* MacMurrough. No, *mi amigo*, all the witnesses who talked were gringos and so the conspiracy against us continues. They are all sticking together and it is only adding fuel to an already raging fire of hatred and mistrust. Talk of a strike is far worse and more urgent than ever and I fear we will see horrible things coming out of this incident."

Manuel couldn't believe it. Perhaps if he had gone he could have prevented this, but no, he thought, the booze and longstanding anger were due to come to a boil, and last night it had.

Esteban Baca Calderón, one of the most vociferous of the handful of revolutionaries who influenced the gatherings and fostered talk of unions and a strike, further incited the crowd.

"Compadres, go home now, show your support for your fellow workers and don't show up for your next shift. We must show that we can stand together and will not tolerate abuse and disrespect any longer."

Calderón concluded his plea and the remaining workers disbursed – many heading home, some continuing into the cantina for a fortifying breakfast of menudo and chicory coffee to help stave off the effects of the alcohol from the night before, and just a very few heading for the mines, because, in spite of everything that happened, they still needed the money to support their families.

Mexico was a curious blend of cultures and had a long and disastrous history of poverty and abuse. The native cultures in Sonora, including the predominant Papago, as well as the Pimas and Yaqui tribes, had long been abused by invaders to their native land. The Spanish conquistadors brought more than civilization and religion to the country of New Spain; it also brought diseases such as smallpox, which the natives could not fight off and which wiped out whole tribes in a matter of decades. There was a well-established caste system in place in the country at this time, evolving from a land of diverse and widely dispersed native Indian tribes to a more centralized European style society with the all of the pleasure and pain that these societies bring.

He thought the tension in the Cantina would be thick, but interestingly, it was calm and serene, almost as though a boil had been lanced and all the tension relieved. He felt sure that many of his co-workers felt as he did; that the trouble makers drank too much on Friday again, and got what they deserved. The voices of dissidence were small but strong, pitting brother against brother, and polarizing the workers against each other instead of against the rich, as was purported.

Manuel was not alone in thinking that this was a good job and better than the life they had before the mines opened, but he too was conflicted in his thinking. He remembered when he was young; his father had come from Spain with promises of streets lined with gold and silver. "Well, the mines are lined with silver alright, but extracting the metal is much more difficult and strenuous than could ever be imagined," he thought to himself.

The stories of Cibola and the seven cities of gold were grossly exaggerated, and building a life in Mexico, the name derived from the dead Aztec nation and believed to mean "center of the moon," was not a center of anything other than contention. "For decades, no, centuries," he thought, "this land has been a place of war; war fought over land, precious metals, boundaries, and anything else that could be fought over. First it had been tribe against tribe, although many of the native tribes were not a warring people, which creates a completely different problem, having no real leaders to show the true path. But how can a nation ever hope to become powerful if it doesn't treat the arts and humanities with the same respect and admiration as it does its' raw power and might? Then the Europeans came, and tried to compel the natives to drop long standing beliefs in their gods and take up Christianity, a religion based on principles very much like what they already had, but with rituals and customs that seemed designed to control thoughts and actions more than focusing on the respect of others. Now it is the rich, including many Americans, who have plundered the land to line their own pockets with wealth, and along the way, almost by accident, creating new jobs and the ability for many of us to do things we had only dreamt of before." It was, indeed, a conflict that Manuel could not come to grips with, but could only reflect on and question. He walked off, with the questions in his mind still unanswered, and headed off to the mines to his job, determined to continue to do what he was paid to do, and maintain a quiet, dignified life as much as possible, given the conditions of the day. He thought once again of Edelmida and hoped he would see her again soon.

When Manuel arrived, he was accosted by Thom MacMurrough, and his blood immediately turned cold. He was shocked to see MacMurrough, but thought to himself that he shouldn't be surprised. MacMurrough was the sort who had no conscience whatsoever, and would simply continue to bully his way through life, uncaring about the feeling of others and how his actions might affect them.

"Manuel, me boy, I suppose you heard about the scuffle we had last night?" MacMurrough asked with a gleam in his eye. "An unfortunate incident, but one that could not be avoided. I'm sorry the lad is gone, but he came at me with one of these new, big Bowie knives, and I had no choice but to defend myself. You understand, don't you laddie?" he exhorted.

Manuel didn't like it, but he had to somehow appease MacMurrough. He had no idea of the repercussions of these actions, but he was determined not to buy into MacMurrough's poison.

"*Señor* MacMurrough, these are difficult times, this is very bad business, and I know that many of my co-workers are very unhappy. I hope that when news of my promotion is announced, that it will relieve some of the pressure." Manuel responded.

"Well, me boy, that's what I wanted to talk to you about. I had a conversation last night with Colonel Greene and A.B. and a couple of the others and we have decided to announce your promotion tonight at the dance. What do you think of that?" MacMurrough asked with a grin.

Manuel was elated and his heart soared. Tonight, while he was with Edelmida, the woman he felt in his heart was right for him, he would be announced as the first ever native manager at the four C's. How proud she would be! He was sure his friends and family would be so happy and proud and perhaps some of the tensions of recent weeks would be eliminated. He would work to make changes and his fellow workers would see things improve.

"*Señor* MacMurrough," Manuel, replied, "I am honored of course, and I am so pleased. I look forward to the announcement tonight – and tonight of all nights, for there is a special lady who I will be with and I know it will make her proud as well to be with me," he continued enthusiastically.

"I know, me boy," Thom replied with a twinkle in his eye, "I'm sure all of your people will

177

be proud. Why don't you take the rest of the day off today and get ready for the big event tonight. Starting Monday, you will be part of the management team."

And with that MacMurrough walked Manuel back up the path toward town, slapped him on the back, and headed to Casa Greene for breakfast, and not the poor mans stew, but a proper Irish breakfast of eggs and ham, with real coffee and toast, satisfied with himself and the plan he set in motion, and wondering if Edelmida would be serving today.

When MacMurrough got to the mine after an excellent breakfast, with no sighting of Edelmida, he learned that some of the workers had called in sick. Production would be effected and that would not do. Colonel Greene had recently sold additional stock in the company to new investors and productivity increases were important to boost revenues to cover this expansion. Some said the Colonel was overselling shares, but he continued to grow the business and set up ancillary businesses, allowing him to move investment funds, revenues, and costs amongst his various ventures.

Then, additional new investment dollars would allow the Colonel and A.B. to upgrade equipment and increase the number of rails in and out of the yard to get product to market more quickly. Westward expansion and demand for metals was at an all-time high and competition was stiff.

MacMurrough knew this "sick out" was a direct effect of the incident at the cantina the night before, and he also knew he had to take action to prevent it from spreading further – twenty percent of the workers were out and this could not be tolerated. He marched off to speak with Colonel Greene to discuss what punishment he could impart.

At the same time, the miners who did come to work that day were surprised that Manuel wasn't there. He was known to be one of the most dedicated workers and never became embroiled in politics. Some thought Manuel might not be the smartest, and maybe even a little slow at times, because he would not engage in any discussion about workers' rights, and never seemed to complain, no matter how trivial the task or how many hours he worked.

But Manuel was just stoic. As a good Catholic boy, he had been raised to be God fearing and to accept what came to him without complaint, and what many took for slowness in Manuel was really his ability to contain his feelings and soldier through any situation, regardless of the obstacles in the way.

Manuel's father had died in a mining accident when Manuel was only five years old, so his memories of him had long faded. Many people said that Manuel looked almost exactly like his father did at the same age. His mother did the best she could for the boy, but she had to work, and so

Manuel, as an only child, grew up alone much of the time and learned to do things in a quiet way. His mother, a staunch Catholic, raised him by the churches' rule and taught him to accept God's will, and suffer in silence. He wasn't what would be called a mama's boy, but without a father figure to help guide him, he had a soft side that was more pronounced that most boys his age and this turned him inside himself even more.

His trust that good would win out over evil often got him into situations from which he could not extricate himself and he was often a target of ridicule and physical abuse by others. Manuel grew up to be a strong man, and his years of swinging the axe in the mines gave him added bulk and strength. He was strong and silent, and, as an adult, that made him a person to be respected by his peers.

So the fact that Manuel did not show up for work on this particular day fed conjecture that he had finally had enough and was taking his stand. This rumor spread throughout the community and gave credence to the impending strike, fomenting talk of a more widespread action to protest working conditions and individuals rights.

All the while, Manuel was at home praying to God to thank him for his good fortune and oblivious to the rumors surrounding his absence. He was washing his best clothes for the dance and counting the hours until he could leave to meet Edelmida, his little songbird. Her friends had nicknamed her Sparrow, because she was always humming a tune as she worked in the kitchen.

At *siesta*, he lay down and tried to get some rest, but he could not sleep, tossing and turning and dreaming of the wonderful things to come with Edelmida and his new job as a manager. "Yes," he thought with satisfaction, "starting tomorrow my life will be like a dream come true," and with that he rolled over with a smile on his face and thought again about his beautiful little sparrow, Edelmida.

Meanwhile, MacMurrough was looking for Colonel Greene, who had just left for his annual hunting expedition with his business associates and some of the investors from New York. The Colonel knew how to throw a party and made a specialty of the care and feeding of his millionaire friends, who were heavy investors in all of Greene's enterprises. The colonel made sure that these men had the finest of food and liquor during these retreats, and sent his best carriages to take them to Greene's private Pullman train to whisk them off to the Sierra Madres for a week or two of hunting, drinking, and camaraderie.

The Colonel had a penchant for the fine life, and made sure that he and his investors always had the best of everything, is spite of the increasing unrest back at the camps.

MacMurrough, meanwhile, was forced to speak to A.B. about the sickout. A.B., who was scheduled to meet the Colonel and the entourage in a day or two after clearing out some unfinished business concerning inconsistencies in the accounting books, famously disliked MacMurrough and vice versa. It was no secret within the management team that A.B. wanted MacMurrough out. He never liked the Irish anyway, as he thought them to be lazy drunks, and he believed MacMurrough was hiding something from them at all times. A.B. would grudgingly admit that MacMurrough was anything but lazy; in fact, he seemed to have an unlimited amount of energy which he exhibited from morning till night, and always seeming to be busy and rushing here and there with no apparent reason. He had that wiry, kinetic energy that exuded from his freckled skin, but A.B. was distrustful and suspected that half the time MacMurrough was drunk. He was just such a good drunk that no one could tell the difference when he was drunk or sober, and his capacity for alcohol was legendary. He was known to confiscate tequila from the workers, which was becoming more and more popular, and replacing mesquite as the liquor of choice, despite its higher price tag. It had a smoother flavor and texture than its fiery cousin, and was more convenient now that the Cuervo company had developed the *pachoncitas*, the small flask-type bottles that fit into the baggy pants of the workers. MacMurrough's stockpile of *pachoncitas* grew, and A.B. knew he would mix the contents of different flasks to fill them and sell them back to the workers for much less than the price of a new bottle. The workers, of course, knew this also, and it gave them an even greater reason to hate and distrust this man.

MacMurrough hated A.B., who always got in his way when he wanted to speak to the Colonel. While MacMurrough believed in using an iron fist when dealing with the miners, both A.B. and the Colonel rose to power and prominence working the mines, and empathized and preferred employing the approach of camaraderie and *simpatico* as the tools of effective management instead.

MacMurrough believed he would eventually get the Colonel to agree with his way of thinking and would allow him more use of force, particularly since Greene was away so often. But as A.B. was there to reinforce Greene's tendencies, MacMurrough had no chance to change his mind. And now, he had to talk to A.B. about the strike. Well, perhaps his ruse of giving Manuel the day off could be used to his advantage.

"A.B.," Thom began breathlessly as he ran into Casa Greene from the steamy morning, with sweat glistening on his brow, "we have a situation at the mine and I think we have to take drastic action before things get worse."

Fall hated it when MacMurrough called him A.B., he did not consider him a peer and would have preferred if he addressed him more formally. Perhaps he would give himself a title and

183

MacMurrough would have to address him as "Director," or "Lieutenant" to Greene's Colonel, which is what he really was in practice, but no matter, he would deal with this peon and finish up his business so he could leave for the hunt with the Colonel.

"Yes, MacMurrough, what is it?" he demanded harshly.

MacMurrough replied quickly, "Many of the miners have called in sick, as many as 75 of the 250 who are scheduled, and production is suffering, the lines are uneven, and there is general chaos. I think strong tactics are required to take control of the situation immediately. They are probably using the attack on me yesterday as their excuse, thinking we will respond to their demands."

"Yes, and I suppose the fact that you killed a man might have caused some upset. Did it dawn on you at all yesterday what kind of reaction it would spark when you took that knife and slaughtered him?" A.B. replied hotly.

MacMurrough thought to himself, "What an imbecile. Any real man knows that, in the heat of battle you fight to survive, not contemplate life choices." But he held his tongue and replied "A.B., I thought he was going to kill me, I simply tried to defend myself and it was purely an accident. Any man would do the same, why, even Colonel Greene himself shot a man at the OK corral."

A.B. did not bother to respond. He knew that there were plenty of people available to help

184

subdue the attackers yesterday and that the knifing wasn't necessary. Besides, they were all very drunk at the time and no real threat to anyone. Instead, he responded "What is your recommendation?"

"Well, the situation is very bad. Even Manuel Carreras is not in work today and…""

"What!" screamed A.B., as his face turned as red as the clay on the banks of the San Pedro, "the person you recommended we announce tonight as the first ever native worker to become a manager at the mines? What have you done?"

MacMurrough knew then that his plan had backfired. He had intended to use Manuel's absence as a lever to show how serious the problem was, and get A.B. and the Colonel to agree to his methods, which worked very well on the Intercontinental Railroad. The Chinese workers wouldn't dare defy him, for they knew he would beat them unmercifully if they dared to disobey, but the idiot Fall turned the tables on him and made it seem his fault. And he was the one who was attacked!

"Listen, A.B., you and Colonel Greene refuse to take these people in hand. I have proven methods, and that is why the Colonel brought me here in the first place. I'm sure he would agree with me on this one, and let me do my job the way I see fit," MacMurrough concluded with as much force as he could muster.

"Well, he's not here, and I'm in charge and I'm equally sure he would talk to the people first, as he always has, and appeal to them, one miner to another. So, here is what we are going to do; go get Manuel and bring him directly here to me. We will announce his promotion tonight and I will address the workers on the Colonel's behalf. There are to be no more altercations with any of the other workers, and no more manipulation. Are we clear?" A.B demanded.

"Sure, A.B. You're the boss. I'll go and get Manuel." MacMurrough left, more determined than ever to get Fall out of his hair once and for all.

That evening, just before the dance started, A.B. made an impassioned speech that would have made the Colonel proud. He announced Manuel's promotion to wild applause and spirits in the room soared. He talked about Manuel meeting with him at the Casa and the two of them going over strategies to improve conditions at the mines. MacMurrough was nowhere to be found, and all of Manuel's friends and family gathered around and brought him drinks and toasted him endlessly into the night. They now thought they knew why he wasn't at the mine today, and understood that only positive changes could be ahead for all of them.

A new day was dawning for the Four C's and the hope was that Manuel would be able to represent their wishes with the management team and invoke some changes in working conditions.

Manuel drank and smiled and joked with all of his friends, and he had more fun that night than he had in quite some time. But there was one question which was nagging at him and put a damper on the entire evening, although he did not let it show, as he wondered "Where is Edelmida?"

While the dance continued long into the night, Edelmida was at the chapel praying for forgiveness and saying rosary after rosary at the Stations of the Cross. She had been raised to be forgiving and turn the other check, but in this case the Old Testament held the key to her redemption and at the stroke of midnight, as the mission bells tolled, she returned to her room with the genesis of a plan on how to address Mr. Thomas MacMurrough. Edelmida's blood boiled whenever she thought of him, which never ceased, even for a minute, ever since her attack. Her heritage of Spanish blood on her father's side and Papago Indian on her Mother's side, had instilled in her a resolve and belief in retribution.

"This *gringo*," she thought, "will not get away with another rape of my people." She went to bed, and for the first time felt she would get through this horrifying episode and fell soundly asleep while plotting her next steps.

Sunday, at Church, Manuel saw Edelmida as she walked back down the aisle after she received communion. He tried to catch her eye, but failed. Edelmida did not lift her head and the scarf that she wore shielded her face completely. Manuel could not receive communion himself because he had had too much to drink the night before and drunkenness was a sin, so he would have to wait until the following week, go to confession on Saturday, and finally receive next Sunday. His celebration raved on until the wee hours of the morning and he could not say no to those who wanted to buy him a drink. He had tried to nurse his drinks, but friends and relatives would toast him with shots of tequila and it would have been rude of him to not at least take a strong sip with them as they drank. Manuel decided to try and speak to Edelmida as church let out to see why she had not attended the dance the previous night. He was confused and perplexed because she had seemed as excited as he was when they last spoke.

But when the church service ended, Edelmida was nowhere to be found and Manuel headed home to his family dinner with conflicting emotions of elation for his promotion and hope of things to come, and sadness and frustration in regards to Edelmida and the mystery surrounding her sudden withdrawal.

Over the course of the next several days, Manuel was consumed with his work, and while he thought of Edelmida often, and prayed he might see her in the morning or evening, she did not make an appearance. Manuel was now invited to the Casa Greene for dinner as a part of the Management team, which he loved, for the food was fresh and fabulous and the setting magnificent, but there was a hole in his heart and an empty feeling in the pit of his stomach, for he longed to see Edelmida again.

He discretely inquired as to her whereabouts when he saw one of the kitchen workers, but all he could uncover was that she had taken ill and had not been in all week.

Manuel settled into his new job and the hours were long, but the job hadn't really changed for him all that much. He had the new title and more pay, but he was still supervising the workers, and only the native workers at that, the American workers had their own foreman. Still, the miners seemed happier and more productive, in spite of a small contingent that continued to try to stir unrest and claimed that Manuel's promotion was a smoke screen and he was being used as a puppet.

Manuel hadn't seen Thom MacMurrough since he spoke to him about the promotion. He was off recruiting new workers for the mine, which seemed to be an ongoing process. Miners would come and go as steadily as the sun would rise in the morning and set in the evening. Colonel Greene always had an eye towards expansion of one of his businesses, and this made the process that much more challenging. The Colonel was due to head back to New York in a few weeks, where he would undoubtedly raise more capital to continue expansion, and would need the new workers to help with the building and organization.

189

On Thursday, as Manuel was heading home from work to shower and get ready to head out to the Cantina for the evening, he saw Edelmida coming down the path towards him. His heart skipped a beat and he thought it must be his imagination, for he had all but given up the thought of seeing her again, and he believed that he was the reason for this – perhaps she had second thoughts or believed the lies of the revolutionaries who talked of his "puppet management."

Instead, Edelmida strode toward him with a purpose and a defiant gleam in her eye. She looked even more beautiful than he remembered and seemed to fairly glow in the fading light of the afternoon.

"Manuel," she called out to him excitedly as she came closer.

He began to run towards her, and as they met he put his arms around her and picked her up off her feet and buried his head in her neck muttering "Oh, Edelmida, I am so happy to see you." He was worried about being so familiar with her, but she returned the hug and then gently pushed him away.

"Manuel, I am sorry I was not there to celebrate with you last Saturday night. I came down with a very bad fever and had to stay confined to quarters. I was too weak and feverish and felt as if I were in a dream all week. As I got better yesterday, I thought about sending word to you, but decided to wait and see you myself. I'm sorry if you were worried," she gushed breathlessly.

In truth, Edelmida had spent the week in remorseful reflection, at first embarrassed, and then, worried. Her emotions continued to change and grow, and each day she strengthened until she eventually became angry and resentful, at what had happened to her at the hands of *El Diablo*.

She vowed that the shame she felt would forever be her secret, that no one would ever know, and she would find a way to avenge the attack she suffered. Coming out of her raw emotions and lack of sleep, and overcome by grief, she hatched a plan to stop the only other person in the world who knew what happened that night from ever revealing what had occurred.

Her presence on the kitchen staff would come in handy in her plan, which was still rudimentary in her mind, but she had become obsessed and thought constantly about how she could get back at MacMurrough. Even now, while talking to Manuel, it never escaped her mind. Edelmida knew she had to act quickly for she feared that *El Diablo* would be the type to get drunk and brag about his conquests.

Tomorrow would be Friday, payday, a night of drinking and partying, and Edelmida had to figure something out before then. For now, though, she was happy to be talking to Manuel.

"I will be going back to work on Monday. I spoke to Luisina and she wants me to get completely well before working in the kitchen. I would like to think she is thinking of my well-being, but I'm afraid she only wants to make sure I am not contagious. So, I am free to go to the dance with you tomorrow night if you still want to see me."

Manuel's heart felt as light as a feather. "Of course, Edelmida, I would be honored to escort you to the dance. This time, may I walk you from the Casa to make sure you arrive?" he said and winked at her.

"Of course," she laughed, "be there right after work, and I will make you something special to eat before we go." And with one final squeeze of his hand, she left him, and Manuel went back to his barracks with his heart soaring, counting the seconds to Saturday night and his time with Edelmida.

Francisco watched all this with concern from behind the stone wall that lined the entrance to the Casa. There was something wrong with Edelmida beyond her illness, and his gut feeling told him it was because of MacMurrough, but he didn't know what it could be.

He liked Manuel and Edelmida and thought they were a great couple. Both were hard working, religious, and family oriented, and more than a little naïve.

"Of all the people here at the mines," he thought to himself, there are few more deserving of happiness. And they are so much alike, there are none as oblivious to the dark side of the world as these two." And with that thought, he headed off to his office to see if there were any further exploits of Thom MacMurrough, or whatever his real name was.

On her way back to her room, Edelmida stopped in at Casa Greene. It was *siesta* time and there was no one around, so she went through the kitchen and into the drawing room. She stopped for a moment and drew in a sharp breath as she once again came upon the bejeweled cross, and remembered the incredible story that Colonel Greene had told of how it came into his possession. She hesitated only a moment before reaching up and snatching it off the wall, quickly hiding it under her *quechquémitl*, a poncho-like garment that was usually worn only for special occasions. Edelmida had worn it this day, because meeting Manuel had, for her, been a special occasion and she wanted to look her best.

She knew in taking Colonel Greene's Amulet that she was taking a step to eternal damnation and would never see the gates of heaven, but she followed the advice of the Old Testament and was determined to trade an eye for an eye.

She quickly left the Casa and hurried back to her room with her prize. Shaking and breathing shallowly, she hid the cross under her bed and went off to execute the rest of her plans for vengeance on *El Diablo*.

Chapter Ten
Retribution

"Compadres, it has now been weeks since Manuel Carreras was promoted and we have seen no changes at all in the conditions in the mines or the treatment of native workers. It is time to rise up with one voice and make ourselves heard."

The morning sun was beautiful on this fine day in early summer and Pedro and Manuel were heading towards church for Sunday worship. Esteban Baca Calderón, along with other revolutionaries, had been trying to incite the miners for months. When Calderón had first arrived in Cananea, he met and befriended Manuel Diéguez, a local merchant with an agenda of his own. The two organized the labor party PLM (*Partido Liberal Mexicano*), and were attempting to rally the native miners from Cananea with other mines in the region. Calderón was a great orator and he could rally the workers as no other in Cananea. His only real rival, both oratorical and politically, was Colonel Greene. Calderón was trying hard to gain a foothold and sign up miners to join the union and strike for better wages and conditions, but the path was difficult because they were afraid to lose their jobs, which was all they had in spite of the inequities and danger.

195

Regardless of the relative strength or weakness of the union, each time a quorum of workers would consider taking action to strike for better conditions, something would happen to quell the unrest. However, the spirit of revolution was in the air and the last management ploy, the "promotion" of Manuel Díaz Carreras, only had a very short term impact. The expectation had been set that real change would finally occur and conditions and pay would improve, but in the past few weeks nothing had changed at all.

Manuel was widely respected and well liked, but he was too reserved to invoke any kind of real change at the management level. The position which was created for him to help reduce tensions, and offer some hope of advancement to the *mestizo* class was an empty gesture and his actual job did not vary much from what he had been doing before, which was supervising the removal of matte and transportation of the raw material to the surface. The only real change was that he was now allowed to take meals at the management table at Casa Greene, a visible act that struck a chord of relief with the miners.

Colonel Greene was not the operational leader at the Four C's; he left that to his managers like A.B. Fall, Francisco de Torres, and Thom MacMurrough. He perceived his role to be that of visionary, a raiser of capital for expansion and new ventures, such as the lumber company which supplied the materials for building the mines, and the cattle company, which supplied food for the workers and their families. Although Greene had grown up in a well-off suburb of New York City, he had worked the mines for years and led a rough and tumble life of his own and he traveled throughout the southwest deserts in pursuit of gold and silver mines. He became the copper king, but even Greene had no real interest in the metal at first. It was serendipity that he came upon it, and fortuitous that this occurred at a time when copper was coming into great demand due to its conductive properties. So, although the Colonel was sympathetic to the miners' grievances and understood their concern, he left the decision on operational changes to others.

Manuel and Pedro listened with interest and observed the reaction of the crowd. There was much nodding in agreement and whispering among the men, griping about conditions and the lack of change. In spite of these emotions, the reality was that the mines were growing and expanding.

"I don't understand, Pedro," Manuel commented as *Señor* Calderón continued to incite the crowd. "Colonel Greene has been operating the mines for years now and it has brought jobs and growth to the area. We are all doing much better than before; jobs are plentiful, the pay is better than anything we have seen, and the railroads are bringing in people, goods, and food. Why is everyone so unhappy?"

"Manuel," Pedro replied, "in some ways you are so naïve. Of course things are better, but better for us? No. The ones who are doing well are the Americans who take our jobs at much higher pay, while we clean their toilets and do their laundry. We have given up much of our freedom for the meager paychecks we receive. Díaz may have opened the country to expansion through industrialization, but he also ensured that the Americans and the rich *Peninsulares* share all the wealth while the rest of us toil and labor for meager scraps. We are viewed as third class citizens and only those of us with some Spanish blood in our veins are given any real work to do with only a tiny bit of responsibility. The rest of us are given menial and demeaning jobs at very low pay and very long hours. But maybe most important of all, the pay and work is not equal. We are being exploited on our own land."

"Look," Pedro continued, "before the mines were producing at the rate they are now, and copper was exported to the States, we used what we needed and lived a simple and free life. When the rains came, we moved up into the hills where we could cultivate the fruits of the land and tend to our flocks. When the weather was dry, we were free to pack our belongings and pack our mules and horses, and return to the river banks where the ground was fertile, and we could grow all the grain and vegetables we needed for our meals, with maybe enough left over to bring to market. Our existence was like that of the great hunting birds; free, mobile, and reliant on only ourselves and our intelligence."

"But Pedro," Manuel interrupted, "we now have stable homes, not tents and adobes, with running water which is clean enough for us to drink, and money in our pockets to buy tequila and not have to drink everclear. We have a place to bring our sick; doctors and medicine, not herbs and *curanderos*. Yes, we may have less mobility, but before it was forced, dependent on the weather, and there was never a guarantee we would be able to grow our crops. Everything was left to chance and the only education we had was passed from one generation to the next. Now, we have people from all over the world, from places we never knew existed before, bringing food, techniques for growing and mining, that we never considered. Medicine, education, and growth. Our children will see and do things we could never imagine," Manuel concluded.

"Oh, *mi amigo*," Pedro responded "much of what you say is true, but the price we pay is too high. We live near poverty while the Americans and Porfirian cronies make all of the money and treat us all as peons. Enough of us have died in the mines, and what about all Yaqui brethren who have been kept in slavery and removed from their lands to profit the rich Americans? You are right, we are becoming more educated and with that education

199

and knowledge comes the ability to see not only what we do have, but also what we do not have. All over the world, countries are growing and expanding and people are fighting for their rights. The old ways of accepting our position in life is no longer acceptable. This is our land and you are I are fortunate to be *Mestizo*, with a Spanish father and a native mother, offering us the best of both worlds. Our class is accepted and we have more than many, but the past forty years of Porfirio Díaz's rule has taken its toll on this country. Mexico is rich in resources, but its people are poor, and the gap between the classes is growing wider and wider with each passing day. We will never be respected as a country on the world stage if we don't take back control of our destiny and eliminate the corruption that has taken hold because of the greed of a few."

"The Spanish and Americans have shown us what we can do with our resources, but why should we work for them? Díaz fuels economic growth by selling off what is ours instead of encouraging native people to build new businesses and exploiting our resources. The Mexican people are becoming the working class for the rich, and the rich are almost never Mexican. First, we give more than half of our country away to America, now we see our people working for these same Americans, or worse, migrating to America where they can build business and use their talent and intelligence for the personal gain they cannot achieve here."

"The Jesuits gave us faith, hope and education. It is time for Mexicans of all backgrounds, whether native or of mixed blood, to unite and share in the wealth that naturally belongs to us." Pedro continued, "I know you want things to stay as they are today, with your new promotion and Edelmida in your life, everything is going well for you now. Change is a difficult thing. But, as a people, if we continue on as we have, we are doomed forever to be ruled based on the desires of others. No Manuel, I love you like a brother, but in this you are wrong. We need to stand up for ourselves." And with that, Pedro turned and walked off to listen to Calderón talk about revolution and what happened in France and the United States in the last century and how it is now Mexico's turn.

Manuel shook his head, lifted his chin, and marched off down the road to the chapel where the Franciscans now held services. When the Jesuits were expulsed and recalled back to Spain by King Carlos III in 1767, there was a period when all the good work they had done went unfulfilled until the Franciscan order took up residence in many of the Missions which had fallen into disrepair, and began to offer services once again to the faithful.

Pedro's words stuck in Manuel's mind. He could not shake the sense of what he heard, and yet, he did not want change. Things for him were going very well right now, and he wanted the rest of the world to feel the same way. He arrived at the church

201

and went directly to the statue of the Blessed Mother. Manuel always went to her to pray, because he believed that Mary was the most important figure in his Catholic religion. She had carried a child conceived without a human father, and raised him in absolute faith as the one, true son of God, only to live to see him treated brutally; beaten, tortured, punished, and put to death in a savage manner marked by mob violence. After witnessing this horrible death, she saw his body mysteriously disappear from a sealed, stone burial crypt, in order for him to be reunited with his rightful father in heaven. She did all of this with dignity and resolve, never complaining or denouncing her faith. She was a true pillar of faith and stoicism, and Manuel admired and revered her perspicuity and heroism.

"Blessed Mother," he intoned, "please guide me on this path. I am confused and the conflict within me is tearing me apart. I know that some of my confusion comes because of my personal gain. I am making more money, and have more influence, than any of my peers have ever had, and I believe I can use this influence to make changes in the mines. But I am concerned that I may not be able to make the real changes required to advance my people and I want to help and make a difference in people's lives and the future of our country."

"Please guide me in the right direction and help me make the right decision for my family and friends and for all the people of Mexico." Manuel made the sign of the cross and knelt and prayed for direction until the morning had passed and the church began to fill with those in the city who believed.

Meanwhile, Edelmida was about to leave for services when suddenly, Luisina broke into her room. Edelmida!" she cried out, "come quickly, I need your help at the Casa."

"What is it, Luisina? Edelmida replied, afraid for the worst.

"Colonel Greene's antique cross – it is gone!" Luisina cried out. "I must alert the staff and call Francisco, the head of security. We will need to search Casa Greene and all of the workers' quarters. The cross could only have been taken by someone who works at Casa Greene," she continued breathlessly. "Oh, Colonel Greene will be furious" Edelmida agreed, "and I hesitate to think of what A.B. will do with the Colonel out of town."

Edelmida was petrified. Here was Luisina in her room with the cross just under her bed, talking about a search of the quarters and her plan wasn't even fully thought out yet. She cursed herself for her stupidity. She should have thought this through. If they found the cross in her room, she would lose her job, her reputation, everything she had ever worked for, and the prospect of jail. Certainly Manuel would never speak to her again. She had to think quick and come up with a plan, and that had better include a way to pin this on *El Diablo*, but first, she had to get Luisina out of her room.

Thinking quickly, she responded, "Luisina, let's go back to the Casa to the dining room and check there first. Perhaps someone moved the cross while cleaning and forgot to put it back on the wall."

She shepherded Luisina out of her room and went to back to the Casa to search the dining room and kitchen area to no avail. This gave Edelmida the time she needed to concoct a simple, yet effective plan.

After they got to the Casa and searched all the likely places where the Amulet could have been left, Edelmida said, "Luisina, I'm afraid you're right, the cross is gone. I will go get Francisco right away. Why don't you call all the workers back to the Casa and I will explain to Francisco your idea of searching the quarters. I'm sure Mr. MacMurrough can help with assembling everyone. I will stop by his quarters on the way and ask him to help you as well."

Luisina thought this was a solid plan and headed off to round up the workers.

Edelmida ran off as quickly as she could and went to her room. She removed the cross from under her bed and hid it under her *quechquémitl*. Running as fast as she could to *El Diablo's* quarters, she knocked on his door frantically, calling out "*Señor* MacMurrough, Luisina needs your help at Casa Greene!" She did this so he would not think she was there for any other reason. He came to the door, and when he saw her, his eyes went wide and a cruel smile spread across his face. Just as he opened his mouth to say something, Edelmida blurted out angrily, "*Señor* MacMurrough, as much as I despise you for what you did to me, I am here to tell you that Colonel Greene's antique cross, which was hanging on the wall in the drawing room, has gone missing and is feared stolen. Everyone seems to believe you stole it. You need to get over there right away, before they come looking for you."

A look of disbelief came over his face and the smile disappeared and was replaced with a dark scowl. "That's ridiculous" he stammered, "why I …"

Edelmida cut him off. "*Señor*, there is no time to stand here and talk to me. You must go to the kitchen at Casa Greene right away and speak with Luisina. Francisco is on his way as we speak." she finished forcefully. And with that, MacMurrough grabbed his walking stick and hat, and raced off to the Casa without another word.

Edelmida worked quickly. Once *El Diablo* was around the corner, she glanced around, saw no one nearby, and entered his room. In one swift motion, she removed the cross from under her garment and placed it under the mattress of his bed. Then she left, slamming the door shut on her way out. She knew that even if someone saw her, her cover story would deflect any suspicion.

She then ran to Francisco de Torres' room and pounded on his door over and over. "I'm coming, I'm coming" he called out and opened the door. "What is it that's so important during siesta?" he questioned. Siesta was taken very seriously in Cananea and even the Americans took advantage of the break, although it was typically taken after the midday meal. Francisco did work odd hours, however, so it was not unusual for him to take *siesta* when he could.

"*Señor*, there has been a theft at Casa Greene. Colonel Greene's antique cross has been taken from the drawing room wall. Luisina is rounding up the workers for questioning by you and we need you to come quickly." As he grabbed his hat and pulled the door closed, she leaned over to him and whispered in his ear "I heard someone say that *Señor* MacMurrough did this to get back at the native workers for the troubles they have been causing."

"Just like MacMurrough" he thought to himself, "trying to stir things up so he can justify his heavy handed tactics. A.B. is right, this man can't be trusted." On his way to Casa Greene, he stopped by to alert A.B.

Together they walked into the kitchen to find MacMurrough, Luisina, and all the kitchen workers, including Edelmida, standing around the counter and talking over one another excitedly.

"Silence," shouted A.B., and everyone stopped talking at once. MacMurrough walked over

206

to the two as if he were a peer and above suspicion and said "Colonel Greene's cross is gone and I have heard that people are accusing me, and no one admits to taking it. You know how loyal I am to the Colonel. I would never even contemplate such a thing," he concluded.

"We'll see about that MacMurrough," A.B. replied harshly, "and when I said silence, that applied to everyone, including you," he finished, as he glared at him. MacMurrough shut his mouth and sat at a stool by the counter. "Now," A.B. continued, "who discovered the cross was missing?"

Luisina spoke up "I did *Señor* Fall. I was prepping for dinner and checking the table settings and had just walked into the drawing room to check on the liquor supply when I saw the cross was gone. It was obvious immediately, and I ran for Edelmida since she is closest. I also thought she would be the best person to help me search for it. Edelmida has lots of energy." Several of the girls giggled, for it was true, and Edelmida was often teased about it.

"Alright," A.B. quieted the crowd again. "Everyone stay here. Francisco and I will search the Casa and each of the barracks, and you will be free to go after that."

MacMurrough looked up expectantly, but didn't dare ask the question, as A.B. addressed him, "MacMurrough, you are to ensure no one leaves this room – and I mean no one." And with that A.B.

and Francisco de Torres left the room and began their inspection.

Once the Casa and all the workers rooms were searched, and nothing had been found, they were about to head back to the kitchen to release the workers when Francisco commented, "A.B. what about the comment MacMurrough made when we first arrived? Do you think someone is setting him up for this?"

A.B. replied, "Plenty of people have reason to want to see MacMurrough take the fall, but I don't think anyone would be foolish enough to cross him, and even if they did, it would take an enormous amount of nerve and a cool hand to steal that cross and set him up, but you're right, we at least need to check his room."

A.B. returned to the Casa Greene kitchen soon after by himself. "You are all free to go. MacMurrough, come with me. You and Francisco and I will talk to the other workers who weren't on shift." And with that the crowd disbursed, back to work or to their rooms, and A.B. and MacMurrough started towards Ronquillo.

As they strode down the dirt road in silence, A.B. led them past the barracks and stopped at the door leading to MacMurrough's room. "Let's stop in at your room for a minute, MacMurrough, there's something I want to discuss with you."

MacMurrough was pleased. "Maybe A.B. is finally seeing my value" he thought to himself, "certainly this may be the time to take harsher

208

methods on the workers, to stop this type of felonious behavior."

As the door opened, Francisco stepped forward, grabbed MacMurrough by the wrist and boomeranged him into the room, sending him into free-fall as he landed on the floor at the foot of his bed. A.B. slammed the door, bent down and took the Bowie knife out of its scabbard. They then both stood against the door with their arms folded across their chests and scowls on their faces.

"What the bloody hell!?!" MacMurrough shouted. "What is wrong with you?" What is this all about? Are you both insa …"

"We'll ask the questions," A.B. interrupted. "Francisco, please show him what we found."

Francisco lifted the mattress and said, "This is what this is all about, MacMurrough. Colonel Greene's cross."

MacMurrough stood up and gazed down at the bejeweled antique cross and stammered, "This is a set up, you have to know that. Why would I ever be stupid enough to hide that in my own room? I mean, if I took it, which I didn't. I'm being set up here," he protested.

"That may be true, MacMurrough," A.B. raised his voice in distain, "Although the lord knows you have done some truly stupid things during your tenure here. But no matter, your effectiveness has been compromised. You cannot command respect after this. We can't keep it quiet,

209

so your time is up. You are to pack your bags immediately and leave Cananea, Sonora, and Mexico, forever. If I see or hear from you again, you'll regret it," he spat out. "Stop at the bursar's office on your way out and Francisco will escort you to the border."

"You're making a mistake, A.B. When Colonel Greene gets back, you'll be the one in trouble. You haven't heard the last of me," he vowed.

Francisco slapped him on the back of the head and said, "MacMurrough, smarten up. We can charge you for this theft and slap you in prison with the rest of the vagrants, thieves, and murderers. How long do you think you'll last there? Be thankful we're letting you go."

As MacMurrough packed, and he and Francisco opened the door to leave, a crowd, which had gathered outside the barracks, cheered and applauded with cries of "*hasta la vista*" and "*cojale*, MacMurrough" accompanied by whistles, raised fists, and items thrown at MacMurrough's head.

Francisco and MacMurrough mounted up and rode out of town at a gallop and MacMurrough thought to himself, "I am not done yet, someone set me up and I have a good idea who it was. She has not seen the last of me," and with that, they took off in a cloud of dust, to the cheers of the grateful crowd.

Chapter Eleven

Te Quiero

The news traveled fast back to the Casa, as Edelmida helped to prepare for the evening meal. It was to be a light dinner since most of the staff would be attending the dance, or, if not, would be making their own plans for the evening. Luisina told her to place one less setting as *Señor* MacMurrough would not be joining them. She smiled and winked at Edelmida, which gave her pause. She smiled back, however, and a part of her was very happy, as she congratulated herself silently on her own cleverness.

Still, she was hurting inside and remained worried and upset. What if Manuel were to ever find out? She was no longer a virgin and this would bring shame on her if it were ever public knowledge. Edelmida knew she could never wash away the hurt and shame she felt, but her actions were a step towards healing and she was determined to take advantage of this momentum and concentrate on building a happy and safe existence for her and her family.

Tonight she would be with Manuel and felt a tingle of excitement below her waist; a feeling she had never known before.

That evening, when the meal was done and her work completed, Edelmida rushed back to her room. Strange that, only hours before, she was fearful of what she had done, taking the Amulet with no plan and only fear and hatred in her heart. Now she felt light and almost cheerful. *El Diablo* was out of her life, all of their lives, and she had the dance with Manuel to look forward to.

When Manuel showed up to take Edelmida to the dance, she looked radiant. "Sparrow, you look beautiful," he stammered.

"*Gracias, Señor*," she replied coyly, "and may I say how handsome you look."

They walked towards the dance chatting amiably about the events of the day. The removal of Thomas MacMurrough was like a breath of fresh air that blew through the camps. Everyone seemed happy, relieved, and relaxed, the issues of unfair pay and hazardous conditions, and the political environment surrounding Díaz's rule all melted away for the evening. This would be a time of fun and laughter. The tequila was flowing and the band played exceptionally well this evening, forsaking the *corridos* and playing only *Maríachi* tunes that were keeping everyone on the dance floor. The usual fighting that seemed to accompany the excessive drinking was absent and everyone was enjoying themselves and having a wonderful time.

Edelmida and Manuel danced almost every dance, and didn't dance with anyone else. The women were all playful and colorfully dressed in their finest garb, many with mantillas on their head and taps on their feet. The men were all scrubbed, and had their hair slicked back with no hats, and ruffled shirts, which were typically saved for the most festive occasions. The party-like atmosphere was contagious and all the town seemed to be happy and carefree, releasing their emotions with abandon.

As the evening wound down, Edelmida softly asked Manuel, "Can you take me home now?" They walked slowly through the warm night air, with the stars twinkling brilliantly bright above them and the moon three quarters full, giving off a soft glow that lit the way down the packed earth path.

As they came to Edelmida's doorway, she said "Manuel, I had the most lovely time this evening. I wish this night could last forever."

And he responded, "My little sparrow, nothing could be better than this night, but I promise you, as long as we are together, I will keep you safe. I will always be there for you. May I see you again?"

Edelmida laughed and said "of course," and they kissed goodnight and she went to her room with a smile on her face and a light heart. Back in her room, she felt as she hadn't in weeks. She no longer felt she had to hide under her blanket and lay awake all night long, fearing the worst. She knew that Manuel would protect her and take care of her, and for the first time since the rape, she was able to sleep through the night.

After that first night, she and Manuel became an exclusive couple. They saw each other every day and learned all they could about each other and shared each other's hopes and dreams, which were essentially the same.

Edelmida was able to compartmentalize her feelings, and separate the violence of MacMurrough from the gentle lovemaking of Manuel. She likened this in her mind to the Trinity; the concept of three persons in one. Their romance was a whirlwind and they married within weeks. When they finally made love after the wedding, she had none of the vestiges of guilt or shame that she felt after *El Diablo*. She was able to give herself, body and soul, to Manuel without a thought of her past. She loved Manuel completely and felt as if she had been in a bad accident through no fault of her own. That is why she could not only separate out her feelings but also keep her secret and bury it deep within her.

Neither Edelmida nor Manuel had any desire to travel or move away from their home as their ancestors must have. They were not of a privileged class, but they felt that way sometimes, fantasizing that they were full blooded Spanish *Peninsulares* with the greatest of privileges. The native Indians had the lowest rank in the caste system of Díaz's Mexico, and both Manuel and Edelmidas' parents had Papago blood. They were afforded no formal education and could land only the most menial of jobs, if they could find jobs at all. Many times, the natives would sell hand made goods or vegetables which they cultivated from the harsh and unforgiving land.

The Spanish blood of Manuel and Edelmida gave them above average height and the handsome features that exemplified their European background, although Manuel displayed more of his Indian blood with a somewhat flat nose and eyes spread farther apart than Edelmida. She was very fortunate and blessed with wonderfully erect posture and a straight, petite nose which gave her an air of superiority, although her temperament and demeanor was considerate and humble, and she possessed a wry sense of humor.

They both desired a very staid life completely filled with work, church, and perhaps, someday, a family. They desired nothing more than that, because they wanted to be able to give their children so much more than they had growing up. They even thought that perhaps they could afford an education for a son if they were so blessed.

Edelmida's plan was to continue to work in the kitchen after having children, as it was one of the few jobs in Cananea with the hours and flexibility to allow that. Plus, the job required special skills, and not everyone knew their way around a kitchen as Edelmida did.

While they talked of these things and the future, Edelmida was worried deep inside. She was torn about what happened with MacMurrough and whether she should tell Manuel, but she was afraid he would leave her, or worse, tell others, which was the thing she feared most of all. Edelmida had not even told the priest in her weekly confession, which in itself was a sin, compounding one sin on top of another. She had vowed that night never to reveal what had happened under any circumstances, so she strengthened her resolve and determined she would never share her secret with anyone, and, in fact, would deny anything ever happened either way. Even if *El Diablo* himself were to come back and try to brag about his conquest, who would believe him after what had happened? No, it was better forgotten and put behind her forever.

Edelmida's life fell into a comfortable rhythm after that night at the dance. Each day she would work, although it was hard to think of it as that because she loved what she did so much. After work she would spend the rest of the evening with Manuel. Most of the time they would simply spend time at the common area of the barracks, playing games, or joining in discussions about politics, or who is dating whom.

Occasionally, they would go to the cantina or attend a bullfight, or *fiesta brava*, as it was so magnificently named. She had heard that bullfights were much maligned in America, and she understood why. It was a brutal sport, if it was sport

216

at all, and the horror of the gorging of the horses by the bulls and the brutality inflicted upon the animals was horrifying to her. Of course, most of the men loved the events, and Manuel was no different. Why blood sport was so attractive to them was beyond Edelmida's comprehension. "The reputation that the Spanish and Mexicans have for macho blustering could almost put *El Diablo* to shame" she thought bitterly, "the difference is that *El Diablo* performs horrifying deeds on unsuspecting females while these fans simply watch and cheer on the horror."

While Mexico City had become a Mecca for the fights and had a magnificent new stadium, which was filled to capacity and drew crowds from all over the world to witness the spectacle of the events, Cananea was a sleepy town in comparison and the events were crude and modest in scope and not very well managed. It made money, for sure, but the cruelty to the animals was even more horrific than it would be in better run facilities. For the miners, bullfighting was an expensive sport, for the bulls cost a lot of money to house and maintain, and the matadors worked for a percentage of the gate. Of course, the stands were segregated, like everything else, with the natives on the sunny side of the stadium and the American workers on the more expensive shady side.

The venue could hardly qualify as a stadium. It was a walled area with stands of dried mud, stone, and wood on either side of the viewing area. There were a few food stands selling *quesadillas*, *tacos*, and *meundo*, as well as a place to buy cold drinks and tequila. It was a full day's affair to attend the fights, with three bouts held per day, the last featuring a matador of some prominence fighting the most threatening bull in the region. The bulls were bred for fighting and, by law, they could only be used once, ever, for a fight. Once they had experienced the dance with the matador, they were either killed, or in rare instances, if the bull were courageous enough, put out to pasture for breeding.

Since Colonel Greene had been managing and expanding the mines, he had interests in other business ventures to support his workers, and he owned thousands of acres of ranch land where he raised cattle for food and clothing. This was an ideal place to allow the bravest of the bulls to run wild and procreate, and Greene had numerous bull studs in his stable.

The cattle produced meat, milk, and cheeses, and, when they became too old to be productive, leather for clothing and saddlery. Colonel Greene had many ways to make money from the mines and the workers; selling services back to his company and the families who worked there, and from the sports and services the workers spent their hard-earned money on, thereby essentially recycling back to him the money he paid them to work.

Edelmida had been in the kitchen one day, and while butchering a chicken for the evening meal, talk turned to the bullfights. Edelmida was never a fan but the sous chef, Tepin, hated the fights with a passion, and went off on the subject with venom. It was a well-known fact that the bulls were kept hungry for days to weaken them, and often drugged or given laxatives to weaken them further before the fight. She vented her feelings one day while in the kitchen with Edelmida, "Although the bulls are almost always killed at the end of the fight, they suffer horribly for hours, and even days, before the fights begins. The horses are treated no better and often have to be put down afterwards, if they survive the fight at all."

Edelmida had always thought the "ballet" of the bullfight was a farce. "Edelmida, you know I am a horse lover, and so is Luisina, which is why we do not serve *carne de caballo.* For the horses, it is much worse than for the bulls, if you ask me. They are covered with a *peto*, a thin, coarse, horse blanket, that is supposed to protect them from the thrust of the bulls' horns, but it really does nothing more than hide the wounds from the fans. These poor animals, originated on this continent, yet were extinct here, until about 200 years ago when the Spanish arrived and brought them back in as domesticated animals. They are prized and well respected in Europe and in the U.S., where horse racing is considered a genteel and wealthy sport. Yet here, where these macho men view this spectacle as if they, themselves, were the *matador*, use these same animals to taunt the bulls, yet it is the horses who bear the brunt of the horns' thrusts and die in humiliation and defeat."

It turns out that the sous chef's brother was a *picador,* one of two horsemen that jab the bull with a lance during the first stage of the fight. He was tragically killed when he missed his spot and the bull threw his horns into the horse's flank, under the *peto,* and delivered a death blow sending the horse to the ground and falling on her brothers' legs. He was unable to extract himself and escape. The bull trampled on both the brother and horse, killing her brother in seconds.

The thought of the whole spectacle sickened Edelmida, who felt that, while God's creatures may be made for food, they were never meant to be used for a kill sport. It was a conflict she acknowledged within herself, that she could understand butchering an animal for meat, but could not understand the insulting, cruel and humiliating behavior of killing or maiming for fun and profit.

Manuel, on the other hand, thought the bullfight showed the superiority of man as an animal, and believed that the sport was truly man against beast and the ultimate test of strength and bravery. He took Edelmida to the fights on a few occasions, but it was the one area on which they could not agree, and eventually he would go with his *compadres* and she would do other things.

When they were dating, before they were married, on Saturdays when the fights were not being held, or Manuel could not afford to go, they would meet to go to confession, and then go their separate ways to prepare for the dance. They always arrived and left together and never danced with anyone else, and in this way, were very different from most of the others their age. The renegade atmosphere at the mines and the surrounding town made it nearly impossible to maintain a normal, family existence. Cananea, indeed all of the region, revealed a dichotomy of emotions and activities, and Edelmida and Manuel were no exception. The influx of outside influences and cultures and the differences between the macho posturing of the miners on the one hand, and the strong pull of the penitentiary posturing of the Church, gave even the most conscientious a plethora of choices to make day in and day out.

Like most people, Edelmida and Manuel had their fears and insecurities, and, even though filled with the best intentions, they would make mistakes which drove them to attend Church on Sunday and ask for forgiveness. The fact that they were both young, had no family guidance, and the enormous peer pressure so common among the young, had them appearing as the ideal couple while harboring the same intense desire that all young adults face.

On Sunday they would go to Church together and receive Holy Communion, a conceit that Edelmida allowed herself to keep up the pretense that nothing had happened to her that constituted a mortal sin. Then they would have a meal that Edelmida would be allowed to prepare from scraps of the menus served at Casa Greene that week.

Both Manuel and Edelmida were without a family and it was common in the harsh and unforgiving climate of Cananea, to marry young and conceive children. The hostile environment at the mines made this seem particularly urgent. Most young adults had lost at least one family member, and inherently knew that progeny was the best revenge on death.

Manuel went home that night and knew he would ask Edelmida to marry him. He would do so soon, because he knew how special she was. His love for her was deeper than he could ever have imagined and there was no reason to wait and put off the inevitable. The environment at the mines encouraged these family ties, knowing that doing so would ensure future workers without having to recruit from outside the town. A cruel way to establish an unusual workforce, but a necessary evil, and one that worked for the both the miner and the mines.

"Yes," Manuel thought to himself, "I will ask her next week and we will get married a soon as we can."

Chapter Twelve

Revenge

Thom MacMurrough left Francisco at the border at Nogales, a town that was torn in two by the Gadsden Purchase in 1853. The purchase was named after James Gadsden, who was ambassador to Mexico at the time. The purchase of this stretch of controversial border was desired by the U.S., to facilitate the building of a new transcontinental railroad along the southern route – a plan strongly influenced by Jefferson Davis, the future President of the Confederacy, who was then-president Franklin Pierce's Secretary of War. Davis was a strong proponent of a southern-route transcontinental railroad, and if this had become a reality, the outcome of the future War Between the States may have had a very different outcome. It also represented an attempt by the U.S. government to appease the new Mexican nation after the Treaty of Guadalupe-Hidalgo which was the outcome of the Mexican-American war of 1846-1848. The terms of this Treaty were largely dictated by the U.S, since the interim military Mexican government was newly established, and had no real power or leadership to fight for their rights. The U.S. was granted the territory which was composed of Texas,

New Mexico, Arizona, and parts of Colorado and California, in exchange for $15 million, which the Mexican government badly needed to help repair the war-damaged areas of the country.

The Purchase split many cities including Nogales, Laredo, and other border towns, leaving families to make decisions on where to live and work. It was a gut wrenching time for many natives, and the U.S. government gave these families only one year to decide their fate and that of their future generations.

MacMurrough was sitting in a cantina on the new U.S. side of Nogales, sipping a warm *cerveza* and a shot of tequila while plotting his revenge.

He was furious over the set-up that had been constructed against him, and of course, never considered the fact that he deserved a far greater punishment. He was already plotting his revenge and his target was A.B. Fall. He knew in his bones that it was Edelmida who set him up and he almost couldn't believe it, since she had been such a shy and honest girl. But he knew he would never be able to get to her within the confines of the Four C's, and, besides, he had punished her enough while he was there. No, he would settle with A.B. and make sure that he paid the price of ousting him from his position at the mines.

As MacMurrough wandered to the U.S. side of Nogales, he realized he would miss Mexico. There were palpable differences on the two sides of the border; the music, food, and atmosphere was markedly unique once you crossed the Mexican border, a border that had changed much over the past few decades.

The peso was not accepted on the U.S. side of Nogales, so MacMurrough had to cash in his pesos for U.S. Dollars, and it didn't go far. The exchange rate heavily favored the dollar, by a two to one margin, and he would have to find a job quickly or run out of cash. For all of MacMurrough's failings, and he didn't see them as anything other than personality traits and not wrong at all, he was not a thief. He had always worked an honest day for an honest day's pay. He knew that many of the men from Cananea had family near the border, some in Nogales and some as far away as Tucson. To avoid any conflict or detection, he decided to head further east, perhaps to El Paso and cross the river to Ciudad Juarez, which he heard was a growing town with lots of work. It was rumored that a new rail line was to be built to carry the goods to the more lucrative and larger markets further east. Besides, he heard there were many beautiful *Señoritas* there and he had been many days without a young girl to make him happy. So, he took his bags and struck out for El Paso, using the time to plot his revenge.

At this very moment, Colonel Greene was in El Paso making arrangements to bring a new rail line in to help with distribution of copper from the mines in Cananea. A global recession had hit him hard last year and the price of copper was depressed, making it difficult to raise new capital. His sources in New York were wary of copper mining projects, and he was finding it more and more difficult to turn a profit from the mines. Greene started to turn to other, more lucrative projects associated with mining to shore up revenues and show some profitability. His chief financial officer, a person interestingly named MacMurrough, had been manipulating the books at the mines in order to show increased revenues and profits.

Greene was challenged to continue this trend in spite of the worldwide financial crisis and the weakening of the price of copper. He was aggressive in developing ranches to feed the townspeople and miners, a lumberyard to supply the building of homes and barracks, and other ancillary service businesses to capitalize on the growth of the area and encourage his people to spend the little money they made in the mines at his other businesses, thus recycling his funds and increasing profitability. Since virtually nothing was produced locally, everything had to be handled by the Company's transportation system which operated between Cananea and Naco, a border town about 45 miles northwest and just a few miles from Bisbee, Arizona.

With MacMurrough out of the picture and Colonel Greene away so often on fund raising and new ventures, life returned to some semblance of normalcy in Cananea and at the mines, although, in their world, death and deplorable conditions were the norm. Little could they know that they would one day look back on these times as the good old days.

Luisina returned to the Casa and began to prepare the midday meal now that MacMurrough was run out of town and things had returned to normal. As she passed through the drawing room on her way into the kitchen to see about the table settings, she passed by the empty place where the cross had been and wondered, in all the commotion, where had it gone?

Part II

Cananea

1906

Chapter Thirteen

Cananea in Conflict

"Mama, can you take me and the twins up to Casa Greene this morning? You promised them you would take them to the kitchen for a while just before your prep time. I told them I'd ask and walk with you. Can you take us, *por favor*?"

Edelmida looked at her oldest child and could hardly believe what a beautiful young woman she had become. At 16 years old, with the long dark hair she had inherited from her mother, and her God-given intelligence, which was transmitted to the world through her clear, green eyes, she had quickly blossomed into a poised and attractive young lady right before her eyes. The maturity she had gained from her years of observing people who visited Casa Greene from all over the world gave her a demeanor and wisdom far beyond her years.

"Of course, Carmelita. You are right, it is long overdue. I spoke to Luisina yesterday and we can go there for 30 minutes, no more, before we have to start lunch prep after the breakfast cleanup is done. Hurry and get Juan and Rosita scrubbed and dressed. Put them in their Sunday clothes just in case Colonel Greene or one of the managers of the Four C's comes into the kitchen. Hurry!"

Raymond F. Cavanagh

Carmelita jumped from her chair at the kitchen table with a big smile and ran from the room shouting, "*Gracias*, Mama. Juan! Rosita! We're going to the Casa."

Whoops and laughter emerged from the other side of the kitchen door as Carmelita's seven year old twin brother and sister came around the corner, fully dressed, scrubbed, bright eyed, and ready to go.

"We just knew you would say yes," Carmelita trumpeted. Indeed, Edelmida's oldest child was fast becoming a woman. Not only was she intelligent and mature, but she was resourceful and persuasive. Edelmida knew she would go very far in this world and that made her extremely proud. She was already fluent in both her native Spanish, as well as English, and she could converse a little in the Papago tongue.

Manuel was, of course, very protective of his oldest daughter, but not nearly so much as Edelmida. The devastating experience she had endured at the hands of *El Diablo* years ago at nearly the same age as Carmelita was now had ensured that.

She gave Carmelita everything she and Manuel could afford; sacrificing what they could to enable her to experience things they could have only dreamed of at her age. The struggle they went through for food and shelter when they had grown up was vastly different from the world Carmelita knew. The explosive growth of the mines and the town of Cananea, which had grown faster than any city in the region, including those in Arizona, with the possible exception of Bisbee, had assured that there were always jobs that paid wages to buy essentials. Of course, the working men always complained about being paid less than the *Americanos*, and, it was true that the hideous miners' disease had taken its toll on families. But what it gave back was a chance to get out of Cananea, maybe move into America, where even a poor mestizo could find work and improved conditions from the harsh work environment and difficult life at the Four C's.

Fortunately, the exposure to both the good and bad of all that Cananea could offer, from the elaborate and elegant events at Casa Greene, to the near poverty, harsh and dirty conditions at the mining operations and homes in Ronquillo, had turned Carmelita into a well-rounded and well-grounded individual with sensitivity and compassion.

In all the years since *El Diablo* was forced from Cananea, Edelmida had never breathed a word of what had happened to anyone. Although she did come very close once, just six weeks after Carmelita was born. Edelmida had fallen into an inexplicably depressed state and could not shake the depths of her despondency. She was at such an emotional low, that, at one point, she had contemplated taking her own life with a poison she had taken from the kitchen at Casa Greene.

She believed her depression was some type of punishment for what had happened to her and that God was punishing her for her sin. She didn't understand what was happening and could barely look at the child she had wanted so desperately. Her life had become one long, endless nightmare and her melancholy was unbearable. All of her friends and family would come by to try and cheer her up, bringing food which she wouldn't eat, and regaling her with stories of the events in the kitchen at Casa Greene, but all to no avail.

Of course, she could never even think of telling Manuel what had occurred, for he would be completely devastated. Her thoughts would vacillate between feeling that he would shut her out forever, to believing he would forgive her and understand that she had been victimized and the events that had occurred were completely out of her control.

Manuel and Edelmida had grown amazingly close after their first night together at the weekly dance. Not only did their relationship explode like a supernova physically, which is expected of young love, but their commonality extended to their religious dogma, intellectual stimulations, and even political affiliations and beliefs. They had grown incredibly close in so many ways and even at such a young age, Edelmida was only now just thirty-four years old, had shared all of their most intimate thoughts and fears, loves and hates, insecurities and convictions, and future plans and dreams.

She could never imagine sharing what had happened to her with Manuel, or anyone else for that matter. She had buried the pain and shame deep within her heart and her mind. She rarely let it escape into her consciousness, and when it did, she pushed it back, further and further each time. She didn't realize it, but what had occurred served to make her a much stronger and more driven person. She was determined to give her children all she could and more. She pushed education, and, through reading and storytelling, encouraged them to leave Cananea when they came of age and go to the United States where they would be able to become whatever they wanted to be.

Carmelita was already showing that the fruits of these labors were blossoming. She had an unquenchable thirst for knowledge and, besides doing very well at the Catholic school, she read voraciously outside the classroom. She also shared Edelmida's love for music. Although they could not afford a musical instrument, and so had no formal training, her voice was sweet and throaty and filled with emotion and had the ability to attract and hold people's attention.

Carmelita was already trying to talk her mother and Manuel into allowing her to go to school in Tucson once her studies at the Catholic school were completed. She had no fear of going to new places and seeing new things. To Carmelita, she believed that anything that one wanted to accomplish could be accomplished if they set their mind to it. The concept of money and where to stay, not to mention clothing and food, were inconsequential. The vast majority of workers in Cananea barely got by with the money they made, and by comparison Manuel and Edelmida were very well off. Manuel made a bit more than the mine workers and even some of the office personnel at the mines due to his supervisory role, although it was still less than comparable work done by an American worker. Edelmida had the privilege of access to Casa Greene and often brought them food and other goodies which were well above the quality and quantity of what other families could afford. Consequently, things had come fairly easily to Carmelita compared to others in her circle and she never gave a thought to where the money would come from.

She was also, by far, the most beautiful girl in all of Cananea, as well as one of the smartest and most charming. She was very bright and often heard the arguments among her people about inequities in pay and the political landscape which had proliferated under the Díaz regime. She had grown ever more liberal in her thoughts and often was heard applauding the thoughts of some of the more radical leaders in Cananea. She never really thought any of this would directly correlate to her own life and economic situation, and believed with all her heart that she would find a way to get to the U.S. and gain her rightful place among the wealthy *norteamericanos*.

This was an area where Edelmida was torn. She wanted her children to pursue ever greater things, things she and Manuel could never even dream about, because they had no knowledge of the vastness of the possibilities, but she was paralyzed with fear at the thought of Carmelita going out on her own. She feared people like Thom MacMurrough.

A year after Edelmida's postpartum depression, which had lasted only three weeks but felt like a lifetime, it became apparent that Carmelita's "baby blue" eyes were not going to ever turn brown like her parents. Manuel had dark, almost black eyes that illustrated his Indian blood, but Edelmida had soft brown eyes that were very expressive and conveyed an almost ethereal quality. They would turn stormy if she became angry, and almost seem to take on a liquid chocolate quality when she was laughing.

Carmelita's eyes, on the other hand, had turned a soft grey/green with little flecks of gold in her pupils.

Edelmida was alarmed at this manifestation, as she thought that not only would Manuel question this, but so would everyone in the community. She was never completely sure if Carmelita was Manuel's child or had been conceived on that awful

235

night when she was brutally raped by *El Diablo*. In her heart, she always believed she was Manuel's natural daughter and she loved Carmelita with all her heart, but there was always a lingering doubt and this may have caused her to overcompensate and give her more than perhaps she should.

Carmelita was born just seven months and two weeks after Edelmida discovered she was pregnant but showed none of the expected signs of immaturity. The doctor was a kind man and very patient, but he had to treat everything from scorpion bites, to birthing babies, to silicosis, and could give Edelmida no explanation for a premature birth of what looked to be a full term child. This only led to Edelmida's further confusion over the paternal identity of her newborn. Edelmida was convinced it was this uncertainty that had led to her depressed state after her daughter was born.

""Mama, are you alright? Can we go now?" little Rosita piped up, breaking Edelmida out of her reverie.

"Of course, children. Let me get my *quechquémitl* and we'll leave right away."

She gathered her covering and ubiquitous flask of sugar water and tea and scooted the family out the door. As they walked down the path towards Casa Greene from their company owned bungalow, one of the perks of Manuel's position at the Four C's, they observed two men standing at the side of the road apparently arguing about money. Edelmida tried to steer the children out of earshot, but

Carmelita heard some of what was said, "five pesos and eight hours of work, viva Mexico," mumblings about long hours, short pay, and inequality between the Mexican natives and the international workers, particularly the *norteamericanos*, although there were workers from other countries as well, and these were paid as outside labor and also at higher wages than the Mexicans.

Carmelita knew there had been trouble at the mines recently, much more serious than the usual griping about pay. There was a growing faction led by the radical workers Esteban Baca Calderón and Manuel Diéguez, who were representative of the emotions running through the entire country of Mexico at this time. The thirty year rule of Porfirio Díaz had certainly improved industrialization, but at the cost of creating deplorable working conditions for most of the working poor. Díaz and his Liberal political party long operated on the principle that the only way to fully develop Mexico's resources was to encourage foreign investment. Díaz ruled as a *Caudillo*, a politician who ruled by military force and whose will was law. Under the Díaz regime, commonly referred to as the *Porfiriato*, Mexico was as stable as it had ever been, but the vast majority of people throughout the country were poor with little means to improve their lot in life. Díaz himself was a *mestizo* and born into poverty. He was educated at the Institute of Science and Art in Oxaca, and was studying law when the war between Mexico and the

United States broke out. He found his true calling in the military, fighting the French during the reign of Maximillian.

As she listened to the two workers, Carmelita thought about the many friends at the nuns' school she attended who had lost fathers, brothers, and other relatives at the mines, either in accidents or to the dreaded lung disease, silicosis.

No one wanted to admit it, but they would all prefer that if anything tragic had to happen, and they prayed night and day that nothing ever would, that a quick and near painless death in a mining collapse or explosion would be better than the protracted and excruciatingly slow death that came with the lung disease. Those afflicted would ultimately be home night and day, coughing, hacking, and spitting up phlegm and blood until finally, mercifully, the rattle in their chests would become too much for them and they would give up their spirit to God above.

Edelmida took note of Carmelita, who was clearly trying to hear what was being said. She was at that age when she was no longer oblivious to adult events, and old enough to understand, and even rebel against, injustice. Edelmida could only hope that she was still too young to do anything about it.

In fact, it seemed that everyone was powerless to do anything about it. During the past ten years, the unrest had worsened and the gap between the Americans and the Mexicans was growing deeper and more emotional with each passing day.

The copper mines and Colonel Greene's other ventures had grown and prospered as the turn of the century brought westward expansion and the advent of the railroads throughout the south and west. The proliferation of electricity, and the industrial revolution, both of which depended on the relatively cheap but excellent conductive properties of copper, helped to fuel the need for more and more of the semi-precious metal.

But it was not without its cost. Colonel Greene and his partners had struggled mightily in the early years to develop the mines in Cananea and the surrounding areas without the advantage of rail lines to support transportation of goods both in and out.

Costs in Mexico were lower than in other copper producing areas in the world, giving the fours C's a distinct economic advantage. Greene's first mine, the Cobre Grande, was managed by the Colonel's good friend and technical wizard, George Mitchell. George, and his brother Robert, were from Swansea, Wales, the self-proclaimed smelting capital of the world. George's methods were so proficient, that he could bring matte, a combination of copper and up to fifty percent of other minerals, to market at a much lower cost than his competitors.

However, the expertise Greene needed to keep the plants running did not exist in Mexico at the time, and he had to import workers and smelting experts from around the world.

Besides running the Cobre Grande, George held a patent on a water-jacket smelting furnace which was more efficient than those used up to that point in time. Colonel Greene's ability to befriend people and inspire confidence in future success was a critical part of why Mitchell partnered with him. George already had a measure of success on his own selling the furnaces, and now that he and Greene were partners they had both the technical know-how and the ability to woo investors.

Greene always thought big. The mines of Cananea, particularly Cobre Grande, where George Mitchell was enthusiastically cranking out production with his new smelters, required that the goods get to market quickly and efficiently. This need for expeditious delivery applied to other holdings which he had acquired as well. Greene had used his money and influence to purchase extensive holdings in the region under different company names. His companies could then sell goods, one company to another, to provide needed food, lumber, and, most importantly, water, to keep the manufacturing process productive.

At one point in 1901, he decided to build his own railroad to move these goods. He had proposed building a new line to E.H. Harriman, owner of the Southern Pacific railroad, and was laughingly turned down. Construction of the Cananea-Naco line was pushed through aggressively and service was inaugurated in January of 1902. By July of 1903, Greene's line, the Cananea, Yaqui River, and Pacific Railroad, became part of Harriman's Southern Pacific system.

Greene was competing in a global market, and keeping costs down was important to him and his investors, but because of his distance from major shipping centers and the rural nature of his facilities, the one major area that he could affect for keeping costs low, was labor. Labor costs in Mexico were extremely low, and particularly in the Sonora region, which was just beginning to expand and grow after the Gadsden Purchase. Díaz' policies of attracting foreign investment and offering tax incentives made this a very attractive place to do business and the mines under Colonel Greene's and George Mitchell's direction and technological advances gave them world class status in the burgeoning world of copper production. Railroad expansion, westward movement, and the growth of electricity, all contributed to the chain of events that ensured success at Greene's ventures in Cananea and the surrounding area.

Since the Colonel had to attract workers from outside the region, he had no choice but to pay higher wages to bring them to Cananea. The harsh conditions, extreme heat, lack of services and transportation, and a serious, ongoing concern regarding the lack of running potable water forced concessions to outside personnel. Economically,

241

although revenue and output were increasing, allowing Colonel Greene to attract more investors, his cash flow was suffering, and he could not invest fast enough in the new technologies necessary to stay competitive. To offset these difficulties, he had to pay handsomely, and the American workers were very well paid and not shy about letting everyone know.

Consequently, Greene's cash flow continued to suffer, and in spite of his efforts to offer better living conditions to the native workers, they refused to move out of their self-contained community. Due to this resistance, the disparity in pay and benefits between native workers and imported labor worsened year over year, creating greater animosity and increased prejudice.

Most of the Mexican workers lived in a small town called Ronquillo, which was located in the valley between the mesa and the reduction works, where the raw material from the mine was processed. The area had grown without any type of plan or supervision and was a collection of shacks and hovels with unsafe and unsanitary conditions. In spite of Colonel Greene's attempts to move the workers to better living quarters close to the mine shafts, they refused; preferring to stay close to friends and family, as the town became a breeding ground for unrest with increased leanings towards revolution.

The children of Cananea were not immune to, or ignorant of, this state of affairs. So many families had been affected by death or severe illness that it was almost an expectation that some form of tragedy would one day occur to each of them, and at each event; parties, weddings, and funerals, the men would argue endlessly about the injustice and inequality of work and pay.

One day, while Carmelita was supposed to be indoors cleaning the four room bungalow that was provided to her family by the Four C's, she snuck out the back door of the kitchen and stood at the corner of the house, out of sight of a group of men gathered across the street. She had heard raised voices and was curious as to what the ruckus was all about. As she carefully peaked around the corner, she saw one man speaking, surrounded by others who seemed to be hanging on his every word, shouting out their agreement and approval. She recognized him as Esteban Baca Calderón, who had been making quite a name for himself in the town. He was trying to organize the workers to band together and form a union, with the primary complaint demanding equal pay for equal work.

"There are those who say that all societies have inequities and that the wealthy, ruling class is responsible for making decisions that affect all of us. To this I say ¡no más! The proletariat deserves the right to decide their own fate! Rise up with me, amigos and fight for your rights. Equal pay for equal work. Do not shirk your duties to yourselves and your families. Now is the time to open your eyes to the line of reason. If the situation is bad, it is yours to remedy. A people which goes to sleep in timidity awakens in conquest."

Carmelita had heard this type of talk for as long as she could remember. Her earliest recollections were of her father bringing home his friends, and the arguments that ensued about the inequities of privilege between the proletariat and the capitalists. The Porfiriato certainly helped Mexico improve its' status in the world markets, but it did so on the backs of the natives which were used for cheap labor and given little of the wealth in return.

As Calderón finished his impassioned speech, one of the Mexican workers turned his head swiftly, as if he knew someone were spying on them, and just saw a wisp of dark hair as Carmelita ducked her head back around the corner of the building. Her heart beat rapidly as she turned and ran back into the house, hoping the worker did not know who she was or what she had heard. She entered her small crowded home and ran to hide in her room. As time passed, she relaxed her breathing, relieved that she had not been found out.

This had occurred weeks earlier, but it still gave Carmelita a chill when she thought of how close she had come to getting caught listening to the revolutionary rhetoric.

"Mama, can we please go now?" she questioned excitedly.

"Of course, Carmelita, we were looking for you so we could leave. Let's go, we won't have much time before I will have to get you back here so I can help prepare for the midday meal."

As they started up the brown dirt road, which had been packed down hard and dustless after years of use by workers trudging to and from their workplaces, they came across three cowboys that they had never seen before, straddling the path and blocking their movement forward. They were dirty, as if from a long ride, and could have been ranch hands hired to work the Colonels' horse ranch which serviced the needs of all the townspeople in Cananea.

Edelmida took the children's hands and slid to her right to pass by, but as she did they shifted their stance and spread out to block their access. Edelmida stopped and looked up at one of the cowboys and said in her broken English "Excuse me, *por favor*, I am taking my children to the Casa where I work, and I cannot be late." She thought for certain that mention of Colonel Greene's residence would cause them to move out of their way.

The cowboy in the center was several inches taller than the other two and had long brown hair braided in the back, Indian–style, with a leathery face and a chipped front tooth. His head was capped by a filthy, tan, Montana peak-styled hat, and he wore dark brown boots, which were muddy and ragged. He wore them with his pants tucked into the

245

tops which rose up to just below his knees. He looked at Edelmida with hard, flat, black eyes and said "*Muchacha*, you are married to Manuel Díaz Carreras? Where can I find him?"

Edelmida thought about ignoring him, turning in the other direction and taking the children straight home, but was concerned about creating a disturbance, and so, instead, decided to try to use an innocent approach to find out what this was all about.

With a smile pasted on her face, she said, "*Señor*, Manuel is at the copper mine where he is a foreman, but I will see him at noon when I will be bringing him his lunch. Can I tell him what this is about and who is asking?" she asked as sweetly as she could muster. There was something sinister in the way he looked at her, and she knew this was not a social call or that it could have any good purpose at all. He looked at them with caution as they paid particular attention to Carmelita, who was a young beauty with physical attributes that always caused men to gawk at her.

"*Sí, Señorita*. Tell him that Jack Durand from El Paso is looking for him. He doesn't know me but I have a message for him. I need to deliver it personally. Tell him to meet me tonight at *Caballo Loco* at sundown. I will speak to him then." With that, he turned on his heel and marched away with his two cronies following behind.

"Mama, who was that man, and what does he want with Papa?" Carmelita queried. She knew

246

as well as her mother did that something was wrong and she meant to get to the bottom of it. But Edelmida belied her own concern and tried to make light of it.

"I'm sure it's something about the horses for Colonel Greene, *pajarito*, you know your father has a very important job and does more than just mining now. Don't worry, we will find out soon enough." She shooed the twins to hurry them along so she could give them all a quick tour before getting them to school at the nunnery, and get back to the kitchen on time to begin her prep work.

However, underneath her cool exterior, Edelmida was quite concerned. Anyone working at the Four C's would know where to find Manuel. This cowboy was clearly sending a message to Manuel by confronting his entire family.

Something was very wrong, and she was quite uncomfortable at the way Cowboy Jack, as she thought of him, thinking he was a gringo, had leered at Carmelita.

Edelmida never saw Manuel during the day, but she would do it today. She planned to go to the mining office with his lunch and ask if she could see him under some pretext about goings on at the Casa. It would be implied that she was there for A.B, and no one would question why and risk the wrath of A.B. Fall.

For surely Colonel Greene was not the disciplinarian at Cananea. He had always played the card of the former miner who struck it rich, and kept peace with his workers for all these years based on the goodwill he garnered from being a miner as they were. Greene was extremely popular with the workers and professed to be a miner, not a businessman, but he was chameleon-like and just as comfortable in the boardroom as in the mines. He was a great delegator and left the chore of dealing with difficult situations to A.B. and Francisco.

After Edelmida gave the children their tour of the kitchen, she bundled the twins off to play group and Carmelita went to the church where she practiced each day with the choir for Sunday Mass.

Half an hour before Manuel's scheduled lunch break, she asked Luisina if she could bring a lunch to Manuel as a surprise to celebrate the 17th anniversary of the day they met. Luisina was never one to say no to such a romantic notion and with a promise from Edelmida to be back before lunch was served at the Casa, reluctantly agreed.

Edelmida hastily placed a few tamales and some beans in a container and rushed off to the mining office to find Manuel.

When she arrived at the office, he just happened to be there already, and as he turned a surprised look came upon his face. In the 17 years that they had known each other, she had never come to see him, so he reacted strongly, knowing instinctively that something was wrong.

"Edelmida, is everything all right with the children? What's wrong?" he asked as the smile disappeared from his face.

She explained to him about Cowboy Jack, but couldn't remember the visitors' last name. She explained to him about the confrontation, and told him about the proposed meeting at sundown at the *Caballo Loco cantina*.

Caballo Loco was not a place that Manuel had ever been inside. With only a few places to go in Cananea, there were clearly gringo places and locals-only places. You didn't go where you didn't belong, and Manuel thought to himself that he would never see someone named Cowboy Jack at *El Charro Cantina* either, which was exclusively the province of the Mexican workers.

Just as Edelmida had done with the children, Manuel downplayed the significance of this to her, and insisted it had to have something to do with mining operations. Manuel had no real enemies and his role as peacemaker for the naïve workers made him a friend to the locals and the gringos alike.

He thanked Edelmida for delivering the message, and the delicious looking lunch, and told her to go back to work and not to worry. He would find Pedro and together they would go to the meeting. He promised her to go home first to see the children and asked her to prepare a quick bite to eat beforehand.

Edelmida reluctantly left, although she did feel better after seeing her husband and hearing his reassurances. However, something was nagging her in the back of her mind as she hurried back to the Casa, keeping her promise to Luisina to be back before lunch was served.

Meanwhile, Manuel went to the office and spoke to his new supervisor, a man named Judd Thurmond, who had known Colonel Greene in New Mexico a few years before he bought his first mine in Cananea. Judd was a back office man primarily, who was well liked and great with people.

When Thom MacMurrough was summarily dismissed, the Colonel, along with A.B., Francisco, and other trusted advisors, decided not to replace him, but rather, expand Judd's responsibilities. It gave him more money, which encouraged him to stay, and accomplished the added perception of another promotion for Manuel, as he was now one step closer in rank to the Colonel. All of the workers, particularly the Mexicans and Indians, had strong orientations towards hierarchical structure reinforced by their Catholic upbringing, believed in a hierarchical system of power.

Manuel was hoping Judd could shed some light on the mystery of Cowboy Jack, or perhaps find out what it was all about. Judd was a bit older than most at the mine, nearly fifty, with kind, soft eyes hidden behind half glasses that were perennially perched on his long, thin nose. His straight, close-cropped brown hair was flecked with gray and he had the beginnings of a bald spot at the crown of his head that he tried to hide with a bowler, when he wore a hat at all. He spoke softly, and when he listened to someone speak, he would stay quiet even after they were done speaking. This often led to learning even more information than the speaker originally wanted to share, and gave him a hint of that person's perspective as they would continue to talk to fill in the gap of silence. Only then would he ask simple but pointed questions to get to the reason behind the emotion.

When Manuel told Judd what little he knew, Judd nodded, adjusted his glasses and waited. When it was clear that Manuel had nothing more to say he finally spoke. "Manuel, I have not heard anything about this, and can't see any reason one of the cowboys, especially a gringo cowboy, would need to meet with you. It is strange. I'll tell you what, I will speak with Francisco this afternoon and see what he has to say and get back to you before you leave for the day. He has ears everywhere, and if this has anything to do with the Four C's, he'll know. And if it doesn't, he'll want to know."

"*Gracias, Señor*" Manuel replied, "I will stop in before I leave tonight."

That evening, when the shift whistle blew, Manuel went back to see Judd Thurmond. He wasn't there, but he left a message for Manuel that he had written out for him in Spanish, to be sure there was no misunderstanding. It read; "Manuel,

251

Francisco knows of no official reason for this meeting, but he does know something about Cowboy Jack. He says you and Pedro should go and he will have eyes to watch out for you. Judd"

Manuel was a little surprised that Judd was not there to discuss it with him but felt comforted that Francisco was aware of the meeting. He left to find Pedro and prepare for his meeting with Cowboy Jack.

Chapter Fourteen

El Paso

For the past sixteen years, Thomas MacMurrough, now Declan Cassidy once again, had bounced around the southwest, ventured out to the west coast, and ended up back in Texas. After he was run out of Cananea, and had crossed the border into Nogales, he headed northwest to Phoenix, just to put some distance between himself and the unpleasant situation that occurred in Mexico.

He seethed whenever he thought of Edelmida and the Amulet, and how she had set him up, and his behavior reflected his increasing anger. His job in Cananea had afforded him a fair amount of disposable income and he had a high visibility job that brought him prestige, at least among the peons. After his ouster, he was never able to reacquire such a high paying, prestigious job, and spent most of his time as a laborer. Pay in the U.S. was much higher than in Cananea, but so were living expenses, and the mistake he made when he first landed a position in Phoenix was in understating his compensation and not asking for enough money. He had spent very little time in the States after his deportation from Ireland, and had

253

been in Cananea long enough to have forgotten the difference in value of the peso to the dollar. This was particularly disquieting to him, since the primary issue at the mines was money, and the differences the Americans were paid versus the native workers. Once he established his value in the U.S., he had a tough time getting the money he felt he deserved. He also never achieved the status he had in Cananea, and did mostly menial jobs or worked hard labor to increase his earnings.

Phoenix proved to be less than he had expected. A small city of only fifty-five hundred residents, half of them Mexican, he was looking for something new and exciting. Declan stayed and worked in Phoenix at various odd jobs, saving his money, and dreaming of the day he would finally move out of the dust bowl of Arizona to the verdant and fertile lands of northern California, and the enticing and exciting ventures that he hoped lay ahead.

He heard great stories about California, particularly San Francisco, a tolerant city that had grown from a small village to a bustling community of over a quarter of a million people after the gold rush of forty-nine. The city was considered by many to be the "Paris of America," and it offered a taste of something for every type of appetite, a welcome change for Cassidy from the backward towns he had inhabited since coming to America.

He had remained fairly well-behaved since he left Cananea, in part because there was little in the way of female companionship to be had, but also because he feared there might still be eyes on him so close to the border. Colonel Greene and his men had friends everywhere, and Phoenix was too small a town, a place where his actions could easily be observed without his knowledge.

After he spent three years at hard, manual labor, working on the railroads, or in jobs related to mining activities in the area surrounding Phoenix, he finally had saved enough money to realize his dream, and struck out for San Francisco. Cassidy had now re-established his rightful name, put the past behind, and found himself in a bustling city with an endless number of possibilities open to him. His experience with mining and railroads was welcome in the city, where horse and buggy threaded its way around cable cars and automobiles, the latter of which were fast becoming commonplace. It didn't take Cassidy long to gravitate to an area of the city that housed the lowest class of vile and despicable characters, a section which was known originally as Sydney Town, but more recently as the Barbary Coast.

The area attracted petty thieves, prostitutes, cutthroats, whoremongers, murderers, and tramps of every kind and orientation. It was an area frequented by sailors coming to port from Asia and Australia looking for booze and women after months at sea, and it was a place where the practice of shanghaiing was raised to an art form.

255

Raymond F. Cavanagh

Many a sailor who came to port to release the tensions of his journey by sleeping with loose women and drinking a weeks' worth of whiskey in one night, awoke the next morning with not only a hangover, but on a ship heading back to the far east. The task of this form of kidnapping was practiced by "crimps" who were paid handsomely, by the body, to provide sailors for service. Once a sailor was on board a vessel, it was illegal, under penalty of imprisonment, to abandon ship, regardless of the method employed to get him there. The crimps would contract with a vessel's Captain, and use any form of persuasion, including trickery and deceit, to get a sailor on board, sober or not.

This led to the common practice of enticing the newly arrived to "crimp parlors," places where sailors could come and drink cheap booze and enjoy plentiful sex with the ladies of the parlor. Often, the sailor would find himself indebted to the crimp parlor and have to work off the debt by taking another tour on the high seas. The crimper would keep the sailor drunk, and, most often, lace his booze with laudanum or opium, and coerce his signature on a document agreeing to another tour, agreeing to tithe several months' pay to the crimper. The crimper then sold the unsuspecting sailor to the captain of a ship at an inflated rate, so he would make money off the ship's captain as well as the sailor himself.

This was a lucrative racket, and there was plenty of blood money to be made off each new and unsuspecting body. San Francisco harbor was so choked with ships that had come into port with treasure seekers, that finding sailors to return was very difficult, which led to this barbaric practice.

Cassidy was a notorious and expert crimper and received money not only from the sailor wages and the inflated fees he charged the captains, but also from the crimp parlor itself, and the girls who charged for their services. Cassidy had built a reputation which gave him ample opportunity to make money, but which also made him a feared and hated man. There were many crimping parlors and infamous crimpers by the time Cassidy hit San Francisco, and only a very few were women.

Cassidy had always been drawn to women, but on the San Francisco Barbary Coast, there were few young enough or inexperienced enough to suit his taste. He found himself increasingly looking for women of Mexican or Spanish heritage, but these were few and far between in this area of the country, so he would often go to Chinatown and find the smallest and youngest girl he could find, and fantasize about her virginity.

After several years in San Francisco, he had made, and lost, a substantial amount of money and was beginning to become bored with the lifestyle, and, although he could hardly believe it himself, he missed the desert and the *Señoritas* of Mexico. He regularly found himself waking up in the middle of the night with visions of the gold Amulet, and a woman with dark hair and eyes taunting him and holding the cross just out of reach. When Cassidy had this recurring dream he would go to Chinatown, find a young girl, and with each encounter subsequent to these dreams he became more demanding and violent.

Cassidy's behavior finally caught up with him again when he contracted with a very young streetwalker named Soo Li, whom he brought back to his apartment near Grant Street and brutally raped several times over the course of a night.

Soo Li was decimated, but alive, when she got back to her pimp who was connected to the Wang Fu clan, a dangerous gang of street punks who were noted for opium smuggling, numbers running, and prostitution. After 14 years in San Francisco, Cassidy had at last run out of luck. He was on his way to the crimp house one evening, when he was approached by the gang and confronted. He did his best to talk his way out of this latest trouble, but to no avail. Cassidy was severely beaten and left for dead. If it hadn't been for a passing patrol who called an ambulance to take him to the morgue, thinking him dead, he would not have made it. He had sustained serious internal injuries, including a ruptured kidney, several broken teeth, two broken ribs, and contusions over his back and abdomen.

He also suffered a broken nose and concussion, and had lost several pints of blood by the time he arrived at the clinic on the waterfront, where he had just enough luck left to have drawn a doctor who revived him and treated his wounds. He spent two months in the clinic recovering, and, in true fashion, rather than vow to change his ways when he got out, he dreamt of moving back to the southwest where things were more relaxed, and gangs were not yet so well organized.

When Cassidy was finally released from the clinic, broken and bent but still alive, he spent the next five weeks crimping at a furious pace and doing nothing else. When he felt he had saved enough money, he jumped a train heading east, where he planned to head back to El Paso, a place where he had lived and worked on the railroads before arriving in Cananea.

He traveled south and east back to Phoenix, where he spent a few days negotiating to buy a horse and supplies with help from a former co-worker, who helped him negotiate a deal that proved almost too good to be true. He wanted to get out of town as soon as he could and get to El Paso, but had to wait until the deal he struck was concluded. The price he was quoted for the horse, supplies and extra clothing was cheap, and he didn't bother to negotiate, although he did wonder if the horse's true owner knew about the sale. It was an art form to change brands on stolen cattle and horses, and this brand looked good enough to pass.

He arrived in El Paso after two weeks of near constant riding; hot, dirty, and exhausted, but

259

with a plan to strike back at his enemies in Cananea. He had convinced himself that all his troubles were caused because of what Edelmida had done to him, and the longer he was away, the more convinced he became.

The long ride, which he made at a very fast clip, took him over mountain ranges, arid desert, and across the plains, and gave him ample time to reflect on what had happened in Cananea. The region he traversed was still rampant with Apache, and the tribe was still one of the most feared threats in the area, more so than the scorpions, tarantulas, and other wildlife that peppered the region, but Cassidy's luck held and he arrived unscathed.

Cassidy remained in total denial of his responsibility, for either his behavior or the errors of his ways, and the hurt he inflicted on his victims, both emotional and physical.

During stops on his journey east, he picked up information on his former employers in Cananea when he stopped in the small villages and towns for food, or just to rest and take a break from the constant, burning rays of the incredibly hot sun. As he got closer to El Paso, he learned that Colonel Greene had recently been there, and also in the sister city of *Ciudad Juarez* right across *Rio Bravo del Norte*. He had been drumming up political and financial support for his latest venture, a train that would run from Cananea to Juarez, to help with distribution of the copper matte.

Cassidy knew that Greene had multiple enterprises in various stages of completion and success throughout the southwest from Tucson to Cananea, down to Hermosillo, up through Bisbee, and as far east as El Paso. Greene had effectively built the city of Cananea, whose population had climbed from almost nothing to 20,000 people by 1906, and his reach to build an empire of enterprises throughout the region was coming to fruition with alarming speed. The Colonel had multiple mining companies besides the Cobre Grande and the Cananea Consolidated Copper Company (the Four C's). By 1906, his interests included Greene Cananea Copper Company; Greene Consolidated Copper Company; Greene Consolidated Gold Company; Greene Gold-Silver Company; Greene Cattle Company; Sierra Madre Land and Lumber Company; the Cananea-Naco Railroad; Cananea Realty Company; and the Cananea, Yaqui River, and Pacific Railroad Company. His holdings also included the rights to 2.5 million acres in Sonora, and the water rights to the both the Aros and Yaqui Rivers, meaning he could sustain all of his enterprises without little outside help, save ongoing financial investment. He constantly needed new cash flow to continue to build and sustain his businesses and appease his investors. It wasn't exactly fraud, but the house of cards that were his holdings were fragile and seemed to require an inexhaustible and constant influx of funds to stay solvent.

Cassidy's scheme was to infiltrate Greene's enterprise in El Paso, counting on the distance from Cananea to keep his identify anonymous. He intended to pay back A.B. Fall and Edelmida, both of whom he blamed for his troubles. He checked into a boarding house on Utah Street in El Paso, the main street in the tenderloin district. He soaked in a hot bath, then, feeling relaxed and refreshed, headed down the street to the local barber for a much needed shave and haircut.

He then headed off to the Parlor Cantina to see his old friend, George Ogden, who he knew from days gone by when he helped to build the El Paso Northeastern Railway line. George was a big man, both tall and heavyset, with red hair, a luxurious handlebar mustache, and an outgoing and boisterous personality. Ogden was well liked by all, but especially the ladies. The Parlor Cantina was run by George, but owned by "Madam" Tillie Howard. Tillie had been born Mathilde Weiler in Wisconsin, and both her parents died when she was very young. Although she had surviving relatives, she ended up living at the home of neighbors who treated her poorly, and by the age of twelve, hopped a freight train and spent several years riding the rails.

Once she reached adolescence and her body formed, Tillie became a "caboose girl," a prostitute who worked the trains, traveling from place to place and person to person, doing what she had to for money, food, and clothing. It was a surprisingly lucrative way to survive, and Tillie sold her services only to the most well-heeled gentlemen. Somewhere along the way, she changed her last name to Howard, and eventually became the mistress of one Willie Sells, owner and trick rider of Sells Circus, but he deserted her in San Antonio, and she lit out for El Paso. She arrived in town with a large amount of money from her escapades, which she used to purchase the Parlor Cantina from the well-known Madame, Alice Abbott.

Tillie's place was known to be an elegant, high class establishment, and she treated her girls very well, paying them a salary to keep them honest, as opposed to the commissions paid by other Madame's. The Parlor was legendary for its high class demeanor, as Tillie did not tolerate vulgarity, loud behavior or drunkenness. This had the dual effect of preserving the illusion of class and keeping her high-paying customers happy and satisfied. Her place was well appointed with imported glass chandeliers, mahogany furniture, velvet curtains, and original oil paintings. Each bedroom had a brass bed, full length mirror, wash basin and stand, and an armoire. Butlers and maids served drinks from silver trays.

This was not the type of place that Cassidy would normally frequent, but he had known George from the early days when he worked the railroad

263

and thought he could count on him to "hook him up" with a girl of his choosing.

As Cassidy walked into the Parlor, he heard a booming voice call out, "MacMurrough – I told you never to set foot in this establishment again." George Ogden stepped out from behind the piano with a scowl on his face and a menacing look in his eyes.

"Georgie, old sod, you must be joking. After all the money I spent in here when we were bringing the trains through, and the clients I referred to you? That one little skirmish before I left town was nothing compared to what I've seen here. Besides, it was just one of the whores." he cackled.

George was not only large, but tough, and he would brook no trouble from any man. He was extremely close to Tillie, and was the primary reason she had been able to stay in a rough business in a tough town. They were so close, that many people thought them married, and some thought George was the owner and Tillie only the Madam. The Parlor was known as the most genteel of the brothels in town, and the girls were always of the best background and refinement for their craft. No amount of tolerance was shown to any sort of rough behavior.

"I meant what I said last time, MacMurrough – Out!" he barked back.

"George – I just got back in town, I have no job yet, and not much money, but I am lonely, and would like to go someplace to get with a woman. It

264

has been too long a time. Can you just tell me where I might find what I am looking for?"

George knew what he was looking for, and all his instincts told him to throw MacMurrough out on his ear. But he had been a good and lucrative customer in the early days of the cantina, and George always had a soft spot for those from the British Empire, the birthplace of his own descendants. Besides, he knew that MacMurrough could create more trouble that he was worth.

"There's no place here in El Paso for your tastes, MacMurrough," he bellowed, "go over to Juarez - to Paco's Place and see what you can find there - and don't come back," he scowled.

Cassidy took the hint, if you could call it that, and headed out the door for Juarez. He thought that George was right – your money went at least twice as far, if not more, in Juarez, although you had to be careful which woman you picked. Mexico did not have the medical facilities of the States, in spite of the fact that it was only a few miles away.

Juarez was not a sleepy little village. Located just across the *Rio Grande*, it was a bustling city much larger than its sister city of El Paso. He found Paco's Place, which was a run down, shot-and-a-beer hall, with harsh lighting, plain pine-board walls and floors, and a beat up piano, horribly out of tune, where a toothless old miner in tattered clothes pounded out barely discernable tunes loudly, and with little regard for maintaining a rhythm.

The place was sparsely furnished, but was fairly crowded with miners, cowpokes, and assorted ne're-do-wells playing poker, keno, and eucre, with money changing hands at every turn. Cassidy looked around and to the back of the cantina, where he saw a maiden who commanded his attention. Her makeup and clothing were similar to what the other girls in this place wore, but somehow she attracted his attention, and he kept turning to stare at her again and again.

The few women that were visible in the cantina were heavily made up with blue mascara on their eyelids, overly rouged cheeks to cover pockmarks and scars, and colored hair that could only have come out of a bottle, as there was no comparable color in the natural world.

The outfits the women wore were designed to take your eyes off their faces at any rate, and focus on other assets. The long dresses were raised in the front to show their lace petticoats, and short enough that one could see their high heels and even a glimpse of leg. The bodice of the dresses were so low cut that it was miraculous that their bosoms didn't fall out of them, and with many of the girls you could see more than a little of the pink areola surrounding their nipples.

Cassidy walked over to the woman he had noticed, and as he approached, he realized why she held his attention. She was much older than the women he would normally be attracted to, but this one looked like a trashy version of Edelmida, and his blood immediately surged within him.

She smiled as he approached and he took note of her crooked and yellow teeth. "Hello, me beauty" he began, "and what might your name be?"

"*Señor*, I am Consuelo, and I would be happy to be your date tonight," she replied slyly.

Cassidy's mind was running a mile a minute, and he was imagining Edelmida as he said, "Not tonight, deary - but tomorrow night. What is your usual rate?" he asked. They negotiated a price for the entire evening which was less than he would have paid Conchita for just one hour with one of her girls back in Cananea. "But I have one request for you me lovely. Shall we discuss it over a drink?"

"As long as it does not involve animals or unnatural acts, I am happy to oblige *Señor,*" she answered, and they took a table in the back to discuss what was on Cassidy's mind.

Meanwhile, back across the Rio Grande in El Paso, George Ogden went down to the Western Union office and sent a telegram to his good friend and frequent customer, Francisco de Torres, informing him of the visit by Cassidy. Although MacMurrough had changed his name and effectively eliminated his recent past, the likeness on the poster that was passed around the various bars and bordellos from Cananea to El Paso and as far west as Bisbee, offering to pay for information on MacMurrough's whereabouts, showed a pretty good likeness, and his unique looks and demeanor made him an easy target to spot. Ironically, George Ogden was also a red haired man, but his frame was much larger and he was considered a handsome man, particularly in comparison to Cassidy/MacMurrough's scrunched up face and broken pug nose. A few choice questions about where MacMurrough had been the last few years was enough for George to be pretty certain that this was the man they were keeping tabs on at the Four C's.

The next evening Cassidy went to Paco's, to room 6 A, and knocked gently on the door. He was turned out in his finest clothes, although that wasn't much; leather boots, worn and with a need for new soles, yet freshly polished; a white shirt that was well worn but clean; a black wool vest; and tan, heavyweight poplin slacks.

He carried a used .45 Colt long-barrel single shot revolver which he bought from a retired Army officer before heading off into Indian territory on his way to El Paso from San Francisco. A custom scabbard held his trusty Bowie knife which he had named "The Peacemaker," and was anything but, that went with him everywhere, even to bed.

Consuelo opened the door and his first glance at her caused Cassidy to suck in his breath. By no means beautiful, she nevertheless looked remarkably like a poor man's Edelmida. Her eyes and natural hair color, which had returned since

Cassidy requested she wash the dye out of her hair, looked just the same. Her dress was simple and conservative, and looked like the dress she would wear going to church on Sunday, if, indeed, she ever saw a church at all. The way she held her body and her dimensions were identical. The structure of her face, space between her eyes, and shape of her nose, was all the same, and if one saw her from her left side or the back, she could easily be mistaken for Edelmida. But when she turned, and he saw her full face or from the right side, the pockmarked cheek and yellow, crooked teeth made her look completely different and she would never be confused as the more beautiful and confident Edelmida.

"*Señor*, I hope you are pleased and that I have honored your requests, although I feel naked dressed like this and with no makeup or hair coloring," Consuelo commented with a shy look in her eyes.

"*Señorita*, you are perfect. I hope you are ready to indulge me." Cassidy smirked. At first, Cassidy was aroused by this woman, although, to her bewilderment, he repeatedly went behind her to fondle her, but as their clothes came off and his passions increased, he became rougher with her and began pulling her hair and throwing her from one side of the bed to the other. "So, that's how you like it, *Señor*? O.K., but not too rough," she pleaded.

269

"Call me Thomas!" Cassidy demanded in a loud voice. "Call me Thomas, and tell me you love me," and his voice became louder and more insistent. He bit her neck and squeezed her hard, and she felt his passion but knew this was not about sex. He began to hurt her and squeeze her throat tighter and tighter and tossed her about the bed like a rag doll. There was no sexual connection at all, although he was engorged and his eyes were wild with frenzy. Consuelo was as large as he, and probably as strong, but he had a wiry strength and she was no match for him.

She begged him to stop, but he was beyond reason. He grabbed his ""Peacemaker" and held it to her face twisting the point near her cheek.

"You bitch!" he screamed at her. "You forced me to do this. You are the source of all me troubles and you will pay. Tell me you are sorry. Beg for my forgiveness." Cassidy was beyond all reason - he alternated between sudden violence and threatening her with the knife, to groping and exploring every inch of her womanhood. This lunacy went on for what seemed like hours to Consuelo, until he finally took her from behind with brute force and finished his business quickly.

As he lay on his back breathing hard, Consuelo threw her dress over her head hurriedly without bothering with undergarments, grabbed the rest of her clothes, and ran out of the room screaming "¡Cabrón! ¡También! ¡Loco Hombre! Don't ever come to this place or near me again!"

270

He let her go and smiled contentedly to himself then fell asleep with dreams of Cananea and young women and jewel encrusted gold crosses with different colored stones for each of his conquests.

Cassidy awoke with a start, disoriented and confused. He focused his eyes and strained his ears to hear what had awakened him, but he didn't have to try very hard, for he heard the click of a hammer being slowly pulled back on a gun right next to his head.

As he looked up, he saw a tall hombre with long, black, braided hair covered by a leather wide-brimmed hat, a chipped front tooth which could be seen through his scruff of beard, and flat black eyes boring back into his. In his left hand was a Colt .44 pistol, cocked and ready to fire.

"Is this the one, Consuelo?" he whispered in a low growl.

"*Sí, mi hermano*. That's the sick pig I told you about." Consuelo replied with venom in her voice.

"*Pendejo* – my sister here tells me that you hurt her and I am here to repay you and show you what it's like to be defenseless and abused." He held up Cassidy's Bowie knife and twisted it near his right cheek so the light from the morning sun shone off the blade. "Go ahead, give me an excuse to use this," Jack Durand said menacingly.

Cassidy was confused, and knew he had to think fast. Here was what looked like a half breed *mestizo* claiming to be the whore's brother. They were in Juarez, where he could easily be strung up for his actions without the benefit of a trial, if he wasn't tortured and killed first, and he had to find a way out.

Frantically, he stammered, "*Señor*, I meant no disrespect. I was caught up in the passion of the moment by the beautiful *Señorita*. I offer my sincere apologies. Is there anything I can do to show my regret and make everything right again?"

:Consuelo…?" Durand began.

"*Sí, sucio marrano*, you can pay me a week's wages and I won't turn you over to *la policía*" Consuelo spit out angrily.

A calm and knowing look came into Cassidy's eyes as it dawned on him that this was a shakedown and there was nothing he could do about it.

He didn't have the money, so he had to improvise. He had a gun pointed at his head in a house of ill repute in Juarez, with two Mexican nationals between him and his weapons. There was no chance he would ever make it to the border, even if he did escape. Death would be infinitely better than rotting away in a Mexican jail, where he would die of dysentery before anything else, and then in his weakened state would be sodomized brutally.

"I have a deal to make with you, and you will make much more money than what you are asking for, but it will take some work. Since I just got into town, I don't have the money on me," he lied convincingly, "but I have a way to get it if you are willing to help me. Otherwise, turn me over to the police if you must." he bluffed.

Cassidy knew that if the hombre was going to shoot him, he would have done so already. He was counting on the fact that the two of them wanted money more than justice, and shooting a gringo, even in a dump like this would bring trouble and the *Federales*.

Durand and Consuelo exchanged a glance and he nodded to her slightly. She lowered her eyes and slowly dropped her head in acquiescence.

"OK, *chico*. Let's hear your story, and make it good, you only have one chance." Jack responded.

Chapter Fifteen

Rail Wars

Colonel Greene had been to El Paso the week before Cassidy arrived, evaluating the possibility of building a new rail line between Juarez and El Paso for the purpose of importing his copper matte to the U.S., and controlling its' transportation between the two cities. A.B. had traveled with him, and together they hired an agent to petition the city council to franchise the building of a new street and railway system.

Having successfully completed that task, and after giving direction on what he wanted to accomplish, Greene headed back to New York to work on attracting new investors for his enterprises, and left Fall in charge of the project.

The agent, a local man named Josiah Heywood, who had been a prospector in the heyday of gold prospecting and knew everyone who was anyone in El Paso and Juarez, came back to A.B. after meeting with the city council to report his findings.

"Stone & Webster, the Boston based engineering firm, has been running an electric streetcar for the past 4 years, but they have done nothing to expand the service in spite of the tremendous growth of the twin cities. There is a new station being built at the end of San Francisco

274

Street, and, at a minimum, they would like to expand service to the new Union Station." Josiah reported.

A.B. misunderstood the council's intent and responded, a bit disappointedly, "So, they won't grant us a franchise, because Stone & Webster already has existing streetcars?" He knew the Colonel would be back in a heartbeat to fight that decision.

"On the contrary," Josiah replied, "just the opposite, in fact. They feel that the current supplier has been too lethargic and has not reacted to the growing needs of the city. The population here has grown fourfold, to over 20 thousand people in the last few years, and they desire better service to keep up with expanding demand."

What Josiah didn't explain, was that the city council felt that by offering a franchise to Colonel Greene, operating under his corporation, the Sierra Madre Railway, they would spark a race to see who could lay down track quickest and control the business, thereby setting up a competition and getting the maximum amount of track laid in the shortest amount of time.

The concept seemed to work as the council expected, but caused a nightmare for the twin cities during the construction phase. Traffic was snarled and streets disrupted and torn apart to make way for new track as both Greene's company and Stone & Webster raced to the finish of the project.

Colonel Greene had left and chartered A.B. to run the project, and he authorized all the resources of his vast holdings to stand behind it.

A.B. immediately hired hundreds of workers, and rushed to lay down ties and rails in all directions, beginning in Juarez and creating havoc everywhere.

The frenzy continued for a week, as both firms begin laying track, disrupting traffic all throughout the main streets and avenues in El Paso, and causing incredible frustrations for existing businesses.

After A.B. had laid miles of track through Juarez and into El Paso, the labor bosses of the project announced they were cutting employee wages from $1.50 per day to $1 for unskilled workers, ostensibly to save money and bring the project in under budget. One of these bosses was a man named Declan Cassidy, who didn't report to A.B., but to one of his site managers, and who managed to stay far away from senior management of the project and on the front lines supervising the laying of the track.

Cassidy had recently taken to wearing one of the wide brimmed hats made by John B. Stetson's company in Philadelphia. These hats suited the hot climate of the west, and was designed for a variety of functions that cowboys, drovers and ranch workers needed. It also served the purpose of covering ones identity with its broad rim.

It was a radical departure from the bowler he favored in Cananea, and unless someone was specifically looking for him, he would be very difficult to recognize.

The announced reduction in pay for the workers on the rail line was not well received, and, as a portent of things to come, the workers formed a picket line and went on strike. After a tense weekend of picketing and negotiation, a compromise was reached with representatives for the rail workers. The unskilled laborers would still receive $1 per day, but steel workers would make $1.50 per day. Although this was really a victory for Greene and the Sierra Madre Railroad Company, work continued, and the laborers seemed appeased.

Shortly thereafter, Stone and Webster successfully completed their line from San Francisco Street to Union Depot. They had won the race and A.B. halted all work on Greene's behalf. Greene's Sierra Madre Railway Company simply halted work and walked off the site, leaving unfinished rail lines and supplies, which Stone and Webster then purchased. There was some who suspected that the entire enterprise was simply a profiteering maneuver on Falls' part since he never really seemed to believe the Sierra Madre would be able to displace the franchise that the Boston firm held in El Paso. It wasn't until years later that Fall admitted that the venture had allowed him to personally pocket over $100,000.

277

Now that the project was over, Cassidy was again unemployed, and it was then that he ran into trouble and convinced Jack Durand to travel with him to Bisbee, AZ.

Cassidy had convinced Durand and Consuelo of the existence of a "fantastic, antique gold cross encrusted with enormous rubies and worth at least $250,000, if not more, just in metal and jewels alone."

Cassidy explained, "Sixteen years ago, I was employed by the Cananea Consolidated Copper Company - the Four C's – do you know it?" Durand nodded his head. "Well, I was accused of stealing an antique cross that was made of ornate gold and jewels. It was owned by Colonel Greene who now owns many businesses in Cananea, El Paso, and elsewhere. You know about him, too?" Again, Durand nodded. "Well, the bitch who set me up was the wife of one of his *mestizo* foreman, her name is Edelmida Carreras. She was a bitching whore before she married him, and she stole the cross and pinned it on me. The head of security at the Four C's was a guy named Francisco de Torres, a strange bastard whose mother was Spanish and his father, white. He was all over me and had it out for me from the start. They found the cross under my bed, which I know had been put there by the whore Carreras. They looked no further, and I became the scapegoat. I know that Edelmida, who had access to the place where the cross was hung since she worked in the kitchen at Casa Greene, set me up for this. Interestingly enough, after all this time, the cross is still missing. Apparently, after they found it in my room, it was misplaced again. Both Torres and Greene's right hand man, Albert Bacon Fall thought the other had taken it back to the Casa. *I* think Edelmida still has it." He finished with a smug look of self-satisfaction.

"Interesting story, Cassidy. But if she has it, why hasn't she sold it for the gold and jewels? Why keep something like that that could be found and get her in much deeper trouble than even you are in now?" Durand's logic was inescapable.

"Not everyone is as mercenary as you, Durand. Edelmida may be a whore, but she is deeply religious. You know the type – acts all sweet during the day, goes to church, dresses coyly, but once the sun goes down and you get her alone, she is a wild woman. Look, she even left scars on me back from her clawing." He lifted the back of his shirt to show Durand scars that looked like they were caused by fingernails, which had been healed for a long time. Of course, they weren't from Edelmida, but Durand didn't know that. Cassidy couldn't speak two sentences without telling a lie. He seemed to be in capable of it.

Cassidy continued, "The piece is a relic. The rumor is, it was given to the ancestor of a priest by Cortés himself. If it *is* the religious relic everyone thinks, then its value is much more than the price of the gold and jewels to the Church. I'm sure that at

279

some point in the not too distant future, when this is all forgotten, the cross will show up once again and be displayed in one of the missions, maybe even Guadalupe."

"Alright, Cassidy. It's worth a trip to Cananea to see if what you say is true. It will be easy enough to find out, and if you're right I will take this as payment for your erroneous ways. If I do not come back with the cross, I will hunt you down and kill you like the dog you are."

Cassidy couldn't be seen anywhere near Cananea, and was afraid to even cross the border into Sonora, Mexico, so it was agreed he was to go to Bisbee, along with Consuelo for insurance, and find a buyer for the Amulet. Although Durand didn't trust Cassidy near Consuelo, he needed to keep an eye on Cassidy, and Consuelo knew how to handle a gun. "She should have had one when she first went to Cassidy's room," he thought to himself, "and all this could have been avoided, but perhaps things are working out this way for a reason. Maybe there is some truth to this story. Cassidy certainly seems to believe there is a cross made of gold and jewels, and the only real question seems to be – where is it?"

Durand could have just killed Cassidy then and there and be done with it, but he had no way of knowing if his story was real, and it was certainly worth finding out. Either he would find the Amulet or not, but either way he would come back and find Cassidy and kill him for what he did to his sister.

Durand harbored no illusions about what his sister did for a living, and the danger it presented. In Mexico, you did what you had to do to survive, but Cassidy was pure evil and had clearly stepped over the line. He would not be forgiven, either here, or in the afterlife.

For his part, Cassidy knew that Durand also could not be trusted and would be tempted to get the cross and head back to El Paso leaving him out of the reward for all his hard work. Having his sister nearby was the only insurance he had that Durand would return. "Cassidy, if you try to lay one hand on her while I am gone, I'll make you suffer for weeks and kill you little by little. I will take you out to the desert and take out your tongue so I won't have to listen to your screaming. You will be stripped naked and have no food or water. I will cut off one finger a day and feed it to the buzzards to give them a taste of your flesh, then each of your toes, and last, your manhood. Then I will bid you *adios* and leave you there to the rest of the scavengers who will pick your bones clean until there is nothing left and even the marrow will be sucked clean from your bones."

Durand smiled a cruel smile and looked as though he hoped Cassidy would try to make a move on Consuelo. Cassidy knew he would, and could, do all he said, so he promised to keep Consuelo close but would not touch a hair on her head.

"*Señor* Durand, you have my word, but I must have yours, that you will bring the Amulet back to me in Bisbee. Otherwise, your precious Consuelo will suffer the same fate as that you just described."

Durand didn't think that Cassidy had the temerity to pull off that kind of torture, but he knew the kind of torture he *could* put Consuelo through, and he would never allow that to happen to his sister.

"Don't be a fool, Cassidy. Consuelo is as good with a gun as any man." He turned to his sister.

"Watch your back" he said, as he handed Consuelo his pistol. The two nodded slowly, and each went on their way. Cassidy tried to take Consuelo by the elbow, which she gruffly shook off, and pushed him ahead of her as they walked towards Union Depot and the train to Bisbee.

Bisbee was the home of a competitive mine to the Cananea Consolidated Copper Company; the Copper Queen Mining Company, one of the largest mines in the United States. Greene also had operations in the town and was planning to open a smelter to refine his copper for shipment to the north. Bisbee had a booming population of over 20,000 making it the largest city between St. Louis and San Francisco. It had been named for Judge DeWitt Bisbee of San Francisco, who backed the original mining venture, although the Judge never saw the town. It earned the sobriquet "little San

Francisco" but not because of where the Judge was from, but rather because of its climate, culture, and overall quality of life.

Durand was to go to Cananea, find out who had the cross and where it was located, steal it, and bring it back to Bisbee. There they would remove the precious stones and fence the metals and jewels separately. Cassidy was convinced that Edelmida still had the Amulet because of an interchange he heard between A.B. Fall and Francisco de Torres as he was about to leave town.

A.B. had ridden up to Francisco just before he escorted Cassidy out of town and pulled him aside, but because they were both on horses, their whispering could still be heard slightly by Cassidy and he heard him ask Francisco, "where did you put the Amulet?" Francisco looked at Fall, cocked his head, and shrugged as if to imply "I don't know, I thought you had it." At that, Fall spurred his horse hard and reined him sharply left to head back to the camp.

After the exchange, Francisco went back to Cassidy and led him out of town. Cassidy asked "what was that about?," but Francisco just ignored him, and continued to ignore him the whole time on the trail to Naco, the border town where they would cross on the way to Bisbee, which took the better part of a day.

After Durand arrived in Cananea and confronted Edelmida, he was certain Manuel would show up for the meeting at *Caballo Loco.* He hired two local goons for a nominal fee to help him n the event of any confrontation. These two goons were nothing more than muscle to back him up and would be gone right after his work was done.

He arrived at the saloon well before sundown so he could be early for his meeting with Manuel to observe if he was alone or brought company.

As he waited, he went over what Cassidy had told him of what had occurred, and why Manuel would know where the cross could be found. Cassidy was convinced that Edelmida had it, and if Manuel knew its location, Durand would be able to find out or die trying. Durand didn't realize that Francisco had already been informed of his presence in town and had eyes on him everywhere he went.

The story Cassidy had told was a simple one and partially based in truth, although he didn't really know how close to the truth he was. Durand reviewed the details to see if there were any holes in the story. He was told that Edelmida, who worked in the kitchen at the big house, Casa Greene, had set up Cassidy by stealing the cross and hiding it in his quarters, then reported it stolen and led the chief of security, Francisco de Torres, to his room.

Cassidy had to tell Durand about his name change, and that he went by the name

MacMurrough while n Cananea to avoid any confusion. As he offered his explanation, Durand just looked at him with heavily hooded eyes and nodded quietly. It was common practice to change a name when moving to a new town in this part of the country.

Cassidy explained that Edelmida set him up. "Because her husband, Manuel, was named the first Mexican supervisor at the mines at my recommendation, but he was lazy and could not control his workers. Production on his line was the lowest in the camp and something had to be done. I had several conversations with Manuel about this, but his *mañana* attitude was too much for me and I told him to shape up or be fired.

His wife, Edelmida, used to be the town whore, and she's the one who came up with the idea to set me up. When they found the cross under my bed, and, Durand, let me tell you - it is a beauty indeed - Francisco handed it to Edelmida to hold while the arrest was made. Later, when he asked her to hand it back, she said she had given it to A.B. Fall. Francisco asked him and he said, yes, she had handed it to him, but he had laid it down on the sofa to bring back to the Casa later and after returning to my room, it was gone. He thought Francisco had picked it up. I know the whore Edelmida has it, but she is too dangerous to approach. She has screwed every lawman in town and is known to be protected. Better to go after that lazy slug she's married to,

Manuel. With the proper incentive I'm sure we can make him talk." Cassidy concluded.

Durand bought this line of reasoning, for why would Cassidy lie? If the Carreras did not have the Amulet, Cassidy was going to die by his hand anyway, and Durand would be able to get back to Juarez from the American side of the border with no fear of retribution. If they did have the Amulet, Durand would have to find a way to kill Cassidy before he had a chance to do anything to Consuelo, and would then take the cross back to El Paso to break it down and fence the pieces. Durand could just take care of Cassidy now and be done with it and go after the Amulet on his own, but he wanted to see the look on the hombre's face as he held the bejeweled object, just before he sent him to his final reward. Besides, there would still be money to be had from Cassidy in either case.

Just as the sun was dipping into the western sky, Manuel and Pedro approached the swinging front doors of the *Caballo Loco* cantina. Time in rural Mexico was not the same as on the other side of the border. In Mexico, you started your job when the whistle blew, but no one except the managers watched the clock. If you finished one job, you started another regardless of where the sun sat in the sky. Time was not judged by a clock. On weekends, you traded the job for which you were paid, for another where you took on the responsibilities of home, family, and church. Time did not matter the same as in the States, it was judged not by

286

beginning and end but by finishing one responsibility and taking up another. The concept of *mañana* was not one of laziness, but one of priority, which was completely misunderstood by the Americans.

On the inside of the saloon they could hear chairs scraping across the broad wooden floors, raucous laughter, and a rollicking piano playing a tune entitled "*Mary's a Grand Old Name*" from a brand new Broadway hit show "*45 Minutes from Broadway*" all blending into a cacophonous blend. Colonel Greene loved this song, after having first heard it on Broadway while living in New York at the Waldorf hotel, and often sang it to his wife, Mary.

Mary Proctor was Colonel Greene's second wife. His first wife, Ella, had died of cancer on Christmas Eve in 1899 while away trying to recuperate in California. Some say she never recovered after the death of her beloved daughter and namesake, Ella.

Mary was the adopted daughter of Mr. & Mrs. Frank Proctor, Frank being a long time sheriff of Pima County. Frank and his wife had adopted her, after she was orphaned. Mary had been named for her grandmother, Maríah (Mar-eye-ah) Benedict, but in the southwest it was invariably pronounced Ma-ree-ah, the most prominent woman's name in the region. However, Frank and his wife wanted her to have an English, rather than

287

Spanish name, so they shortened the name to the Anglican Mary. Mary had been the fifth child and only daughter of Albert Case Benedict, one of Arizona's true pioneers who had married Georgia Alvarez, whose family owned substantial ranching interests throughout the Sonora region.

As Manuel & Pedro walked into the cantina, all conversation slowly died out and the piano faded to a soft tinkling and eventually stopped altogether.

In spite of its Spanish language name, *Caballo Loco* was a predominantly gringo cantina and Manuel and Pedro did not belong there, in spite of the fact that Manuel was a supervisor and generally liked by all. Pedro felt completely exposed and feared the worst, and was just about to grab Manuel's arm and run from the place when he heard a voice call out, "Manuel, thanks for coming by. Wait outside and I'll be right with you," called Francisco de Torres. Pedro breathed a sigh of relief, and although Manuel seemed puzzled, he took his arm and they both headed out the door as the sounds gradually returned to normal.

Out in the street, it was quiet and dusk was just beginning to settle in, casting a warm amber hue over the mountains overlooking the town of Cananea.

From the western corner of the building, they heard a voice call out, "Manuel, come around the corner here so we can talk openly away from the gringo cowboys."

Manuel and Pedro squinted into the setting sun, but could not see anyone, and thought it must be Francisco or one of his men. As they turned the corner of the building, rough hands grabbed him and closed over his mouth, while a second man knocked Pedro unconscious with the butt of a gun.

Just then, Francisco came out of the cantina and looked up and down the street, but did not see Manuel or Pedro anywhere. Confused, he went back inside to see if anyone else had seen which direction they went.

When the two had initially arrived at the cantina, Jack Durand had acted too late to intercept Manuel and his friend before they entered the bar, and he figured it was just dumb luck that they came out shortly afterwards without incident. This time, however, he was ready for them. Once he had the two of them in hand, he said to Manuel, "*Señor*, I have your wife Edelmida, and your daughter Carmelita, hidden out of town under guard. If you do not do exactly what I say, they will both die. Do you understand?"

Manuel, having trouble breathing, with rough hands covering his nose and mouth, nodded slowly.

"Now I will take my hand off your mouth and you will not say a word, *¿comprende?*"

Again, Manuel nodded his assent. Durand and his two hired hands marched Manuel down the hard packed dirt backstreet, and out behind the

289

blacksmith shop which was closed for the day, leaving Pedro lying out cold in the alley next to the cantina.

"Manuel, your wife is the one who noticed the gold cross that hung on Colonel Greene's wall was missing, correct? Don't say anything, just nod yes or no." Durand demanded.

Manuel shook his head, no. He knew that Edelmida had been involved in the incident, but it was Luisina who had noticed the Amulet was missing, not Edelmida. "Manuel," Durand tried again, frustrated, "now, again, nodding only, tell me the truth this time. She hid the cross and pointed the finger at Ca.. ahh, MacMurrough, correct?" Durand nearly used the name Cassidy which would have meant nothing to Manuel. Again, he shook his head no.

"This is getting us nowhere. Jose, Miguel, take him to the stall behind the shop and we'll beat the truth out of him."

As they choked a dusty bandana into Manuel's mouth, Francisco and two other men, with Pedro groggily stumbling behind, came around the corner from the alleyway, guns drawn. "Hold it right there, *amigo.*"

He instructed his deputies, Jose and Miguel, to tie and gag Durand's cronies using thick hemp rope. They then tied Durand and secured his hands to his legs to restrict his movements.

"What's your name, *amigo*, and what's your business here in Cananea with Manuel?"

290

Durand just glared and said nothing. Francisco took out a pair of handcuffs and cuffed Durand's hands behind his back, and pushed him to his knees.

"Manuel, what is his business here?" Francisco prompted.

Durand, struggling against the cuffs and rubbing his wrists raw, looked up at Manuel and spat out, "Say nothing, *amigo*. Remember what I said."

Manuel closed his eyes and thought of his wife and lovely daughter at the hands of these monsters. He looked from Durand to Francisco and back again. He was torn and didn't know what to do. Pedro had been unconscious and hadn't heard Durand's threats, and Manuel had no way of knowing if Durand was telling the truth about holding his family or not. Clearly, Durand had no real idea of the truth behind the story of the cross, although he wondered how he knew about it at all. Manuel was torn, but if he didn't speak at all, Francisco would put Durand in the Cananea jail, and if his threat were real, his family could perish.

Finally, he made a decision and turned to Francisco. "*Señor* Torres, can I have just a few private words with *Señor* Durand, *¿por favor*? I may be able to help clean up this mess" Manuel pleaded.

Francisco stared at him and chewed on this for a few moments before responding.

291

"Frisk them all thoroughly boys. Look for hidden knives and derringers."

He waited while the men complied and pulled out a boot knife and the pistol from Durand's holster.

"O.K. Manuel," Francisco continued, "don't get any closer than three feet from the hombre and say what you have to say. Durand, if you make one move that I don't like, it will be your last. Jose, Miguel, Pedro, take up positions at ten feet surrounding them." Francisco was taking no chances and Durand knew his only chance was to comply.

In whispered tones, Manuel told Durand what he knew about the theft of the Amulet, and Edelmida's limited role in what had occurred, and although he really knew nothing of the situation between Edelmida and MacMurrough, he knew there was bad blood for some reason and he revealed that to Durand as well. He also informed him of the troubles MacMurrough had with women and the management team at the Four C's.

Durand was no dummy. He knew that what Cassidy/MacMurrough had told him were a bunch of half-truths. He now knew for certain that the cross existed, but was convinced Edelmida had little to do with its theft, and even more convinced that Manuel had no idea of its location.

As they concluded their brief discussion, Durand straightened up and asked Francisco, "*Señor*, do you know the location of this cross?"

Francisco looked at him and thought for a moment. "After we found it in MacMurrough's bunk, it was somehow mislaid. We believe it is in Cananea and whoever snatched it sixteen years ago hid it, and is waiting for the heat to cool down, but as long as Colonel Greene is here, that won't happen. The theory is that the anarchists have it and will eventually try to fence it for its gold and jewels, and when they do, we will find out. The reward Colonel Greene has offered is very rich, and there are few people who are willing to cross him. You never really know who is in his employ. Why do you ask?"

Durand responded, "MacMurrough set us up for this. He told me lies to get out of his own trouble with me in El Paso. If it's all the same to you, I will leave town quietly to go and deal with him myself. He's in Bisbee waiting for me to go back with the Amulet. Manuel, we do not have a quarrel with you, and I lied about having your wife and daughter. I was lied to, and I will fix the problem with MacMurrough."

Manuel and Francisco exchanged glances and Manuel replied "I will go home to make sure everyone is safe, and if no one has been harmed I will go to the jail and talk to Francisco and he will decide your fate." They nodded and Francisco, Jose, and Miguel marched Durand and his cronies off to the Cananea jail.

Manuel turned to Pedro "I'll walk you to Doc's on our way home so he can take a look at you and make sure you're all right. If all is well, I will head to the jail after. Meet me there, if you are well enough, and thanks for your help today."

When Manuel arrived home, everything seemed normal. The children were drawing pictures of the mountains on foolscap, and coloring them with paint made from iron oxide runoff from the mines, and Edelmida was fashioning her tamales of cornstalks and ground up leftover meat. When she heard him enter and she saw he was alright, she rushed to him and hugged him tight. "Oh, Manuel, I was so worried. Is everything alright? What happened?"

Manuel himself was relieved, and so happy to see that everything was normal at home and there was no threat that his heart fairly burst in his chest. He hurriedly told her what had occurred and asked if she had any idea why MacMurrough would tell such lies and asked if she knew anything more about the cross.

"Manuel, I swear, the last time I saw the cross was the day it was found in *El Diablo*'s room. MacMurrough hates me, but why, I don't know. I had no dealing with him outside of meals at the Casa." Edelmida had grown accustomed to telling half-truths or lying outright.

"Well, he may finally be getting his just rewards. I need to go down to the jail and speak with Francisco. I will see you later this evening.

Keep the children here and put them to bed early so we can talk later," Manuel said as he hurried off.

When he arrived at the jail, Pedro was already there. "The Doc says I am too hard-headed to have suffered any real damage, and my brain must already be scrambled or why would I be here working the mines? I'll be O.K. He gave me something for the pain and told me to rest, but first I wanted to see what Francisco is going to do. Everything O.K. at home?"

"*Sí*, fine" Manuel replied.

When Francisco came out to the office from the back of the building where the cells were located, Manuel gave him the information he received from Edelmida.

"No surprise," he commented "MacMurrough was always a liar and a fraud. Durand just told me he goes by the name of Cassidy now. Well, if you have no objection, I think we should let Durand go and do his business with MacMurrough or Cassidy or whoever he is. Durand is one bad hombre but his quarrel is with MacMurrough, not us. His cronies are just local hired guns and I'll keep them locked up for a day or two until we're sure Durand has crossed the border. O.K.?"

Manuel nodded in agreement and he and Pedro left quietly to go home and get some rest. Manuel and Pedro, and probably Durand, all had the same thought running through their heads.

"Where is the cross?"

Edelmida was worried as she waited for Manuel to come home from the jail. She knew she had to tell him something, but felt she could not tell him about the rape and her concerns about Carmelita. She had just put the children to sleep and was formulating her ideas when Manuel burst through the door.

He took a bottle of mescal from a cabinet and poured a little into a glass for himself. Edelmida rarely took a drink, and when she did it was usually a weak mix of cactus juice and pulque, a milky drink fermented from the juice of the maguey plant, part of the agave family. Manuel gave her an update and extended version of what occurred with Durand, and his release to go to Bisbee to deal with MacMurrough.

"Edelmida, I know there is bad blood between you and MacMurrough, and I don't know exactly why, but there is obviously more to the story of the gold cross than what you have told me. Is there anything more you want to share with me about this?"

Edelmida took a deep breath, took a glass from the shelf in the kitchen area next to the small bare wooden table that served as both kitchen table and general purpose workspace, and half filled it with water poured from a jug wrapped in goat skin to keep the liquid cool. She held out the glass to Manuel and said quietly, "pour me a very small amount of that mescal into my water glass, *por favor*."

After he did so, and handed her the glass, she took a gulp, set it down, sat back, cleared her throat, and said, "Manuel, MacMurrough - *El Diablo* - is an evil man. All of the women and the wives of the workers talk about him. The stories are legendary and horrifying. I won't give you the details, but he has done horrible things to many women, and not just those at the bordello. Something had to be done and I - I couldn't help myself. I took the cross off the wall and hid it in *El Diablo's* room. I whispered to one of the kitchen workers, after the theft was discovered, that I wouldn't be surprised if *El Diablo* had taken it, and the belief spread like wildfire. I was not at all surprised that they would search his room and, of course, I knew they would find it. I'm sorry Manuel, but I would do it again if I had to," she said defiantly.

Manuel sat back, picked up the bottle of mescal, and poured himself another two fingers. Edelmida held out her half-full glass and asked him to pour her another dollop.

Emotions were running through him, but he finally responded, saying to her softly, "I understand Edelmida. We have all heard the stories and know what an evil man MacMurrough could be, and it seems he believes you are behind the theft. Why he would select you, of all the people who hate him at the camps, I cannot guess, but you may want to think about that and think about what would happen if you were to ever run into him again."

Edelmida thought about this a second, then raised her glass to Manuel and as they toasted she said, "When it comes to my family, I am a lioness, and I will forever protect them from whatever possibility of harm may befall them," and choked down the glass in one swallow.

Manuel sipped his glass and looked at her over the rim and thought to himself, "I'm glad she's on my side."

Chapter Sixteen

Revolution in the Air

The latest edition of the anarchist weekly, *Regeneración,* was published and distributed, contributing additional inflammatory rhetoric designed to incite the workers throughout Mexico. The incendiary writing of the Flores Magon brothers, who had moved their operations to St. Louis in 1905 to escape prosecution from the Díaz regime, was sparking more unrest among those increasingly supporting thoughts of revolution, and strengthening ties with the socialists, anarchists, and revolutionaries in the U.S.

The International Workers of the World (IWW), a group of radical labor unionists, anarchists and Socialists, which was founded in the U.S. the same year that the brothers moved operations to St. Louis, heavily influenced the Mexican labor party, *Partido Liberal Mexicano* (PLM), which adhered to the principles advocated by the Flores Magon brothers and promoted anarchy and civil disobedience.

Although the Four C's was one of the largest mining camps in Sonora, there were other mining interests and businesses scattered throughout the region owned by a number of different companies.

299

Virtually all of them were owned by foreign corporations that made their profits off the backs of the Mexican workers, thus setting up a scenario that made it ripe for revolution.

For years, proletarian unrest was fomenting around the policies of Porfirio Díaz, whose dictatorial rule as *Presidente* of Mexico was nearing its end. Initially a rebel against the government himself, he envisioned himself as an autocratic leader who could bring his nation to world class status and take full advantage of its natural resources by encouraging foreign investment. Díaz had run his initial campaign on a platform of reform, no re-election, and respect for the constitution.

The years prior to Díaz' rule, Mexico had been racked by wars with France and Spain, internal strife between the Spanish settlers and Indian natives, and the U. S. border wars. In less than 40 years prior to Díaz' reign, the U.S. border had extended to take more than half of Mexico's land mass, and established the U.S./Mexican border at the Rio Grande.

Although Díaz' initial leadership intentions were good, he rapidly came to the belief that he needed to have foreign investment and expertise to truly bring Mexico into being as a world class country and take full advantage of its' natural resources. To this end, he encouraged foreign investment, offering tax incentives and other considerations in order to build out the railroads, improve the mining of precious metals, and enhance oil and gas exploration. This approach led to rapid economic expansion at the expense of the lower class, contributing to the caste system, and an inequitable disbursement of wealth and privilege. This was a major cause of the civil unrest gripping the country. Factions were spinning up independently from the South, throughout Mexico City, and in the North, disparate, but all gaining strength. Once these factions began to coalesce, the strength of the whole would begin the fight against the government and privileged class.

Cananea was no exception, and a microcosm of the rest of the country, and unrest was rapidly becoming more and more visible as the union stepped up their efforts to create divisiveness as anarchists rallied the workers. The added tension created by the theft of the cross and Thom MacMurrough's unpopularity, only added to the long list of grievances of the workers. They now felt that their families were being threatened as well as their livelihood.

The rhetoric of revolution was not lost on Manuel or Edelmida, for they had much to gain and little to lose by siding with the new liberal party. Both of them knew, although they would not say it out loud, that Manuel's "promotion" was that in name only, and except for the pittance of increased pay, it was nothing more than a token. Manuel had been treated with respect, but after all this time, with no changes made in attitudes, pay, hours, or opportunity, it was well known that this stop-gap measure instituted by MacMurrough was a tool to hold down unrest and fight fire with fire against the uprising anarchists. For the anarchists were not only fighting against the Porfirio and the Díaz machine, but also against all of the investors from outside the country who were taking profits and giving nothing back to the community.

More importantly, the talk and activity was not lost on Carmelita and her peers. About to complete her catholic school education, she, like many of her age group, was about ready to go out into the working world. Politics, social issues, and mores were very important to the next generation and they had strong feelings and beliefs about the direction that the country was headed.

The PLM and other factions appealed to them and the fact that Díaz had been in office for three of their lifetimes, contributed to the insurrection of the young and growing population. In spite of the conservative teachings of their Spanish Catholic heritage, this new generation was headstrong and felt that they were to be the first real generation of Mexican blood, not claiming the caste orientation of *peninsulares, criollos, mestizos*, or natives, but as Mexicans and a people unto themselves, a right they had earned after centuries of turmoil, invasions and insurrection. They created new music which spoke of revolution, and wrote *corridos*, which were sung throughout the land, one person teaching it to another, with stories about outlaws and those who challenged authority. The stories were mostly based on truth and only enhanced the reputations of anyone who provoked the status quo. This generation would prove to be the ultimate undoing of the years of repression and poverty.

Díaz kept the resistance in check by the expansion of his armed, rural police, the *Rurales* (*Guardia Rurales*), a ragtag group that numbered only a few hundred in the early part of his reign, but which he expanded to over 2,000 men by the turn of the century. Many of these were captured bandits who had been recruited into the employ of cleaning up the same behaviors they had previously exhibited. To that end, they often used unnecessary force, and ruled under the guise of *ley de fuga*, the law of flight, which afforded them the option to shoot, upon flight, a convicted prisoner, but was often abused and used to contain or kill anyone who defied them. They had earned a reputation as a ruthless band that would brook no resistance, a profile that was fostered by Díaz.

On an unusually cold day in early June, the sun was just coming over the horizon when Carmelita took her bother Juan and sister Rosita by the hand, to walk them to the school they all attended which was run by the Catholic nuns. The growth of the town of Cananea had been explosive in the past few years and had boomed to over twenty thousand, requiring an increase in schools, markets, and other necessities to satisfy the needs of the community. Although Mexico, in general, had a very poor track record in education, in spite of Díaz' lip service to the need, Cananea had the Catholic Church to help with education, and both the foreign workers and the natives were able to take advantage of this, although in disparate locations. Carmelita was fortunate to be one of the few who continued to go to school after her elementary education was completed. Each year the Franciscans took on a few of the most promising students and taught them in theology and practical sciences, saving them from having to go to work in the mines or one of the other businesses owned by the Four C's. Carmelita could afford this because both her parents were alive and worked at good paying jobs by Cananea standards.

"Come along, Juan. I need to drop you off quickly so I can get to class early." Carmelita pleaded. Of the twins, Juan was the one who liked to dawdle and was always late or holding Carmelita up from where she had to go.

Carmelita had become surrogate mother to Juan and Rosita, but not because Edelmida was a bad mother, rather, because she was always working. After years of trying, the twins were born nine years after Carmelita, almost to the day. Rosita was the first born, but only just barely, a fact that she never let Juan forget. Twins were extremely rare in Cananea and, because they were not identical, over time most people did not think of them as twins at all despite the fact that they were the same age. Physically the two were very different, with Rosita inheriting her mothers' height, long, black hair and light brown eyes, evidence of her European heritage. Juan, on the other hand, had his father's features, and was shorter than Rosita with a thick chest and the black eyes exemplifying his Papago background. His legs were short, making it difficult for him to keep up with the long legged Rosita.

Life in the kitchen at the hacienda was a job that had some flexibility, but Edelmida had to be there to prepare for all of the meals, and dinner often kept her there until after 9 o'clock. Manuel was at the mines from before 8 in the morning, due to his foreman responsibilities, and left after 8 at night. This was one of the main grievances of the miners; they wanted to shorten the day to an eight hour shift. Ten hours was a long day even for Manuel, who no longer had to swing a pick and shovel. For those workers inside the mines, who had to cull the precious minerals from the dry red clay, the heat, dirt, and dust was excruciating after such a long day.

Manuel would often come home after work and have a meal that Edelmida had already prepared and fed the children, then head back out to the cantina to meet with others, using the excuse he was discussing work at the mines.

Carmelita knew that he was really attending the PLM meeting she had heard so much about. It was no secret within the native community that the miners had been discussing a strike, and although Manuel was a foreman, and technically part of the management team, he had grown seriously disenchanted with things of late and was espousing many of the beliefs of the Flores Magon brothers.

"Carmelita, why are we in such a hurry?" Juan asked breathlessly.

"I need to get to choir practice. We are singing at the wedding of Felicity Montoya this weekend and we have to rehearse a new song before and after school. Hurry." Carmelita exclaimed and walked even faster to stem any further inquiry.

Juan, Rosita, and the rest of Cananea all knew about Felicity Montoya. Her uncle, Luis, was owner, or *hacendado,* of a sprawling hacienda near Alamos, Sonora, named *Hacienda Las Mercedes*, approximately 120 miles from Cananea. The Montoyas were the richest family in town, and were one of the elite *Peninsulares*, having migrated from Spain to New Spain in the late 1880's after having been given farm land in exchange for political favors at home.

All of the land contained in the *hacienda* had formerly belonged to native tribes and had been confiscated when the Spanish invaded and conquered New Spain. The *hacendado*, or *patrón,* received all of the profits farmed by the peons who came with the land as a part of the grant.

The people who farmed the land were paid only a pittance. These were the former land owners and this practice was the most hostile representation of the rich exploiting the poor and a primary reason that the proletariat revolted against the establishment to spark the revolution.

They shipped their crops to the U.S at a handsome profit, in spite of the challenges of bad roads and hot weather which was an enemy of fresh produce. Luis Montoya had come to Cananea on an extended visit to discuss expansion and funding of the rail system with Colonel Greene, and used the town as his base of operations until plans were completed.

The Montoya children were attending the Catholic school and would remain for the entire school year. Mercedes Montoya, was a few years older than Carmelita, but they were friendly in spite of the age difference although they were both strong willed and often conflicted. Carmelita came to know her through her brother, Alejandro who was in the same class as Carmelita and was infatuated with her.

After she dropped the children off at their schoolroom, she hurried down the road towards the church where they usually took choir practice, and ran instead straight past the church into a side alley that ran between the church and the school building. There she met with Alejandro and three of the others who were in the choir.

"Alejandro, did you bring the paper?" she asked breathlessly.

"*Sí*, Carmelita it is right here," he responded. He bristled at the thought of one day owning a piece of the hacienda, and taking advantage of his friends he went to school with today. His rebellion was a cause for concern in his family, with good reason. Today, he held in his hands the newly arrived newspaper, *El Centenario*. They had published the text of Baca Calderóns' speech he gave to the newly formed revolutionary society called the *Union Liberal Humanidad* on the fifth of May, a holiday in Mexico that celebrated the Battle of Puebla, when the Mexicans defeated the French.

Calderón once again rose to the occasion with his gift of oratory and incited the workers. "Now is the time to open our eyes to the light of reason and to leave off lame lamentations. If the situation is bad, it is yours to remedy it. To resolve to do so - that is all. A people which goes to sleep in timidity awakens in conquest....Do not vacillate. The laurels of triumph will adorn your brow. Long live the Republic! "

These words resonated with the miners and other workers at the camp. The word also spread to other holdings of Greene's, and although the workers genuinely liked Colonel Greene and believed he was a miner more than a businessman, Calderón's words could not be ignored. Greene was a U.S. citizen and had been living in New York for the past few years, so the conclusion of Calderón's speech was telling: "Teach the capitalists that you are not beasts of burden – the capitalist who, in every way and everywhere has displaced us with his legion of blue eyed blondes."

Carmelita finished reading this and declared, "We must stand up and fight for our freedom. We have seen our Fathers and Mothers work and slave for little money while trying to give us the best that they can. It is time for the youth of Mexico to stand united and support their efforts. We need to spread the word of the revolution and change the world and our future. Are you all with me?" she pleaded, and was satisfied when all eyes turned towards her and nodded yes.

__Chapter Seventeen__

Carmelita María Ríos Carreras

In Cananea, Carmelita was almost as well-known as Colonel Greene. She was a striking young woman who had inherited the very best features of her mixed heritage and had a tall, well rounded physique, raven black hair, very straight teeth, which was quite unusual for a non-European, penetrating grey/green eyes that seemed to sparkle as she spoke, and a lovely singing voice that was earthy and hypnotizing although somewhat thin and high pitched. Her waist was very narrow and accentuated both her hips and breasts. Her fingers were long and thin, as were her legs. Carmelita could not hide her natural beauty and physical attributes and this made her a target for every man in Cananea, for she was truly beautiful and desirable.

She was the only soloist in the choir, and loved to sing with the Church, and was a stout believer in the Catholic religion. Her looks contradicted her predilection to her chaste beliefs and, although she did not try to hide her charms in the way she dressed, neither did she accentuate them. She was first and foremost dedicated to family, and her outgoing personality ingratiated her to all she met.

Even the women, who would ordinarily be jealous of her, did not harbor any ill feelings, because Carmelita did not seem all that interested in boys, and was never flirtatious. She was too busy. She was a virtual mother to the twins during the week, preparing them for school and walking them there on her way to her own class, and after school she either went to the Church for choir practice or went to the company store where she worked as a clerk.

The manager of the company store, Geraldo Tomaso, loved Carmelita for what she was, but also because she brought in so much business. Men would come in to the store after work, whether they needed anything or not, just to look at her. Geraldo had tried to get her to come to work for him full time, and at a handsome wage, but she was focused on finishing her classes with hopes she would one day be able to leave Cananea and Mexico, and set up a life for herself in the United States.

Carmelita was always well turned out. She couldn't afford new clothes very often, but she had her pick of the used goods that Geraldo sold. The American women who visited or lived at Casa Greene would sell their used clothing at a very fair price to help the company store and hope to improve the overall look of the women in town. One thing that could be said of Colonel Greene was that he was generous to a fault. When he had money, he would buy gifts for his family and friends, and even though there was severe unrest at the mines in Cananea, it was a fact that the miners there were paid better than at any other mine in Mexico. His hunting trips were legendary, and he often hosted the wealthiest men in America at Casa Greene, as the women would visit with Mrs. Greene and spend their time enjoying the warm days and cool nights on the mountainside.

Mrs. Greene encouraged the women to bring their old clothing to Cananea to be sold at a fraction of the original price to the miners' wives so the town would look as respectable as a mining town could be. It was a wonderful gesture, but the people were so poor that they could barely afford food, much less finer clothing.

Carmelita took full advantage of these items and was always there to get first pick when the new clothes came to the store, and it didn't hurt that her physique was closer to that of the American women than the *mestizos* who shopped there. She would often mix outfits and pair the peasant blouse, which her mother made for her with colored ribbons, and skirts that she bought cheap at the store. Geraldo always gave her an "employee discount" although such a thing did not exist, because he knew that people came to see Carmelita. She was tall and thin and her skin was so fair as to be almost white, and she held herself with a regal air about her and her shoulders back and her head held high. She seemed oddly out of place with the *mestizo* and native women of the town and if you didn't know it or look too closely at her hands, which were workers hands with chipped polish and callouses, you would think she was a wealthy American who had come to visit.

Her dream was to be a singer in a local nightclub, and eventually to marry and settle down in a small home that she could call her own. She was like her mother in that way, both dreamers and singers and with visions of things that most people could never imagine could become a reality. Carmelita was determined to make her dream a reality. It would take an act of God to stop her doing what she wanted to do, and her sights were firmly set on the future.

Every night when she went to bed, as she said her prayers before sleep, she asked God to help her find a way to become what she wanted to be. Her mother had told her that the U.S. border was less than 75 miles away, less than two days' ride on horseback. She knew she could get to the border once she had her money saved, and she would find a job in a store, or maybe even singing in a cantina.

One evening in the middle of the week, when Carmelita arrived at the company store for her shift, she was nearly run over by a miner who was running out of the store screaming at the top of his lungs.

"You common thief, your prices are outrageous! If I had the time and money I could go to Naco and find the same items for a tenth of what you charge. Keep your cheap, lousy merchandise. I'll wait until I can buy a quality product for cash."

With this invective he went stumbling off muttering an apology beneath his breath, "*Disculpe, Señorita,*" to Carmelita.

She was used to such emotions. The company stores were a necessary evil in Cananea and in many parts of Mexico, and were run by the companies who had built operations in remote locations and paid low wages. People were upset with the structure and necessity of company stores, including Carmelita's parents.

The company (in this case it was the Four C's, but the practice was prevalent throughout the remote regions of Mexico at various mining operations, textile mills, and others) would lease property to a third party at a fairly high rate and the workers were required to buy from the company store.

The company issued scrip or *vales* in advance of the workers' pay that could be used only by that person to buy goods. At the end of the week, when pay was issued, the value of the *vales* was deducted from their pay.

The cost of these goods was often higher than in a competitive environment and frequently the quality was poorer. The company received a commission from any purchases, and by advancing the scrip to the workers kept them indebted and also guaranteed that a portion of their pay was, in essence, paid back to the company. The miners felt this was a paternalistic practice and a form of indentured servitude.

This was nearly as large an issue for the workers, and almost as great an incentive to strike, as the long hours and low pay. This practice, called *tienda de raya* had been outlawed by the Mexican government and was seen as a device to exploit the workers, but as with many laws in Mexico, exceptions were made if a case could be argued. One of Greene's Vice Presidents had gone to Mexico City, where Greene was well liked and respected and had many, many friends, and argued that the system was necessary because a large percentage of laborers and employees were so poor that they could not wait until payday to purchase necessary food and other goods and the *vales* helped them between pay periods. The argument was successful and the practice continued. None of the government negotiators ever brought up the concept of paying higher wages or paying the workers more frequently to help them out as an alternative to the scrip, which only helped the PLM further incite the peons to revolt.

"*Hola*, Geraldo." Carmelita called out as she entered the shop for her shift.

"*Hola*, Carmelita. I am happy to have you here. I suppose you saw Paco leaving just now?" Geraldo asked.

"*Sí*, he did not seem happy" Carmelita commented.

Geraldo responded "No one seems happy with the prices we have here at the store, but I have to keep prices high because my rent is high, and the only way to get my goods here is to use company transportation. There is no way I can do better than what I am doing, but no one seems to believe that. I try to buy goods of a little lower quality to keep costs down, but then I get complaints about that. Then we have the beautiful clothing that Mrs. Greene has donated, but I cannot give them away and it is a luxury for so many. I just don't know what to do. If you weren't here, I don't think anyone would ever come to my store, except for the fact that they have no other choice."

He shuffled back into the storeroom and just as he disappeared, Julio Esperanza ran into the store shouting "Carmelita – come quick. Your mother is very sick and had been taken to the infirmary. Your father needs you right away!"

Carmelita dropped what she was doing and ran out of the store with Julio, shouting back to Geraldo that she had to leave and didn't know when she would be back. She didn't know if he heard her or not, but now was not the time to worry about that.

"Julio, what's wrong?" she asked as they ran down the path that led to the infirmary. Fortunately for Carmelita, the company store was located close to the grouping of municipal buildings where the infirmary was located as were other service businesses, such as the bank and blacksmith shop.

"I don't know, Carmelita, I was told to run and get you quickly. I know nothing more" he replied.

Carmelita entered the sparse three room building that housed the infirmary for the mining company. This was a place where injuries and other ailments were triaged, not treated. It was small and cramped and always full. The mining company also supported and ran a small hospital that was located on the road out of Cananea heading toward Naco, a small town that was split at the border, as many had been after the Gadsden Purchase, and which retained the same town name on both sides. It was located close enough to get there in an emergency, but far enough that it was not a constant reminder of the illnesses and injuries suffered every day in the mines.

She saw Manuel, and immediately ran to him. "What's wrong, papa?" she asked breathlessly.

"Your mother, Carmelita, the doctor is not sure, but it seems she is having a problem with her kidneys. He thinks there is a problem with her blood and it is causing complications, something to do with blood sugar. It is a common ailment among our people, but she has never been diagnosed with this. He calls it diabetes and that she has probably had this for many years and says it can lead to kidney failure." Manuel responded.

For all the seemingly backward ways of much of the country, Cananea was so close in

317

proximity to the U.S., and there was such a large American population, that some of the services that were available to the residents of Cananea were far superior to that of the rest of Mexico. The infirmary and hospital were among the things that had advanced in the area as the population grew and the mines made more money, but this had occurred out of necessity due to the high incidence of injury and disease, an irony not lost on the organizers of the workers unions.

Carmelita was stunned. This was so sudden. Her mother was so young and vibrant, only thirty four years old. She could not imagine her having a health issue.

"Can I see her, is she going to be O.K.?" she asked her father.

"*Sí*, my child, she asked for you." He hesitated then continued, "Carmelita, it is not good. I know this is very sudden, but the doctor says she is in a very serious condition and they do not have a cure. All those times she was carrying her flask of sugar water and tea, we thought it was just her way, but the doctor says she did it because she needed the sugar even though she may not have known that. They say there are new methods being tried to treat this affliction, but they would have to transport her all the way to the United States and with the roads as they are, she would never make it. Be strong, my child. Show her your love, and not your fear," Manuel counseled.

Carmelita gingerly opened the door to her mother's room and stepped in quietly. "Mama?' she called quietly, "are you awake?"

""Come in, my child" Edelmida whispered.

"Mama..I…"

"Hush, Carmelita. I spoke to the doctor and my condition is not good. I didn't even know I had this problem, even after having all three of my children, but they tell me it can come on later in life and I guess that is what happened to me." Edelmida looked drained and almost pale. Her lips were swollen and had turned very dark and her skin by comparison looked yellow. Her eyes were red and her hair was matted with sweat. Carmelita had never even seen her mother sick before, so this came as a complete shock.

"Mama, is there anything I can do to help?" she pleaded.

Carmelita was only sixteen, but she was a very bright woman and extremely mature for her age. She could not face the possibility that her mother was so ill and might die. She began to pray silently to the Lord, asking him to help her, to make her, Carmelita, sick instead of her mother. She suddenly felt so alone and empty, as if she had no home, no life, no happiness.

"Carmelita, listen to me. I have something I have to tell you." Her mother started to cough and there was a tiny bit of spittle tinged with blood at the corner of her mouth. Carmelita began to shake,

319

but willed herself to look strong in spite of what she felt inside.

"Carmelita, you are my oldest child and one of the strongest people I know, man or woman. I need you to carry on for me and take care of your sister and brother and father. Manuel is a good and strong man, but he is useless with the children. Things are very difficult now here in Cananea and you are our best hope for the future. Do you feel up to the task?" Edelmida asked sincerely.

"Mama, I … I don't want you to talk like this. We will get you better. You will be fine if you just rest a while and …."

"Carmelita – *pajarito* - listen to me. I know how you feel. I lost my mother when I was born and never even knew her. I cannot tell you how important it is to me to have you, and what you have meant to me. We are closer than any two people I have ever known. Even more than me and your father." Edelmida had tears well up in her eyes and had to choke back the emotion rising up through her chest.

"Carmelita, promise me you will take care of everyone. Promise."

Although she could barely speak, she quietly choked out the words, "I promise, Mama."

Edelmida closed her eyes and took a deep breath. She lay so quietly that Carmelita wasn't sure if she was still breathing. With her eyes still closed, she said in a soft, sad voice "Carmelita, *parijito*, before you were born, I had an unspeakable thing happen to me. Something I have been so ashamed of that I have never told anyone about it, and only two people in the world even know this happened to me. I need you to promise me that you will take what I tell you to your grave and will never tell anyone what I am about to say. Can you promise me this, Carmelita?"

Carmelita was confused. She knew her mother to be a devote Catholic, dedicated to her family and of the highest moral character and strength. She could not imagine that she may have done something to be ashamed of.

"Of course, Mama. I will not breathe a word to a soul. What happened?" Carmelita replied somberly.

Edelmida told her daughter about the brutal rape by Thom MacMurrough/*El Diablo*, and how she had repaid his repulsive act by stealing and hiding the Amulet in his room, and drawing attention to him by whispering to the kitchen staff, who had then spread the suspicion. She described not only his actions and the unspeakable horror she suffered, but every detail of his looks, the shock of red hair, his bony, wiry body and the knife that he always has at his side. She told her of her deep depression, and the difficulty she faced in trying to get her life back together. She spoke rapidly and without pause, keeping her eyes closed the entire time and barely stopping to take a breath. When she had finished her soliloquy, she paused, slowly opened her eyes and, with her head down, stole a glance at Carmelita.

Her daughter was staring into the middle distance with her sparkling grey/green eyes pondering what she had heard. Her mouth was open slightly and she was pale and seemed frozen in place. The legend of the missing Amulet had been part of the folklore of Cananea since she was born. It had been passed down from person to person in whispers, and was never discussed out loud in public. The story was considered by many to be just that – a story that had become legend with no basis in reality. It was the type of story that teenage girls told to each other at night when the lights were down, to scare each other in the wee hours before sleep. Slowly, she turned to her mother and asked the one question Edelmida was hoping to avoid, "Mama, when did this all happen?"

"Carmelita, you have to understand that all of this happened before I married your father. The reason I tell you all this is because the Amulet was never recovered. I heard that *El Diablo* always suspected me of setting him up, but he has no proof. I thought he somehow got hold of the Amulet and would try to retaliate, but that never happened. I wanted you to know all this, because perhaps someday you can search for it and it will bring you good fortune. It is a lucky piece and everyone who has had it has benefited by it in some way."

Edelmida began to breathe heavily and shut her eyes tight.

"But… Mama," Carmelita hesitated. Could he be my father?"

<u>Chapter Eighteen</u>

Blood and Water

Cassidy was waiting in Bisbee for Jack Durand to return. He was sure Durand would have possession of the Amulet, and Cassidy had buyers all lined up for the gold and the gems. He didn't want to take any chances that someone would recognize the piece, or worse, that Colonel Greene would have a reward out for its return. Greene had substantial holdings in Bisbee, where one of his companies was a clearing house for importing his copper matte and transporting it to refining operations across the U.S.

Cassidy knew that, once broken up, the item would bring a pittance of its' real worth, but it would be more than enough to give him a fresh start. He thought about where he would go next and considered heading down to the Argentine Republic which intrigued him greatly. A number of his allies in Ireland had emigrated there recently, and he had heard wild tales of the *Señoritas* of Buenos Aires and a new dance called the tango, which was said to be very sexual and arousing.

Bisbee was growing into a large town, but Cassidy knew that Greene had eyes everywhere, so he was careful to keep a low profile since he had a feeling that there was a watch put out by Francisco de Torres in the event he showed near the border within range of Cananea. Cassidy grew a pathetic looking, straggling beard and moustache, for his Irish complexion did not allow for much hair growth, and with the Stetson he had been wearing, which was now soiled and beat up, he passed through town shunted and not given a second glance.

He avoided any thoughts of young women and spent his time at the fringes of society looking for the right parties to buy the gold and gems with no questions asked. It was a little difficult to do, for most people with the kind of money he needed wouldn't touch a treasure like this if they had any inkling of its source or true value. So Cassidy decided that when he and Durand got to Bisbee, they would sell one of each jewel to a different buyer spread out over a week or two. They would also melt down the gold by dropping a few ounces at a time into cool water to create nuggets, and sell those a little at a time to avoid any possibility of identifying a single source for their wealth. Durand hit upon an idea that Cassidy embraced and wished he had thought of himself.

There were plenty of new "miners" in these towns, those who had come from the East seeking their fortunes. The magazines and news stories painted a picture of easily found wealth by simply panning for gold, a task that, in reality, brought little wealth at all. However, the nuggets that these plebeian newcomers were panning for were not

325

finished pieces of gold, but rather raw rock, which took a true eye and knowledge to detect. Durand conceived of a plan to sell a real gold nugget culled from the amulet to these amateurs at a low price. The nuggets would be shiny and bright, which is what most of them expected, trusting them with the piece to have it appraised with promises of many more to be acquired when they verified its value. They would then manufacture false "nuggets" by the pound and sell these to the gullible greenhorns at a premium, thereby doubling to tripling their take. Cassidy was thrilled with idea and since they would be travelling from small town to small town, detection was considered to be minimal and worth the risk.

Cassidy didn't trust Durand any more than Durand trusted him, but he did believe that if anyone could find the Amulet, Durand was the one. Cassidy had looked into Durand's background and rumor had it that he had been a member of Díaz' famed and feared *Rurales* and had worked for the Russian madman, Emilio Kosterlitzky, the Moscow born mercenary who was legendary for his effective repression of insurrection through violent means. Kosterlitzky was a master in the art of *ley de fuga*. Evidence of this had been told many times about an incident that occurred when he and his men were patrolling through Ronquillo and a fight broke out between two of the Mexican workers, most likely fueled by liquor and caused by a common interest in a woman. Kosterlitzky evaluated the scene with disdain, then looked at the last two men in his patrol and nodded. They dropped off the line, rode to the disturbance, and proceeded to shoot the two instigators dead on the spot, thereby abruptly ending any further incidents. The two then re-entered the line as before, and the entire troop proceeded off as if nothing had happened. Such was the reputation of Kosterlitzky as a cold, calculating Cossack who took no prisoners and did not tolerate any type of anarchistic behavior.

Cassidy knew that Durand was of a similar mind, and that he would not hesitate to do what was necessary to advance his means, so he developed an alternate plan to deal with Durand when he arrived back in town. Cassidy had no friends, at least no one he could trust, and so there was no way that he could be alerted to Durand's approach.

After his years of training with the Irish insurrectionists, he had honed his instincts and he had a plan to divert Durand while he attempted his treachery.

Back in Cananea, Durand jumped on his steed and said his goodbye to Francisco. "Torres, thanks for being fair with me. In the *Rurales*, we would not be so forgiving. If you are ever in El Paso or Juarez, and need anything at all, let me know. I have friends everywhere there, and we can do or get you just about anything you need. *Adios, muchacho.*"

327

Francisco waved and watched as Durand's horse churned up the dry, brown, silica-laden dust, and galloped off to his meeting with Cassidy. Torres wondered what would happen when the two met and Cassidy found out Durand didn't have the cross. His bet was on Durand, and that would suit his purposes fine. With Cassidy out of the way, the mystery of the missing cross would finally be over. He would spread the word throughout the southwest, and make sure that everyone knew that Cassidy had taken the Amulet and been done in by Durand.

He thought to himself, "I think I might take Durand up on his offer. El Paso is a fun loving town with a growing need for security, and it's remote enough from Cananea to suit me. Easy to get across the border too, if I need to. I have waited sixteen long years for this drama to play itself out and my patience will be worth it. The anarchists are getting ready to pop and I don't want to be here when they do."

Meanwhile, Carmelita had left her mother after several hours of questions, crying, pleading, and praying, and all that changed was that Carmelita came away for the first time in her life wondering about her true father. She always knew she was different from the others, but had assumed it was due to the Spanish blood of her ancestors. She was not the only child who had vestiges of other races evident in her physical appearance.

Throughout all of Mexico, across the mountains, deserts, and plains throughout the region, without regard to borders, were a mix of different heritages, races, and colors. Although brown-eyed, brown-haired people were by far the most common, there were plenty of people of all ages who had red, and sometimes blondish hair, with light colored eyes.

Her mother had spoken to her of the cross and how she had duped everyone and put the blame on MacMurrough. She spoke of her loss of faith, and worry about Manuel, and what he would ever say if he were to find out what happened. She talked about her depression and desire to take her own life to spare that of others, and about her joy when the twins were born, ensuring that no matter what, Manuel had one child of each sex for certain. She spoke of the mystery of the missing cross and Colonel Greene's despondency over its loss, and the feeling that a precious artifact was lost to the world forever, and it was all her fault.

She finally said to Carmelita "*El cariño*, you are the love of my life. I am so incredibly proud of you. You are smart and beautiful and strong, and I wouldn't trade you for anything in the world. If your father and I hadn't met when we did and got married, it would not matter.

You are my first child, and I love you very, very much. I had to tell you this, because I fear I won't be here much longer. I could not go to God

329

with this heavy burden on my heart. He may not let me into heaven, but I'll go knowing I told the truth, and did everything I could while here on earth, to protect you and my family and keep you from shame. Please do not judge me Carmelita. Go with God your whole life and do what is right. I will always love you, my angel."

Carmelita left her mother with a broken heart. Not for herself, but for all the pain her mother had to live with for all these years. She walked alone with her head down not knowing what direction she was heading, or how long she had been walking, as she contemplated what to say and do when she next saw her father.

As she continued walking, she realized "First, I have to find out who my father *IS*."

Her mind grew clearer the more she walked, and her resolve grew stronger as she made a vow to herself to find out the truth.

"I will find this *El Diablo*, and when I look into his eyes, I will know if I am his or not. There is no other way to do this, I have to find out where he is, and I know just the person to help me. Francisco has always liked me, and although he has a tough exterior, I know he tell me where I can find MacMurrough."

With that, Carmelita lifted her head, only to find she was about to turn the corner at the blacksmith shop at the edge of town, not too far from the jail where Francisco could often be found. She decided to go and talk to him about

MacMurrough under the guise of asking about the Amulet. Everyone in Cananea knew of the Amulet, the history of how Colonel Greene came into its possession, and how MacMurrough was ridden out of town for stealing it.

Everyone also knew it had been missing for sixteen years, and most, who believed the story, thought it was still somewhere in Cananea. Carmelita would ask Francisco if there was any possibility that MacMurrough had hidden it and would come back for it. She would tell him that she was afraid, because of the rumors she heard about his way with young women, and wanted to be alert to the possibility of becoming a victim, as so many had before. Francisco would help her, and she could probably find out where MacMurrough was located.

As she came around the corner, she heard the smithy clanging out a beat on a heated horseshoe with his hammer and tongs, and looked up to see Francisco talking to a man on horseback with braided hair and a peaked hat. She immediately recognized him as the man who had detained her mother, the twins, and herself.

As she stepped up her pace, the stranger pulled on the reins of his horse to turn the head of his steed, and galloped away churning up a cloud of dust. Carmelita called out to Francisco, "*Señor* Torres!"

Raymond F. Cavanagh

He turned and saw her approaching, and the corners of his mouth turned up just a little, but not into what would ever be called a smile.

He called back, "Carmelita – what are you doing here at this time of day?" He thought she should be in school.

She came up to him, and with a serious look on her face, asked innocently, "Who was that man? He looked familiar."

"Oh, that was just an hombre from El Paso who had some business here with Colonel Greene. I'm sure you don't know him. Why are you here Carmelita? What's wrong?" he asked as he studied the look on her face.

Francisco scared a lot of people with his eye patch, somber disposition, and imposing size, but he had known Carmelita since she was an infant and he always seemed to have a soft spot for her. She didn't know why, but she always felt he knew something that he didn't share. Carmelita was very comfortable with him and knew that he would protect her at all costs. Theirs was an unusual friendship, if it could be called that, with Francisco more than twice her age.

She tucked away the comment about El Paso and asked him, "Have you heard about my mother? She is very sick."

He looked at her and slowly nodded his head.

"*Señor* Torres, my mother told me about the evil man, MacMurrough. She's very worried that he

332

hid Colonel Greene's cross and will come back for it someday, and she's frightened for me. She thinks that if he comes here and sees me, he will know who I am because of my resemblance to my mother, and will try to harm me. She has me worried and I don't want her to die with that on her mind. Can you tell me anything about this MacMurrough?" she pleaded.

Francisco inhaled a long breath through his nose and held it for what seemed like minutes. When he finally let it out, he got down on one knee and looked up into her grey/green eyes, and could see the gold flecks sparkling in the waning hours of the evening sun.

"Carmelita," he said while looking straight up into her eyes and holding her gaze, "MacMurrough will never bother anyone ever again. Of that, I can promise you. I can also promise you that the gold cross will be accounted for soon, and everyone will know that he did not hide it here. Do you believe me?"

Carmelita did believe him, but she had to know more, she had to know where MacMurrough was, and why Francisco could be so sure.

"Of course, I believe you *Señor*, but how can you be so sure? Do you know where the evil man is? How do you know we'll ever find out about the cross?"

Francisco stood up and took her slim hand in his and told her, "That man you just saw came from

Bisbee, where he had problems with MacMurrough. MacMurrough had the cross, but broke it down for the jewels and gold and sold it all. He told that man to come and let me know that we will never see him or the Amulet again just for spite. He wanted to let me know that the Amulet IS lucky and he got all the luck. He said a few other things about me and others that are not for your ears, but he especially wanted me to tell Colonel Greene. I'm afraid the Colonel's head will pop when I tell him all this. He, and almost everyone else, always believed that the cross was still here in Cananea hidden somewhere. MacMurrough said he is leaving the continent and that we'll never find him."

"I struck a deal with this hombre who has no use for MacMurrough. It is now my job to wait until the man who just rode away sends me a telegram from Bisbee confirming MacMurrough was there and has now gone. If he has not left, then his job is to capture and hold him and I will meet him in Bisbee to enforce justice."

He looked at her and shook her hand as if to say "this is a pact between us," and his lie was so convincing, that he almost believed what he had told her himself.

"OK" Carmelita agreed. "I see why you're so sure. *Gracias*, *Señor* Torres. I will tell my mother that you have assured me he will not be back, and that the cross will be in safe hands. She will be able to go to her rest peacefully."

She gingerly took her hand out of his, waved, and turned to head back in the direction of her mother's sick room. Now she had to find a way to get to Bisbee quickly.

__Chapter Nineteen__

Truth or Consequences

It was at the time Manuel and Pedro were about to attend the PLM meeting earlier that day that Manuel had received the message that Edelmida was seriously ill. "Pedro, go on ahead without me. I know there's a vote to strike tonight. Tell the union you have my vote. I only hope it's not too serious with Edelmida. She's never been sick for as long as I've known her. If I don't get back here before the meeting ends, come find me and tell me what happened."

"*Sí*, Manuel. Give Edelmida my best wishes and tell her I'll keep her in my prayers," Pedro responded.

Manuel hurried off to the infirmary where he spent time with the doctor before seeing Edelmida.

"It's not good Manuel. I don't really think she's going to last the night, but I can't tell her that. I sent a telegram to a doctor in Bisbee who's well known for treating this type of disorder, and I'm hoping he can give me some guidance, but I haven't heard back yet. I suggest you spend a little time with her and give her all the support you can. If there's anything at all you want to discuss with her before she dies, I suggest you do it now."

Manuel was stunned. "Die?" he thought to himself. "How could she die? She's young and vibrant. A pillar of strength. How could someone who is so tough succumb to anything like this? She had defeated one of the meanest people either of us had ever known, Thom MacMurrough. Well, there is no time to think about this, I have to go in there and be strong. I have to show her strong resolve, so she will have strength."

Manuel took a deep breath and entered the space behind the curtain where Edelmida laid on a bed made of corn husks and rabbit fur on cross beams of unfinished boards. He smiled at her, and bit the inside of his cheek to keep from reacting to the way she looked.

"My little sparrow," he began gently, for her eyes were closed and he didn't know if she was asleep. She turned to look at him and smiled.

"*Hola*, Manuel. Sorry I can't get up to give you a kiss." They looked at each other and he held her hand and kissed her lightly on the forehead.

"Edelmida, the doctor says he sent a note to another doctor in Bisbee and he thinks he ..."

"Hush, Manuel" Edelmida interrupted, "you don't need to try and cheer me up. I've made my peace with the Lord and I'm ready to make my peace with you. I need to speak with Carmelita as soon as she can get here. Have you sent for her yet?"

"No, I'll send for the children after you and I spend some time…"

Again Edelmida interrupted, "No, I don't want the twins to see me like this. They're too young, and I want them to remember me as I was, not as I am now. Carmelita is a young woman. Strong and smart. I need her to be here for me. Can you get her right away, *por favor*? I know you don't want to hear this, but I don't really think I have much time left."

Manuel looked at her with sad eyes, and inside, his heart was breaking, but he agreed and sent for Carmelita.

He waited while his wife and daughter spoke for what seemed like a very long time. Manuel loved them both very much and knew that they always had a very special relationship. He could never quite put his finger on it, but there was some type of bond between them that he could never penetrate. He always felt a little distant from Carmelita and could not understand why her ties to her mother were so much closer than they were to him. His friends with girls all told him that the special bond was between a father and his daughter, yet Edelmida and Carmelita had a bond that he was not a part of. It was so much different with the twins. Edelmida loved them as much as anything in the world, but it was a clear, mother-to-child affinity. With Carmelita, it was much more, they were mother and daughter, but also close friends and they shared an intimacy that transcended that

338

unique and special bond that a father could never understand.

Carmelita finally came out, after speaking to Edelmida for what seemed like hours.

"Carmelita, you were in there for a very long time. What did your mother say to you? Do you think she'll be alright?"

"Papa, mama is very strong, but I'm afraid she won't be able to beat this horrible thing that's taken over her body. She said I will need to be both mother and sister to the twins and I should help you in any way I can. And for that, she said I'll need the patience of a saint. She asked me to pray to God that the mines won't take you away, and to make sure the children grow up with a strong faith."

"She wants to be sure they get a good education so they can move to a new and better place. Mama would never leave Cananea, but she wants more for her children. She made me vow that I would take care of them and somehow, some way, move them across the border. She wants you to go with us and make a new home no matter what the cost."

Manuel hung his head and choked back tears. He and Edelmida had long talked about packing up and moving, but neither one of them had much English, and with the children it would be so difficult that they could never seem to find a way to make it happen. They had no money and lived off the mines using *vales* to pay for their food and

339

clothes, thereby indebting them further to the company store. It seemed they would never get out from under the debt and could only dream of moving away with the family to start a better life.

Manuel went back into the area where Edelmida lay and spent a little more time with his wife. After what seemed like minutes, but was actually hours the doctor told him to go home, that Edelmida needed to rest. Reluctantly, he said goodbye and kissed her goodnight.

"I will be here early in the morning, my sparrow," he softly whispered in her ear. "Sleep well and dream of me. I will pray you are better tomorrow."

Manuel left to go home and tell the children about their mother but when he got there he was surprised to find that Carmelita wasn't there. Instead, the sous chef from the kitchen at Casa Greene, Tepin, was watching the children and didn't know where Carmelita had gone; only that she "had an errand to run."

Manuel thanked her for watching the children and said good night wondering where Carmelita could have gone at this hour as her poor mother lay dying. As Tepin was leaving, Pedro came running down the street towards Manuel, calling out "They voted to strike! The PLM and the Mine Workers Union both had the votes to strike!"

As he came closer, he slowed down his gait. In a more conversational yet excited tone continued, "A date hasn't been set yet, and it was decided to

340

try one last time to negotiate. But no one believes it will not happen. We're going to strike, At long last we will see about an honest day's pay for an honest day's work. The terms demanded will be five pesos per day for eight hours of work and naming a percentage of our people as supervisors."

As he came to Manuel's side, he saw the look of despondency on his face and said "I'm sorry Manuel. What's wrong? How is Edelmida?"

"She's not good Pedro. I'm very concerned. The doctor doesn't seem to have much hope. He's trying to reach a doctor in Bisbee to see if there's another treatment, but hasn't heard back yet. Carmelita spent quite a bit of time with her, but now she isn't at home and I don't know where she's gone. The sous chef from the Casa who works with Edelmida, Tepin, tells me that she had stopped in to her adobe and asked her to watch the twins while she ran an errand for her sick mother. That's all I know, and I can't imagine where she might have gone. Now I'm worried about her as well. Can you do me a big favor? Can you stay here while I go look for Carmelita? There's a bottle of mescal in the kitchen and you're welcome to enjoy it while I'm gone. The children are already asleep."

"Of course, Manuel. Just stop at my place on your way and let my wife know where I am. Take your time. I'll stay all night if you need me to. Let me know if there's anything more I can do to help."

Manuel walked towards town and fell beside Tepin, escorting her to her adobe. Along the way they asked everyone in their path if they had seen Carmelita. She was so well known in town that he was sure he could find someone who would have seen her. He passed the cantina, which was packed to overflowing with people spilling out the door, whooping and shouting about the strike and calling out to Manuel to come in for a drink.

He just walked on by with his head down, waving them off. "Fools," he thought to himself, "don't they know that the whole town will know about the strike, and the security officers will do whatever they can to stop it? What are they thinking?"

He shook his head at them and when he got a little farther down the road, he poked his head into the company store and asked Geraldo if he had seen Carmelita. "*Sí*, Manuel, she was here. I heard about Edelmida's illness. I'm very sorry. Carmelita came and asked if she could borrow some money. She said there was a doctor in Bisbee who might be able to help, and she had to catch the train to Naco, and then another to Bisbee. She was in an awful rush. I thought you knew about this, no?"

Manuel dropped his head. He should have known Carmelita would take such a direct approach. But she had never ventured far from Cananea, and had never been on the train before. He was surprised that she would do this now.

Edelmida's doctor must have told her about the specialist in Bisbee, and she decided to take matters into her own hands and go and see if she could get her mother the help she needed.

"Geraldo, do you know what time the train leaves?" Just as he finished asking the question the train whistle blew and Manuel instantly realized it was leaving the station. The two men looked at each other blankly, but there was nothing they could do. There wouldn't be another train until morning, and a horse or wagon would take too long. Besides, Manuel couldn't leave the twins and Edelmida. He supposed he could ask someone to go after her, if he could find anyone who was sober enough.

"I'll need to talk to Francisco de Torres in the morning," he thought to himself. He wondered what Carmelita was possibly thinking. He dejectedly headed back to his home and his children, wondering what could happen next.

As the train left the station, Carmelita stared out the window wondering if she was doing the right thing. She was a little scared, but also excited, knowing that she had such important business in Bisbee. She had told Geraldo at the company store that she was going to Bisbee to find the doctor and make sure he contacted Edelmida's doctor in Cananea, but she knew that no doctor would be able to save her mother now. She also knew that the doctors agreed to speak to each other the following day on the house phone from the Four C's offices.

In her heart, she knew that nothing could save her mother's life now, and her more urgent need was to confront *El Diablo*. She believed in her heart that once she had the chance to look in his eyes, she would know if he was her father or not. She could then return to Cananea and tell her mother what she had learned, and send her to her final resting place in peace.

It had been an emotionally draining day, finding out that her mother may die soon, and then that her father, after all these years, may turn out not to be her father at all. She knew that Manuel would find out where she had gone, but she had two good reasons to go, and nothing was going to stop her. She thought to herself "By tomorrow night I will have had a look into *Señor* MacMurrough's eyes and spoken to the doctor in Bisbee about my mothers' condition. I will talk to *El Diablo* about my mother and I will know if he is my father. Only then will I have to decide what to do."

She turned to look out the window and fell into a deep sleep, where she dreamed of golden pagan idols that sprang to life and chased her through a strange town with narrow streets and into the mouth of a mine shaft. As she ran deeper and deeper into the dark and stale smelling hollow, she heard the timbers give way and felt the bumping earth beneath her feet shift as she realized the roof had collapsed, trapping her in the dark.

She woke with a start and found herself shaking, with saliva oozing from the corner of her mouth. She looked about her wildly trying to get her bearings, but the train droned on, and all the other passengers were either asleep or absorbed by a book or a deck of cards.

She settled back down and laid her head back trying to get some rest, but her mind was working too fast. The best she could muster was to close her eyes and try to imagine what it would be like to meet MacMurrough. She prayed that her dream wasn't a premonition of things to come.

Back at the border in Naco, Jack Durand decided to spend the night thinking about how he would handle Cassidy when he got to Bisbee. His horse was spent. Naco was only a few of hours ride south of Bisbee, but he wanted to arrive fresh in the morning and face Cassidy on his own terms. He found a room down the street from the stables, and went off to the local saloon for a bite to eat and a beer.

He suspected that Cassidy was planning to double cross him. It was either that, or he had already skipped town after succeeding in sending Durand on this wild goose chase. But Durand knew men like Cassidy, and he knew in his heart that Cassidy believed the cross was in Cananea and he would be waiting for Durand's return. To Jack, that meant Cassidy had a plan to get the cross from him and kill him, because that's just what Durand would do. He also knew that if he didn't show up with the cross, Cassidy wouldn't wait. It would be a

345

showdown, and if that happened, he had to be sure he knew that Consuelo was safe.

Durand had to come up with a counter plan and figure a way to neutralize Cassidy, and be rid of him once and for all without jeopardizing his sister. As he sat sipping his beer, forsaking anything stronger so he could keep a relatively clear head, he could never imagine the role that Carmelita would play in the drama about to unfold.

As Durand sat in the saloon plotting his next move, Cassidy sat in Bisbee, biding his time, and waiting for word from Durand. He cursed himself for not suggesting that Durand contact him when he was on his way so he could prepare, but knew the first thing he would do when he arrived in town was look for his sister, Consuelo. He would have to be ready on a moment's notice of his arrival, so he couldn't enjoy the fine whiskey and women of Bisbee this night, and he also had to keep a very close eye on Consuelo. Without her as insurance, he had nothing, and she was a cagey character. He thought to himself, "If I were Durand, I'd come into town early, no later than noon, while the town is bustling with people. I can't trust him. There's no reason why, once he has me out of the way, that he can't line up his own sources to sell the jewels and gold, or just take the cross back to Juarez with him. He'll look for Consuelo, so I need to keep her close to use as an exchange for the golden cross."

Carmelita's train approached Naco in late afternoon as the sun began to cast long shadows and imbued a burnt orange cast over the town. Naco was much smaller than Cananea, and one of the many border towns that had been torn in two when the U.S. took territories from Mexico after the Treaty of Guadalupe Hidalgo and the Gadsden Purchase expansion.

Carmelita knew that Colonel Greene had operations in Naco, as well as in Bisbee, and it made her feel a little safer that so many things seemed familiar, since the towns had so much in common. She also felt that there must be people in town that she would know from Cananea, although she would never expect to see any of them.

Geraldo had been very generous and had given her enough to get to Bisbee and for a hotel and food for the night, but she had to be very frugal. If she ran out of money here, it would be very difficult for her to get back.

Crossing the border was still easy, but the rumor was that things would become more difficult for Mexicans to cross into the U.S. The influx of workers into the States to work on the railroads, and the easy passage between the two countries was going to become more difficult. It was always easy to go north to south, but anyone heading into the U.S. from Mexico was now being watched more closely. It was said that this year, 1906, they would initiate more formal border crossings here at Naco, as well as Nogales, and other smaller border towns.

Many of the larger towns, like Juarez/El Paso already had strict guidelines for crossing.

When Carmelita inquired about catching the next train to Bisbee, she was disappointed to learn that the last train had already left, and the next one wouldn't leave until ten o'clock the next morning. She noticed a stagecoach station attached to a small barn across, and just down the street, from where she had crossed the border. She headed in that direction determined to find a quicker way to Bisbee. Carmelita knew that the ride to Bisbee only took a few hours, so she decided to see if she could take the stage that night and find a place to stay, in order to awake refreshed and begin her search for MacMurrough early in the morning.

She approached the stagecoach and saw a young man with his head down, cleaning the wheels and undercarriage, who appeared to be much younger than she. "*Perdón, muchacho*, do you know when the stage will be running to Bisbee, *por favor*?"

The young man turned his head, looked up, and saw Carmelita standing there with the fading sun behind her. The vision of her in a white peasant blouse and a long cotton dress of patterned material, with scarlet ribbons in her hair and the most beautiful light colored eyes he had ever seen, that seemed to sparkle at him as she spoke, took his breath away.

He slowly straightened up, and stammered, as he tried to get his tongue around his words.

"*Señorita*, the stage only operates every other day from here to Bisbee, on the way to Tombstone. It is usually booked well in advance. The Apache tribes cause us great problems, so the times are staggered to make it difficult for them to know when we will be passing through. Can I help you find a hotel to stay the night and we can check availability in the morning?" he finally managed to say.

She looked at him and thought he seemed to be such a nice young man. He had short straw colored hair, like she had never seen before, and very light skin with a few brown freckles across his nose. His eyes were sky blue and he had pronounced front teeth, and he seemed to whistle when he said "*Señorita* and stage." He was a good six inches taller than her five foot six inch height and the corners of his mouth were upturned as if he had a perpetual smile.

"I need to get to Bisbee tonight" she said urgently. "I know it's not very far. Isn't there some other way to get there?"

""Ma'am, it's right dangerous to go out after sundown, The Apache, they don't like people on their land at all, and if they come upon you at night, there's no tellin' what might happen," he replied. "There's a couple nice hotels in town I can recommend, and I can get you a good deal too."

He gave her a grin and started to walk towards the town, when she raised her voice and called out to his turned back in a demanding tone, "Who owns this coach?"

He turned back to her and softly replied "Why, I do Ma'am. My Pa used to run the stage to Tombstone and back every other day, but he got killed by the Apache, and when the horses run back here, I took up the trade. It is all I have left. My Ma died on the journey out here from Tennessee."

He looked so young and vulnerable that Carmelita could not believe he ran this stage through such a wild and dangerous country.

"How old are you, if you don't mind my asking?" Carmelita inquired.

"I'm eighteen, Ma'am. My name's Gideon, Gideon Riot. I know – it's an unusual name. Rumor has it that our ancestors started a riot after the revenuers tried to tax them for selling moonshine, and the name stuck and became legal somehow. I don't know if that's true, but I sure get a lot of funny looks about it. I've been running this stage every other day, except on Sundays, for the past three and a half months now. I've learned to shoot real well, and I've turned aside every attempt to hold up the stage, although in truth, it's only happened twice. Believe me, Ma'am, I would take you if I thought it was safe."

Carmelita was on the verge of tears. So much had happened in such a short period of time and her emotions were hanging by a thread. She approached the young man and told him the whole story of her mother and MacMurrough and why she had to get to Bisbee right away. She said that she knew Durand was on his way there, and had to get there as soon as she could, or she feared he would kill MacMurrough and she would never learn the truth.

He looked at her and then at the sky as the sun was cresting at the tops of the horizon and asked, "Is that all your stuff with you, right there?"

She nodded, and he bent down and picked up her clothes which were wrapped in a serape, and tied with rope and said emphatically, "Let's go right now. It'll take us a little more than an hour; we'll be taking a roundabout route. We won't take the coach, we'll take the buckboard, which is open, so if we run into any injuns they'll see we have no goods with us and might let us by. This is their mealtime, and we might get lucky. Can you shoot?"

Carmelita looked at him as a laugh bubbled up from her chest in spite of the seriousness of the situation. His boyish good looks, and funny little whistle when he talked made it all seem kind of comical, but she knew it was dead serious. She shook her head no.

Gideon went to the barn, quickly hitched up the horse to the buckboard, threw her bundle of clothes in the back, and handed her a thick woolen blanket. "Here, cover your head and let the blanket fall to the floor. If any injuns see us, I don't want them to know you're a woman."

He took up the reins and with a loud "Giddyap!" slapped them on the horse's back and they took off like a bullet from a gun headed for Bisbee.

Chapter Twenty

Discovery

Warm arid air and a brilliant blue sky greeted the day of Saturday, May 5, 1906 in Naco, Arizona. This was the date that Mexicans in Puebla celebrated their victory over the French, who had invaded Mexico after their failure to pay debts accumulated during the Mexican-American and Mexican Civil wars. The French, as well as the Spanish and English, had supported the effort for Mexico's independence. However, former Mexican *Presidente* Benito Juárez, whose country was virtually bankrupt at that time, had decreed suspension of payments to the supporting countries for two years, and met with immediate resistance from the lending countries.

France lead the resistance against this offer, and the three countries signed the Treaty of London and sent expeditionary forces to Mexico to demand payment. The Spanish and English settled and accepted Mexico's offer to issue warrants to settle the debts in the future, but the French did not, and invaded the country in an effort to further to expand its empire under the leadership of Napoleon III. The Mexican militia, led by General Ignacio Zaragoza, defeated the French at the Battle of Puebla, but the defeat was short lived and the French eventually marched on Mexico City and installed Maximilian I, a member of the Imperial House of Hapsburg-Lorraine, and ex-Archduke of Austria, as Emperor of Mexico. His reign lasted only three tumultuous years, marked by insurrection, and he was overthrown by the forces of *Presidente* Juárez and his ally, future *Presidente* Porfirio Díaz. They were aided in this quest with financial backing from the United States, which had itself recently emerged from a civil war, and had just recently turned its attention back to its neighbor to the south.

Maximilian's wife, Carlotta, suffered an emotional breakdown and went back to Europe to rally support for her husband. He had been virtually abandoned by the French, but her efforts proved unsuccessful and he was eventually executed by the Mexican forces. Thus, the fifth of May became an important and festive day of Mexican national pride.

Jack Durand woke just after dawn, had coffee and a biscuit at the hotel bar, and saddled up for the quick ride up to Bisbee. Unlike Naco, which had one road in and out of town, Bisbee was a bustling town of twenty thousand people, and there were many ways to approach it undetected. He was ready for Cassidy, and eager to get the bastard, although he was unhappy and frustrated that he did not find the cross. Someone knew where it was, and he would find out who, but first it was time to take care of Cassidy once and for all.

Meanwhile, up in Bisbee, on the south side of town close to the Copper Queen mines, Cassidy awoke and knew in his bones that this was the day Durand would be back with the Amulet. He had chosen this location because Durand would have to pass through the area to get to the center of Bisbee, no matter what route he took to the center of town. The Copper Queen mine was the sole reason the town of Bisbee existed, and while the road past the mines eventually split into several different routes leading to the town, offering multiple routes to the center, only one road led from Naco to Bisbee before the split.

He had a premonition that something big was about to happen, and he went across the hall to Consuelo's room to see if she was awake and would like to take some breakfast. They had managed to stay apart, but close enough, for each to keep an eye on the other, and this would be the first time he would ask her to spend any time with him. They had each taken a room in a boarding house on the outskirts of town, across from each other at the back end of the hallway. The owner stayed in a suite at the front end of the hall by the head of the stairs, and there were only two other bedrooms in the house, each between the owners suite and Cassidy and Consuelo's rooms. To get in or out, one had to go downstairs through the living room, which was

355

kept locked between the hours of 9:30 at night until 6:30 in the morning. It would be difficult, if not impossible, for either of them to get away without the other knowing. Most of their days were spent at the boarding house passing time reading, whittling, or helping with chores just to keep busy. It was hell for them both, but there was no other choice.

Just as he was about to knock, Consuelo flung open the door and pushed a gun into his face.

"Whoa, whoa – no need for that. I just came to see if you wanted to have breakfast. I have a feeling we will see your brother today, and I need some good news. Like you, I can't wait to get out of here, split the goods and move on."

He gave her his best smile and cocked his head a little to the side. In spite of Cassidy's evil side, he could be charming when he wanted to be. A little elf of a man with his shock of red hair and diminutive size, he seemed to be no threat at all. The day was beautiful and she was hungry, and also felt that Jack would be there soon, so she saw no harm in sitting in the parlor over coffee and a home cooked meal.

"*Sí, chico*, I hope this is the last time I will have to see you. You first," she replied, uncocking the gun and hiding it in the folds of her skirt.

As they went down the stairs to have breakfast and wait for word from Durand, Carmelita awoke in a little hotel in Bisbee square. Stretching and yawning, she felt alive and full of energy, and wanted to run right out the door to find

356

MacMurrough and then head over to the doctor's office, before he got too busy with patients, so she could ask him if anything could be done to help her mother's condition.

She and Gideon Riot had arrived after a three hour ride through a dark and moonless night. Only the howl of the coyotes and the screech of an occasional bird broke the silence. Each time they heard a sound, Gideon would tense up, and she knew he thought it was an Apache warning call. If they were observed at all, they were allowed to pass, for they arrived without incident, and the hotel they chose was cheap, but clean.

"Are you awake, Gideon?" she called out, not quietly.

On the floor of Carmelita's room, under a rumbled mass of blankets, she heard a muffled sound "hmmpff." Having only enough money for one room, Gideon had slept on the floor on the extra blankets and pillow from the bed. Carmelita could not turn him back out in the chilly desert night to return to Naco, and after the hours in the buckboard, felt she knew him well enough to trust him. Besides, he had shown his true mettle by taking her at all to begin with. On the ride out Gideon talked quite a bit, in whispered tones, about his parents and the trip out from Tennessee in a covered wagon six years ago, when he was just twelve. He came from a place called Johnson City, which was a crossroads for railroads north to south and east to west, making

357

it a popular and fast growing town. Carmelita thought it funny that he came from places with so many "s's" in their names, and Gideon seemed to be just whistling away every time he said "Tennessee or Johnson City."

He explained to her, "My father was from the Appalachians and most of the family were bootleggers. It was said they made the best home-made whiskey in Tennessee and sold it to folks from Bristol to Kingsport. That was part of the problem, they sold it without tithing to the government for taxes, and it landed my uncle and cousin in jail. My Pa didn't take up the family business, he worked for the railroad. Specifically, the East Tennessee & Western North Carolina Railroad, nicknamed the Tweetsie, partly because of its whistle."

He grinned as he finished that mouthful, as if he knew how absurd it sounded whistling out those words, but Carmelita just looked at him as if she were fascinated, never hinting at the humor of it all.

Carmelita knew nothing about such things as bootleg booze. In Mexico, the alcoholic drinks that were available were not home brews. Pulque, Mescal, and Tequila all came from the agave plant, and it took eight years to cultivate, mash, and refine the various liquids. They were cheap, but were prepared by others, not a home brew. She learned that Gideon and his father did not carry on this dangerous, albeit lucrative profession. He explained that his father had always been fascinated by the power and movement of the big engines. His family had loved the rural atmosphere that mountain living represented, but as Johnson City grew, it became more and more politicized and populous, and his "ma and pa" decided to head out west where they heard there existed a pioneering spirit like they remembered from the Tennessee of their childhood.

"Naco is a nice town, but so different from Tennessee, which has green trees everywhere, with rolling hills and valleys full of deer, turkeys, and all kinds of critters. I miss Tennessee, and I'm saving my money in the hope I can go back in another year or so."

Gideon went on to describe the countryside, the people, and all the things he loved about his place of birth. His heart was clearly still back in Tennessee, and Carmelita marveled at his words and wished that one day she might be able to see such a place. For now, however, Carmelita was focused on her mission and what she needed to do.

While Gideon went down the hall to void himself, Carmelita freshened up from a wash basin in the room and applied a light coat of makeup, although she did not need to rouge her cheeks, since her color was high owing to her excitement.

When Gideon returned, he asked "What's your plan, Carmelita? I don't need to get back until Tuesday for the stage, so I'm happy to help you here and take you back to Naco when you're done, how can I help?"

Gideon was more than smitten with Carmelita, and most likely would have driven her to Canada, instead of Cananea, if she had asked.

She smiled at him sweetly and replied, "*Mi amigo*, I never expected Bisbee to be so large and busy. I thought it would be easy to find MacMurrough, but now I'm not so sure. I could use some help, particularly since you have the buckboard. My plan is to visit the sheriff's office and describe MacMurrough and see if he can help in any way. Can you take me there?" She turned to him expectantly and gave him a smile that melted his heart.

""Of course, Carmelita, but let me ask you something. You say that this MacMurrough fellow is one bad hombre. Don't you think he'll go back to his old habits? I'll tell you what, I'll take you to the sheriff's office and drop you off, and I'll go to the south side of town and inquire at the bordellos and saloons. I'll meet you outside the sheriffs at high noon and then we'll head to the doctor's office, OK?" Gideon said with more confidence than he felt.

"*Sí, Gracias, Señor* Gideon." Carmelita then described in detail what she had been told MacMurrough looked like. "I hope we find him soon, so I can look in his eyes and know if I am of his blood, God have mercy on my soul."

As Gideon and Carmelita climbed up on the buckboard, Durand was approaching Bisbee from the south side of town. He had never been there before, but had heard it was about as large as El Paso, so he knew the task of finding Cassidy was going to be difficult before he ever got there. He had a strong sense about Cassidy's tastes and the type of places he could be found, making the task a little easier.

As the sun heated the red earth and dried the dew on the sparse grass and plants, he saw the buildings of the town looming ahead. He noticed that the approach road passed several buildings on the way to the fork, including a boarding house and saloon on the west side of the street and a blacksmith shop and dry goods store on the other, and wondered if Cassidy was smart enough to hole up there while he waited. He figured that he was since it would give him line of sight to anyone passing through on the way to town.

Cassidy and Consuelo, meanwhile, were seated in the small dining room at the boarding house, enjoying their early breakfast, but not speaking to, or even looking at, one another. Cassidy had positioned Consuelo with her back to the window and he with his back against the wall, able to see anyone who might pass by outside. The boarding house, run by a woman named Molly McIntire, was situated on the west side of the entrance road when approaching Bisbee, and the morning sun shone into the front windows, so they could not be seen from the outside until at least noon, when the sun passed overhead. Cassidy's plan was to catch a first glimpse of Durand as he rode into town and then make sure Consuelo was secured in her room. He would make some pretext of needing to go next door to the saloon for a drink to calm his nerves, and would follow Durand and wait for him to put up his horse and was on foot. He would watch him from behind to see if he would remove the Amulet, which he knew he would not leave in his saddlebags. If he took out a wrapped object, he would know he had it, and would set his trap, if not, he would know he failed, and would confront him with his "Peacemaker."

Gideon, meanwhile, dropped Carmelita off at the sheriff's office, waited until she entered, then headed off to the seedier, south side of town, where the bordellos and saloons were all located within close proximity to one another, which made Gideon's task easy. He had the same thoughts as Durand, and figured that if MacMurrough was frequenting one of these places, he probably frequented more than one, and it wouldn't take much to find out where he stayed.

Durand, meanwhile, came into view of Bisbee on horseback, and, after scoping out the outcropping of buildings, decided to approach the first group of buildings he came upon from the rear on the western side of the street. He was afforded this luxury since he rode in on a horse, instead of a carriage or coach, so he could take almost any approach he wanted, roadway or not. He stopped a few hundred yards from the first group of buildings, to allow his horse to rest a bit and observe any activity. He approached the buildings on foot, and knew that he had no easy way to escape detection if Cassidy was inside one of the buildings looking out. His best hope was to hug the back sides of the buildings until he made his move.

Several carts passed by in the street heading south filled with workers in mining gear, apparently heading to the Copper Queen mine. Durand had already figured that most of the activity in this part of town was geared toward the miners, who worked about a quarter mile south of where he was now, and that the rooming house, saloon, and all the other services in proximity catered to mining interests. It would be the perfect place for Cassidy to wait for his arrival. He watched and waited wondering if Cassidy would show his face, or if he would have to make the first move.

Cassidy was inside enjoying his breakfast omelet made with peppers, cheese, and smoked bacon, and looked up from his meal frequently to see if there was any activity that would attract his attention, glancing down to grab another forkful of eggs and quickly looking up again. He had a premonition in his bones and could not shake the feeling that Durand was nearby. He kept one eye on Consuelo, hoping she would tip her hand if he was.

363

For some strange reason, he was now feeling that the Amulet was not in Durand's possession. His blessed Irish mother told him he had the "gift of sight," and it did seem that he often knew things before they happened.

As Cassidy enjoyed his breakfast and Durand carefully approached the entry to town, Gideon stopped at the first saloon that he came upon, in an area delineated by a large gap between buildings and around the first bend on the way south of town without direct view of the center. The saloon was called the Crazy Horse Saloon, and based on what Gideon had heard of MacMurrough, this could be just the type of place he would come to drink. He walked through swinging wooden doors into a dimly lit place that smelled like stale beer and strong perfume. There was only one old prospector in the place, apparently passed out with his head down on the table, and a two thirds empty bottle of whiskey in front of him. Gideon called out, "Anybody here?"

From out of the back shuffled an old man with a hunched back, a fringe of grey hair around his bald head striking out in all directions as if each strand had its own destination, and a long, full moustache, streaked with grey, that curled up at the ends almost to his eyes. "What'll it be?" he asked, and hacked a cough into the air.

"I'm looking for someone…" Gideon started to say and was interrupted brashly as the old man said in a loud voice, "If I had a nickel for every

364

tenderfoot to come through here looking for someone, I'd be living in France with Lily Langtry," he coughed out, and started hacking again from deep in his chest.

Gideon knew he would get nowhere with this type of questioning, so he ordered a shot and a beer. "And buy a beer for my friend over there as well," he said, indicating the drunk in the corner.

"Big spender," the old man mumbled under another cough.

"Look, I'm here trying to find my girlfriend's uncle. He left his wife in Mexico, and we think he's hiding out somewhere around here. She just wants to talk to him. Can you tell me if you've seen a wiry, small boned man with bright red hair who speaks with an Irish accent? He usually carries a Bowie knife."

The old man looked up at him and squinted, as if trying to determine if his story was real. "There is one *hombre* that fits the description, but he doesn't carry any weapons. The only reason I know is because of the hair color. Not too many like that around here. You wouldn't even know it because he always wears a big Stetson, but he takes it off, polite like, whenever he has something to eat. Stays over at Molly McIntire's rooming house. Doesn't come out much, but likes to have a drink or two on occasion. Likes the girls, young ones, but only talks about it, hasn't touched any of 'em. " He turned away, hacking again, until Gideon thought he would pass out from the effort.

"Thanks, old man. Give these to my friend." he said indicating the drinks, and rushed out of the saloon to find Carmelita.

Chapter Twenty-One

Strike

"A.B., we have major problems at the mines. The workers are buying into the talk of a strike that the PLM is advocating, and it's said it will happen early next month. It's all the talk at the dances and in Ronquillo. Manuel tells us he can no longer influence his workers. Besides, he is very distracted with his wife on her deathbed, and his daughter, Carmelita, has been missing for three days. I think we need to alert Colonel Greene about the potential for a strike." Francisco delivered this in one breath, with uncharacteristic urgency.

A.B. looked at Francisco and nodded his head slowly. Things were coming to a head here at the mines. After all these years, in spite of the tremendous growth in revenues and expansion of the town, it was a month to month effort trying to keep things running with cash flow issues and employment problems, such as drunk and unreliable workers. He always knew he would eventually have to involve the Colonel, and he was pondering how to approach him. Greene was a man who always thought he could reason with the miners, being of their ilk and paying higher wages than other mines in the country. As he thought about this, he observed Francisco who seemed to be lost in thought.

"I've been waiting for the right time to make my escape" Torres thought to himself. "It has been a struggle keeping the Amulet under wraps all this time. The temptation has been great to leave Cananea, melt down the gold and jewels, and sell them off little by little as I worked my way to Spain to live on the *Costa del Sol* for the rest of my life, lying in the sun with beautiful *Señoritas* to keep me company. The timing has to be right. If I ever left suddenly, it would be suspicious, and Colonel Greene has not spent one day without cursing the loss of his precious cross and having me tear up the town looking for it. He has eyes everywhere, no one knows better than me, so conditions have to be right to take my leave. The country is about to explode, and the new regulations that have been imposed on border crossings will make it impossible to bring the Amulet into the U.S. legally. I will now have to head to the Gulf coast, and take a ship to New York, then to Spain. Fortunately, I have saved enough money to do this without needing to melt the Amulet first. I'll do that in New York, where it will never be questioned. It's just a matter of time before the strike occurs, and when it does, I will take the Amulet from its hiding space and leave immediately for the coast." He looked at A.B, who nodded as if he had made his decision, and then marched off to talk to the Colonel, wondering what Francisco had been contemplating.

Francisco had been clever and kept his mouth shut about the Amulet. In the excitement of the moment, when MacMurrough was being arrested, no one noticed it when he had slipped the item under his tunic as they were rushing out of the room. He put it in his saddlebag while getting out his cuffs, and waited two excruciatingly long days before ever attempting to retrieve it, and put it in a proper hiding spot.

The hiding spot that Francisco had eventually chosen was a risky one, located at the base of Colonel Greene's casa. The foundation of the home was constructed of rows of large multi-colored local rock, cemented together around the perimeter with strategically placed footings, under a wooden floor laid on top of it, which allowed for air flow to keep the house cool.

Francisco had waited until the middle of the night to remove one of those stones carefully, digging out the cement and placing the Amulet in the hollow just beyond the stone. He then painstakingly replaced the cement, wetting it with water and mixing it with the dirt surrounding his feet to ensure it retained an aged look. The stone was blue, which was unusual enough, but he marked it by poking a chink out of the upper right quadrant and filling that with a mixture of dirt and stones. It was virtually unnoticeable, and he had counted on the fact that no one would ever suspect that the Amulet, if it indeed was still in Cananea, would be hidden on Colonel Greene's property.

As A.B. rushed off to inform the Colonel about the insurrectionists, Manuel and Pedro had just left the meeting of the PLM, and were heading out to the cantina for a drink, to discuss the strike and talk about Edelmida and Carmelita.

Manuel had been extremely distraught, and Pedro was trying to get him to relax a bit. There was still no word from Carmelita, Edelmida had lapsed into a coma, and the doctor from Bisbee had still not sent a telegram back to her doctor. Manuel feared she would not last much longer, and he needed to know that Carmelita was safe. Pedro had all he could do to keep Manuel from hopping on the train to Naco, and taking up the trail of Carmelita. He knew in his heart that was wrong, since that would mean leaving Edelmida and the twins, but he was torn as to what was the right thing to do. Pedro's wife had been a saint in helping him with the children, who seemed more grown up every day, as they had to become more self-sufficient.

The union meeting had been raucous, with most of the miners wanting to go out on strike the next day. Tensions were high, the entire country seemed to be revolting against the *Porfiriato*, and a mass insurgency seemed imminent. There were factions springing up all throughout Mexico, stirring up the peons, and pushing revolution against the foreign investors, who were taking all their money across the border. There was both a social and armed revolution underway, and Manuel no longer had even a semblance of control over the workers at the mines any longer. His role as a "supervisor" was no longer accepted, and he became a symbol of all that was wrong in Cananea and all of Mexico. The workers demand for shorter hours and better pay had eclipsed any goodwill that the naming of Manuel as supervisor had brought to the mines. Manuel himself now felt that he had been used by MacMurrough as a token manager to give the illusion of the progress of Mexican workers.

Colonel Greene received A.B and Francisco, and listened to their concerns. Of course, he was aware of the issues, and with his vast network of political contacts, both in Mexico and in the U.S., he could not ignore what was happening across the country. The Colonel knew that some of the insurgency was promoted by unions in the U.S., particularly the Industrial Workers of the World union, a radical organization run by anarchists and communists whose goal was to overthrow the managing class and empower worker solidarity through violence.

Ricardo Flores Magon and his brothers were staunch proponents of the ideas and ideals of the IWW, and used the platform to incite the workers from their relatively safe haven in St. Louis. The precepts and principles of the IWW and other organizations such as the Western Federation of Miners, fed the discontent of the workers in

Cananea and established a mob mentality that was self-sustaining and about to cause the town to implode.

The strike was set for Friday, June 1, 1906, at five a.m., scheduled so the workers could be intercepted on the way to work, if they hadn't already gotten the word, or had a sudden pang of conscience. Both the PLM and the Western Federation of Miners voted for the strike and the stage was set for a walkout. A large group of workers congregated at the portal to the Oversight Mine to prevent any of the miners from entering while other factions obstructed work at the smelters to cease production of the finished matte.

Dr. Felipe Barosso, the mayor of Cananea, received a call from Pablo Rubio, the *comisario* (peace officer) in Ronquillo, that the strike was official. They had been anticipating this action and just the night before, Colonel Greene and his staff; A.B. Fall, Francisco de Torres and others, took possession of a cache of arms, including rifles and hand guns to prepare themselves in the event of a violent uprising. Fall had contacted the Governor in Hermosillo, the capital of the State of Sonora, who instructed his military to be prepared in the event an outbreak occurred in Cananea.

When the officials arrived at the mines, they were met by a group of four hundred excited, cheering miners, shouting out, *"¡Viva México!"* and *"¡Cinco pesos por ocho horas!"* After an impromptu discussion and negotiation with the

372

striking leaders, it was agreed that their demands be put into writing and a formal response would be issued. The crowd was excited, but not unruly, and Barossa and Rubio left to confer with the manager of the Oversight mine, A.S. Dwight, who was expected to meet with the striking miners at ten o'clock that morning.

In the first of many missteps, Dwight flatly refused the meeting stating that the demands were "absurd." The formal letter that the strikers produced was addressed directly to Colonel Greene, and not only demanded fewer hours and better pay, but also contained concerns about having to trade at the company store and named names of those supervisors they wanted replaced.

Colonel Greene responded to, and addressed their demands, by explaining that an increase of 2 pesos per man amounted to almost a half million pesos a year, and would make the company unprofitable and put them out of business. He spoke about the hundreds who were turning out at the mines willing to work for three pesos a day, because there was little work elsewhere in the country. The Colonel was well liked by all the miners, but he failed to recognize that it was not the pure increase that was the root cause of the unrest, but rather the discrepancy in pay between the Mexicans and the Americans.

The leaders laughed derisively at this response, and accused the Colonel of being in the

373

pocket of the corrupt Mexican officials, and lining their pockets with wealth while using unemployment as a ploy to keep the worker down. Their stance was to continue the strike and stop production until they received concessions on their demands.

Manuel and Pedro watched and listened as the most aggressive of the strikers continued to incite the crowd and keep the energy level up for a fight with management.

"Pedro, I am very uncomfortable with all this. We still make more money than workers at other mines, and I know that the government is to blame for allowing foreigners to control our land and pay us a pittance, but I am concerned that this will turn to violence and that will only lead to more violence, and in the end, I don't know that anything will really change."

Pedro nodded his head as he looked at his friend, who in the last few days seemed to have become a shell of his former self. His eyes were sunken and he didn't eat anything at all. His gaze was distant and he could not sleep because he was sick with worry over his wife's illness and Carmelita's sudden disappearance. The doctor had told him the night before that nothing more could be done for her, and it was just a matter of time. Manuel, for his part, thought he had been desensitized to death, having lost parents, co-workers, friends and relatives throughout his life to silicosis, consumption, trauma from mining

374

accidents, and other tragedies, but losing Edelmida was heart wrenching and the disappearance of Carmelita tore him apart. He prayed every day for God to take him instead, imploring Him that if He were a true God, He would take the strong and leave the weak to breathe another day. This is the prayer of all who are about to lose one they love, and that prayer is never answered. His faith taught him that all who die in God's grace are assured eternal salvation, and that, after death, they achieve the purification necessary to be received through the gates of heaven. Manuel was committed to spending the remainder of his life offering penance and prayer on Edelmida's behalf to ensure her path to eternal happiness, but for now, he was angry at his God and all that was wrong in Cananea, Mexico, and the world.

As he moved ponderously down the street with his *amigo* by his side, he wondered where Carmelita was, and why she would leave at this time of sadness and turmoil.

The stage was set for a confrontation with the managers at the mines who were ready for a fight, the insurgency leaders provoking the miners to take up arms, and the political leaders from Hermosillo to Mexico City watching to see what would happen in the formerly sleepy little town of Cananea, Sonora, Mexico.

Chapter Twenty-Two

Confrontation

Gideon Riot literally ran into Carmelita as she huffed out of the sheriff's office after an exasperating hour trying to enlist some help to find MacMurrough. The deputies derided her mercilessly as she haltingly tried to explain her quest. These were a couple of ignorant southern boys who had no tolerance for Mexicans of any type, and in spite of Carmelita's beauty, they taunted her with catcalls and innuendos intimating sex.

"Carmelita! I think I found MacMurrough!" Gideon exclaimed breathlessly. "If the old man I talked to is right, he's at a rooming house called Molly McIntire's. It's early, so if we head up there right now, we might be able to find him."

"¡Andele!" Carmelita replied.

Just then, Jack Durand was approaching Molly's rooming house from the rear. His thinking was that if Cassidy were there, he might be able to surprise him, and if he wasn't, there would be no harm and it would simply be the first place he would ask of his whereabouts. He tied his horse to a scrub brush fifty feet from the rear entrance, and walked slowly towards the back door. He looked in and saw an empty kitchen with a pot of steaming coffee on the wood stove, and let himself in quietly. He heard voices in the front of the house and peeked around the corner to see Consuelo talking to a woman he took to be Molly McIntire.

Carmelita and Gideon pulled up across the street from the boarding house and she said to Gideon, "Wait here for me. I want to see him alone. If I call, come running."

He looked at her doubtfully, and turned as if he were ready to jump down from his seat anyway.

Carmelita grabbed his arm "Don't. I know what I'm doing. I'll be out soon."

As Molly turned from Consuelo and started to head back to the kitchen, Consuelo saw her brother Jack peak around the corner and hold his finger up to his mouth indicating for her to be silent. He slithered into the room, and with cat-like grace and speed, he was on Cassidy in a heartbeat and had his knife to his throat.

"Cassidy, you lied to me" he roared. "The Amulet was not in Cananea. It's still missing, and now you have to pay for the all the trouble you've caused me and my sister. I'm going to your room to take everything you've got, and you better hope you have enough or you'll pay with your life. Consuelo, take this rope and tie his hands and feet to the chair. Here, take the bowie knife, and if he so much as moves a finger, cut him!"

Cassidy could not think of anything to say. He had no hope of getting out of this dilemma, and

377

he was shocked and surprised that the Amulet was not found.

"Durand, I swear," he pleaded "I know the Amulet is in Cananea and that the whore Edelmida knows where it is. Please let me go back with you and I will persuade the bitch."

Carmelita was right outside the door on the porch about to enter, and she could not believe her ears. This must be the man her mother told her about, but who was Cassidy? Why did this stranger want to kill him, and why would he say such horrible things about her mother?

She heard the scraping of the chair, as they must have been tying up the one called Cassidy, as she opened the front door to enter. When Carmelita stepped into the room, all three of them looked up to see the sun radiating behind her back, and outlining her tall physique. Cassidy took note of the outline of her body and the raven black hair cascading to her shoulders, but could not make out any features, with the sun streaming into the room. She looked like a dark angel coming to his rescue, and he felt as if he were in a macabre play.

Carmelita stopped just inside the door waiting for her eyes to adjust to the change in light, and, as she moved, the sun streamed in and MacMurrough lowered his face to avoid the bright light, making it impossible for Carmelita to get a good look at his face. She stared towards where Cassidy sat and asked quietly, "Are you Thomas MacMurrough?"

Cassidy was confused, for how could anyone so young possibly know of the name he used only when he was in Cananea? He was struck by the apparent beauty of this young girl and, in spite of his situation could not help but be aroused by her youth, and wondered to himself if she might be a virgin.

Durand stepped between her and Cassidy and spoke up sharply, "Who are you? Get out of here. This man is wanted and I have come to bring him to justice. Get out before you get hurt."

Carmelita replied with quiet confidence, "I am the child of the woman he mentions from Cananea. I have come to find a man named MacMurrough who raped my mother. Can this be that man?"

"Ask him yourself" Durand curtly replied.

Carmelita came into the room and began to cross the floor attempting to look into Cassidy's eyes, whose head was dropped to his chest to avoid the bright sunlight.

"Are you the man called MacMurrough, who lived in Cananea and worked for Colonel Greene?" she began. "My mother was raped by a man named MacMurrough who answers to your description, and I want to know if you could be my father."

She was almost close enough to see his eyes clearly, and she knew that when she did, she would know the answer without his having to speak.

379

Before he could answer, Gideon came running to the front steps of the boarding house, shouting, "Carmelita, the sheriff followed us here and has his deputies with him. I guess he heard the story you told and wanted to check it out for himself, and found my buckboard. Hurry! We have to get out of here."

Carmelita turned around to look at Gideon, but continued, "Answer me!" she shouted, her grey/green eyes flashing a look to wilt the will of any man.

Cassidy, his chin still on his chest, laughed mockingly, and mumbled out "You are a pretty young thing, and much better looking than your mother. When all this is over, let's see if we can spend a little time together and get to know each other. What do you say?"

Consuelo, who had stood by watching this drama with wide eyed wonder, could take no more.

"You are a pig!" she cried out, and grasping the Bowie knife, she plunged it into his stomach and twisted, causing him to cry out.

"Bitch! You'll pay for this," and he toppled over with the chair and collapsed on the ground.

Durand took his sister's hand and ran out the back door as quickly as he could. Gideon, standing at the door, called out "Carmelita, we must leave – NOW!" But still she resisted.

"Wait, no," she shouted. "I have to find out if he is my father," Carmelita cried out as Gideon tugged her away.

She turned around to face Gideon and he froze, for the look on her face was something he had never seen in a human before.

"Gideon, go get the buckboard and bring it around to the back. I'll be out in a moment. The sheriff will not deny me my right to know, and he will not hold me. I won't allow it."

Gideon looked at her and knew she was right; no sheriff in his right mind would try to hold this possessed woman. Gideon left quickly and she heard him calling out, apparently to the sheriff and his deputies, "two Mexicans from across the border – they stabbed a man inside," and she heard the sound of galloping hoof beats riding after them in a cloud of dust.

Carmelita bent down over MacMurrough or Cassidy, or whatever his name was as his head rested on the ground facing down away from her. He could barely hold his head up and she did not have the chance to look into those eyes to see if he was her father.

She leaned over and whispered to him "Tell me – are you the man who raped my mother?"

He gurgled and spat out blood and turned to look at her with one mangled and bloody eye and said, "Your mother betrayed me and lied about me taking the Amulet. I know she still has it. If you are my daughter, then so be it. I wouldn't know. Go back home, talk to your mother, and get her to tell you where the Amulet is. Everyone thinks it brings good luck, but I know now that it is cursed. When you find it, get rid of it right away. It brings nothing but trouble."

Then he coughed and spit out a little more blood and heaved a deep breath, and turned away. Molly came scurrying out of the kitchen after having heard all the commotion and was shocked at the image before her.

Carmelita looked at her and with great calm, said, "I'm going for the doctor now. I'll send him back shortly."

She heard Gideon pull up in back, and, with nothing more to learn, she got up quickly, looked at him with pity and said "May God rest your soul, whoever you are," and went out the back door to get into the buckboard and look for the doctor.

Chapter Twenty-Three

Loyalty

Manuel was caught in the middle by the impending strike; between his duty as a supervisor at the mines, and that of a Mexican peon worker, which is where his loyalty truly lay. He had to make a decision to strike with the miners or stand with the managers, and this tore him as it was also a choice between his duties to his company and providing for his family, or standing with his core beliefs and his community. The pressure of Edelmida's illness and Carmelita's disappearance weighed heavily on him and his thoughts were not rational and constantly conflicting.

There was hope in his heart, however. The night before, he had received word that Carmelita was on her way home after successfully contacting the specialist in Bisbee and talking to him at length about Edelmida. The specialist had finally gotten in touch with Edelmida's doctor and they conferred on her condition and he had offered a suggestion about treatment. According to the specialist, Carmelita had been in Bisbee the day before and was getting a ride to Naco, then the train to Cananea, and could be expected back that afternoon.

Edelmida's doctor spoke to Manuel about all this, but confided, "Don't get your hopes up just yet, Manuel. Edelmida is in a very late stage, and the treatment is unproven even in early stage patients. We will do what we can and I will let you know if I see improvement."

The twins showed little effect from the events of the past several days. They had always found ways to keep themselves occupied, and it seemed they were absorbed with each other and kept themselves busy in spite of everything going on around them. They seemed impervious to the working of anything outside their world, and almost seemed to float in a cocoon of their own design.

Still, Manuel felt better than he had in days, with Carmelita scheduled to be home and Edelmida getting the treatment they had been praying for. Now, it was time to turn his attention back to his family and put the issues surrounding the strike behind him for a little while. The news of the strike that day gave him a reason to stay home in the morning, and he spent time with the twins waiting for Carmelita's arrival.

The entire town was disrupted by the upcoming strike, and schools were closed and most businesses did not open, expecting some type of backlash from the town managers or the mines themselves. It was not a secret that this was the day that the work stoppage would occur and all sides knew it. The real question was; what type of problems would arise and how would the town managers and mining executives react? The night before the strike was announced, Colonel Greene had signaled for his coach and gone to Bisbee to arrange for reinforcements and all the weapons he could muster, working all night and arriving back at four in the morning. Violence was not sanctioned or condoned, but the possibility was always there, and since Colonel Greene and his minions had stockpiled weapons in the event that violence occurred, it seemed a good likelihood that something would transpire.

It is just this type of fear of reprisal that has instigated confrontations since time immemorial and caused untold bloodshed in the name of defense. The first shot is invariably the one that is unaccounted for, for it is only after that initial encounter when the bodies are counted and the winners declared. It is one of the oldest stories in the history of mankind when one person, group, or nation, with a common interest escalates defenses to protect itself from the potential invasion of a similar group with competing interests. Yet, within any given assemblage, there is invariably a splintering distinction of interests, and at any time factions within the clique can turn one against the other, ultimately boiling things down to individual likes and dislikes and a prioritization of self-interest.

Manuel was well aware of his unique and tenuous position in all of this, and the perception by both sides that he may be sympathetic to the other. He was attempting to avoid it altogether by keeping a low profile and staying home to tend to the twins, visit with Edelmida, and welcome Carmelita home with open arms.

The Metcalf brothers were going to be challenged at the Oversight mine. George and William Metcalf had been working for Colonel Greene for some time and George was not much more popular than Thom MacMurrough had been.

George was the manager of the lumber business, but also responsible for housing, which made him extremely unpopular. His previous experience was as Superintendent of Schools in Tombstone, where he was known to be impatient and capricious in his dealings with both students and teachers.

The Colonel had been attempting to move the miners out of their hovels and shacks in Ronquillo into better quarters in the company barracks, but many wanted to stay among their friends and family rather than the much improved conditions in the barracks. George was the type who brooked no arguments and would not accept backtalk or listen to any of the workers pleas. Will, who worked in the office at the lumberyard, was a much more amenable character, but, unfortunately for him, he stood by his brother and his methods.

As head of security at the mines, Francisco de Torres, and his team, had already been in touch with the authorities in Hermosillo, the capital of

Sonora, and in Mexico City, regarding the impending strike at Cananea. Governor Izabal of Sonora had ordered troops to be dispatched in the event of trouble and had instructed Emilio Kosterlitzky, the mad Russian *rurales* commander who was two days away in Magdalena, to leave immediately for the troubled community.

While the insurgents were doing their best to stir up the strikers, they had arrived, en masse, in their Sunday finest, and altogether were presenting a civil and peaceful demonstration. Colonel Greene addressed them on Main Street and he had been greeted with cheers of *"Viva Mexico"* and *"Viva el Colonel Greene."* They listened to him, for they genuinely liked him and respected his opinion. The Colonel told them that he would be willing to listen to reasonable requests and that the Governor had stepped in and decreed that the strike must be averted. He repeated that the mines in Cananea paid more money to the workers than any in Mexico, and that they should be thankful for what they have and go home to their families in peace, and many heeded this advice and left.

However, the instigators remained and the mood changed dramatically when the meeting broke up. They derided the company, and once again stirred up the crowd. Julio Esperanza, one of the union organizers, incited the miners once again; "The company has made no concessions!" he disparagingly cried "The Americans still make more than we do. The strike must go on if we are to receive justice. The company is making excuses and trying to keep us down. We must fight to protect our rights! We must band together and demand our due. All workers must strike! Everybody!"

By mid-afternoon, the crowd was back on Main Street and they had a plan. They would visit every business in Cananea and recruit workers to the strike, crippling business until their demands were met.

Manuel was visited that morning by his boss, Judd Thurmond.

"Manuel, I am so sorry to hear of Edelmida's illness. If there is anything I, or the company can do to help, please let me know."

"Thank you, *Señor*. We just heard from the doctor in Bisbee and they are trying a new treatment for her, by trying to reduce her blood sugar, but they may be too late. I will let you know as things change, but I thank you for your kind words and concern."

"Manuel, as you know, things are very difficult here at the mines. The strike has begun and the unions are agitating the workers. They are traveling from site to site and going to other businesses in town to create a work stoppage. We need your help as a leader and respected member of your community to try and reason with some of the workers and reduce their ranks. We are fearful that this can escalate if something isn't done. You have heard that Kosterlitzky is on his way here?" he asked.

"*Sí,*" Manuel replied. "I have also heard that the Americans have troops lined up ready to cross the border at the first sign of violence to help stop the strike. That may be the most difficult thing to overcome. If the workers, and especially the union leaders, believe that the Americans will send in troops to our sovereign land to assault our people and assist the American owners to stop to the strike, all hell will break loose, and I don't want to be here when it does."

Thurmond looked at Manuel with sympathetic eyes and thought "He's right, I don't want to be here either," but he had a job to do.

"Manuel, will you at least go down to Main Street and talk to the union leaders and see if there is anything you can do to delay any further action? Maybe talk to some of your comrades and at least try to get them to listen to reason. No one really wants this to escalate except the union, and ultimately that won't do anyone any good."

Manuel listened to his boss. He knew he was a good man, and he had helped him when he needed it, so he agreed to go down to the lumber yard, where he was told the crowd was heading next, to see if he could help.

He once again left the twins in the capable care of Tepin, who had been a godsend to him during these difficult two days. As he approached the center of town on foot, he heard a familiar voice ring out, "Papa!"

He turned to see Carmelita and a young man with blond hair in a small wagon riding towards him.

Before the buckboard came to a stop, Carmelita had jumped off the wagon and ran to her fathers' arms. They hugged and he whispered, "Carmelita, I was so worried about you. Don't ever go off on me like that again."

"I'm sorry Papa. I had to try and help Mama, and I did find the doctor in Bisbee and he promised to call about her condition and see if he could help. How is Mama feeling?"

"She's not good, Carmelita. The doctors did speak and they went over all the possibilities, but the outlook is not good. This diabetes is a killer, and a very difficult disease to control and they think it may be too late to do anything, now that her kidneys are failing. You need to go see her right away. She is in a coma, but I'm sure it will lift her spirits, even in her current state, if she hears your voice."

He looked up at the young man on the bench of the wagon, who nodded a greeting to Manuel.

"I will go now, Papa. Where are you going? Where are the twins?" she responded.

"They are at home with Tepin," he replied. "Things have escalated here at the mines and all throughout Cananea, and the strike began this morning. I have been asked to go to the lumber

390

yard, where they are headed next to see if I can help and get the workers to listen to reason. This madness cannot lead to anything but bloodshed."

"Be careful, Papa. As we left Bisbee and passed through Naco, we saw the Arizona Rangers assembling. It appears they are prepared to come into Cananea to help if there is trouble. I am worried this could be a disaster." she cautioned.

"Don't worry, Carmelita. I'll go and see what the mood is, and if I can't help, I'll go right back home. Go see your mother, and I'll see you at home shortly."

Carmelita jumped back up on the buckboard and pointed in the direction of the clinic to Gideon, who clucked the two tired horses to a slow gait, as she waved to her father.

When Carmelita and Gideon left Bisbee, he committed to staying with her to Cananea to ensure her safety. They got along very well, and she felt safe and secure by his side. She knew there was turmoil throughout the region and agreed to let him escort her.

When she arrived at the clinic, she asked for her mother's doctor, to see if she could find out about the new treatment before she went to her bedside. Gideon went off to the stables to get some feed and water for his horses.

"I'll be back in an hour, Carmelita. Send someone for me if you need me sooner."

Gideon was taken with his new friend and envisioned himself as her protector, although she could clearly fend for herself. As he headed off, she looked at him thoughtfully, then went inside to find her mother's doctor.

"Carmelita, I have to tell you that your mother is very seriously ill, and it doesn't look like any of the methods the doctor in Bisbee suggested will be able to help. Her kidneys are too far gone and I don't expect her to live out the day."

"She's comatose right now, but could awaken at any moment. I suspect that hearing your voice can only have a soothing and beneficial effect on her."

As Carmelita made her way towards her mother's bedside, Manuel was on his way to the lumber yard, where he knew the crowd was heading first to enforce the work stoppage. He assumed the spot was chosen particularly because of the Metcalf brothers, but he supposed it could have been by chance.

As he approached, he saw George Metcalf standing outside the yard holding a water hose. The crowd was marching forward, fronted by three workers holding flags dressed in their Sunday finest. To his surprise he saw his friend Pedro in the middle with the Mexican flag, and on either side of him, a man holding a red flag, and a man holding a white flag.

"We want to talk to your workmen," Pedro demanded of Metcalf.

"Don't try to get past me, hombre," Metcalf replied tersely. "Try, and I'll turn this hose on you."

Manuel started to run towards the confrontation to intervene, but before he got halfway across the street the water hose came alive with a burst of water spewing from its mouth. Metcalf turned it on the crowd, soaking them, the flags, and their Sunday suits. From that point on, all hell broke loose. There were shots fired from both sides, and the crowd rushed at the Metcalf brothers. The melee turned into a free-for-all, with shots ringing out and the fire hose gyrating wildly, spraying all, so no one could really see who was who.

When the shooting stopped and the smoke finally cleared, people lay dead from both sides of the conflict. The Metcalf brothers were lying in a common pool of their combined blood, dead from stab wounds suffered by "miner's candlesticks" – iron tools with long, sharp shafts that were used to drive crevices in the walls of the mines.

Pedro was soaked, but unharmed, as he staggered down the dirt road hearing cries of pain, and seeing diluted puddles of blood being washed away by the still leaking water hose. As he staggered towards the lumberyard, he came upon the lifeless body of his friend Manuel, shot through the heart by an errant bullet.

"Nooooo!" he cried, and sank to his knees, crying and pleading to God not to allow his good

393

friend to die. Of all the people who did not belong here, or deserve to die, it was Manuel Carreras, he thought. Pedro's mind was racing.

"Why was Manuel here? When I left him he was tending to the twins, and preparing to go see Edelmida. How can such tragedy strike such a wonderful and loving family?"

Pedro knelt down on one knee over his dead friend, sobbing, and picking up his hand to hold in his, as he both cursed and prayed silently to his God.

"Lord, why do you take the good when there is so much evil in the world? How can a just and forgiving God be so callous and irresponsible? Why not take the ones who hurt people, instead of the ones who truly love you and honor you? If there is justice, please help me understand."

In his heart, Pedro knew that God was not the one responsible for all this, that people ultimately make their own choices and have to live and die by those choices, wherever they lead. It is by the wisdom of God that gives us this choice and can lead us to where our decisions take us. Sometimes for individual benefit, and sometimes for things we do not see directly. The real prayer is the one that asks for guidance in making the right choice, whether or not it looks more attractive or correct in the short term.

Pedro shook himself out of this litany with the sudden realization that he had to go and find Carmelita and see about Edelmida and the twins. He was not sure he would be able to deliver the news, but he knew they had to find out from someone they knew and trusted, not from rumor or a stranger.

Carmelita was with her mother, who did respond to her voice, and briefly opened her eyes and offered a faint and beatific smile. She barely croaked out with a whisper.

"Carmelita, I'm so happy you're here."

"Hush Mama, you need your rest. I need you to get well soon. We all miss you, Mama."

"Child, I had a dream. I dreamt that you had gone from Cananea to try to find *El Diablo*. I know you have wondered about your father. I have to tell you, *Cielito*, your father is Manuel. He has loved you as no father has ever loved a daughter and sacrificed everything to give you the best he could offer. The color of your eyes comes from your Spanish blood, not from the evil *El Diablo*. Don't ever doubt who your father is. There is no greater love on earth. Your father is not *El Diablo*, *Cielito*. I need you to know that."

Carmelita looked at her mother, shocked. She could not imagine she had guessed what she had done, or how the possibility of *El Diablo* being her father had affected her, but she was grateful her mother had told her this.

"*Gracias*, Mama. I never really wondered about that," she lied, "but I am happy to know how much my true father loves me."

Carmelita kissed her mother on her forehead as she appeared to doze off again.

The doctor appeared "Your presence seemed to have helped her, Carmelita. She hadn't awakened since you were here last."

He touched Edelmida's forehead and turned serious. He took her wrist and touched her on the neck, but could feel no pulse. Carmelita could sense his concern, and, alarmingly, asked the doctor what was wrong. He turned to her and as he did so, he began to raise the sheet over her head.

"I'm sorry, Carmelita, but you must have given your mother a few brief moments of happiness. She has died with a smile on her lips."

And before the sheet passed over her face, Carmelita saw that, indeed, her mother seemed to be smiling.

Francisco de Torres was frantic. Blood had now been spilled, and Colonel Greene had gone around him and contacted Governor Izabal who had the *Rurales,* under Kosterlitzky, on the march. A confrontation would have disastrous effects and cause a full scale revolution.

Captain Tom Rynning of the Arizona Rangers was meeting with the Governor of Arizona in Naco to find a way to intercede in the confrontation. The Arizona Governor wanted to protect the U.S workers and felt he had to try and stop the altercation from happening. If the Rangers were allowed to cross the border as a unit, it would be considered an invasion of Mexico by the United States, and constitute an Act of War.

But Rynning found a solution by suggesting to the Governor that the Rangers cross the border as individuals, one at a time, not a troop, and reassemble on the other side, thereby sidestepping an international incident.

Colonel Greene himself was distraught, and sending messages to everyone he could think of, including *Presidente* Díaz and President Roosevelt.

Torres knew he had to get the Amulet off Greene's property while he still had a chance. It was likely that the unrest would center there and he may never be able to recover it, if he didn't move quickly.

The potential that the Casa would be burned to the ground, or worse, was a distinct possibility. As evening approached, he went to see Colonel Greene at the Casa. He had just learned that Manuel had been shot to death, and Edelmida had passed away from her disease, and knew he had to go see Carmelita as soon as possible, but first he had to convince Greene to leave his home.

"Colonel, I'm not sure how much longer you'll be safe here in the Casa. First thing tomorrow morning we will move your family to safer quarters until things calm down here. With the incursion of troops, we have to get your family to safety. We cannot guarantee security at this location."

"I agree, Francisco. I think we'll be all right tonight, but I would prefer to have armed guards posted outside. Will you see to that?" Greene directed.

"Of course, Colonel. I will personally take first watch at the front perimeter. I'll instruct the men to patrol the grounds through the night in four hour shifts. You and your family will remain safe," he replied as he left hurriedly.

Chapter Twenty-Four

Justice

Carmelita was leaving her mothers' side, and briefly spoke to the doctor about making arrangements, when the wounded and dead were brought into the clinic from the skirmish at the lumber yard.

Gideon had just arrived back from the stables and was about to enter the clinic, when he saw the wagons pull up and transport the dead into the triage room. None of the bodies were covered or hidden in any way. They were carried by hands and feet whether alive, dead, or wounded, into the emergency area. He was just about to turn away from the carnage when his eye caught a glimpse of a face that looked familiar. He turned to look again and was certain it was Carmelita's father, who he had just seen an hour ago, near the center of town. He asked one of the men carrying the wounded the name of the dead man, and he replied tersely, "Manuel Carreras."

"My God," he thought, "it *is* Carmelita's father. How can I ever break the news to her?"

As he contemplated his dilemma, he saw Francisco de Torres gallop up to the entrance of the clinic, bring his mount to a screeching halt, jump

399

off in mid-stride, and barrel into the entrance of the clinic.

He heard him ask loudly, "Does anyone know where Carmelita Carreras is?"

Gideon surreptitiously approached the entryway, slid inside hugging the wall, and saw Carmelita come around the corner and face the man.

"Francisco, what are you doing here?" she exclaimed. "I heard there is a strike and people could be killed. My father has gone to the lumber yard to try to help. Shouldn't you be there with him?"

"That's what I have come to talk to you about, Carmelita. Please, sit down." His face was drawn as he paused, while she gingerly sat on the nearest chair.

"How is your mother?" he asked considerately. She bowed her head and answered.

"She just passed away, Francisco. It was so sad. She was at peace until the end, and she was a good and strong woman. I have to find my father and tell him right away."

"That's what I've come to talk to you about, Carmelita. There is no easy way to say this – your father has died. He gave his life for his country and is a hero to us all."

Carmelita was stunned. "No – that can't be, Francisco! I just saw him a little while ago in town. He was going to the lumberyard to talk to the strikers and try to get them to listen to reason, and push off the strike. No one had any weapons! It was a peaceful demonstration. It just can't be!"

Carmelita looked past Francisco into the middle space and tried to wrap her mind around the events of the past day. It was inconceivable to her that both her mother and her father could be gone so suddenly, in such a brief period of time. Like her mother before her, she lost both parents on the same day. A tragedy that seemed impossible to understand. She did not know where to turn.

Francisco held her hand and whispered, "Carmelita, if there is anything at all that I can do, please let me know. I will help you sort things out and get you help for the twins. Your family will be well cared for by the Colonel, you have my word. But right, now, I need to get you to safety."

Carmelita bowed her head and nodded her assent, not really understanding what was happening.

Gideon observed all this from a distance, and instinct told him to hold back. Carmelita was distraught and she obviously trusted this man and he didn't want to create any additional burden or stress for her. Since this Francisco didn't know him he decided he would continue to observe from afar, and keep an eye on things in the event Carmelita needed him.

Gideon followed Carmelita and Francisco back to her home at a distance, and waited outside until Francisco left. Eventually, he knocked on the door, announced who he was, and entered when summoned, stopping and standing just inside the doorway. He watched with sadness as Carmelita, bent down on her knees, embraced the twins and explained that they had to leave Cananea due to the troubles at the mines. Her stoicism was admirable, but Gideon thought she must be in shock.

"But what about Mama and Papa?" Rosita asked innocently. "Mama has to stay in the hospital, and Papa needs to be here with her," Carmelita explained.

"We can't leave her alone and it's too dangerous for us to stay, so, since I'm old enough, I'll take you to the border and we'll stay there until we hear from them. This will be an adventure. We are going to see if we can cross the border and stay on the U.S. side until things quiet down. Haven't you always wanted to go there?" she asked.

The twins looked at her wide-eyed. Although the U.S. Border was only 45 miles away, it could have been the dark side of the moon for all the natives of Cananea were concerned. Very few had ventured so far from home since the border was established, and fewer yet had been able to cross. The twins soon forgot about the troubles, and although they were worried for their mother and father, they didn't know the true extent of the situation, as is often the case with children. Although they sometimes had bad dreams about it, in the light of day they could not imagine their parents perishing. So off they went to pack their

402

things, for Carmelita said they had to leave as soon as possible.

"Carmelita, it's dark now. We should wait until morning, and let the children sleep." Gideon said quietly.

Carmelita looked up at him as if seeing him for the first time, then got up off her knees and ran to him and buried her head in his chest, and let out a long and heart wrenching sob. She let the tears flow until she caught her breath, as Gideon stroked her raven hair and murmured soft sounds.

"Oh, Gideon, I'm not sure I know what to do. I'm so sad and angry about what's happened to my parents. I know that in Cananea there is always the possibility of death - but to lose both my parents, and on the same day. It is just too much to handle. Thank God you came with me to Cananea. Will you help me find a place with the twins when we head back north? You will help us, won't you?" she pleaded.

"Of course I'll help you Carmelita. You and the twins can stay at my house in Naco as long as you like. We just have to figure a way to get you across the border and…." He replied.

"But we have no money." Carmelita interrupted in a breathless rush. "My parents did well by us compared to most in Cananea, but it was always hand to mouth. I don't know how I'll pay you, and I'll have to find a job, and I don't speak English very well and…"

"Hush, Carmelita," Gideon intoned quietly. "Everything will be fine. You need to think about the twins and leaving Cananea first, and we'll work things out once we're in Naco. Do you have anything to drink in the house to calm your nerves?" Gideon asked.

"My father liked his mescal, but my mother always drank pulque mixed with a little water."

"O.K., then, go pack your things and get the twins to bed and I will fix us both a drink and we can sit and talk about tomorrow."

Carmelita went to pack and get the twins settled. As she spoke to them, the hurt in her chest was palpable, for she knew she would have to tell them about her parents at some point. But for right now, it was much more important to get them to safety and out of Cananea. As she reflected on the events of the past few days, she couldn't help but shake her head in wonder and surprise. She was certainly in agreement with the revolution of the peasants against the powerful politics of Mexico City. She believed with all her heart that after centuries of fighting colonization, the *hacendados* and rich Americans who took the land from the native tribes and *mestizos* deserved to pay for their indiscretions and that revolution was the only path left.

The nuns themselves had taught her of other countries whose poor and destitute had suffered at the hands of the capitalists who ruled the land and took all the wealth, and the people were regarded as

404

heroes when they staged their revolts. Their neighbor across the border to the north was one of the prime examples of this conduct and yet, here they were, victims themselves of this fate, and only a few dozen miles away from their border.

Carmelita knew there were those who were insurrectionists and were attempting to create an atmosphere of fear and hate in order to drive the peasants to strike and create unrest in the country for the purpose of a new world. But she also knew that most of the people in Cananea were aware that their life had improved over that of tilling the land by hand and receiving nothing in return but the fruits of their own labors. The secluded native Indian life of planting, sowing, and reaping, and living off whatever proteins were local, was a thing of the past. Not only was revolution inevitable, but it was necessary in order to advance into the new world which had already arrived in most other countries.

The *Porfiriato* had brought order to a violent country, wealth where there was none before, status on the world stage to deliver the natural abundance of their resources, and opportunity to travel via a new and improved rail system, which encouraged migration and exploration. What it didn't deliver on was the promise to educate the masses to enable them to take advantage of these assets, and improve their station in life instead of shipping off all the resources and profits to the political leaders in Mexico City and outside their own country.

As Carmelita dwelled on these random thoughts, she hurriedly packed up her scant belongings and those of the twins into a large *rebozo,* which her mother had bought her from a member of the *Otomi* tribe of San Luis Potosí, who routinely came to Cananea to peddle her goods. Other than the clothes on their backs and a few additional garments in their possession, she went to her parents' room and took a crucifix from her mothers' side of their bed and a gold *escapulario* depicting an image of Our Lady of Guadalupe from her fathers' side, the only items of any value in the home. She checked for any money they might have stashed away, and found a two peso note and fifteen centavos in one of her mothers' shoes. When all this was wrapped up, the entire contents of the *rebozo* weighed only four pounds, which didn't seem like much to accumulate in a lifetime.

She went back into the living area and found Gideon sitting at the table swirling a small amount of mescal, and a glass of pulque with water set out for her.

"Carmelita, when we were riding here and talking about your life in Cananea, you told me you are friendly with the head of security here, correct?" he asked her.

"*Sí. Señor* Torres. He is well respected by many here in Cananea, and it is rumored he served in the *Rurales* under Kosterlitzky. He does not smile much, so people fear him, but he has always been gracious with me and watches out for me. Why do you ask?"

"The border has become more difficult to cross going south to north. They have built formal border crossings at the major points, like Naco on the way to Bisbee, and Nogales on the way to Tucson. It is still easy to get across on small side roads, especially if you are on horseback, but then you are simply an illegal immigrant and can be sent back. If this was just twenty years ago, it would be easy. When the U.S. bought the land from Mexico after the war, you would have had a choice of which side of the border to live, and for decades passing back and forth between the two countries was not only simple, but most people didn't even know the border existed. Now, it is not easy and Mexicans heading north to find work are being transported back if they are caught. The world is changing. But there are still ways to cross legally, if you have the right connections or enough money. I thought maybe your friend might be able to help us get you and the twins into the U.S. legally before things get any more serious. Already the rangers are at the border waiting for the word to cross to help with the striking miners. Do you think he would help you?"

"I know he would Gideon. That's a wonderful idea. You know, most Mexicans believe the U.S. stole our land by invading and conquering our people in the rural areas, away from our might in Mexico City. We were taught in school about the Americans' "Manifest Destiny" and how they used this as an excuse to take land to stretch their country from one ocean to the other, without regard for the sovereignty of Mexico."

"We had already struggled for centuries attempting to win our freedom from the dominance of the Spanish invaders and others who coveted our land, and took the farmland from the natives who had always lived here, and our neighbor to the north came along, after their own struggles ended, and did to us exactly what they fought against in their own revolution. Many are still bitter about it, and believe another revolution will occur against the Americans in the future. I don't condone violence, but I do think they're right. Maybe not a traditional revolution, but a revolution of the people."

She paused and stared out across the room, lost in thought. Gideon sat quietly and waited for her to come back to the reality of the situation today. After a time, she turned and looked at him with new determination in her face, and he could see the strength in her resolve.

"Come,' she said quickly. "Let's go and find Francisco and see if he can help," and she grabbed his hand and pulled him to his feet with surprising strength.

"What about the twins?" he asked.

"They'll be fine. They're sleeping, and everyone in town is out drinking and plotting, and worrying about tomorrow and what will happen in the streets. No one is going to disturb us at home. Beside, we'll only be gone a short time. Let's go while we can."

Carmelita and Gideon went out into the street and were surprised to see that the streets were deserted, although the excitement and energy lingered, electrifying the air. The whole town was alive with hope, and believed that the incidents of the day would force the company's hand and that they would accede to their demands, although the blood that was spilled was tragic. There were five times the number of Mexican workers as Americans, and the shear strength of numbers worked in their favor. The union insurgents stoked the flames of hope, and ignored the might of the few over the fervor of the many. No one was out on this night; it was quiet, as if the entire town was waiting to see how the events of today would affect the events of tomorrow.

Carmelita knew that Torres must be near Colonel Greene's, if not in the Casa, so they decided to head quickly in that direction. Gideon felt that the buckboard would cause too much noise, so he unhitched one of the horses and they rode double.

"I have never ridden a horse before, Gideon. Is this safe?" Carmelita asked.

"Yes, it's safe, Carmelita. We're just going to walk the horse slowly, as I have done many times with my father when I was young. Just put your arms tightly around my waist and grab hold of the saddle horn. It's not far."

As they mounted the steed, Gideon could not help but feel a tingle to his soul as Carmelita hugged her arms around his waist. He felt at that moment that he would somehow be by her side as long as she would allow it, for no other woman had ever made him feel so alive. Just then she whispered in his ear,

"Thank you Gideon for all you have done for me. I don't know how I would be able to cope with all this without you."

He grinned and replied, "It is my pleasure, *Señorita*," whistling the last word breathlessly and causing Carmelita to almost smile.

The sky was covered with clouds, and there was no moon to be seen, making their journey slow and difficult. They approached the Colonel's beautiful home quietly and stopped by a stand of trees with a view of the front of the home, looking into the parlor. It was impossible to get too close for several reasons, most of them due to the location, for it sat up on a small hill and was fenced in, but also because there were guards surrounding the property on the three sides, but, fortunately, for some reason, not the front. They dismounted, and walked silently, as close as they dared, hugging against the sparse copse of trees that lined the walkway. As they got closer to the house, they saw Colonel Greene, A.B. Fall, and Francisco de Torres, standing inside the parlor, talking heatedly. They were smoking cigars, and Carmelita could see that Colonel had a cut glass tumbler in his hand with what appeared to be some type of whiskey. They tried to get close enough to hear, but it was impossible given the surroundings and the guards. It appeared A.B. was yelling at Francisco and motioning with his hands to the front of the Casa. Francisco stood there silently and took this for a period of time, but then seemed to puff up and appeared to grow in size as he confronted A.B., who backed down, walked away and poured himself a glass of the whiskey.

Colonel Greene seemed to be taking it all in and watching the events unfold, and after a while he spoke to them both, separated as they were on either side of the room. It seemed as if whatever they were discussing had caused serious disagreement, and that Colonel Greene was making a decision.

It appeared to them as if Francisco must have gotten his way, for he shook the Colonel's hand and walked toward the door leading into the foyer as if to leave. On the way, he stopped where A.B. was standing with his drink and extended his hand. A.B. nodded to him, but didn't take the hand, and Francisco left without another word.

Gideon and Carmelita had to scramble to get back behind the brush before Francisco exited the front door. As he left, Colonel Greene appeared in the doorway.

411

"And make sure it's in her possession when you escort her. I don't want another episode like the last time."

"Don't worry, Colonel. This is one promise I intend to keep, no matter what may happen."

Francisco called to the guards, and Gideon and Carmelita could hear him as plain as day as he told them to gather in the rear of the house until he called them back, that he had something to do for the Colonel. They scurried to the rear of the casa, and Francisco went to his horse and retrieved a small garden tool, went back to the brick wall in front of the home, and got down on his knees and starting digging out one of the stones.

Carmelita whispered to Gideon "What do you think he's up to?"

Gideon whispered back, "I don't know, but it seems he's been directed by the Colonel."

Francisco removed the stone he was working, reached into the newly created crevice, and extracted an item wrapped in chamois and tied with leather lacing. He carefully untied the lace and unwrapped the object, reveling a beautiful gold cross with sparkling rubies at each of the end points. Carmelita saw this and sucked in her breath, for she instantly knew this was the Amulet of Cananea that had been long lost and had been a turning point in her mother's life.

At that moment, the moon came from behind the clouds as Francisco held up the cross for the Colonel to see through the window, illuminating

412

the beauty of the Amulet, as A.B., with a disgusted look on his face, turned away.

Carmelita, realizing the impact of what this item had represented and all the trouble that it had caused, stood there for several seconds debating what to do, and finally whispered to Gideon, "Can you take me home now? I want to get some rest before we head back to Naco in the morning."

Without another word, they walked back to his steed, mounted up, and rode in silence back to the home that she would see for the last time.

<u>Chapter Twenty-Five</u>

Farewell

The next morning broke sunny and warm as Carmelita and the twins got ready to leave Cananea forever. The town was buzzing, and workers were all dressed in their finest clothes and ready to hear about the concessions that the mines would make on their behalf. Now they had a martyr and a mission, and the politicians in Mexico City were all aware of what had happened in Cananea and the impact it had on the future of Mexico. It was rumored that *Presidente* Díaz himself might come to town or, at the very least, send a representative to negotiate.

Colonel Greene was going to speak to the miners that morning in a rally at the town center. Gideon quietly packed up the buckboard. He and Carmelita didn't speak a word to one another on the way back that night, or since. She was very business-like and only spoke to the twins to give them direction. Gideon knew she was suffering much from the events of the last few days, and held his tongue waiting for an opportunity to speak with her.

"It must have been hell for her," he thought, "losing both her parents, having to keep it from the twins, moving out of the town she lived in her whole life and possibly to another country, if they could find a legal way across the border, and

414

finally, finding out the location of the Amulet, which had caused so much pain in her family's life."

He also felt he may never see her again after she found a place to settle in Naco, and it broke his heart to think that. She would speak to him when she was ready, and he would be there for her if she wanted him, but for now, it was important to get out of Cananea before things took a turn for the worse.

As the last of the items was packed onto the buckboard, and Carmelita and the twins were in the house saying a last goodbye as Gideon prepared the rig, a knock came on the door and she went to answer it, assuming it was Gideon to tell her he was ready. When she opened the door, her mouth dropped open and she found herself speechless.

"*Buenos Dias*, Carmelita," Colonel Greene said with a serious look on his face. She could see Gideon behind him with a shocked look on his face.

She stammered out "*Buenos Dias*, Colonel Greene. To what do I owe this pleasure?"

"I was so saddened to hear of the loss of your mother and the tragic death of your father. Let me say from my heart that if there was anything I could do to prevent these unfortunate events from occurring; I would have sacrificed myself to do so. As the lord said " 'Do unto others as you would have them do unto you.' "

"I have a something for you as a token of condolence from the company and me, although I know that no act, no matter how heartfelt, can ever replace your family. You see, I too once lost a loved one and I know the tremendous heartbreak it can cause. Francisco, can you join me, *por favor*?"

Francisco came around the corner and walked to the front door, with what could only be described as the loss of a scowl, and could have appeared, to those who knew him well, to be the vestige of a smile, for Francisco never showed any real emotion. In his hands he held the Amulet, which he grasped with the chamois cloth wrapped at its base. He extended it to Carmelita and bowed his head as if in prayer.

Colonel Greene continued, "For the past sixteen years, Francisco has had the Amulet hidden in the base of the stone wall surrounding my home. Francisco, can you explain?"

Francisco looked at her with a forlorn look, and his one, solitary brown eye conveyed all the hurt and sorrow that Carmelita felt within her heart. A tear appeared to be running down his cheek from under his eye patch as he said to her; "Carmelita, first let me apologize if I caused you or anyone in your family any harm. I don't believe there was ever any question that your mother, or anyone in your family, ever had anything to do with the disappearance of the gold cross. Its disappearance was a source of pain for all of us, as it has long been considered a good luck charm, ever since it came here to Cananea."

Colonel Greene silently nodded his head in agreement.

"When the evil MacMurrough was convicted of the theft and I rode him out of town, I knew that he had it in his heart not to let it go, and that someday he would come back to again try to steal the Amulet. I knew it upset Colonel Greene to no end losing this precious item, which he considered his good luck piece, but, as I explained to him last night, he didn't need it for its value, and ultimately he would get over it."

"I argued that point with him quite strongly," Colonel Greene chimed in with a smile on his face.

Francisco continued "So, I hid the Amulet on his property, where, if it did possess good luck for the Colonel, he would still reap the benefits, but the Amulet would be safe and unavailable for MacMurrough to steal. It seemed a perfect plan."

Gideon interrupted, ""Colonel, if I may, I'm just curious to ask why A.B. Fall is not with you?"

Carmelita could never understand why Gideon always chose words with "s's" in them. Why 'just curious to ask" instead of "I wondered," but then, it was one of the little things she loved about him; that he didn't shy away from his impediment. Too many people in life used their shortcomings as a crutch instead of facing them head on. Gideon, of course, neglected to mention

417

the fact that he and Carmelita had seen the exchange among the men the night before.

Francisco answered, "A.B. felt that the Amulet was destined to be in Cananea, that it originated here, although that is open to controversy, but at any rate, somehow, time and again, finds its way back. He felt, quite strongly, that I had no right to take matters into my own hands. Of course, he also knows the value of the gold and jewels and thought it could have made excellent collateral when cash was short and we needed money to run the mines. He is a strong willed and practical man. Although he thought the gesture was magnanimous, he felt strongly that there were other ways to accomplish keeping the Amulet at Casa Greene and protecting its safety. He also doesn't agree with what the Colonel would like to do with the Amulet."

Colonel Greene picked up the story, "And to be fair, let's just say that A.B. doesn't believe that Francisco always had such an altruistic rationale in mind."

He turned and stared at Francisco who thrust his chin up and feigned surprise at this effrontery.

"Carmelita, this cross was essentially won by me on a bet, and from a Catholic priest at that! Francisco came to me with the idea of giving the item to you as a form of compensation for your losses, and to help you start out in your new life and care for the twins. I know that nothing can bring back your mother and your father, and that money is

418

never the answer. But it is the right thing to do, and I insist that you become the keeper of the Amulet. It has a long and interesting history and you are free to do with it what you must. It brought me good luck and fortune in my life, and I hope it will do the same for you."

Carmelita was, for the second time in the last two days, speechless.

"Colonel, I don't know what to say, but I do know what to do with the Amulet. I will return it to the Church where it belongs. My father was right, you are a good man, and you deserve all that life brings you. I thank you on behalf of my family for your generous offer. I will never forget you.

And thank you also, Francisco. You have been a true friend. Can I ask you one more favor?"

"Of course, Carmelita, anything at all," Francisco replied.

"Do you have any connections that can help me get across the border? I understand sometimes these things can be done if the price is right," she asked slyly.

Francisco bowed his head again and said, "It will be my pleasure Carmelita. I have friends at the border in Nogales, so you will have to head northwest, instead of northeast to Naco. I will begin making arrangements immediately." With this, Gideon's face fell and his heart skipped a beat.

The Colonel chimed in, "Carmelita, I cannot tell you how sorry we all are to hear of the passing of your mother and your father's unfortunate demise. I know you must be heartbroken, and still uncertain and confused. Although we all know you as a mature and self-sufficient young lady, we also recognize that, at only sixteen, this is quite a lot for one young woman to handle. I have very good friends all throughout the Sonora region, and many north of the border. Once Francisco has you safely over the border in Arizona, I am going to set you up with some very good friends who have a son about your brother, Juan's age, and they will act as guardians for all of you until you are of age to watch over the twins by yourself. The company is setting up a small trust fund, so you will have money to live a decent life, but you will still have to work. We will arrange for a job at a small café, which I have a financial interest in, on the Arizona side of Nogales. You can work during the children's school hours, but still be home in time for them to help with homework. Don't think of this as uncharacteristically charitable. We offer trust funds for all who work at Cananea, and since both of your parents worked here, you have two funds to draw from."

Colonel Greene's words were true, but his intent was not. In fact, he always had a very special place for Carmelita in his heart. Not just because of her beauty and strong attitude and presence, but because of something deeper.

Carmelita was been born on the same date as his beloved, deceased daughter Ella. He never told

420

anyone his thoughts, but he often wondered if Ella would have turned out as special as Carmelita had. He believed she would have, of course, and always made sure that the Carreras family was well cared for.

This last show of love was dedicated to the memory of his dear, departed Ella.

"Gideon – can you escort Carmelita and the children to Nogales and work with Francisco to get them across the border?"

Gideon, who up to this point in time was staring wide eyed with his mouth in a frown, suddenly smiled and whistled out his response "Certainly, *Señor*. The pleasure is all mine."

Greene concluded, "I have lots to do today and a strike to try and resolve. Francisco will escort you and Gideon and the twins out of Cananea to make sure you are safe. He has also asked two of his guards to escort you to the border to get you through Apache territory. Goodbye, Carmelita, and Godspeed."

He never shared with her the fact that she had been born on the same date as his never-forgotten deceased child.

As the buckboard passed the Cananea town line, Carmelita turned to Gideon and spoke to him for the first time since the night before.

"Gideon, I've been thinking. I'm surprised and shocked by the generous offer that Colonel Greene and Francisco made in giving us the

421

Amulet, but I really feel like it belongs to the church. Once we cross the border at Nogales, can we stop at the *Mission San Xavier del Bac?* It is one of Padre Kino's missions and was my mother's favorite. She went there with the school when they were younger and always spoke of it gloriously. I would like to donate the Amulet to the Mission so all the world can see its beauty and it will never again tempt anyone to commit a crime."

Gideon looked at her and said, "Carmelita, I'll take you anywhere you want to go and I'll stay with you as long as you like. You are the most special person," he whistled, and she laughed as they rode off towards a new life in the United States.

Chapter Twenty-Six

Freedom

1911

Carmelita was busy cleaning tables at the Iguana Café in Tucson, Arizona, five years after she left Cananea for the last time. She worked multiple shifts at the Iguana and had begun singing there weekends during dinner, with a guitarist to accompany her. Today she was working the lunch shift. The table she was bussing had a copy of the local paper, the Graham County Guardian, folded open to the obituary section and as she picked it up, the headline caught her eye.

William Cornell Greene

Colonel William C. Greene died at his home in Cananea, Mexico, Saturday morning, August 5, as a result of complications related to pneumonia. He had suffered three broken ribs and a broken collarbone after being thrown from his buggy when his horse turned wild and ran amuck. Greene, born in Wisconsin and raised in Westchester County, N.Y., was President of the Cananea Consolidated Copper Company, and a self-made millionaire.

423

Special services were held in his honor. His body was taken to Los Angeles, California for burial.

As she finished reading, Carmelita found tears streaming down her cheeks, blurring the ink on the page. She dropped her wet rag and ran out the front door, calling "Gideon, Gideon!"

Gideon Riot was walking up the road just returning from the blacksmith shop where the smithy was repairing an axle for one of two new stages he had recently purchased. The growth of the City of Tucson, and increasing trade between the U.S. and Mexico created the need for more transportation beyond what the railroads could offer, in spite of the revolution which had finally begun in earnest the year before.

"Carmelita, are you alright?" he cried out as he dropped what he was carrying and ran to be at her side. Carmelita and Gideon had moved north to Tucson only a year ago, after spending the past four years in Nogales, on the Arizona side. Gideon had lived in a boarding house after selling his business in Naco and purchasing a new stagecoach for the Nogales to Tucson run, while Carmelita and the twins stayed with the same family that they had been introduced to by Colonel Greene. Once the twins had finished elementary school, they all decided to relocate a little further from the border so the twins could go to public school to continue their education.

"Oh, Gideon!" she cried, "Colonel Green has died."

She broke down completely as she said this, and fell into his arms sobbing uncontrollably. It was as if the Colonel's death had finally allowed her to release all she had kept pent up in her heart in all the years since her parents had died. She had never let anyone see any emotion or sadness after their passing. She had worked long hours, saving money and keeping the twins isolated from the sadness and fear he knew she must have felt.

"I'm sorry, Carmelita. I know how much you appreciate all that the Colonel did for you and the twins, in spite of all the sadness that occurred in Cananea."

"Oh, Gideon. It's so much more than that. Colonel Greene gave my mother a wonderful job doing what she loved to do. He promoted my father as the first Mexican to a management position ever at the mines, he offered the most valuable and precious item he possessed to me and the twins and he helped me start a new life. He was a magnificent man and I owe everything to him. It was not his fault what happened to my mother and father. They both loved and respected him, as I do. I would like to go back to pay my respects."

Gideon looked at her and his heart nearly broke. What she said was true. Her mothers diabetes had nothing to do with the mines and her father died in a freak accident. Although it all happened in

Cananea, none of this had to do with Colonel Greene and his way with people.

"Carmelita, you know we can't go back across the border. We have a nice life here now. If we're careful, we can stay here forever. But it's too risky to go back to Cananea. The revolution has made it far too dangerous to travel anywhere south of the border. Even here, we take some risk."

The revolution had, indeed, taken over the country and escalated in Mexico after decades of uncertainty and turmoil. After more than thirty years, Díaz decreed that México was finally ready to become a democratic country. However, once it became apparent to him that he might lose the election to Francisco Madero, Díaz had him arrested and sent to jail in San Luis Potosí. After the election, which Díaz once again won under suspicious circumstances, Madero escaped and fled to the U.S. There he published his *Plan De San Luis Potosí*, which called for the end of the autocratic Díaz Presidency and an armed revolution and re-institution of democracy.

"We have a good life here." Gideon continued as he tried to reason with her. "The twins are in a nice Catholic school. We're both working and saving a little money to buy property. We're far enough away from the border that we don't have to worry about revolutionary leaders like Pancho Villa, and Emiliano Zapata, who are leading the peasants in violent revolt. The country is a mess and there are no laws, only *ley de fuga.* No, Carmelita, we cannot go back."

She looked at him and nodded her head. She knew how dangerous it was across the border now.

"Gideon, can we at least go to the Mission and pray for his soul?"

"Of course, Carmelita. Let me know when you want to go."

"I want to go now," she replied quickly.

She left the café, waited until Juan and Rosita came home from school, and packed up the wagon for the short ride to *Mission San Xavier del Bac,* known as *The White Dove of the Desert*, the one her mother had visited as a child and had told her about so many times in what seemed like a lifetime ago.

When they arrived at the Mission, they were once again struck by the beauty and magnificence of the buildings. She never got tired of visiting here, ever since the first time she had laid eyes on it when she delivered the Amulet years before. The mission was architected by the same person who built the *Mission San Ignacio de Cabórica* in Sonora not far from where she lived with her parents in Cananea.

"This mission must be the most beautiful in the entire world," she remarked to Gideon as they climbed down off the wagon and looked up at the stark white stucco of the magnificent architecture.

"It certainly is," Gideon said with his unique way of choosing words to accent his whistle. "In

427

fact, *The White Dove* houses some of the most beautiful watercolor paintings in the world. The original ones were painted by the missionaries back in the sixteen hundreds. My father took me here when we first came to the Sonora area. He said this is a world famous mission, known for its splendid architecture and incredible paintings."

Carmelita, with the twins following close behind her, genuflected at the entrance to the center aisle and walked up to the first row of pews, marveling at the incredibly beautiful array of paintings, frescoes, and balustrades.

They had come to pray for Colonel Greene, her parents, and for peace in her home country of Mexico, although she now considered herself an American.

"My ancestors had chosen the wrong side of the border many decades ago," she thought to herself. "If they had stayed where they had lived, instead of moving to stay in their native country, I *would* be American."

She knelt down on the hard, cold granite at the altar, closed her eyes, and bowed her head to pray.

"Lord God, I know you died for our sins, but I ask you to help this crazy world and bring peace to the region. I pray for the souls of my parents, Edelmida and Manuel; for Colonel Greene, who impacted so many lives in so many different ways; and for the soul of Francisco de Torres, who helped me to get to this beautiful place and to safety. And although I know I should never pray for personal gain or to wish someone harm, I pray that *El Diablo*, MacMurrough, rots in the flames of hell forever where he can no longer do harm to anyone. Of this I beseech you, Lord God."

Carmelita opened her eyes as she crossed herself, looked up at the space above the altar and sucked in her breath and swooned, falling down, and nearly cracking her head on the marble floor.

"Gideon!" she screamed, "the Amulet."

Gideon was just coming through the door after putting up his horse, and ran to her side. She pointed up at the altar and saw that the place where the Amulet had been placed years before was empty. Where it had been hanging, there was only an outline of the cross marked by years of dirt and dust. He ran to the vestibule and pounded on the door, shouting out for the priest. As he came running out of his quarters, he saw Carmelita, still pointing up at the altar, looked up, and he opened his mouth in shock.

"It's impossible!" he called out, louder than he had ever spoken anywhere on the Mission grounds. "It was there no more than twenty minutes ago. Just as I was entering the vestibule, I looked up and offered a silent prayer. Who would ever take such a precious and holy relic from the Mission?"

Gideon stood with Carmelita and the twins while the priest sent one of the altar boys to the local sheriff's office to report the crime. They were

429

baffled, as nothing like this had ever happened anywhere in Sonora in any of the Missions. They all held beautiful, sacred, and valuable objects and were considered above reproach from even the most heinous and desperate outlaws. The Amulet was not mounted very high, but certainly high enough to be out of the reach of even the tallest person. It stood at twelve feet above the altar, which itself was four feet high. It wasn't really secured, it simply rested on a wooden pedestal which had a groove carved in its base to hold the cross upright and slanted at a backward angle to keep it in place. Yet, anyone wanting to retrieve the object would need a twelve foot ladder, at minimum.

As they all drove back towards their small cottage on the south side of the outskirts of Tucson, they passed the Tohono O'Odham village.

"Carmelita, I'm going to stop and talk to our friends and see if anyone has seen or heard anything unusual. If someone stole the Amulet for gain, it's a good bet they would try to fence it for the gold and jewels, and no one has better connections than the tribe. Someone here will know, and if one knows, they all know."

Carmelita knew he was right. The reservation was the best place to go to fence precious items. Most Americans had the mistaken belief that the tribe were savages with little or no regard for anything religious. They were wrong. The idea of native tribes being pagan was the farthest thing from the truth. The entire region had

430

been settled by the Spanish Catholics centuries ago, and all of the natives had converted to Catholicism. The idea of native tribes as pagans was a fiction created by the writers of the American West and fostered by the prejudiced settlers who wanted to conquer the land and take the spoils for themselves. In reality, the natives were devout Catholics who abhorred violence.

"Hola, Desi." His native friend waved his hand in greeting.

"Hola, Gideon."

They conversed in a type of broken Spanish which was commonly spoken in the region, but bore little resemblance to either of their native tongues. Gideon was well known throughout the region and he and the natives often spooked the customers on his stage with faked raids. It was a lucrative performance and Gideon received often obscene tips for his braveness in the face of the Indian raids.

Tucson was growing at an incredibly fast pace, and folks coming from the east still believed the stories of settlers facing Indian raids in the 1880's were still true. Gideon and his friends from the Tohono O'Odham tribe did not resort to extremes, but a few whoops and hollers and a quick chase brought sighs of relief from the newly relocated folks when Gideon outran them. It gave the settlers a thrill and brought good money to the tribe and Gideon.

He explained what had happened at the church, and a scowl came over Desi's face.

"Most of the white folks who come out here to settle don't even realize that this is Tohono O'Odham land. The Mission is on the reservation and is considered a separate country from the U.S. We really can't dispense our own justice, but we can enforce our traditions. The Revolution in Mexico has everyone distracted. Most of the law focuses more on border issues than any real crime on the US. side. It is not a very big problem, but it is a nuisance."

"*Sí*," Gideon replied nodding, "things are changing all over and very quickly. So tell me, have you heard if anyone is looking to fence gold or jewels?"

"About a week ago, a gringo came here looking to see where he could fence such items. He didn't have them yet, but said he would soon. He was very secretive and no one here wanted anything to do with him. You know how we take stock in such things, and he gave off a very bad aura. The medicine man said he was of the devil, with his hair the color of fire. We told him we could not help him and he went off to the north, I would guess looking for other buyers."

Gideon stared at his friend for what seemed like several minutes before speaking.

"Hair like fire? Were there any other things about this man that made him seem unique?"

"*Sí,* he had a strange tongue, not just an American accent of the east, more like a person from another country. He was a strange little man and he carried a large knife, as if it made up for his lack of height. He also walks with a cane made of mesquite with a knob made of bone."

Gideon was thunderstruck. "Could it be?" he thought to himself. "Was it possible that MacMurrough had survived the attack so many years ago, and was still out for vengeance? We left him for dead, but we all left in a hurry and no one really knew what became of him. I have to find out if it is possible that it is MacMurrough and he is still alive."

"*Gracias, amigo.* If you hear anything more about this stranger, please let me know right away. If he is who I think he is, I know a little something about him, and he is a dangerous and evil man indeed." With that, Gideon ran back to the wagon and Carmelita. The question he was asking himself as he ran was whether he should tell her at all.

Gideon climbed back up on the wagon and said to Carmelita, "I'm taking you and the twins back to the house. I have to leave right away for Phoenix. Desi thinks the hombre who took the cross went there to try and sell the gold and jewels. I need to find him before he melts down the Amulet."

Carmelita looked at Gideon with horror. He was a brave man when it came to shooting coyotes and getting rid of scorpions, but she could not

433

imagine him confronting the type of person who would steal a valuable artifact from the sacred confines of a church. Such a person would certainly have to be a desperate and dangerous man.

"Gideon, it's not your responsibility to go after this hombre. Do you realize how dangerous it can be? Let's call the Rangers and tell them what happened and have them go after the Amulet. It's the property of the Church now. We don't have to worry about it anymore. It's always been as much a curse as a blessing."

"I'm sorry, Carmelita. This is something I have to do, I can't explain why, but I need to resolve this once and for all, for my own peace of mind." He couldn't tell her of his suspicions about MacMurrough. It would infuriate her and she would insist on going with him.

"I'm sorry, but that's the way it has to be. There will be no more discussion about this."

He pulled his hat down low over his eyes and whipped the horse with much more force than was necessary.

Carmelita just looked at him with wonder and closed her eyes. She knew his mind was made up and there was nothing she could do or say, so she silently prayed for his safety.

MacMurrough was indeed on his way to Phoenix and his plan was to find two buyers, one for the jewels and one for the gold. He didn't feel, after all this time had passed, that there was a need for breaking up the gems to multiple buyers. He had to get rid of the items fast and he would take what he could get and head back east, to New York. The west had proven to be too much trouble for him, and he needed the safety of a large, concentrated population where he could hide in plain sight.

"Those Mexican shites cost me too much. Between the bitches who cut me and set me up, to the bastards who ran me out of the towns, I've had enough. My body will never be the same; the scars are so deep from the surgery to repair my stomach that I can't even walk anymore without this cursed walking stick. I lost half my intestines to those *pendejos*, but I'll get my just deserts. Getting the cross down from the wall in that Church was a cinch. All I had to do was grab the extended wick lighter they use for lighting their sacred candles, and knock it off its' perch. I was in and out in three minutes. They'll never know who took it or what happened to it. I was lucky I saw that article in the newspaper about the cross in the new church. I wouldn't have even seen it if I hadn't heard Colonel Greene had died and looked in the paper for his obituary. It took me a while to get there from New Orleans, but it was worth it."

MacMurrough arrived in Phoenix on the train and made a beeline for the south side of town and found several pawn shops wiling to get him a pretty good price for the gold and jewels as he described them. One of the shops had pressed him on the source of his items. The owner hinted that he had no problems with stolen articles and that sometimes an item was worth more whole than in parts. He mentioned that he would be willing to take a look, and even do the melting for him, if that would be an idea he would entertain.

MacMurrough, still going by his given name of Cassidy, was skeptical. He had been burned too many times, but was tempted by the amount of money the buyer was throwing at him as a possibility.

He said that the market for antique treasures far exceeded the value of the component pieces and at a 70/30 split, MacMurrough would be set for life and able to afford the finest things and all the young virgins he could find. He said he would think about it and let him know.

"I'll be here," the owner said, "tell me how you want to handle it and I'll come to you, if you're more comfortable." That was exactly what MacMurrough wanted to hear and he needed a couple of days to scope out an appropriate meeting place and make sure he had backup in case this was another setup.

Gideon, meanwhile, was fast on his way to Phoenix. It felt like déjà vu, going to another new town and trying to find the evil *El Diablo*, but this time, he felt sure MacMurrough would do what he did before and head to the seedy side of town. He was armed with new information and would be aware that he might go by either MacMurrough or Cassidy, as he and Carmelita heard him called when

436

they were in Bisbee. It only took a few hours for Gideon to get to Phoenix by train, and he knew that he was only just behind MacMurrough, assuming he was here at all, which he felt in his bones he was. He made his way to an area that housed several pawn shops, aided by the advice from a friendly conductor that Gideon befriended, who used to run his own stage before the train put him out of business.

Gideon was a little concerned because he wasn't really handy with a gun. He had only ever really fired his trusty Remington long barrel rifle, which he didn't have with him. He thought about buying a gun, but figured that if he found MacMurrough, he would play it smart and safe and call in the sheriff.

As he approached the south side of town, he decided he would employ a different tactic this time, and would claim he had a very old and valuable golden bejeweled cross that had been handed down for generations in his family. He would use the excuse that he needed to pawn it because he had to get some quick cash.

In the first shop he entered, he encountered a grizzled, middle aged man in a dirty, tan, long sleeved shirt with brown tobacco stains running down his chest. As he approached the counter, the man turned his head and spit a stream of tobacco juice at a copper spittoon in the corner behind the counter. It hit its mark, but it was obvious from the stains surrounding it on the floor, that many times it had not.

As Gideon made his pitch, the clerk said to him, "That's odd. You're the second fella today to come in here with valuable gold and jewels to sell. Mostly, we get odd items, like guns, saddles, and watches. The last guy, though, said he had loose jewels and a melted down gold bar. Anyway, I might be able to help you, but really, the right guy to talk to is Nathan Twomey. He runs the pawn down the street called Twomey's Treasures. He has connections for antique valuables that most of us don't deal with."

Gideon thanked the man, and headed out to talk to Twomey. He was across the street, three doors down from his destination, thinking about how he wanted to approach the situation, when he saw someone walking out of the shop, and at once he knew it was MacMurrough. He still had the Stetson, and the bowie knife strapped to his right leg, but in his left hand he had a gnarled wood walking stick with a dirty white bone handle.

Gideon's blood boiled and he had to fight the rage within him, and forced himself to calm down. He had to think quickly of what to do and how to handle it. He didn't want to let *El Diablo* out of his sight, yet he had no effective way to stop him. He never expected to find him so quickly, and now he had no weapon, hadn't yet talked to the sheriff, and didn't think confrontation was the right approach in any event. Gideon breathed deeply and

438

tried to force himself to think logically. It was obvious that MacMurrough didn't have the Amulet in his possession. Although he had suspected it was MacMurrough who had stolen the amulet, which is why he came to Phoenix in the first place, a part of him hadn't been completely sure. Now he knew for certain that MacMurrough was alive, and he was pretty sure he was the culprit, but he had to see the Amulet to be absolutely certain. How could he even think of engaging the sheriff unless he had proof?

Gideon decided to follow MacMurrough. He didn't exactly know what he would do, but felt sure he would know when the time was right. As he followed MacMurrough, a plan began to form in his mind.

MacMurrough was thinking about how to set up the meet with the shop owner when he entered his hotel and asked for his key. Gideon was standing across the street wondering if he should run for the sheriff now, explain his suspicions, and take him to the hotel. If MacMurrough had the Amulet, then he believed all would be right again and *El Diablo* would go back to jail. But if he didn't have the Amulet in his possession, he would be scared off and would most likely leave the region and go elsewhere to peddle the valuables. That was a risk that Gideon could not take, so he kept watch until dark, but MacMurrough never reappeared.

As he was standing there, deciding what to do next, he realized that MacMurrough never really saw his face before. He had been at the boarding house when Carmelita confronted *El Diablo*, but Gideon never really entered the room, and when he went to the swinging doors to get Carmelita to leave, MacMurrough was already on the ground bent over in pain from his stab wound. He could confront MacMurrough and he doubted very much he would have any idea who he was. Gideon decided to get a room in the same hotel as MacMurrough and keep an eye on him until the amulet made an appearance.

He didn't have to wait long. Later that night, as Gideon sat on the front porch of the hotel whistling and whittling in the warm, but pleasant air, MacMurrough came out of the hotel. Without giving him a glance, he headed off down the street in the direction of one of the many saloons in town. Gideon took all of three seconds before he got up and went into the lobby of the hotel.

"Excuse me," he asked the desk clerk, "I thought I just saw an old friend of mine leave here. Red hair, walking with a cane?" Gideon gave his best smile. "He got that when we entered a bronc busting contest and was thrown. Never walked the same again," and he shook his head sadly. "He used to go by the name MacMurrough, but his wife divorced him after the accident, poor fella. Said he wasn't the same man. So he changed his name to Cassidy. Was that him?"

The clerk looked at Gideon, with his youthful face, blond hair, and innocent expression, and grinned.

"Yes, that was Declan Cassidy. Sorry to hear about his troubles. No wonder he's so crotchety. Oh, sorry, I know he's a friend of yours."

"Well, he was. But you're right, he hasn't been the same since his wife left him. I sure would like to surprise him and pick up his spirits. Do me a favor, would you? I have to go meet someone, so I can't go after him right now – I assume he's gone to the saloon?"

The clerk nodded. He looked no more than eighteen, had light brown hair that was parted on one side with bangs that almost covered his eyes.

"Well, keep it between us that I'm here. I'm going to see if I can buy him breakfast tomorrow. I'm in room 308, what room is he in?" Gideon held his breath to see if the clerk would go for the ruse.

"Well, I'm not supposed to tell anyone room numbers, but if you can help this guy, I don't see what harm can come of it He's in room 219."

Gideon sighed to himself and let out his breath slowly, smiled, and handed the clerk a dollar gold piece.

"Thanks, *amigo*."

Gideon went back out the front door, waving and smiling and headed toward town. Once out of sight. He turned back towards the rear of the hotel and entered through the service entrance. He was

441

able to access the room floors thorough the service stairway and made his way to his room on the third, and highest, floor. There, he picked up his whittling knife and made his way down to the second floor to MacMurrough's room. The locks on the doors were simple warded locks and not too difficult to jimmy open. He inserted the blunt edge of his knife between the bolt and the door jamb and jiggled it smoothly until the lock freed and the door gently swung open.

Gideon was shaking with the fear of being discovered and knew he had to work fast before another guest wandered by, or, far worse, MacMurrough came back. He entered the room and turned on the lamp. The room was located at the back of the hotel, so he had no fear of MacMurrough seeing the light from outside the hotel. He reflected that in his life he had been confronted by bandits and Indians, and had been shot at more than once, but he had never broken any laws.

In spite of *El Diablo*'s physical handicap, he knew he would still be a formidable opponent, especially with his Bowie knife, and Gideon was not interested in testing his mettle in a confrontation with him. Still, he knew he needed to work quickly, but he didn't want to make a mistake in his haste, for he had no idea when MacMurrough would be back.

"I guess I have to get used to referring to him as Cassidy now," he thought to himself. The

442

very first place he looked for the Amulet was under the mattress, and, just as Edelmida had years before, that's where it was hidden. Gideon gently removed it, noting the position it had been placed, and unwrapped it from the chamois cloth which looked oddly the same as the material Francisco had used when he buried the cross. He held it up in the light to get a good look at it. Although he had seen it many times before, mostly hanging in the mission, he was once again struck with awe at its beauty.

Gideon heard a noise, which sounded like boots walking down the hallway, and quickly wrapped the amulet back in the chamois, and hurriedly placed the cross back the way he found it. He extinguished the lamp and stood stock still, breathing through his mouth slowly and listening with all his faculties, but the only sound he heard was the beating of his own heart.

He slowly opened the door and glanced out, but there was no one in sight. He rapidly, yet quietly, closed the door, which had remained locked in spite of his unauthorized entry, and made his way back down to the service door and out into the alley. He then went back around the corner, and bounded up the stairs into the hotel lobby, where his friend the night clerk nodded his greeting.

"You just missed your friend," he noted as Gideon approached the desk. "He just went up the stairs. He's a little slow with that limp of his, so I bet you can catch him if you like."

443

Fear struck Gideon's chest. "You didn't mention me to him did you? I wanted to surprise him."

"No, I just asked him how his night was, but he didn't even offer a hello. Just grumbled to hisself and went up the steps without so much as a word. I'll tell ya, I hope you can cheer him up. That hombre is one miserable son of a bitch." Gideon nodded his head and said good night.

Gideon awoke the next morning before sunrise. He wanted to keep an eye on MacMurrough/Cassidy/*El Diablo* – whatever his name was today – and get to the sheriff's office as soon as he could. Without bothering to wash up first, he tossed on the clothes he wore the night before and bounded down the stairs, out into the street, and ran to the sheriff's office. The night clerk was still on duty and called out to Gideon, who just waved and ran out the door.

The sheriff wasn't in yet, so he spoke to the deputy, a man named Josiah, and rapidly told him all he could about the story of the Amulet and MacMurrough.

"I need you to arrest that man so we can return the cross to its rightful owner, which is the *Mission San Xavier del Bac* in Tucson."

The deputy looked at him funny and drawled out, "Son, do you have proof of ownership? Without it, it will just be your word against his. I can't do anything about this just based on your say so."

Gideon was stunned. It never dawned on him that he had to have proof. He just assumed that once he found the Amulet he would be able to have the authorities confiscate it and return it to the Church.

"Well, can't you send a telegram to Tucson to verify what I'm telling you?" Gideon was incredibly frustrated. After all this time, and the number of horrible things MacMurrough had done, it now looked like he might get away with the theft after all. Gideon could barely contain himself.

"I'm telling you, this is a desperate hombre and he has to be stopped." His whole body trembled at the thought of going back to Tucson a failure and having to tell Carmelita what happened.

The deputy could see the passion in Gideon's eyes and took some pity on him.

"Look, I'll tell you what. You go send the telegram, and have the sheriff in Tucson verify the source as that of the priest at the Mission. I will talk to the judge about impounding the cross with that telegram as evidence until we have it all sorted out, OK?"

It was the best that Gideon could do, so he nodded his head and walked off to the find the telegraph office.

<u>Chapter Twenty-Seven</u>

Resolve

After a leisurely breakfast, Cassidy sent a note to the pawn broker, Twomey, to meet him at noon. In the note, he indicated he would have the item for the broker to view and he should bring some "good faith" money as a down payment. The plan was to meet on the south side of town inside a deserted blacksmith shop. It seemed there were fewer blacksmith shops every day, as people transported more on railroads and automobiles, which, Cassidy thought, were ruining the west.

He planned to arrive well in advance of the appointed time to observe Twomey. Cassidy trusted no one, and he wanted to make sure Twomey was alone, and that he brought money to prove his interest. He wouldn't take any, but needed to have the reassurance of his intent. If so, he would meet with him and set up yet another rendezvous an hour later that same day, with a promise to bring the cross. He would take no chances that Twomey could double cross him.

Cassidy arrived just after 10 am, and spent nearly two hours in the desolate setting, sitting behind the abandoned forge, which once burned white hot as the smithy forged shoes for the horses of his customers. As he sat, he reflected on his past. Cassidy was not an emotional sort. He reflected not on his legacy, which, if he had, would have been abhorrent, but on his "achievements," his conquests of the nubile young women he had deflowered.

He certainly remembered Anne Marie, and a girl named Helen, both of Ireland, which seemed so long ago.

Then, of course, the "royal bitches – Edelmida, Soo Li, and Consuelo." Cassidy could not seem to stay focused on the wonderful experiences such as he had early in life in Ireland. Instead, he dwelled on the troubles he had in Mexico, San Francisco, and El Paso, and could not shake these terrible thoughts from his head. "What good is it to have all these memories," he reflected, "if I can only remember the bad ones?"

Just then, he heard footsteps right outside the entrance to the shop. He scrunched down lower behind the forge, but had a clear line of sight of the door by peaking around the right side of the anvil stand mounted on the forge.

As Cassidy was hunkering down awaiting his fate, Gideon was at the telegraph office hoping to hear back from the Mission and the sheriff. Gideon had also sent a telegram to Carmelita to let her know that he was delayed and expected to be back in Tucson in another day or two. She was to contact his backup driver to handle the work chores until his return. He made no mention of *El Diablo* or the Amulet.

"Gideon, I think this is what you've been waiting for," the telegraph operator held out the paper for Gideon to read. He grabbed it and whooped out a cry.

"Thanks. This is just what I need." The message was from the priest at the Mission and verified the theft of the cross and asking anyone with information to contact the sheriff's department in Tucson. It also stated that a reward had been posted of twenty-five dollars for its safe return. Gideon couldn't know this, but the reward was posted by Carmelita, one that she could ill afford.

He ran to the sheriffs' office and showed the deputy the letter. He looked at Gideon and grabbed his hat.

"The sheriff wanted me to find him right away if this story proved to be true. I explained what you told me and he wants to get to the bottom of this. Let's go see if we can track him down."

As they began walking down the raised, wooden sidewalk, the deputy's boots clunking a dull thud, and his spurs jangling a tambourine tune, *El Diablo* saw two men enter the blacksmith shop.

He sneered to himself "I knew I couldn't trust Twomey. Filthy Irishman - must be from the north – his mother was probably a Brit."

"Cassidy! It's Twomey. I'm here with my appraiser to see if your cross if the real thing. Show your face."

Cassidy was torn. He had specifically mentioned in his note for Twomey to come alone, but he could see why he would need his appraiser. The second man was armed, but so was Cassidy with his trusty "Peacemaker." Since he didn't have the cross with him, he felt there wasn't much to lose. He came out from behind the forge and stood up as best he could with his scarred and damaged stomach.

"Twomey! I told you to come alone. I was testing you to see if I could trust you and it seems that I can't. I'll take my business elsewhere."

The second man moved his right hand down close to his gun belt and said, "Cassidy, I'm Sheriff Taggart. I understand you have some valuables you want to sell. Well, here in Phoenix, we don't take kindly to stolen property, so I just want to check out the goods to make sure you're legit."

Cassidy felt trapped, but he didn't have the cross with him, so he tried to bluff his way out.

"I don't know what you're talking about sheriff. I invented that story to test Twomey. I have some old coins that were handed down from my ancestors, but was told to be extra careful of the pawn shops here in Phoenix. Now I know why. The coins are in Tucson in a safe deposit box. If you like, you can come along with me and I'll show them to you there."

He smiled his best snake oil salesman smile and felt he had both of them beat. There was no way they could argue with his logic.

The sheriff looked at Twomey and just shrugged his shoulders. The bluff didn't work. If Cassidy had any items in his possession, it would be a different story, but they couldn't search his room without some cause. The judicial system in Phoenix was rough, but due process was vitally important to a growing town just about to join the Union.

As they whispered to each other, and it became obvious to Cassidy that the sheriff was about to leave, the door to the shop swung open and the deputy and Gideon rushed into the room.

"Sheriff," the deputy burst out, ""I have a telegram here that verifies that a golden cross was stolen from the *Mission San Xavier del Bac* in Tucson. This man," he pointed to Gideon, "claims he saw the cross here in Phoenix in that man's possession just yesterday."

Before anyone could make a move, Cassidy whipped the Bowie knife out of its' sheath, and made a run for the back door. The sheriff called out a warning and fired a shot that ricocheted off the doorframe and bounced back at the anvil, glancing off its metal surface with a loud ping that reverberated through the room.

Gideon called out, "He's heading for the hotel. He has the cross hidden there. I'm going after him. Cover me."

The sheriff shouted for Gideon to stay put to no avail. Gideon raced across the street, unarmed and without any kind of a plan as to how to stop *El Diablo*. The sheriff and his deputy tore out the front door, both heading to the hotel to try and cut Gideon off before he got himself killed.

Cassidy, was infirmed from his stab wounds, but his legs were still strong and he ran like a madman, in spite of his debilitation, albeit limping and swerving side to side.

They ran down the street trailing Gideon by a hundred yards. Up ahead, the sheriff saw Gideon bounding up the stairs into the hotel. He couldn't imagine that *El Diablo* could have gotten there much ahead of him, but the man was unarmed and young and seemed too green to be able to stop such an obvious madman as Cassidy. They saw them go into the hotel, Gideon trailing Cassidy by only a few yards.

As Gideon approached the door to Cassidy's room, he paused and thought to himself, "It's just not possible that *El Diablo* can escape this time. He's had too many lives and we have all exits covered. I pray that this time we have him AND the cross."

As the sheriff approached the hotel, breathing heavily from the run, the deputy was standing at the bottom of the front steps listening intently. As the sheriff approached, he told his deputy, "You stay here. I'm going to go around

451

back in case Cassidy get away and tries to head out in that direction. This way we'll have all the exits covered."

The sheriff approached the back of the hotel gingerly and all was eerily quiet. He couldn't hear anything at all as he slowly went up the stairs, and he feared that maybe Cassidy had subdued the green stranger. He wanted to be prepared if Cassidy were to come through the door, which he expected at any moment.

Through the door he heard a dull "pffft" and was just about to burst through the door, when it swung open and almost hit him in the face. Peering out at him, smiling and with a smoking derringer in his hand was the young man.

"Come on in, sheriff. We have the thief and the goods."

He smiled and the sheriff followed Gideon into the room.

Sheriff Taggart called out to his deputy, "It's OK, Josiah. Come on up."

Sitting on the floor, with blood gushing out of his left shoulder, was Cassidy. The Amulet of Cananea was sitting on top of the bed with the chamois cloth splayed open exposing the beauty of the cross. The deputy came up behind Gideon and handed the telegram to the sheriff.

He read it and said to Cassidy. "Well, it looks like I have enough to put you away for a long time. I'll have to hold you here until I can arrange to transport you back to Tucson for trial, but this is one time when I caught a thief red-handed."

Cassidy looked up at Gideon and said, "You look familiar, but I don't think we've ever met. You sure caused me a lot of trouble. More trouble than anyone else in my life, and believe me, I've had plenty. When I get out of this, I'm going to look you up and pay you back. What did you say your name was?"

Gideon glared at him and spit on the ground.

"I'll be in heaven a week before the devil tells you I'm dead. I'd better never see you again, or you'll regret it. By the way, Edelmida Carreras wanted me to tell you that the baby wasn't yours."

Cassidy looked at him with fire in his eyes. He had no way of knowing that Edelmida had died and he could not believe that, once again she caused him so much misery and that the cross was again the center of his torment.

The sheriff pulled Cassidy up by his damaged left arm, causing him to shout out in pain "Goddamn it."

Gideon thought that was the perfect expression.

453

<u>Epilogue</u>

Tucson

The trial of Declan Cassidy, as he had to be tried by that, his real name, ran only two days. It may not have run that long but for the repeated interruptions by his lawyer who was a pompous ass who thought that court histrionics could win a case.

He was tried for the theft of the Amulet, but during the course of the investigation, the murder of Luis Hernandez was discovered.

A.B. Fall, who was now Secretary of the Interior, testified via a notarized accounting of the incident. In addition a number of the workers who witnessed the murder were also located and gladly offered testimony resulting in a charge of premeditated murder.

Premeditation was accepted because MacMurrough's knife was not considered a weapon of convenience and enough of his former workers testified he had been out for blood for weeks before the murder.

The jury unanimously found him guilty, at which point Gideon commented, "It wasn't a jury of his peers, because we could not find men bad enough in all the west to sit in judgment."

Carmelita did not attend, and no one in Tucson really knew anything about a connection between her family and the evil charlatan who would stoop so low as to steal a precious artifact from the Mission. Gideon never told anyone all of what happened in Phoenix. He simply stated that he had a telegram from the Mission, corroborated by the Phoenix sheriff, that the cross had been stolen. He gave full credit to the deputy in Tucson, for identifying Cassidy as the culprit and the retrieval of the Amulet.

Carmelita knew that there was more to it than that, but she gave him his conceit. She was content to go on with her business, which was rehearsing her songs. She had successfully landed a job singing in the hotel lounge at night, a dream come true.

"You know, Carmelita, a wise man once told me that as people grow older, they become caricatures of themselves. I guess at the time, I didn't understand what he meant, but now I think I do."

"What does it mean, Gideon?" She asked with a contented smile on her face.

"I think he meant that time exaggerates your good and bad qualities. As a person ages, both the good and bad characteristics of a person are accentuated. If a person has more good than bad, you see much more good. In *El Diablo*'s case, the bad qualities far overtook what good ones he might have ever possessed."

Carmelita nodded her head as if in deep thought. She believed in the devil on earth and was convinced that if ever there was one, *El Diablo* was it.

Both Juan and Rosita were now attending high school, and Rosita was even talking of going to college afterwards in California for medical studies. Juan wanted to stay in Tucson and help Gideon run his business, although Gideon was planning to sell the business since horses and carriages were dying as a means of transportation. Gideon, Carmelita, and Juan discussed that it might be time to invest in an automobile and use it the same way he used the carriages. Juan loved that idea and began to study combustion engines in his spare time.

In the winter of 1912, only 6 months after Colonel Greene died, Arizona was admitted to the Union, the last of the contiguous landmass in North America to become part of the United States of America. In May of that year, Gideon Riot and Carmelita Carreras married and started a new business running automobiles through Tucson to those who needed swift transportation but not could afford a "horseless carriage." They called their new company "Verde Transportation" in honor of Colonel Greene. Their business proved successful and they moved to Green Valley, south of Tucson and closer to the Mexican border, where they built an adobe home and planned to live out the rest of their lives.

Acknowledgements

First of all, thank you to my family - my wife Dianne and my son Greg. I love you both very much and appreciate your eternal love and support.

The process for writing a first novel is always exciting and often challenging. Sleepless nights and jolting awake with characters drawn for me in my dreams. Without the help and support of so many people, it would be a dauntless task to complete.

Thanks to all those who read, reviewed, and spent time documenting my errors and omissions, and made suggestions to make this a better manuscript.

I would like to extend special thanks to Geoff Alexander, who spent many hours from across the country to meticulously review the manuscript page by page. To Karin Wilks and Nikki Markow who took copious notes to help bring the characters alive. To the Jan & Mike Graves for offering a unique perspective by reading the text out loud for full effect. To the Trupp family, Roy Lott, and Sharon LoVan for their encouragement and support. To Christina Ricci for her help with the back cover text. And to my wife Dianne for being a sounding board through the entire process and putting up with many sleepless nights.

Thanks to you all.

Author's Note

This is a book of historical fiction, meaning that some elements are historically accurate wrapped around a fictional premise.

Colonel William Greene was a remarkable person and much of what is written here is accurate based on published reports. The mines exist today as one of the largest copper mines in the world. Many of the troubles that existed at the time this story took place continue to haunt the site today. A.B. Fall was affiliated with Greene at the copper mines and went on to become Secretary of the Interior. He was ultimately responsible for the Teapot Dome scandal.

The Carreras family is all fictional, as are the other players in their drama, such as Thomas MacMurrough and Gideon Riot.

The period in history is depicted as accurately based on written newspaper reports and books published on the subject.

About the Author

Ray Cavanagh spent his early years as a musician and performer. As a member of ASCAP, he had several songs published by Eden Music. The most prominent, "Will I Know You," was recorded by Peggy March and released on Ariola Records worldwide.

Born in Flatbush, Brooklyn, he received a Master's Degree in International Business from Northeastern University, Boston. He traveled the world extensively in his career as a hi-tech executive. Cavanagh founded an Italian wine accessories company, Portovista, which imported glassware from Tuscany.

A recognized industry expert on Security, he has been interviewed as a subject matter expert on many TV stations including WHDH TV Boston, KPRC Houston, WJXT Jacksonville, and WWL and WVUE New Orleans . He has published articles in Security Magazine, SC Magazine, USA Today, the Wall Street Journal and many others.

The Amulet of Cananea is his first novel. He lives in New Hampshire with his wife Dianne. Together they have a son Gregory.

Look for the sequel, "Return to Cananea."